Ijen Kim grew up in Wellington, New Zealand, left to study in Paris and spent eighteen years in Moscow, including thirteen years as a translator for the Kremlin. She has worked as a journalist, knows several European and Asian languages, paints, and writes poetry. She is the author of *The Snuff Bottle Boy*. She currently lives in Vienna.

The Sunset Emperor

Ijen Kim

CRUX
PUBLISHING

First published in January 2020
by Crux Publishing Ltd.

ISBN: 978-1-909979-99-4

CONTENTS

FOREWORD

This is the story of Aisin Gioro Zaitian, who reigned over China as the Qing dynasty's Guangxu Emperor from 1875 until 1908. Historians and writers of fiction, whether in China or abroad, have told this story before, though seldom in objective fashion. Perhaps this is because the period was a stormy one with all its plots, wars, coups and intrigue, and its main characters – colourful and controversial to start with – lent themselves easily to embellishment, blackening or whitewashing, depending on the circumstances.

The period was dominated by Empress Dowager Cixi, and she has tended to dominate the later storytelling too. Here, I shift the spotlight to the boy she put on the throne at the age of four, and to what became of him in the years that followed.

I didn't set out with any "agenda" in mind, had no ready-made heroes or villains, and I found myself wavering this way and that as I read different sources and gathered information. The sources range from archival documents and official court records to diaries, memoirs and accounts from the times. All of these sources are in themselves subjective and selective, distorting information or leaving things unsaid. I drew my version of events through comparison of as many sources as possible, finding the common points and letting logic fill the gaps.

Even historians cannot claim to be entirely objective or have the one true version of events, and novelists are by necessity even more forced to resort to imagination and a bit of guesswork. In as much as possible though, I have attempted to make this story as accurate and objective a portrayal as I could. After all, this was the real story of real people, and I wanted to leave it as I found it.

Chinese emperors are a troublesome lot when it comes to naming conventions, with personal names, era names, temple and posthumous names. The Qing dynasty emperors were Manchus, but they followed the Chinese conventions. Emperors' personal names were taboo and most emperors are known in history by their temple names. The Qing dynasty emperors, perhaps because they are closer to us in time, are more often referred to by their era names, and it is these I use in the novel. Technically, this is incorrect. Cixi and Guangxu did not go around calling each other this way during their day, but it makes things less confusing and is more familiar.

Below, I give a list of the Qing emperors, their personal names, era names and reign dates, to help set the general time context for references in the novel to past emperors and events.

(Ruling from Manchuria)
Nurhaci, 1616-1626
Huang Taiji, 1626-1643

(Ruling from Beijing)
Fulin, the Shunzhi Emperor, 1644-1661
Xuanye, the Kangxi Emperor, 1661-1722
Yinzhen, the Yongzheng Emperor, 1722-1735
Hongli, the Qianlong Emperor, 1735-1796
Yongyan, the Jiaqing Emperor, 1796-1820
Minning, the Daoguang Emperor, 1820-1850
Yizhu, the Xianfeng Emperor, 1850-1861
Zaichun, the Tongzhi Emperor, 1861-1875
Zaitian, the Guangxu Emperor, 1875-1908
Puyi, the Xuantong Emperor, 1908-1911

1

My father walked in the autumn light, birdcage in his hand. Sun slanted mellow through the pavilion and made a golden trail on the water. Sticky-faced in the bamboo, I knelt in the dirt and watched him from my hiding place. He wasn't alone, he came down the path with Sixth Uncle. They were silent. Sixth Uncle had his eyes downcast and my father stared towards the hole in the sky where the light fell through.

They sat in the pavilion. My father lifted the cover from the songbirds' cage and released from within a stream of trills. I kept still in the bamboo. I loved the way the birds performed on call, lift the cover and they came alive, chattering to the gardens until the covers were replaced. Then they fell silent again in the darkness.

My father's angry voice and Sixth Uncle's hard tone pushed the birdsong away. I didn't understand their talk, sensed only that they'd been punished and felt wronged. I watched them, open-mouthed and sad, knowing I'd soon be punished too for the sticky crumbs around my lips and for running off and hiding in the bamboo. My father cursed and made me jump in fright. Sixth Uncle put a restraining hand on his arm. I had only a little courage, enough to steal a fistful of food and escape to the garden, but it trickled from me and the sky took back its golden sun, left me cold and afraid.

Sixth Uncle spied me, came over and pulled me to my feet. I latched my hand in his, my guilty face avoiding my father's flashing eyes.

"He's a good boy this one, so quiet", Sixth Uncle sighed. "Count yourself lucky".

"Don't let him fool you", my father waved a dismissive hand at me. "You never saw such an obstinate child. Ask my wife. He'll make trouble yet".

Winter came and the birds were silent. Muted light filtered through the papered windows and I glimpsed forlorn branches and flurries of snow that turned the eaves white and new. Fleeing to the bamboo was the farthest I'd been. I was only just waking from the arms of nannies and servants. My feet were unsteady and my eyes greedy, running beyond my hesitant body. Nanny carried me through the morning chill to my mother's quarters and set me on my wobbling legs, her voice in my ear prompting me to speak. My mother's straight lips and solemn gaze made me awkward and I reached for Nanny's hand, trying to wriggle away behind her.

My mother was like the caged birds, bundled in dimness and silence. It was better not to snatch her cover free for she didn't sing joyful or glad. Her anxious eyes made me melt away into quiet corners beyond her sight. Peering furtively from behind Nanny, I stole snatches of her presence and she waited for my words, which never came. Her silence was tense. She lived in faded fasting light and cloaked herself in prayers and rites. Her Buddha was like she was, an unsmiling being of choked-up love that only ever showed itself in rules and admonition.

Nanny hurried me away. My eyes had grown large and I wanted to scratch the windows clear and discover what lay beyond, but I was hungry. Sometimes it was just a dull gnawing sensation that I could almost forget, but other times it swelled me up with tears and howls. Then they did as with the birds, covered me too and shut me away in dark places. There, I sobbed and snivelled until the blackness dissolved and I floated in its midst. Sounds came to my ears, new and strange as they seeped through the cracks and walls. The clocks became my friends. Their tick-tick was faint but constant and their chimes put colour in my murky surroundings.

Nanny was as soft and warm as anyone could be in our subdued world. She was schooled into quiet obedience, like everyone who served in our household, but a corner of her still poked free, even if just the simple familiarity and reassurance of her smell and the touch of her hands. She wiped tear streaks from my cheeks and hugged me in her silky folds, but she too held me back when I tried to grab food. It was my mother's order.

Food made my mother nervous and watchful. She feared something but I didn't know what. The servants sometimes broke the rules and sneaked me extra food, made me smile as I gulped down their little gifts, but my mother was vigilant, her anger arriving in jagged bursts of summer thunderstorm fury. The summer sky could change so fast, blue and smooth one moment, strange that it could vomit forth such wrath the next. My mother lit incense and murmured prayers, watched me with her straight mouth, upright and stiff. But the servants stopped sneaking me extra. She had them beaten and made them tremble.

My father was a surer haven, but he was often absent and his eyes were tired when I came before him, hesitant and mumbling my childish greetings. He didn't seem to see much now beyond the ceremonial beads he hung around his neck before hurrying into the new day only vaguely trimmed with dawn. He fingered the beads and looked preoccupied. We were only brief passing moments for each other.

When he was at home, he liked quiet and would shut himself away with his ink, brushes and books. Sometimes he let me in, drew me to his side, directed my staring eyes across the strokes on the paper, read things to me and searched my expression for signs of understanding.

The quiet of our home grew thicker that winter. Perhaps my child's haphazard sense of time stretched days into months and made the winter wilder than before. I was hungry and cold. Sometimes people came to hurry my father off into hushed words and closed doors. My uncles came and went. I wasn't allowed to get in their way. I'd seen them before with festive faces, but now they all had tired eyes like my father and a heavy, serious air.

Voices woke me from sleep one night. Nanny's face in the candle glow peered at me with a hasty and odd expression. I tried to sneak away into the bedclothes, but Nanny's arms came down and pulled me free. There were others in the room, but I didn't know them and they looked like shadows caught up in a bustle of their own.

My mother was there too. She'd turned into one of the effigies before which she lit incense, staring and wooden, and her mouth wasn't straight now but hung open in bewildered forgetfulness. The shadows crowded round and began to dress me. I wriggled in protest and started to cry, but that only sent them into a bigger fuss. They wiped my face clean, straightened my clothes and cajoled me to be quiet and still.

Then we left. My mother had a lost and sagging look. The cold air in the yard pinched the sleep from my eyes. The night tumbled, whipped along by the wind. The strange men wrapped me tight and their steps were fast. I glanced back but couldn't see my mother's face. She stayed inside. More men waited beyond the gate. Some were on horseback. The horses were large and impressive in the lantern-studded night. I wanted to see them better but found myself thrust inside a sedan chair, and the curtains closed around me.

I felt the chair rise and sensed the swift motion of our journey. The chair bearers ran through the darkness, their steps fleet and smooth. Few sounds came through the curtains. The men didn't speak to each other and even the horses' hooves seemed muffled. It was warm within the curtains and the rocking, jogging sensation soon lulled me into drowsiness.

Shards of dream scattered. The curtains pulled back and faces peered in once more. Someone picked me up and we hurried through brief chill and into new places filled with men dressed like my father at dawn, with beads and robes and the official hats with the jiggling peacock feather at the back. I thought I might find my father here too, but couldn't, and felt the tears rise as everything became fragments, faces and candle words that flickered and sputtered.

Two women came close, looked at me all over with reddened solemn eyes. I had to kneel and bow before a coffin. I was small, but I understood from the expression on everyone's faces that this casket contained grief. I did as they wished, bowed my head to the cold ground, and then cried and stamped my foot in impatience. No one seemed to mind my cries. It seemed that to howl away was the best thing to do in this strange place.

The night lost its solidity. Sleep tugged me from its grip and tears misted its outline. Feathers trembled and beads chinked against each other as the men knelt. There was more kneeling and bowing, more words that drifted upwards and hung somewhere in the dimness thickened by heat coming from big brass braziers.

I had almost forgotten that earlier I had lain curled up in my bed, and even the hurried, muffled journey through the sleeping city faded now. All I could think was that I was hungry again, and tired, and I sobbed and sniffed until the night turned so damp with my tears that it crumpled in a wet enveloping heap around me.

2

Someone stood before me. I sensed the shadow as my sleep grew thin.

"Master of Ten Thousand Years, it is time to rise".

I rubbed at my eyes and saw a man looking down at me. He was a little flabby and soft, he smiled slightly. He helped me sit up in bed and see that day had come.

There were others in the room, nannies and eunuchs. We had some eunuchs serving in our household, but these ones were livelier than ours, they came and went and tossed me inquisitive glances. They called me Master of Ten Thousand Years, but I was not master of anything, and certainly not of so many inconceivable years. I didn't want ten thousand years. I wanted to eat.

I could already smell the food. The eunuchs bustled quietly, brought dishes.

"Master of Ten Thousand Years, the food is ready".

I saw this myself. The burst of hot food smells made me dizzy. My mother was nowhere in sight and so I darted forward, grabbed a steaming bun and stuffed it in my mouth.

The eunuch who'd woken me tried to manoeuvre me into a chair, but I wriggled from his grasp, held tight to the bun with one hand, grabbed at a fried cake with the other. The eunuch stepped back and I gobbled as fast as I could, bit at the bun and the cake in turn, eager and frantic until I swallowed too much at once and started to cough and choke. The eunuch seized me and the food fell from my fingers. Then I was in the chair and a nanny fed me porridge.

I was taken to one of the women from the night before, the Empress Dowager Cian. "Empress dowager" sounded like it referred to a shrivelled, age-weary woman, but this woman didn't look very old. She was white-wrapped in mourning clothes but her pale face was pretty and smooth. Her gaze was kindly and a little distracted. She asked me if I had slept and eaten well and I hung my head in silence, the porridge sat heavy in me and the taste of the fried cake was too rich now, even sickening. She said a few things to the eunuchs and nannies while I stared at an ornamental clock that whirred and turned as the black pointed hands pursued their creeping movement.

Cian watched me. "Come." She held out a hand towards me. "Come to Mother".

I stayed where I was. The clock made only a small tick-tick, busy and dry in tone. I'd learned in the dark to hear the layers and subtle notes in the sounds around me.

"Come to Mother," Cian repeated her words.

I kept my head down. The real mother I'd left in the wintry night, didn't smile and her face was taut and tense, not like this empress dowager with her mild, placid expression. The clock chimed, a single crisp tone that hung in the air. This smiling woman called herself my mother when I already had a mother waiting in the night with a lost look on her face. The eunuchs led me away crying.

I was full of tears and my nose ran. The eunuchs didn't notice, and the wet trickle grew. I had to kneel again and I stayed there on the ground, too weak to get up. The other woman from the night before had her turn to sit before me. Would she also say she was my mother? She was another empress dowager, Cixi, and she was pale and sad like Cian, but hadn't the same distracted look. There was a sudden rustle and she got up from her chair, bent down beside me and lifted me from the ground.

"So thin and weak," she murmured. "We'll have to do something about you."

Her voice was light and silvery. I stole a glance at her face. It blurred with my tears, but also with my mother's own face in an elusive hint of resemblance. I closed my eyes and saw so clearly home and Nanny and my mother's admonishing voice warning me not to eat forbidden things and make myself sick. My stomach hurt now. How would I explain to my mother that I hadn't meant to, but the steaming bowls full of dizzying smells were too great a temptation to withstand?

"Don't cry, my son."

A hand stroked my cheek. It was Cixi who spoke.

She called me her son, said it in a murmur more for herself than for me, it seemed. My damp and melting aspect didn't seem to bother her. Her fingers wore the metal glint of sharp-tipped golden nail protectors, but her grasp was reassuring. Only her eyes stayed elsewhere, as if it wasn't really me she held or saw. "My son" was a small word but it came from a huge unseen ocean behind her shining black eyes, a spreading word that grew too vast for my comprehension, still so narrow and tender.

Outside was icy and sullen. Charcoal burned in a brazier but the chill stole its warmth. Though lifted now from my kneeling pose, the cold through the carpet still lingered in me and made me shiver. Cixi felt it, gathered me tighter and let me press my face hard against her until the quiet returned once more.

3

I was borne aloft to the coffin hall in a yellow-curtained chair, eunuchs all around, to perform my ritual kneeling and bows. This new walled world had many rituals and names. The eunuchs told me all these things, their tongues eager with words but their faces hollow.

In the coffin, as I now knew, lay the departed emperor, shrouded and hidden away under wood and layers of lacquer. I doubted he could see all my bows. If the eunuchs were right, he was not even there now.

The eunuchs said he'd ascended on the dragon into the heavens. I imagined him old, stern and yellow, like the other emperors, whose flat-faced portraits also received my bows, sitting astride a dragon and galloping skywards. I doubted he'd return to this shadowy hall, surely more eager now to roam the clouds than to sup on the cold offerings heaped on plates or receive my ritual respect.

This departed ruler was the Emperor Tongzhi. He was Cixi's son. Officially speaking, he was Cian's son too, because she had been the empress and as such was formally the mother of all imperial offspring. She therefore mourned and grieved his loss, but Cixi was the mother who'd brought him into the world, the one who would watch, warn and worry.

Cixi hadn't Cian's elevated status. She had entered the palace as a consort, one of a number of hopeful young women, was promoted in rank after giving birth to a boy, and finally joined Cian as a second dowager empress after Emperor Xianfeng died, leaving Cixi's one small son to succeed him. Now that son, Emperor Tongzhi, was gone too, lacquered out of sight or up in the heavens, and it was I who had to take his place and call myself "your son" in the dowagers' presence.

My tongue was numb and wooden and produced howls and tears more easily than words. Nanny didn't come, nor did my mother or father. I turned into a whimpering ball, crawled back into my familiar darkness and let it suck me into the floating silence. The darkness here was different, much louder for one thing, layered with voices and calls, people coming and going. I added my vain wails to the bustle and fuss, gave everyone tired faces and stole their sleep. The eunuchs and nannies grew sick of me, shuddered and sighed at my stubbornness.

One morning, the eunuchs made me bright with yellow robes, even more anxious than usual to have me clean and quiet. Their chief, eunuch Fan, put on his most cajoling smile.

"Master of Ten Thousand Years, you mustn't start crying today." He wagged a finger at me. "You mustn't spoil such an important occasion. Today you ascend the throne."

Fan put on a solemn air and said I too must be dignified and silent. This throne would probably want my bows and kneeling, like the dowagers, the coffin and the ancestors.

I made myself good and quiet under Fan's watchful eyes. The morning was crisp and gold-edged. We went through the gates that divided our everyday places from the broad courtyards beyond. I sat upright in my chair, peered through the curtains and saw birds wheel in the sky over sun-glistened roofs. Voices cut sharp lines through the stirring air in practised, drawn-out intonation. They called my coming.

Up the steps we went. This hall was bigger, higher, and the air trembled with something grand. Everything lay clear in the morning light and I saw the roofs spread before me, walls, towers, pavilions on the hill beyond, a flash of lakes, darker swathes of trees.

A vast crowd filled the square down below. Officials in their finery, eunuchs, imperial guards, big strange instruments, silent and waiting, gongs, bells and drums, all made a vast frozen picture of meticulous arrangement in which I seemed to be the only living, moving thing, stumbling and reluctant as they bore me into the hall and led me up towards the big carved throne.

The picture and the stillness broke. Voices thundered and roared, rows of heads bobbed up and down, their calls of "ten thousand years!" crashing over me in rolling tumult. Stranded on the enormous throne, I sought refuge from the noise, forgot to sit still and solemn and wanted to climb down and hide. But they wouldn't let me leave. The calls swallowed me in a bellowing flood, my howls lost in the ringing vastness. The heads went up and down, the sun catching hat feathers and silk. I put my hands to my ears and pressed myself into a corner. The golden dragon's head reared over me, its carved claws surrounding me. I closed my eyes and prayed for the throne to let me go.

I fell ill shortly afterwards. My real mother came to see me. The eunuchs' private words drifted my way and I understood that she'd come with Nanny, but they got sent away.

I regretted not seeing Nanny, but was not sure that I wanted to see my mother. I saw her in my feverish recollections, left behind in that stormy night when her sternness fell from her and her eyes turned lost. Perhaps she'd already sensed things in her covered, silent days, read omens in that night's sputtering candles and hasty gestures and knew that I would feast greedily and make myself sick. She knew I was an obstinate child and had said so with her whipping words that made me shrink. The eunuchs' eyes suggested that they too would like to hit me into silence and hide me somewhere far from sight, maybe lacquer me up like Tongzhi so they could doze and sit idle and quiet.

The fever silenced my cries, turned me emptied and limp. Doctors came and went, wrote prescriptions, which hovering Cixi read with vigilant attention, as if one of their medical brethren. She kept me at her side and performed the small routines. She sang to me sometimes too, close to my ear, poured into me her gentle voice, and I let it nudge me into sleep.

They wanted me to forget that there had been other songs, hands and hearts. Perhaps that winter night when they brought me here was supposed to have whirled all those things away in its snow flurries.

I was Prince Chun's son, Zaitian, before that night. Now I was emperor and my name was taboo. Others were not to speak or write it. I received an era name, a title of good omen to clothe the time and dates of my reign just begun. I was now Emperor Guangxu of the Great Qing. I was the Master of Ten Thousand Years and the Son of Heaven.

It meant little to me, a sick snivelling bundle at the dowagers' side. Those days were frayed and thin with the worry on my new mothers' faces, Cixi fussing over the doctors' concoctions and Cian with her prayer beads and appeals to Buddha. Sometimes they ran out of prayers and potions, they just watched me and wept.

4

The foreign woman shone in the sun. Spots of light danced on the floor where she lay, her painted face still wearing its eager expression, porcelain curls with bows and ribbons, porcelain beads round her slender neck. The rest of her lay in scattered fragments. The ticking stopped and the hands were still. Now I could see all the springs and wheels. I picked up the remains of the clock and stared at its insides, intrigued by the neat and careful way all these bits of metal could fit together and come alive.

Eunuch Fan would appear any minute. I revelled in this sudden absence of anyone else around. It was rare. The first clock I tried to smash was too big. I pushed it but it wouldn't topple. Then the one with the porcelain woman caught my eye.

Fan looked panicked when he saw me sitting amidst the shards of glass and porcelain pieces. The ancestors' clocks were precious things, many of them gifts from foreign lands. He admonished me in worried tones and hurried me away.

Life was dull in the Forbidden City. The eunuchs tried to entertain me with plump glossy crickets they kept in little boxes, and they were amusing for a time, but all their tricks and toys soon held no interest. Only the clocks and watches kept their charm, and I continued to smash them, hoping to make them tell me their mechanical secrets.

The summer brought heat-swollen skies, the air still and heavy. Bright flash in the distance, and then the world split about me, like that drowning day on the throne, the sky turned grim and roared its anger. I screwed my eyes tight and screamed my terror.

"It's only a thunderstorm." The eunuchs were dismissive. "No need to be afraid."

The thunderstorms brought my mother back in clanging echoes inside me. I saw her like the shattered porcelain woman, sharp splinters caught here and there in my memories, full of sudden fury. I wanted quiet, not the dark places they shut me away in when I howled too long, not the cold black punishment quiet, but something warm and safe to hide me from the noise and anger. The eunuchs grinned at my stammering fear, deaf to the sky, uncaring of its wrath.

Cixi rescued me, clasped me in her arms until I sobbed myself into silence.

"Come, come, you're not really so afraid of the thunder, are you? Where's your Manchu courage?" she asked, wiping my tears away.

Her question fluttered in me. I was a Manchu, but not yet sure where my courage was, and if I had it. I sat on Cixi's bed and stared at the butterfly in her hair. It was made of jade but looked real enough to flutter away into the sky now cleansed, only the hurried sound of water running from the eaves still there as a last echo of the storm.

She sagged on to the bed beside me, suddenly tired and troubled. I noticed that her face would sometimes cloud with shadows and worries that she tried to keep tucked out of sight. When I called her "mother", it made her choked and sad and she told me to keep calling Cian mother but to call her "father". I did as she asked. "Mother" already belonged to Tongzhi and he'd taken it with him into his coffin.

She sat so close to me but I sensed her shut away, followed her gaze across objects, the brush strokes of a calligraphy scroll on the wall, the golden shine of a foreign clock. I glimpsed a strip of sky beyond the roofs, pink-tinged with evening, then I sneezed and she returned to me, put her hand to my forehead and said she hoped I wasn't catching another cold.

She and Cian fretted constantly over my health. I couldn't sit on the throne if I was always sick, and I had to sit on the throne quite often. I didn't have to do anything, just sit still. This throne was smaller, and stood in one of my own rooms.

Cian and Cixi were always with me, but out of sight behind me, hidden by a thin yellow curtain. The official beads and feathers came at dawn, all those kneeling men and rustling robes, they took turns letting words roll from their tongues. They looked at me, but in reality, spoke to the two dowagers behind the curtain.

I tried to sit straight and still as instructed, but my head turned heavy and I dozed and woke again, usually when the dowagers' voices came from behind, making some remark. I sneezed vigorously and everything went silent. Prince Gong, my Sixth Uncle, raised his eyes and cast a quick, probing glance over me. The others kept their eyes down, but Prince Gong was bold and watchful.

Behind me, the dowagers stopped listening to the men and seemed to try to curl their eyes through the curtain and around the carved back of the throne to check that all was well. I drew my legs up, wanting to turn around, pull back the curtain and let them see me, but Li Lianying, the chief eunuch, appeared from the shadows and motioned discreetly for me to keep still. I thought him tall, thin and unpleasant, but his manner was soft and restrained, his voice oily smooth, and he knew all the rules.

The early air had a faint chill in it. Cian's eyes were red. I came to her hoping to find her happy. I knew that Cixi was already with Buddha and the ancestors, weeping and praying. Cian was the same. They were both crying for their departed husband.

I knelt before Emperor Xianfeng's portrait, ordered to perform the mourning rituals too. His portrait image had no beard or moustache like most of the others, though he wore the same yellow court robes and beads. The ancestor portraits all looked a lot alike, but each emperor nonetheless had his own expression. Xianfeng's expression was slightly shy and meek. I bowed my head and tried to look sad, as befitted a death anniversary.

When the French and English foreign devils invaded Beijing, Xianfeng had to flee for safety with his court. The foreign devils burned the Summer Palace, looted and destroyed, and it all made Xianfeng grow so sad and sick that he died.

My eyes spilled tears too. It wasn't so much the story that made me cry as the sight of my empress dowager mothers filled with sorrow. Cixi sang me no song when evening came. She got me ready for sleep in silence. I slipped a hand into hers, made her stop and look down at me. She had protected me from the thunder and I wanted to console her.

"I won't let any foreign devils come and make you sad."

My voice always came out hesitant, the words not wanting to take firmer form on my clumsy tongue.

Cixi smiled and said this was the way for an emperor to talk. But her eyes didn't seem to believe my words. I saw it in the way she looked at me. Not just now but often, a doubtful look, and though she was kind, hid me from the thunder, kept shrill sounds from my ears, looked after me when I was sick and soothed my frequent tears, I sensed nonetheless that I was not what I should be, not what she hoped to see.

5

I faced south and waited, seated at a small table in the room where the grand councillors came to pour forth their tedious morning words to Cian and Cixi behind the curtain. The room was different now and I awaited my teachers for the ceremony of commencing study. It was time, according to the ancestors' rules.

The dowagers instructed me how to behave. The emperor faced south because he was in this world like the North Star in the heavens. Our world repeated the greater universe beyond, and every person and thing had to keep its proper place and order, otherwise there'd be no harmony and we'd all descend into chaos. The emperor thus always faced south, just as the palaces all faced south and the road ran south from the great palace gates in a straight line to the Temple of Heaven. The emperor had to be solemn and serious, no wriggling and fidgeting, no glancing about here and there with wandering eyes. I sat up very straight and put on what I hoped was a suitably stern expression.

The teachers arrived. One of them stepped forward, Tutor Weng. He wasn't as old as I'd thought all the teachers would be, but his pointy beard and serious look made him seem older, and his slow, grave movements would have suited an old man.

He took a writing brush and the four characters of "Great peace under heaven" emerged in clear strokes on the sheet of paper laid out before me. He dipped the brush in the ink again and wrote four more characters, "Open and Just Rule". Then it was my turn and he guided my hand as I copied the characters.

Prince Gong quoted from the classics about being a virtuous sovereign and ruling the earthly domains following

Heaven's way. They wrote that out before me too. Their faces were happy to see me so wide-eyed and attentive, though their words were misty and not as clear as their brushstrokes.

I already knew some characters, and books were not unfamiliar. Not that I could read them yet myself, but others read to me, and lines from the classics had already traced furrows in my mind. Cixi had often lain paper before me and written characters. She read to me from the Book of Songs too. It talked of faraway things, mountains and countryside, homesick men gone to battle, lonely women with sad eyes searching the horizon, praise for wise kings and sorrow over bad ones. The lines from her mouth wrapped a whole distant world. She too wrote characters with a firm hand and practised gesture, and, following her movement, staring beyond into the lamplight, I remembered my father, brush in hand, scanning my face for understanding.

Sometimes those memories took flesh. The dowagers could grant permission and my father and mother would be summoned from their hazy place beyond the walls and become real again before me. It wasn't the same though. We spoke ceremonial words and it was hard to know what else to say. My parents stayed distant, knelt, bowed, thanked the dowagers for their great kindness.

My mother kept her face locked up and lips clamped tight. I understood now why I'd seen a tiny bit of her in Cixi when I first arrived. Cixi was her older sister. She'd used her standing with Emperor Xianfeng to help win her younger sister a prestigious match with Prince Chun, Xianfeng's younger brother. But Cixi and my mother were so different in character. I sensed no warmth between them and they didn't really seem like sisters at all.

It was supposed to be a special occasion when my parents came, but I felt no wish to prolong it. It only made me confused inside. I couldn't follow them home again, but belonged here with the dowagers and the portrait of Emperor Xianfeng. I was their son now.

The astronomers chose another auspicious morning for my commencement of daily study. The sky was still dressing in dawn when we went to the ritual hall, where I bowed before the image of the Great Sage, Confucius, the teacher of all teachers. My head ached and I wanted to sleep.

I soon hated the dawn, urged the hours to pass swiftly and hurried the clock hands with my gaze. Eunuch Fan was merciless, his scrubbed morning face pulling me from warmth and dreams. Darkness and chill waited beyond, and so did Tutor Weng and his colleagues with Confucius and the classics.

I was quickly weary of the classroom. Tutor Weng's words faded into a distant drone. I had music in my ears instead. The eunuchs knew the places beyond, the city streets and shops, from where they'd brought me a pleasing new thing, a little box which, when opened, played a tinkling melody while a slender woman twirled round and round. She was like the porcelain woman on the clock I'd smashed, a foreign woman with blue eyes and yellow hair. She perched on tiptoes, bared her legs like no one here ever would, and turned endlessly to the music.

I liked the tune. Its meandering sweetness soothed my ears. The eunuchs said there was a shop in the city where a foreign man sold curious objects from the land called Europe, far away across the western ocean, and it was from him that they'd purchased the little box.

The melody settled in my head so much more easily than Confucius' long-ago words. I raised the lid over and over, and the woman smiled at me every time.

My hand twitched in anticipation. I had plans. When the morning finally lifted its dull classroom cover, I'd go to take the box apart and find out how it worked. I wanted to see where the music was hidden. I thought of my afternoon pleasures ahead and the melody swallowed Tutor Weng's voice. He snatched me from my reverie and told me to concentrate.

I stared at him a moment. I'd had enough of the books and the sticky school hours today. His voice turned persuasive, and I ignored him. He urged me. I turned my face to the wall and shut him from my sight. This was much better. Now there was no Tutor Weng, no book to recite, and I could stand a long time in my corner, floating in the melody that played inside me.

My eyes squeezed tight, I twirled like the foreign lady, carried along in a sweet stream of music, no walls around me, no sighing cajoling tutor behind me. I was stubborn and I would win. If I was Master of Ten Thousand Years and all these people bowed before me, I could surely make them mine, make them twirl for me like the foreign lady did, make all the mornings mine too and read books only when I felt like it.

6

"So, you don't want to study?"

Cixi's voice had lost its usual light and silvery sound. I knelt before her.

"You want to grow up into a muddle-headed emperor?"

I shook my head vaguely and stole a glance at her face. Anger darkened it in a look that recalled my mother when the storm broke inside her. The maids standing on either side of her kept their heads down, still and tense. One held her water pipe, the other her tea.

I doubted Tutor Weng had told her about my refusal to study. It must have been Fan. Fan was always at the classroom with me and saw my protests. He was a eunuch, anyway, and I had already learned that eunuchs were like that, deceitful and vicious.

"Well, go on, speak!"

I opened my mouth but nothing came out. Cixi fixed flashing eyes on me. Her anger gave way to something less distinct, a mixture of worry and disappointment. This was the reign of Guangxu, the "Glorious Succession." It was the era title they'd chosen, two small words fat with dreams of keeping our ancestors' shining legacy burning bright. But these two small words would become just a shrivelled husk if I did not prepare myself diligently for the task.

I hated the eunuchs. I took the music box apart and lost the melody. Inside were springs and wheels, like in the clocks, but I couldn't work out their secrets. The eunuchs carried the pieces away. My head had no hiding place now. Cixi's angry words scratched and chafed me and my tears fell on to the shining floor.

My tears were frequent. The urge to sleep turned my head heavy. The dull gnaw of hunger stole my attention. The eunuchs were like my mother, anxious not to have me eat too much. They often let my food grow cold and I felt nausea well inside me when I tried to eat it. Chill got into me and stuffed me up with ache and fever. I coughed and sniffed incessantly. The eunuchs didn't care. Fan pushed me into the dawn regardless. He was soft and round, spoke in coaxing tones, but he prodded me with rules and he was used to me now and let my tears flow past him with weary resignation.

I couldn't wear my tutors down as easily as I'd imagined. It was I who got worn down fast. I had to memorise the classical texts, reading passages aloud over and over until I knew them by rote.

My glorious ancestor, Emperor Kangxi, who was also just a boy when he ascended the throne, used to recite each passage 120 times to fix it in his memory, and later made his sons do the same. My tutors had trouble getting me to do it even ten times. It wasn't that I didn't want to learn, but my tongue stumbled and my strength was in such small supply. It was tiring to read aloud, recite, remember, and I wilted, turned silent and wooden.

The tutors would give me a chance to venture outside and stretch my legs a while in the fresh air. I seldom moved though, sat in the corner with drooping head and eyes half-closed as snatches of dream came and went in curious procession.

It worried the teachers that I was so motionless and preferred to dissolve myself this way rather than roam a little with the sky and the leaves outside. Tutor Weng said Tongzhi had been different, full of life and movement and always ready to seize the chance to lay aside his books. Tutor Weng was tutor to Tongzhi before being appointed to teach me. He was just a young man when he first got that job. His father, a noted scholar, was one of Tongzhi's teachers, but then he died and the court asked Tutor Weng to take his place and continue his work.

He must have been an impressive young man to win such favour. It seemed he'd liked Tongzhi. The way he spoke, I imagined Tongzhi might come running in any minute, flush with laughter. Tutor Weng obviously hadn't expected his young charge to leave the world so soon, and I glimpsed regret in his eyes.

His colleague, Tutor Xia, stood before me now and had the brushes and ink ready for practising calligraphy. The pause was over, but I stayed where I was, obstinate in my corner.

One of the palace clocks was decorated with a mechanical man who began to write a line of characters on a scroll each time the hour struck, and I felt like that man, stiffened and bound by dull repetition.

Tutor Xia looked annoyed. His tone grew impatient but he was silenced by the sudden entry of a eunuch who announced the arrival of Prince Chun, my father. I hadn't expected this. Here he was, suddenly beside me once more, but he kept himself distant and serious. Cian and Cixi had put him in charge of my studies and he came now only to pinch me with reproach.

I wished he'd leave, not because I cared nothing for him, but because his voice dug deeper into me than my tutors' sighs. His memory was easier than his presence and I kept my head down, anxious to avoid the disapproval in his eyes.

He made me obedient for a time. I wrote my characters and read my books. But his voice soon faded from my mind and I retreated once more into silence and refusal. He came on several occasions, dutiful, rubbing me in shame. The emperor wasn't supposed to weep and sit in sulky silence. The emperor was supposed to shine with wisdom and virtue, like Yao and Shun from the ancient days, noble rulers who'd made the land prosper and were so perfect that even the greatest of later monarchs only hoped and strove to follow their example.

I wasn't Yao or Shun and didn't want to be emperor like the clock man diligently writing the same sentence every hour. I hated this place.

They continued the old punishments, smothered my cries and hid me to grow dry from tears and sink into tired compliance. They fed me fat on virtue, learning and filial piety. The eunuchs threatened me, saying the thunder god would take me if I disobeyed, and as if to prove their words, there would come a crashing and banging on the other side of the wall. Fan would nod at my fear with his I-told-you-so look. Later, I realised it was the eunuchs themselves creating that din.

I ran from them one day, left Tutor Weng with his mouth hanging open and the eunuchs gone into a flurry of shouts. With tear-blurred eyes, I stumbled onwards, my fists clenched in sudden determination. Only there were gates and guards every way I turned, and the pursuing eunuchs were already close behind me. They pounced on my hesitation and laughed at the idea that I should have thought to escape.

I was soon back at my place in the classroom. Tutor Weng looked grave. He placed a cool hand on my forehead.

"I think you have fever."

His voice was quiet and concerned.

"We won't read any more today," he said.

I nodded, gratefully, looked up at his face and saw that it was real in its feeling. He caught my look and smiled.

He was closer after that, more willing to let me rest. He saw that I had a naturally good memory and a curious mind, and he understood that I learned faster when he put the books into his own words and made them come alive. He gave their pages greater flavour and graspable meaning. I remained reluctant and silent but he seemed to realise that sometimes I was just too tired or ill. My father came less often. It seemed he didn't enjoy these supervisory duties. I was glad of his absence. Having his gaze on me only made things worse.

But I couldn't avoid my empress dowager mothers. They were always fretting about my studies. Cian didn't probe so deep. She was as if a clock woman, predictable, familiar to me in her workings. She fussed a lot about rules and appearance and liked to talk about the ancestors and how important it was to respect the order they'd established, but her words stayed much the same from one day to the next, faint in their impression.

Cixi made long faces when she saw me, and sighed like my tutors. She was silent and I sensed her troubled. I assumed it was I who'd stolen her glow, for she looked weary when I came and didn't even reproach me. I should have been glad to taste her heavy silence rather than her lecturing tongue, but I saw how grey and dimmed she was and couldn't help feeling guilty.

Tutor Weng announced one day that we were all going to pray for rain. He said it was the rain that made Cixi troubled and silent. The skies had been clear for weeks now. I was curious. He spoke of places where floods had left people homeless, and other places besieged by drought and famine. People starved in Henan and Shanxi. I had no idea where Henan and Shanxi might be, but I pictured the starving people easily enough, knew their hungry feeling, listless eyes and gnawing ache inside. I saw them staring up at the mocking blue sky and begging it to grant them rain for their crops.

They looked to the emperor for help. The emperor was the Son of Heaven and could speak on their behalf to the stingy sky. We would all pray for rain, Tutor Weng said, and we would not eat meat, humble ourselves and turn the sky generous and wet.

I felt sorry for the starving people. Usually, when Tutor Weng talked about the emperor it sounded dry and removed, just something out of the books, but back in my own rooms that evening I pictured the hungry people and it struck me then that I was the Son of Heaven and it was to me that they appealed.

I began to pray. The eunuchs wanted me to get ready for bed but I made them wait while I talked to the sky. The next day was bright and cloudless. The heavens ignored me. Perhaps they did not consider me the Son of Heaven. Tongzhi had flown away and I was maybe just Prince Chun's son and not really an emperor at all. But I was stubborn and continued my efforts the next evening. Sleep-tugged, I fought my tiredness and made myself as Tutor Weng had said, solemn and humble, praying earnestly, begging the rain to please come and share its riches with our hungry lands.

The morning was dark and I thought the eunuchs had woken me too early. My ears seized the muffled patter beyond and I jumped from my bed and ran as I was into the yard. The sky was thick and leaden and the rain fell steady. I raised my face and smiled, lifted my hands to its cool stream, ran through its wetness, excited and grateful. I was the Son of Heaven and the people would not starve now.

"What are you doing running in the rain like that? You'll catch cold!"

Fan appeared, looking alarmed, and the eunuchs hustled me back inside. I protested, dripping and annoyed that they'd snatched me from the rain's embrace. They didn't understand. They all thought I had become emperor on the cold morning when I sat miserable and scared on the big throne in the Hall of Supreme Harmony, but I only really became emperor in that damp grey dawn, jumping in the puddles of my yard and smiling at the bountiful sky.

7

I learned to sit straight, carried in my chair through gates and passages, borne aloft to present my greetings to my dowager empress mothers or take my place before my waiting teachers. The motion was familiar now and so too the close and narrow contours of the palace world.

The outer court was the place of vast squares and grand ceremonial halls. Further on was the great expanse before the Meridian Gate, cut through by a shining ribbon of water. I seldom went to the outer court, let alone to the places beyond, where officials rushed about in endless bustle. The walls and towers rose, more gates, and beyond them the moat, and only my imagination could take me further, into the city streets. Not even rituals got me out of the palace for now. They were delegated to relatives who performed them in my stead. I was still small and stayed hidden away.

Our days passed mostly in the inner court, compressed into a dim jumble of buildings tucked away behind yet more walls. It hadn't always been this way. When Emperor Xianfeng was alive, Cixi and Cian used to spend long months amidst the gardens and lakes of the Summer Palace outside Beijing, but those places were largely in ruins now.

There was Rehe too, beyond the Great Wall. The court used to move there every year to hunt and escape the summer heat but no one wanted to go there now. It got a reputation as an unlucky place. My great grandfather, Emperor Jiaqing, died there. He set out on his usual hunting trip, arrived in Rehe, and suddenly died, just like that. It was to Rehe that Emperor Xianfeng fled when the foreign devils invaded Beijing. Cixi and Cian spoke little of it, perhaps because they returned from Rehe as widows, their husband's coffin following, their splendid summer home destroyed and only the Forbidden City left to take them in its cloistered welcome.

We had the Imperial Garden to amuse us. Cian would walk there in slow and stately promenade when the weather was fine. Cixi had a vigorous stride and would go there even in the rain or snow, her serving girls and eunuchs trying to hide grumbling faces as they hurried after her with the chairs, umbrellas, tea, food and so on that followed us everywhere.

Sometimes she sat in a pavilion, listening to one of the educated eunuchs read stories, and sometimes she was full of bustle and inspection, examining plants and flowers and giving orders to the gardeners.

I preferred to go there on my own. I was never truly on my own for there was always a procession in tow, but I learned to flatten them from my vision and turned them in my mind into no more than a whirring string of mechanical parts like the wheels and springs in the clocks I took apart.

I liked to go there just after the storms had passed. There was a pavilion where I'd sit and watch the water burst from the pipe end into the pond below. I dissolved in that fat flood running forth. The water sang and the pool rippled. The rushing sound hadn't the storm's bludgeoning anger but was glad and free in its haste, leaping into the pond. Gradually it slowed to a tinkling trickle. I melted in that silvery stream. It made me think of my name, Zaitian – a tranquil flow of water. I hoped to be like my name, calm and steady on my journey.

But this journey didn't look so calm. I knew that my prayers had brought the people only brief respite. I heard the rumours and whispers of famine, floods, drought, rebellions and tension on the far-off borders with the cunning foreign powers. I already knew that the heavens smiled upon good emperors and rained misfortune upon bad ones, so that even if they could still hide in their guarded splendour their unhappy people would finally rise up against them, and heaven's mandate would pass to someone of greater virtue and merit. It was in the books Tutor Weng made me read.

I wondered how humble I had to become for the heavens to cease their cruelty. I fasted and prayed and yet it was not enough.

One day, Tutor Weng bade me read aloud as usual, and I obeyed, but my voice was quiet and dull.

"You know this character?" he looked up, seeing that I had paused and was staring at the page.

I nodded. It was "Luxury".

"I don't like this character," I said. "I like 'Frugality."

He stared at me a moment in what looked like surprise and then broke into a slow spreading smile and praised me for these wise words.

His voice was encouraging and his eyes had a sudden glow. In his gaze I had seen worry, weariness, good things too, simple care and concern, but here was a golden spark that seized me in an embrace warmer and tighter than his arms could ever give.

Cian and Cixi praised me too when they heard what I'd said in the classroom. I was happy to be praised, but I wanted my words to be real. I meant what I said and longed for us to be frugal and simple. All the good emperors in Tutor Weng's books were modest and content with little, but we had such riches around us, more than we could ever need, and it worried me. The heavens would surely continue to punish us if it was we who grew fat and replete, and not our vast lands beyond.

I was happy to find an ally in Tutor Weng. He tried to give me examples to follow, not just Yao and Shun who never left the remoteness of legend, but my own forebears, Kangxi and Qianlong, under whom our empire had grown and prospered. He made them leave their places of incense and offerings and gave them flesh. They had lived here in these same palaces, real people, each with their own story. I especially liked hearing about how Kangxi had started out just a boy on the throne, and in difficult times, and how, through his diligence and resolve, he became one of the wisest rulers China had ever known.

"I will be like Kangxi," I declared.

Tutor Weng beamed. "This is my greatest wish," he said softly. "It would be a great fortune for the dynasty."

I was happier after that, knew purpose and future, knew why I had to study. The classroom became my home and Tutor Weng not just my teacher, but also my friend.

8

It was theatre day. Cian nibbled at small cakes and her placid face wore a carefree look in the cheerful sunlight slanting in. She smiled at me, put a sweet-filled bun in my hand and motioned for me to eat up and enjoy myself. I glanced at Cixi but her attention was on the actors and not on me or the cakes. Cixi wanted me to eat proper food, not the sweets and buns that Cian liked to pick at. I put the bun up my sleeve, thinking to enjoy it later in private.

I was thinking too of how to escape the theatre. The gongs, drums and cymbals clanged and banged and the actors' voices grew too shrill for my ears. My head throbbed. We always had theatre performances on festivals and holidays. It had long been a popular pastime in the palace.

One of our dynasty's earlier rulers, Kangxi's son Emperor Yongzheng, who also liked frugality, banned the nobles and officials from having private troupes and spending their days watching theatre, but even then, the palace stage hadn't stayed empty. Emperor Xianfeng had had a passion for it, and the two dowagers continued his choice of entertainment.

Cixi especially loved it. She dreamt up her own scenarios and decor and liked to give the eunuch actors her suggestions. Theatre days were among the rare moments when I did not have to study. I was supposed to accompany the dowagers on these occasions and share their entertainment.

I would have preferred the classroom at that moment. Study had grown more wearying lately, with lessons stretching right through the day now. But I liked to think of Tutor Weng waiting for me. He returned to his hometown to take care of his family graves and I realised then how much I needed him and missed him. I ignored my other tutors while he was gone, neglected my studies and hardly spoke until he came back. He seemed touched by my affection.

Cixi peeled herself away from the actors and tried to turn my attention to the stage. The theatre wasn't all just entertainment. It could tell history and teach morals. If I paid attention, I'd see the same things that I read about in my books, wise sovereigns vanquishing foolish ones, virtue rewarded and rebellion punished. Cixi was in a good mood and there was no lecturing reproach in her tone. She just wanted me to enjoy the performance and soak in the right values at the same time. Tutor Weng made the same exhortations, only without gongs and clamour. My head ached and I wanted to leave.

"What's the matter? You want to go?" Cixi noticed me all fidgety.

I hesitated. She frowned, her look suggesting it was wrong of me to want to escape the dowagers' presence so soon.

"Uh…I want to read," I mumbled. "I'd like to go to my books."

"Oh, you want to study?" her face relaxed and she nodded. "Hmm, it's good to see your diligence. You may go then, if that's what you want."

I breathed deeply as the noise faded behind me. I refused the sedan chair and all the trailing eunuchs. We didn't have to be ceremonial just now and I wanted to walk. Ice lay here and there in the shady corners. The sky was bright and the roof tiles sparkled in gay colour. The bitter wind blew slicing gusts, making me hunch over and draw inwards. Fan hurried behind me.

I spied a magpie perched on a naked branch, saw it leap into the air and land on one of the big lanterns the eunuchs lit in the long passages at night. It watched me with bold eye, perhaps knowing it was sacred to the Manchu people and no one here would harm it. Magpies weren't ordinary birds to us. It was a magpie that brought the heavenly red berry to the maiden

Fekulen, who ate it and gave birth to my people's first ancestor. This one had nothing to deliver, just sat cocky and unafraid as I crept closer. Glossy feathers, head tilted, it seemed to laugh at my approach, but I sneezed and it flew away.

"Let's get out of this cold before you get sick," Fan fretted.

They always wanted to hurry me onwards and keep the wind from flushing my cheeks bright with chill. I looked jealously at the sky where the magpie had gone, wanting to follow it, numbed, cold-pinched but real. Tutor Weng said I shouldn't chafe so much at the protective wrap of rules. When snow fell, I refused to let the eunuchs clear it from my path, deliberately wanting it to hinder my feet and turn damp on my skin. Alone in the fat flakes, cold curtain around me, no road laid smooth ahead, I liked that taste of winter harshness that put a sudden glowing strength inside me. I tried to explain this to Tutor Weng, but wasn't sure he really understood what I meant.

It was probably with Tutor Weng in my thoughts that I came to the empty classroom now. Only the big clock broke the silence. There was a shadowy filtered feeling in the air and the furtive light turned me lethargic. I sat staring at the characters of a poem mounted on the wall, dutiful sentiments from my father's hand.

Cixi would be happy to think me absorbed in my books. I knew her better now. She was stern with me, too stern at times, but that was Tongzhi's fault. The eunuchs gave him gossip-stained flesh and their nasty tongues painted him spoilt, lazy, a dismal student and rebellious son. But they'd liked him, much more than they liked me. Like Tutor Weng said, he'd had a lot of life and movement in him, and that had no doubt appealed.

Eunuchs had lying mouths. Tongzhi hadn't really been so dismal a student, he'd just been too free, too hard to tie down, and that was what they held against him. It mightn't have mattered if Cixi had been an ordinary mother and Tongzhi just her son and not the emperor, but such was not their fate.

An emperor's schooling was a serious matter. I knew that Tutor Weng and Cixi were less than happy with the results their first attempt at raising a model monarch had produced. It seeped out of hints dropped here and there. They feared past errors of lenience and indulgence. I was their second chance and they wanted to get it right this time. I understood now that when Cixi reproached me, it was really Tongzhi's memory she saw, but this knowledge made me no less timid before her.

The eunuchs said Tongzhi had hated the Forbidden City and often tried to sneak away. He'd left it for good now. They took him in grand procession to his tomb and buried him with his empress and piles of finery and objects to serve him in the life beyond. He was seldom mentioned. All that remained was the reign title that dated the events of his years on the throne and the sadness and worry that slid in and out of Cixi's eyes.

Tutor Weng praised Cixi and Cian and draped them thick with virtue. Tireless through long years of labour for our country, they awaited the day when I would relieve them of their burden and become the wise young emperor in whom they could entrust our dynasty's fate in all peace of mind. That was why I had to study. I would be an undutiful son if I did not heed my imperial mothers' worries and hopes.

I remembered the sweet bun Cian gave me and took it from its hiding place. She had looked young and fresh in the sunlight before at the theatre, not bent under any cares of state, and Cixi too had had laughing eyes. I did want to live up to their hopes and take the burden from them so they could watch theatre anytime they wished and laugh.

I placed the bun before me and suddenly felt my stomach tighten in some new fear, dank and suffocating. I wasn't sure why they'd chosen me to be emperor. I wasn't sure I could do it.

They spoke the things of state in language they assumed I little understood still, but I knew more than they thought.

I knew that all our prayers did nothing and the people still starved, still fled drought, floods and locusts. I knew the generals were sent to quell rebellions. I knew the Russians occupied bits of Xinjiang and ignored our demands to give us back our land. They thought us weak.

The strains of the theatre echoed and jangled in my head. I didn't want the bun now and gave it to Fan, who knelt in thanks and looked surprised, knowing what lengths I went to usually to snatch occasional delicacies, sometimes even stealing buns from the eunuchs, sneaking into the room where they had their food out and racing away with my booty.

"Are you feeling ill?" Fan asked, holding the bun and giving me a dubious gaze.

I shook my head. I couldn't share my fear with my empress dowager mothers, or my tutors, couldn't say I was afraid to be emperor, afraid to be alone one day with all the suffering and disasters. I couldn't even face a thunderstorm alone. Tears pricked my eyes and I bit my lip, tried to hold them back. All I knew how to do was cry.

"You don't look well to me." Fan observed. "We should go back to your palace rather than sit here."

His tone was kind enough and I even caught a flash of pity in his eyes. He too saw not an emperor but just a weak little coward of a boy always in tears. The thought angered me. I slammed a fist on the table in frustration and made Fan jump in alarm.

"Master of Ten Thousand Years, you mustn't do that. You'll hurt yourself," he said, hasty and reproachful.

"Go away! Leave me alone."

He stayed where he was and continued muttering about how we ought to go back to my palace and rest. What kind of emperor could I be if not even a eunuch would obey me?

"Get out!"

He blinked at my yell but didn't move. I grabbed a ceramic pot for writing brushes and hurled it at him. It was empty and shattered on the floor.

"Don't you hear me? Get out! Get out of here!"

My voice, usually so quiet and reluctant, swelled and filled the room. Fan lowered his head, backed away a few steps but did not leave. I laid my face on the table and sobbed.

9

My hand was tight in Cian's grasp. Mild wind stroked our faces, pines and cypresses danced, and mountains rose up all around, their peaks pushing at the smiling sky. I tugged at Cian. The spreading view made me want to leap unfettered, roll in the scratchy grass, run to the far edge of the sky and see what lay beyond. I grew so stiff in the chair as we made our slow way over the hills from Beijing, spending the nights at wayside lodgings specially prepared for our procession. The restlessness bit me now and I tugged again at Cian's arm.

"I wish we could run." I made my eyes big and appealing.

She laid a restraining hand on my shoulder. "This isn't the place for running, it wouldn't be proper," she said gently. "Don't forget where we are and why we've come here."

I nodded. We weren't on a pleasure tour but on a ritual visit to the imperial tombs. Our earlier ancestors were buried in Manchuria, but that was before our people crossed the Great Wall and moved the dynasty's capital to Beijing. Emperor Shunzhi, the first of our dynasty's emperors to rule from Beijing, came hunting out this way and the landscape's grandeur impressed him. He let fly an arrow towards the mountains and said that where it fell, there would be his tomb. I wondered if the ancestors ever came out of their dark places to delight in the nature above, or if they just stayed put with the mounds of dusty riches from the Forbidden City.

I should have known, of course, that Cian would stay proper and rule-bound, even with the mountains all around. Cixi was the one more likely to run, let the wind and wildflowers peel her of rank and lure her back a moment to whatever simpler things she'd known before entering the palace. Cixi had cracks and layers that gave glimpses of her younger self, whereas I couldn't picture Cian a girl once, unless a porcelain one, sweet and delicate in its pretty, unchanging aspect. She would never run, let her headdress go askew and grass catch at her clothes.

I sensed tension between Cixi and Cian, but wasn't sure why. Our lives were so tightly bundled in ritual respect that it was hard to know what anyone really thought or felt. We lived very separately and presented a smooth, etiquette-polished surface to each other.

Perhaps sickness had made Cixi irritable, the tiring journey, growing stiff-limbed from all that sitting. It took so long to get there, and all for a brief stay full of rituals at the altars, and then the mountains were already behind us once more and we grew numb again. Finally, we entered the city gates, the streets emptied for our passage and the symbolic stream of yellow sand spread before us on the road our procession took.

The mountains lingered with me long after our return. I saw them as Shunzhi must have done before he fired his arrow and the mausoleums rose. I didn't need a tomb, only the nature and vastness.

In the Forbidden City, I had but small pieces of that nature, this sky rosy with morning, the lanterns only just extinguished. I was already up to start my day's routine. I wasn't like Tongzhi, seeking to escape, but after that brief mountain-ringed broadness, the walls here seemed to close in on me in their purple-hued indifference. We turned through the gate towards Cixi's palace and I prayed she would be well.

"She is still indisposed," the chief eunuch, Li Lianying, met me with a sigh.

I tried to peer past him to the room where she lay. The mornings had become a fat pile of my fruitless arrivals, Li Lianying coming out each time to send me gently away. I wanted to call out to her, run into the room and throw myself on her knees at her bedside. I was ready to play the loving son, not in dutiful performance, but in anxious sincerity so inflamed over these darkened days that it burned inside. Li Lianying wouldn't let me pass. He shook his head regretfully and kept the way barred.

Tutor Weng poked a hole in my glumness, left his place in the classroom and came to my side. His hand stroked my head and I couldn't help but cry, thrusting my face into his beard in instinctive search for shelter.

Cixi had flashing black eyes that turned me timid and a tongue that hurt, but without her the world was shaky and crumbling. She was bigger than her stature, firm and strong, the one who always seemed to know and decide, and I didn't understand how she could lie ill so many months, how it was that neither the palace doctors nor even the renowned physicians called in from far and wide could make her better.

At least I still had Cian. I came to her now with my morning greetings. The air was gentle and laced with spring. Cian was a little like my mother in the shallow taste she gave life, whittling it down to rules and a dry flavourless piety, but she never had my mother's lurking storms. There was a comforting constancy about her and I sometimes came to spend simple moments at her side and be a son of more than ritual words alone.

I had come to her the previous morning and she had received me as always, brief with me as over all these months of Cixi's illness when she was left to be the only one in charge, taking care of duties previously shared. The flowers in her yard smiled as gaily as ever, but the faces were different, strangely silent and subdued.

Cixi waited inside, grey and stricken. Cixi had risen from her sick bed and Cian was dead. It had all happened only a short time before. Her placid smile was gone now, a clenched and rigid expression in its place.

I came to Cian every day during the mourning time, closed my eyes before her coffin and pictured her sunlit and alive. I was as if the pale and dead one myself in my white mourning clothes.

I reproached her silently for following Shunzhi's arrow so soon. She hadn't run when we'd had the sun in our eyes and the breeze on our skins, but that was only so as to cheat me. Her gentle smile as she held me back against the shining mountains had hidden her own secret plans for escape.

Now, we were the restraining hand holding her back while the ritual number of lacquer layers was applied to the coffin and the monks kept their chanting vigil. Auspicious characters wrapped her, talismans threaded into the burial shrouds to help speed her on her way to better lands, though I knew she'd lie as patient as she had been in life, anxious that all the proper rituals be observed before we let her go join the ancestors.

It was all too sudden and unexpected. The sombre looks and muttered fears over these last months had been for Cixi shut away in her palace, silent and wilted. Cian had seldom been ill and it was all in a single day that she fled us. She cancelled the morning audience, took to bed and died as the night fell.

Days and months blurred together in my head. Night fell upon me too. The eunuchs' muffled laughter followed me into the yard. I liked to read books at this hour, letting their pages nibble the evening away until my eyes grew heavy. But tonight, I laid my book aside and went out to where the moon hung low and wan in the chill clear sky.

The cold air was good, soothing my hand where I'd scalded it, clumsy with the water for my tea. The eunuchs not only disliked me but had no respect for me either. I was not Tongzhi to waste frivolous hours in games with them and make friends of them. With Cixi ill and Cian dead, there was no one to keep proper watch on them and they let their putrid nature run free.

Inside, they were like the stink that clung to their bodies, foul and perverse. I found their stench in the history books I read, learnt how they'd ruined the country and brought down dynasties. Fan and the old eunuchs were gone, but the new ones were worse. Complacent in their smug impunity, the coarse strains of their laughter and chatter sullied the clean night. It was maybe a trifle to pour tea, make my bed, or do any of the other small tasks of life, but doing these things myself made a lie of the title they gave me. They called me master and emperor, but placed no substance in the words. The substance was in the acts of service, and those they told me with mocking look to perform myself.

I couldn't help the choking hurt, the tears that made the moon swim cloud-misted a little. The indifference stung most. I told Tutor Weng how the eunuchs forced me into the thickest clothes they could find, bundling me tight in winter layers until I dripped and suffocated in heat. I could hardly move and it made them laugh to see me such a foolish round ball, sweating and desperate.

They let me go hungry, brought me dishes grown cold that they knew would make me vomit, and if I stole food and managed to stuff it into me before they found me, they'd grab me and shake me about, saying that would keep me from getting sick.

When I did get sick, they ignored it and hid it with their lies. They were shrivelled of feeling and morals inside and being beaten was the only thing they understood. That was why I went to Tutor Weng. I wanted the eunuchs beaten. Tutor Weng was reluctant, gave me a few comforting words but found my humiliation insufficient cause for bothering Cixi with demands for the eunuchs' punishment.

He worried about my studies and my subdued mood. It was Cian, he supposed, who put the frequent tears back in my eyes. Sometimes she did. I thought I'd go with her back to the mountains. The astronomers chose the date for her coffin to leave the Forbidden City. It would have been a perfect time for the journey, with the autumn clear and firm and the mountains richly dressed for our welcome. I was looking forward to going there again, even if it was for a sorrowful purpose, but Cixi said at the last minute that she was too unwell. Prince Gong and some of the other relatives were sent instead to accompany the coffin. It wasn't the same and it made me sad.

I had often gone to Cian for nothing more than a moment of her mild presence. I knew from my investigations of mechanical things that objects only functioned well if all the different components were in balance, properly adjusted and fitted together. Cixi's absence through illness had sent the mechanism awry, and Cian's death had the same effect.

Tutor Weng could understand a grieving son's sorrow. He still grieved for his own parents long departed, a model of the filial virtues he taught me. But bigger things weighed on my mind. Had I spent all this time committing Confucius to memory without digesting the fundamental principle that each member of society had to keep his place and perform his duty?

I studied history and knew that many, including my own ancestors, had warned against the eunuchs and their poisonous power. Could I become the ideal ruler Tutor Weng hoped to nurture if I didn't demand respect and punish injustice? Could I be like Kangxi if not even lowly eunuchs obeyed me and I had to be my own servant?

The cold came through my clothes but I stayed where I was, leaning against a column, my face turned to the sky. The moon was a little higher now, it would shine on the mountains where the ancestors lay. Kangxi and Qianlong were there too. I saw their mausoleums when we made our visit and pictured them now, soft silhouettes in the gentle glow, the trees around them still full in form, chosen especially because they held firm and green through the winter, beating death a little every year. My trees were bare, bowed to the season, cutting still thin figures against the night. Like me. I turned then and hurried inside.

10

The New Year had just passed, as tedious as always. I went from one altar to another with prayers and rites before the gods and ancestors, made reverent prostrations before Cixi with the imperial relatives and high officials in tow, and got followed around the Forbidden City by a whole cumbersome procession.

We sent the kitchen god on his way to report to the Jade Emperor up in heaven. I didn't want to let the eunuchs sweeten the kitchen god's mouth with honey to turn it sticky and keep it closed. I wanted the kitchen god to report everything as it really was, hoped he'd open his mouth wide and speak all the truth about the eunuchs so that if I couldn't punish them at least the heavens would.

We always ate together at New Year and I never liked it much, preferring to eat alone. We ate dumplings, like people all around the country. They were just a simple dish, but symbolised the union between old and new.

Normally, I'd have been impatient for the New Year period to end, but this time was different because Cixi had finally recovered from her long illness. My stern and demanding "mother", she intimidated and stifled me, and yet I was even glad of her presence now after those long, lonely, worry-filled months and was eager to have her restore some order to our world.

Now, the rituals were over and the routine resumed with the dawn audience. This time though, the grand councillors were so surprised that they forgot to keep their eyes lowered. Their faces came alive and they stared a moment before dropping to their knees and beginning their ceremonial prostrations.

What surprised them so much was to see us together, Cixi and I, sitting beside each other on the same seat. It was the first time. Cixi sat very erect and I tried to hold myself just as straight. Her eyes were bright and her face shone.

I sensed the glow on my own cheeks, spreading through me as the grand councillors got to their feet and brief silence fell. Cixi's voice rang out in the quiet. Her singsong tone was back. She spoke of the auspicious moment, our skies clear and peaceful, this happy time, and she surveyed the heads now slightly bent in proper pose.

Her words were everyday words. Everything in the palace was supposed to be auspicious and happy. Half of life and language seemed taboo, as if by speaking in euphemisms or not speaking at all, we would avoid the world's misfortunes. But this morning felt different and Cixi's words rang strong and true.Cixi praised my progress in my studies and said we would hold morning audiences together this way from now on to prepare me all the sooner for when the regency would end. I wasn't thinking then of future ends or beginnings and only wanted this trusting moment to continue.

I knew Cixi had doubted me in the past and wondered if she'd really made the right choice by taking me from her sister's storm-edged eyes back in that winter night. But she spoke with pride now and praise in her expression. I saw the proud glow on Tutor Weng's face too. He had been appointed to the Grand Council the year before, a post added to his duties as my tutor. It was easier for him to hide his smile in his beard. I knew this mother and son picture made him happy and I vowed anew to live up to his and Cixi's expectations.

Only would I ever fulfil these hopes?

Inside, I still carried my mother's storms. The oscillations sometimes came so fast, so furious. There I stood in the classroom, blood dripping from my hand. Tutor Weng rushed to my side, eyes bewildered. All my vows and sincerity were as easily smashed as the glass face of the classroom's clock. But

I couldn't fully explain even to myself where these sudden fits of violence came from, let alone give Tutor Weng any coherent answer.

My confidence often faded as fast as the blood had flowed from my self-inflicted wounds. I'd see in my head Cixi's praise-filled face, hear her strong, ringing voice laying a bold road to the future, and behind her, the ancestors, my predecessors on the throne, would rustle and take form in the shadows.

They came more and more often now. I escaped to my quarters and lay pressed into the dimness of my room. It was a hot, still day outside and I was supposed to be out on the long path between the walls, attempting to be a Manchu on my horse under the anxious eye of my instructors.

The Manchu part of my studies included the language, of course, the edicts and instructions the ancestors had left, but also lessons of a more active and martial kind. The ancestors had left orders to preserve the warrior skills that had won our people so many past victories, and so horse riding and archery were essential parts of the imperial education, but I was not a good rider and sought excuses to avoid those lessons. I preferred the bow and arrow. I wasn't strong but when I mustered my concentration my aim was good enough. I pleaded a headache this time, and it had seemed real out there in the sun, though it subsided fast enough here in the shadows. It was more just a pretext to hide for a while.

I called for tea. Ren brought it, one of the eunuchs I hated most. He was quiet today, kept his eyes down. Tutor Weng wouldn't report them to Cixi so I denounced their faults myself. I beat them myself too. They were an insolent lot, but their audacity did not stretch to defending themselves against my sudden bursts of rage. On occasions I left them bloodied, chastened, hurled things at them, kicked them, bruised and tore their faces.

All these little incidents got Tutor Weng upset. He asked me where these fits of anger came from, but I just hung my head in silence. I could never speak easily at such moments, I jammed up inside and knew my tongue would stammer.

Tutor Weng's look spoke his concerns clearly enough. Time moved fast even when I smashed the clocks and whatever else was at hand. The regency would end and his eyes asked with worried gaze what sort of emperor I would make.

I sipped my tea and sensed the shadowy presence of the emperors who'd also once lain here staring at the hanging curtains. Tutor Weng had brought them closer with his lessons. He'd talked about my grandfather, Emperor Daoguang, and the trouble he'd had with the British, who'd attacked and ravaged our country for the sake of the opium they wanted to sell on our market.

Emperor Daoguang had been a conscientious and frugal ruler. Some of his officials, on the other hand, had been rampantly corrupt. The official portraits showed him gaunt and sombre. I supposed he must have lain in this same room, in these same shadows, knowing the English cannons were massacring our people.

I learned about what was happening in the country not just from Tutor Weng now but also from the memorials that had become part of my study. These memorials were the name given to all the reports, requests and proposals that officials sent in from the different ministries and from out in the provinces.

The memorials showed me a wider world. I once knew Europe only from the palace clocks and the curious toys the eunuchs brought me from the foreign man's shop. The clocks' intricate decoration took me on journeys through lovingly crafted details of the distant countries from whence these gifts had come. They offered a fairy tale world of sweet accord, harmless symbols of a civilisation that fused mechanical precision and gentle beauty in harmonious blend. Now though, I knew it really was just a fairy tale.

During the months when Cixi was sick, she had made me hold the audiences by myself, but the officials never said much, and nor did I. They bowed and I told them to rise and asked if all was well in our lands, and they said it was. Now, with me and Cixi together, their speech grew dense and detailed. They spoke about war.

War with France. The French had occupied part of Vietnam, which traditionally had paid us tribute in return for protection, and declared it theirs. Tutor Weng believed we should fight the French and I agreed. The British had come with their opium and war and finally forced Emperor Daoguang into a peace deal. Everyone had hoped they would retreat after getting what they asked for, but they had returned, this time with the French, their appetites and demands even bigger than before. That was when they set the Summer Palace aflame and sent Emperor Xianfeng into flight.

Cixi was cautious though. When it came to foreign affairs, her most trusted advisers were Prince Gong and Li Hongzhang. Prince Gong had been in charge of foreign affairs ever since Xianfeng left him to negotiate with the British and French after they occupied Beijing and the court fled. Li Hongzhang had been a governor general in the provinces. The imperial clan didn't trust him much because he was Chinese, not Manchu, but Cixi valued his experience, and that was what counted. Tutor Weng wasn't Manchu but he didn't like Li Hongzhang either and suspected that Li cared more about protecting his private financial interests than about protecting our borders.

Cixi was reluctant to fight, but nonetheless, she berated the officials vigorously for our army's debacles down south. They looked foolish in their court finery, grown men of venerable bearded aspect, wearing the same chastised-little-boy expression I knew so well from my own face.

I'd been afraid to stammer my sentiments and have her eyes cast me the same withering look they threw the officials' way. Her anger grew and her fighting resolve firmed though.

Finally, I sensed us in accord and my indignation at the French tore words from my tongue. The officials stole glances at me at these moments, knowing only the silent boy, curious to hear the future ruler. As for Cixi, she was pleased to see me take such interest in events.

I drew maps and followed the developments. Neither we nor the French had formally declared war, but men were fighting and dying even so. Prince Gong was getting blamed for our defeats. I didn't share his hesitations about war, but I felt sympathy for him. I disliked most of my relatives, but Prince Gong was different. He had a bold nature and knowledge of the world that appealed to me. Cixi valued him, but didn't really like him personally. He didn't have the right character to please her, was too abrupt, overlooked the small things, the little marks of respect that maybe seemed trifles to him, confident in his birthright as an emperor's son, but that mattered a lot to her.

Meanwhile, my studies continued. Tutor Weng had another memorial for me to read. I stared at the rows of characters. Soon they'd be real, not material for my classes but submissions from officials, on which I'd write my imperial decisions with the special vermilion ink reserved for the emperor's sole use.

Tutor Weng was patient, waiting for me to read, but only the clock ticked. His tone remained polite as he repeated his request for me to begin, and his eyes flickered over me, slightly surprised. I threw the memorial aside, senseless heap of paper, leapt from my seat, ignored his pleas for calm and left the room. He and the eunuchs came after me and tried to tie me down again with their strings of reasoning words. I refused, feeling the anger roll out of me in hiccups.

Tutor Weng looked sad and baffled. He couldn't understand why I'd erupted so abruptly now when for months I'd been attentive and hardworking. He didn't realise that it was he who'd set me off.

There he was, calm as always, as if Cixi's latest edict didn't concern him at all and he hadn't just been dismissed from the Grand Council and stripped of all his duties except for that of teaching me. Prince Gong and most of the grand councillors had been fired too, but Tutor Weng acted as if all was normal and there was nothing to stop me getting on with my study and preparing for my future rule.

No one told me much. I had to collect hints and rumours. Cixi had pressed me to take an interest in all these practical matters of politics and state affairs, but she too turned so stingy with her words now. Her edict had sparked such a blaze of tongues and emotions, and they couldn't hide this from me. My father had been appointed to head the Grand Council. I felt loyalty to him, of course, and yet I knew that many officials were calling for Prince Gong's return and thought the old councillors more competent than their replacements.

I hoped to hear firm conviction and solid reasoning from Cixi, but she gave me such a tired, reluctant look that I felt almost guilty for poking around in her thoughts. She offered me no conviction at all, just resignation on her face and talk of compromise, balancing between the different sides, and making sacrifices.

"It's not easy to learn," she sighed. "But it's necessary. Do you understand?"

I nodded, but I didn't understand and I didn't like her answer. I understood vaguely that this too was the stuff of my history books – factions, plotting and intrigues. Prince Gong and Tutor Weng were the sacrifices, and my father in some way or other had had a hand in making them fall.

I felt like I was studying so hard only to fill my head with contradictions. I was supposed to emulate Kangxi, but at my age Kangxi pushed his regents aside to rule on his own, and a few years later, when his advisers tried to talk him out of war, he ignored them, firm to his resolve.

The whole thing unsettled me. I didn't want to become a blade of grass blown this way and that by others' ambitions and intrigues. I wanted to truly decide and not just decorate memorials with neat clear strokes in the vermilion ink that was mine alone, as if I cared for this vermilion privilege.

The eunuchs mocked me. Some of my own relatives little hid their contempt for what they thought just a sickly timid boy who'd not even learned to ride a horse properly. I kept myself hopeful and told myself it wasn't a burden to be emperor but a chance to make my country and people strong, a chance that would soon fully be mine as the end of the regency drew closer. There was no other sense to my life. It was for this that they had brought me to the palace, and for this that Tutor Weng made his daily efforts in the classroom. But Cixi's attitude shook my hope and sparked the shapeless anger that I vomited up now at Tutor Weng and his lessons that had lost their meaning.

I left the classroom but had nowhere to go. My anger dripped slowly away. The eunuchs said that Tongzhi found ways to slip out of the Forbidden City and escape his burdens for a time, but according to them, he only went off to the entertainment district to forget himself a while in the brothels. That appealed to me even less than Tutor Weng's lessons, and I soon made him smile again with my studious zeal.

The unofficial war with the French became official. The little man in the clock, who wrote his line of characters when the hour struck, was a small Chinese figure fashioned by European hands. I hadn't wanted to become him, but it was he I most resembled now.

Everyone was busy rehearsing the ceremonies and preparing the entertainment for Cixi's fiftieth birthday. I stole away from the hubbub and practised my calligraphy. I was too tired to read, but this I could do like the little mechanical man, dip my brush in the ink and write. Cixi's birthday preparations pushed the war aside and I felt like I was devoting my energies to the wrong thing at the wrong moment, but I had no choice. The most I could do was slip away when the theatre began and let the ache in my head subside a bit as I guided the brush down the paper.

This was how we fought war. We drowned the battle sounds in the din of festive music and spent our time on song, dance and ritual. Our forces were finally turning the tide and driving the French from their strongholds in Vietnam, but even the news of our victories came too late. Li Hongzhang, worried about what the Japanese might be up to in Korea, suggested cutting a deal with the French while the going was good. Cixi agreed.

I had a sour choke in my throat. Cixi's eyes were sombre. They all revered and praised her, but secretly, I wasn't so sure anymore that she was as wise as they all said. She'd hoped to celebrate her fiftieth birthday with pomp and pageantry, but the war cast a dampening pall over everything.

11

The moment finally came. I sat beside Cixi at audience. Everyone was silent. She gave me a significant look and began to speak.

"The Emperor has come of age and his studies are drawing to a close. Next year in the first month, the accession ceremony will take place."

My heart fluttered. I kept my face still but I was smiling inside. Cixi's eyes flitted over the grand councillors. I tried not to look at my father. He seldom came to audience and I saw little of him. He kept his gaze to the ground. We never had a chance to speak much other than formal words and I could only guess at his thoughts. Emperors' fathers were usually emperors themselves and already dead, and so his situation was strange and uncomfortable.

Suddenly, he stepped forward and knelt. I stared at the hanging lantern, its tassels shaking slightly, flicked by some ripple of air. My father's voice implored Cixi to delay this momentous event and continue her wise regency. My heart fluttered again, this time in dismay. I saw his bowed head and kneeling figure and snapped my eyes back to the trembling tassels.

He tugged at my attention with silent urging. I tried to ignore him. What was he doing to me? Anger and disappointment swelled in me, but were quickly followed by another thought. There was Tutor Weng in my head with his books and endless talk about the ancient sages.

Of course, my father's act was just another of the ritual gestures. Back in the golden bygone days, the wise ruler Yao announced he was stepping down and passing the throne to Shun, and Shun, being of modest nature, refused three times before finally accepting. You always had to refuse politely first and so my father was no doubt trying to nudge me into joining his words as a formulaic mark of gratitude for Cixi's long labour. After all, she'd kept up her taxing vigil for years, head not drooping and eyes alert. Even weary and worried she always came to audience erect and perfect, her headdress not a fraction crooked, fresh and shining in her robes and jewellery.

My father knew she liked these displays of esteem. That was partly why he was on the Grand Council now and Prince Gong was not. In any case, Cixi dispelled my doubts by issuing an edict later that same day confirming her announcement. I would begin my rule in the New Year on the day the palace astronomers deemed of best augur.

My joy came too soon. I hadn't yet learned to read the real meanings behind words. The air in the classroom grew heavy as Tutor Weng talked filial duty. He and my other tutors had joined my father and the grand councillors in begging Cixi to continue her regency and he wanted me to add my support. I stayed silent and vague. Cixi was following Shun's example too and had rejected the officials' appeals, and I just kept my head down, waiting for the fuss to die away.

Tutor Weng didn't let up.

It was back to the old days of playing stubborn games. It was harder though to play stubborn with Cixi herself. Her room was fresh with gentle morning cool and summer flowers, fruit piled neatly in bowls, even the maids were light and crisp behind their lowered eyes. I knelt and presented my greetings as always. Cixi bade me rise, her voice quiet and expression thoughtful. She rested a hand on the memorials stacked on the table beside her.

"They keep coming," she sighed. "You know what they ask, and you know too that it is not my desire."

I swallowed hard and waited for her to go on.

"Your tutors say you are clever." She gave an ironic smile. "But of course they do. It would reflect poorly on them if you weren't. They do think though that you still have much to learn. And they say your Manchu needs improving."

I was silent, eyes lowered like the maids who'd retreated discreetly to the background. I beat my eunuchs when they angered me, and with Tutor Weng I had smashed things, run away or gone sullen into my corner. I couldn't do any of that with Cixi.

If all I heard about Tongzhi was true, he never learned to read a memorial properly whether in Manchu or Chinese, but he had been allowed to rule, and Tutor Weng and all the court hadn't implored him to beg for his mother's continued instruction. Cixi kept a constant eye on my studies, more watchful than ever these last months. She examined everything I wrote, and she'd made no complaints. My teachers too had seemed happy with me and it was only now that I suddenly became such an unfinished work in whose hands they were all so afraid to place the country's destiny.

"What a difficult situation." Cixi looked not at me now but at her flowers. "I have made plain my desire and yet they continue to implore me. These are not easy times. All this uncertainty and agitation, it's no good thing for the court or for the country. I fear the consequences if I ignore the voice of so many…And you," she rested her gaze on me again, "what are your thoughts?"

As if she expected me to speak the thoughts clanging inside me at that moment. It was an empty etiquette question and I gave my hollow formulaic answer in response. "Your son leaves it to your wise decision," I said, my voice hardly more than a whisper.

"I'm asking you to speak your mind." She tapped the memorials with her finger. "This is your affair, our affair. What do you think?"

I stared at the jewel-encrusted surface of her slender nail protector. Memory dripped from its sharp tip on to the pile of memorials. Hands that held me long ago when I was a sobbing frightened child. She had chosen me and she had guided and watched over me all these years. What if she meant it? What if she hoped to see from me precisely a sign of strength and resolve, an echo of Kangxi, who, when he'd been younger than I was now, had swept his regent aside to rule on his own?

"I...I think..." The words caught in my throat and I felt the stammer coming as I summoned up my courage.

And there it came, the faint impatience in her gaze, the doubt in me, the disapproval. Perhaps I was wrong and she wanted to see me meek and compliant. I felt trapped and cheated. Was I supposed to be son or emperor? I wanted to be both, but there were so many contradictions.

I hesitated until her prodding gaze became too much. I had the impression she could sense the conflict inside me, and could sense too that I did not want to give in so easily. In the end though, I swallowed my anger and nodded my agreement with the memorials. She sighed and called for the maid to bring tea.

She announced her agreement that day. The edict said that we had beseeched her, and she therefore graciously accepted to supervise me in government.

The skies cracked and split that evening, raining a violent torrent that swallowed and battered the night, thunder coming in endless deafening rolls. I called the eunuchs close and ordered the room shut tight. The storm went on and on and I trembled. No anger inside me now, I murmured my pale shaking submission. Even the heavens thought me unfit.

On the road to Tongzhi's tomb, just outside a small village, stood a little temple. I'd passed it, no doubt, on my way to the tombs, but I'd never been inside. Not everyone had been happy with my being selected as the new emperor. The throne was supposed to pass to the next generation down, but Tongzhi and I were of the same generation. To get around that bind, I was declared Xianfeng's heir, and when I had a son, he would be heir to Tongzhi, so that my cousin's spirit would not be left disconsolately roaming the world with no one to perform the needed rites for him.

That hadn't been enough for one of the censors. He had taken that road towards the mountains, come to that village and entered that modest temple as evening fell. There, he wrote a letter of reproach, took poison and left his corpse in an ultimate protest against Cixi's violation of the dynasty's rules.

Listening to the thunder outside and contemplating my new predicament, I couldn't help thinking that perhaps he'd been right, that former censor who took himself to the dim-lit temple and prepared to abandon his life amidst the statues, incense and offerings.

During Tongzhi's years, they had finally suppressed the Taiping uprising that had ravaged huge swathes of the empire for so long. They had started modernising the government and military and given the country new hope and confidence. Right from the start though, my reign had brought only disasters, unrest and war, all signs that the heavens did not want me on the throne. Maybe Tongzhi had been a lazy student, roamed the brothels, and wasn't the model sovereign Tutor Weng aspired to fashion, but he'd had all the legitimacy of our laws and traditions.

12

"It must be an auspicious moon. It's rare to see one so perfect." The eunuch stopped fiddling with the cape he was fixing in place around my shoulders and stared at the darkness still gathered thick beyond the windows.

"I don't see any moon," I said.

"It's ready," the eunuch finished with the cape. "I saw the moon from the yard before...I've seldom seen it so bright."

I saw it too when I came out into the yard. It was golden and rich. The astronomers had chosen well.

A myriad of lanterns and a stately procession carried me forth. My heart was smooth in the cloudless dawn. I knelt before the ancestors' portraits and the many heads behind me touched the ground too. By the time we reached Cixi's palace to present our respects, the sky was a great glad arch of unruffled blue.

It was a solemn moment when I took my place on the throne in the Hall of Supreme Harmony and everyone bowed, the air ringing with their cries of ten thousand years. From out of it all fell the fragmented recollection of the wailing child trying to hide from the noise all those years before, but today I shone, upright and still, face glowing like the early moon of rare perfection. The musical instruments arrayed down below hadn't played on that long-ago day, ceremonially present but silent in mourning for Tongzhi. They played now.

I was not dampened even at the banquet put on for the Mongol nobles. Such events were a tedious duty on other occasions, but this day had a lustre nothing could tarnish. I knew of course my diminished status, half a year gone by since Cixi decreed that I would rule under her instruction, but the day came momentous even so and I felt somehow grander and stronger.

Those feelings soon fled. I was back in the classroom and Tutor Weng turned a slightly irritated gaze me way.

"Emperor, you're not listening to me, I see."

He wanted to talk about my first ploughing ceremony. I'd had enough of ceremonies. They seemed the sole purpose for which I existed. I remembered the very first time I ever saw him, not as old as I'd imagined he was going to be. He looked older now. I remembered too the moment when I'd brought a smile to his face, declaring I would be like Kangxi. Fine sentiments, but we were so far from the reality.

Tutor Weng had had me read all those history books. Had he thought too about the notions that might take shape in my mind and the traces their pages would leave?

Kangxi, really just a boy still, had removed his regent quite literally. Oboi had played that role, a tough and distinguished Manchu warrior, but with ambitions and a political agenda of his own. Kangxi and a bunch of youthful guards at the Forbidden City, they'd plotted an ambush, lured Oboi to their side, captured and imprisoned him.

I wasn't Kangxi, and even if I'd had his determination and courage, my regent wasn't some outsider to the imperial family, no matter how feared and respected, but my august mother the Empress Dowager, to whom – Tutor Weng had insisted all these years I was dutybound to display the greatest obedience and attention.

I half-closed my eyes and let the classroom clock's rhythmic tick push Tutor Weng's voice into the background. Recollections from the day before were still fresh. Rocked gentle on the water, I saw the eunuch at the oars, and for a moment he was just a youth, no older than me, as he raised his face to the spring sky, arms working away. He became just a boy caught up in the splash of the sun-speckled water and completely forgot me, it seemed. His happy flush dimmed only when he glimpsed Chief

Eunuch Li Lianying standing on the other shore, waiting and eager to show me the progress on the island.

Cixi's new project restoring the parks and palaces in the lakes area just west of the Forbidden City. Tutor Weng was always urging me to show an interest in that too, though I was far less adept at this than Li Lianying. He had a gift for reading Cixi's moods and speaking the words she wanted to hear, and she'd wait impatiently for his updates on the restoration work.

"Emperor, this uncaring attitude, this is not what I expected to see from you," Tutor Weng said, the reproachful note in his voice sounding stronger now.

What would he say if he knew that my thoughts had drifted back yet further into history, all the way back to the Han dynasty and Empress Dowager Lu.

Passed on down the centuries, hers was a notorious and chilling tale. In her bid for power, she poisoned the son of a rival consort. She turned the unfortunate consort into a "human pig", cut off her limbs, nose and ears, blinded her and made her mute, then had her thrown into the latrines. Her own impressionable son, the new emperor, was so sickened and afraid after seeing what happened to the consort and her son that he abandoned all interest in affairs of state, fell ill and died, leaving Empress Dowager Lu to make a string of subsequent youthful emperors puppets in her hands, their lives brief and bleak.

"Emperor!" Tutor Weng fixed me with his stare.

I couldn't share with him these thoughts of Empress Dowager Lu. Cixi encouraged me as much as ever to show interest and be active. Only it was hard to know how, hard to see my place when everyone continued to look to her alone. My apathy would have delighted Empress Dowager Lu, who quite literally killed any signs of initiative.

"Is this the kind of emperor you want to be?" Tutor Weng sighed. "Think of what this ploughing ceremony means to the ordinary people. If you don't put your heart in it, don't make it sincere, then it's just a hollow act, empty and false. Is this what you would give your people? Is this all they are worth to you?"

I raised my head. He fingered his beard and contemplated me with a sad look. It wasn't hard to read his sadness, the sadness of a man afraid to see the fruits of his labours spoiled. His words shook me. I hadn't forgotten myself leaping in the rain when it answered my prayers to come and save the starving people. If the people suffered hunger, I suffered too, and if they suffered cold, I suffered too. Those were words I wrote in one of my classroom essays once. I recalled my brush sincere and my heart earnest as I set out those thoughts and so many others like them.

I ploughed my furrows in the special field at the Temple of Agriculture, princes, officials, all the huge suite around me, even selected common peasants came for their one rare chance to set eyes upon their sovereign. But, wilted and sad inside, what would ever grow in my furrows?

The summer came, harsh. Beijing and all the land around were drought-scorched and the crops shrivelled away. The people would go hungry. And all we ever did was pray for rain and organise emergency food handouts for the starving, year after year as the disasters kept coming. I still preferred frugality. Yao and Shun, those ancient yardsticks of imperial virtue, lived in simple huts, wore the dress and ate the food of the common people. I'd have had us do the same if I could, but even my small attempts to trim palace budgets and shear a little of the luxury from our lives only caused new conflicts.

The work in the Western Gardens was already swallowing a lot of money, and then my father suddenly proposed rebuilding part of the old Summer Palace outside the city. Tongzhi had announced the same grand plans when he'd begun his rule. The court had opposed him, pleading that the treasury couldn't bear the expense. Tongzhi had backed down eventually and settled for restoring the Western Gardens instead, but his death had ended the project and it stayed forgotten until Cixi revived it after the war with France.

No one opposed my father the way they'd opposed Tongzhi.

"We simply haven't got the money for it," I ventured, when I got a chance to speak with him.

"We'll find the money," he said. "You know she never liked living in the Forbidden City. It'll be a place for her solace and rest after all these wearying years."

No one liked living in the Forbidden City, dark and cold in winter, hot and stuffy in summer, narrow and cloistered.

"We won't rebuild everything," my father tried to reassure me. "Only the part that Emperor Qianlong had built for his mother's sixtieth birthday. It'll make a fine act of your filial devotion."

"Yes, but at what cost?" I protested.

"Some things are worth more than money spent," he said, giving me a meaningful look.

"You do want your august mother to have her well-deserved rest, don't you?"

Slowly, I started to glimpse reason in my father's plans. The best empress dowagers in the history books were those who went quietly off into retirement, offered advice when called on to do so, and otherwise spent their days in virtuous and apolitical pursuits such as needlework, growing flowers and copying out Buddhist sutras. Our dynasty in particular had always been adamant that women had no place in government. In past dynasties, if it wasn't eunuchs who caused ruin, it was meddling palace women.

Was my father just trying to stay on Cixi's good side, or were his spendthrift ideas a hidden way of clearing the road for me, his son? Either way, we had no money for it and it made aches and lumps under my skin and kept me wakeful at night.

My father too had aches and worries under his skin. I didn't realise in time how deep and serious they were. It all hit home at the morning audience, when Prince Li reported that my father lay in bed, limbs swollen, fever-gripped. We'd known for a while that he wasn't well. Cixi showed concern and sent palace doctors to see him, but she would not open the gates for me.

After the audience, I waited in the classroom for Tutor Weng. He was such a familiar, trusted figure and I let my sorrow burst free before him. Tutor Weng tried to comfort me now as best he could. He went often to see my father.

"Tell him I have him constantly in my heart. Take him these words." I implored him, hearing that he would go to see my father again later that day.

He promised to do my bidding. It was the most I could give my father, a tiny handful of words carried by others from within my walls.

It looked as though he was dying. He wanted to see me. Cixi ordered the officials to make preparations. She would accompany me back to my old home herself. It wasn't far from the Forbidden City to my father's residence, but I could not, like Tutor Weng, tell the chair bearers to take me there this very instant. Another week went by before the gates finally opened and I retraced the steps of thirteen years before, the streets once again clad in winter. I peered through the curtains and saw the escort, men on foot, men on horseback, buildings closed and blank, people chased away. They weren't supposed to watch the emperor pass. I wondered a moment if they had cleared the streets on that long-ago windswept night or if some solitary figure had huddled to the cold-scoured walls, moving clear of the hurrying procession, as unaware of imperial presence as the sleeping boy behind the curtains.

My father was in bed. When we came in, he attempted to get up and kneel.

"Goodness, stay where you are, there's no need for ceremony," Cixi motioned hastily for him to lie still.

Even here there was no undoing ourselves. We could be father and son at most in a squeeze of the hand and look in the eye. My brief presence at his bedside was itself a kindness he'd hardly dared hope to see. It was hard for him to talk, but he thanked Cixi for her boundless mercy and tried to show himself ever the loyal subject. He wasn't old, not yet fifty, but he looked exhausted, swollen and finished.

The memory of these places was supposed to have been scrubbed from me. Cian and Cixi had been quick to wipe away the small scrap of my life that lay beyond the Forbidden City. That was why they had been so reluctant to let my mother and my old nanny see me back then. They'd sought to smooth the way ahead by trimming from me the rough bits that might catch on the palace walls and keep my feelings divided. I'd had few memories in any case, and none so hard to part with.

I hadn't expected to find the little boy still hiding in the bamboo. The gardens were smaller now with my grown perspective, but even after all this time they remained intact inside me. And the little boy was there, kneeling in the dirt, peering through his rustling curtain at the songbirds and the grim men in the pavilion. My father and Prince Gong in the wavering autumn light, I hadn't understood their anger back then. That would have been the autumn when they'd battled with Tongzhi over not squandering the treasury's money on rebuilding parks and palaces. Perhaps Tongzhi, too, had really only hoped to give the empress dowagers a pleasure place and retirement park to keep them out of his way. He hadn't counted on his uncles' opposition though. He died soon afterwards, the one sure way he found to flee a life he hadn't sought.

I felt sadness press inside. My father too still sat with his songbirds in the pavilion and I still didn't understand him, only watched him from my hiding place and hoped he'd make the birds sing. He had a cautious heart. He refused to ride in the apricot-coloured sedan chair Cixi bestowed on him. The apricot shade was so close to the yellow hue reserved for imperial use alone. It was too high an honour and he deemed it wiser not to ride around Beijing looking like an only slightly paler imitation of the emperor himself.

When I became emperor, he stood down from all his posts and stayed out of sight until Prince Gong's fall from grace during the war against France. He hadn't been able to dream like Prince Gong once had of becoming Emperor Daoguang's successor, too young still, never really in the running. Even less could he have imagined his own son on the throne. They said that when the dowagers announced my name on that wind-tumbled night my father was so taken aback he fainted and had to be helped out of the room and sent home.

His calligraphy hung on the walls here, sentiments of modesty and virtue, like the lines he'd had put up in my classroom. I was not so naive anymore as to imagine him as smooth inside as the flow of his brush strokes or as pure and free of ambition as the words he wrote. Perhaps that's why he remained in the autumn light, his face clouded but his eyes still looking to that hole in the grey where the sun fell through.

I found him in the study too, among the books, heard his long-ago voice reading out loud, trying to spark something in my silent staring expression. It wasn't me he read to now, but to the two little boys who fixed me with shy and curious eyes. I was as shy and curious as they were. I knew of them, of course, but it delighted me to see their sudden smiles, hear their childish words and have this chance to be slightly less the emperor and a little bit their older brother.

My father had taken a secondary wife and these two boys were her sons, though as tradition dictated, my mother, as the principal wife, oversaw their upbringing. I recognised their timid looks in her presence. I was my mother's only living child. Her first two died before I was born. She had another two after I became emperor but they also died. Her last son died of hunger at about the same age I was when taken from her on the dowagers' orders.

She was calm now. With Cixi, her older sister, she was quiet, formal and polite, and I felt the coldness between them. I felt sorry for my mother but didn't want to look at her. She seemed serene, locked quiet in her rigid piety, but I knew her tense silence and sudden violence. I was afraid to be her son. Cixi had no patience for her. They were too different. It was strange to think that had I not been made emperor, I too would long since have starved to death. I was already on my way there when they came for me that night.

13

Speckled with light, the carved wood absorbed me in its chiselled embroidery. Cixi's face was tinged with ceremony but at the same time gentle, with drops of private memory pushing to the surface. I stood at her side and drifted away in the wood's lace-like beauty.

She coughed faintly, enough to turn my face her way. Her smile was brief, not for anyone else to glimpse, just a little squeeze of encouragement and hurried reminder of what I was to do.

She gestured at the girls before us.

"Make your choice," her voice was warm and rich like the wood. "Take this sceptre and present it to the one you deem most fitting."

She lifted the jade sceptre, symbolic emblem of fortune and desire fulfilled, from the table before us and placed it in my hands. I'd let my attention wander in the wrong direction, entranced by the ornate southern timber instead of by the "fine maidens", as girls selected for the palace were called. They were Cixi's little garden, a handful of the sweetest flowers she'd picked especially for me from among the Manchu girls sent in for inspection. No less carefully arranged than the room's decoration, they stood before me now with their eyes modestly downcast.

They were very still, the faint sway of the tassels hanging from their headdresses the only movement. Faces down, painted beauty, dark dot on the lower lip and cluster of earrings, my glance swept stealthily across it all, I as reluctant to raise my head now as they. I stared at the sceptre in my hands. The picture that took sudden form in my mind was not deliberate, for it was not a respectful thing to undress my aunt and adopted mother of her august status and peer into her past, but it was there before me even so.

In an echo of my present, Emperor Xianfeng had once stood at the empress dowager's side, the same fortune-giving emblem in his hands, and among the painted frozen girls had been a "fine maiden" from the Yehenara clan, the daughter of a minor official from Beijing. I wondered if Cixi saw the same ripples of the past, looked over the bowed heads now and measured her own fate's strange twists.

Her eyes urged me to step forward and do my duty. The question of my marriage had hovered on her lips for months now and she had long since begun the preparations. I became a lump of stone before her whenever she mentioned it, obedient, but with no interest in my eyes. My father's illness had given me temporary respite from her plans. The heavens did sometimes answer my prayers though, my father recovered, and marriage returned to Cixi's tongue.

We had stood together one morning, buried in memorials, appeals from provincial officials desperate enough to stop pretending that all was well in their domains and speak their real woes, people made homeless by an earthquake in the south, hunger in Beijing and its surrounding province after another drought, rising costs making everything worse. It was hard to read it all, but I made an effort to concentrate as the clock ticked the silent minutes away. Cixi raised her head, stared at the clock and the wallpaper, and I saw a tear slip from her eye.

I thought it was the memorials with their sorrowful news. She watched me a moment.

"Why do you fear this marriage so much?"

Her voice was soft and invited me to share my heart. I didn't doubt her sincerity, but couldn't admit to her how hard it was for me to muster the courage to speak in her presence. I feared revealing myself only to see her disappointment, hear her dismissive tone, and have her realise that for all her efforts to refashion my life I would never be more than her hopeless sister's son.

"Don't you trust me to make you a happy match?" she asked.

"Of course I trust you," I hastened to assure her.

"Then what is it you fear?"

I was silent.

She sighed. "I see your reluctance, but you know the day must come. This rule under my instruction will continue so long as you remain unmarried. You know they have always gone together, marriage and personal rule. Are you going to let me finally retire after all these years?"

It was a tired look she had given me then, a small bleak smile.

I nodded and mumbled a few words about being ready to do her bidding.

"Then I will proclaim the happy event," she said briskly.

"I welcome your edict."

"You know I am arranging a new selection of 'fair maidens.,'" Her tone was slower again.

"Yes…"

"No, I haven't changed my mind." She caught the flicker of hope and question in my eyes. "I am still settled on my choice. It's the consorts we need to see to."

Her choice stood before me now and she had her head down like the others, but she still looked taller, thin, shoulders hunched.

Jingfen. I was silent when Cixi first said her name. It had come as no surprise. She'd started talking about Jingfen as soon as the marriage question swelled big in her head and she'd put together a little list of potential brides, Jingfen among them.

"I think she is highly suitable." Cixi had spoken confidently then, describing the merits of Jingfen's character; mild, quiet, well-mannered, clever enough. "But you know Jingfen," she'd said cheerfully. "You know yourself what a sweet-natured, decent girl she is."

There was nothing I could do but nod and agree. Tradition did not give me a say in these matters. Now I was supposed to go to Jingfen and place the jade sceptre in her hands. Not Jingfen anymore, they would have recorded her clan name only, the same as that of Cixi herself, Yehenara. She was my cousin, the daughter of Cixi's brother Duke Guixiang. A few years older than me, a thin quiet girl, I couldn't really know her as Cixi suggested. I had seen her and had exchanged a few vague pleasantries. But I knew for sure that I didn't want to marry her.

Under the selection rules for the "fair maidens", she shouldn't have been there in the first place. She was too old. But Cixi had her heart set on it. The selection rounds were just a formality, to whittle down the number of girls who might become concubines. Cixi took care of that herself. She saw I showed no interest anyway and left me a handful to choose among now, for ceremony's sake. I had my instructions: present the sceptre to Yehenara and pick two consorts from among the remainder.

Wooden, I stood foolishly, clutching the sceptre and knowing I couldn't place it in Yehenara's unwanted hands of my own accord.

"Your son cannot decide," I murmured, doing the old "polite refusal" thing. "Such an important decision is yours to make."

She shook her head. "The decision is yours," she said firmly. "Make your choice".

I stepped forward. The jade sceptre seemed heavy in my fingers, the air was stuffy and I felt dizzy. I glanced back, saw Cixi with a waiting look and glimpsed Imperial Princess Rongshou further back in the shadows, her thin impassive face watching me. She was Prince Gong's daughter. The husband Cixi had arranged for her died no sooner had they married. She watched me now with her widow's eyes.

Blood ran to my head in throbbing sensation, the light was bright now, swirled around me and caught all the sparkling bits on the girls. I didn't know where to look. One girl speared me. She raised her gaze slightly and it seemed to me that her mouth wanted to laugh. Our eyes met for a moment and I could see that she was fighting back a smile. Her mouth twitched, no doubt in childish amusement that after all she'd pictured – the emperor was just a boy clutching a silly sceptre and looking like he wanted to fling it away and race from the room. She was my choice. I stepped towards her and reached out my hand.

"Emperor!"

Cixi's voice rang out in brief exclamation. My hand fell and I turned, dazed, ears buzzing. I saw her silent signal. Go to Yehenara. Wooden again, my head empty, I didn't see Yehenara before me but handed her the sceptre. That was as much as I could do. Cixi tried to draw my attention to the two red embroidered purses that lay on the table, waiting to be presented to the concubines of my choice, but I stood staring blankly at everything around. I was dimly aware of Cixi telling the widowed Princess Rongshou to take the purses for presentation, but didn't really register in whose hands she placed them.

14

Ragged voices and hurried movement jolted me from sleep. "Master of Ten Thousand Years, the palace is on fire!"

The eunuch entered with a panicked face. I sat up abruptly, expecting to see the air aglow with flames, but the only light I saw was from the lanterns in the scurrying eunuchs' hands. The night danced with wind and snow.

"Where's the fire?"

"Uh…" the eunuch stared about him as if also searching for the flames. "I don't know exactly."

"Then go and find out."

He disappeared, then came back with reassurances that we were not about to burn. The fire was not in the inner part of the Forbidden City, where we lived, but in the outer court. Daylight looked sad upon it, the blackened remains of the Gate of Supreme Harmony, snow streaked dirty all around. The fire had begun in the storehouses, destroyed the gate and spread to the surrounding buildings.

There was shock on all the faces, but Cixi looked especially crumpled, not wanting to believe that such calamity could befall us with the wedding day so close. Though I cared nothing for the pomp and splendour and didn't even want this marriage, I saw her stunned gaze and couldn't help feeling sorry for her. The marriage of a reigning emperor was a rare and grand event. She had planned it so carefully and could not conceive of her elaborate arrangements unfolding amidst rubble and ashes.

Murmurs and rumours came in a dank trickle between the narrow walls. Not some eunuch's negligence or fateful accident had started the fire, but heaven's wrath. Some officials were so convinced of heaven's flaming finger that they plucked up the courage to put their names to the charges they made and sent in memorials accusing the court of wasteful extravagance and spending money on projects of little public worth instead of on the things that mattered.

Personally, I believed the heavens had good reason to punish us for our financial sins. Even Cixi, though unhappy with the memorials' audacity, seemed to agree that the fire was a warning and ordered the rebuilding work at the Summer Palace stopped.

Money really was in short supply. Tutor Weng had been appointed to the Board of Revenue and was always going around gloomy-faced these days. The wedding gobbled enormous sums. I had to review all the presents, gifts for the bride, gifts for her parents, had to watch it all loaded up and sent off with suitable escort to Duke Guixiang's residence. Horses, armour, bows and arrows, bolts of silk, gold and silver, items for court dress, food and drink for the banquets Duke Guixiang was expected to hold at his home, all went off with my ceremonial blessing.

There was no time to repair the damage from the fire and no changing the wedding day from the auspicious date the astronomers had set. The most the workmen could do was erect a hasty shell, an empty facade to make it look as if the real buildings were there. I too was an empty facade, my heart absent, but I looked like a real emperor in my full regal attire as I mounted the throne in the Hall of Supreme Harmony, ready to formally confer the title of empress on Yehenara. Night still hung heavy and the great crowd performing their prostrations in the cold beyond would perhaps not notice the deception.

My bride was supposed to arrive at dawn, entering the Forbidden City as the new morning broke over the dazzling pageant within. I was the symbolic dragon and she was to be my phoenix. Even the sedan chair that bore her to the palace was called the Phoenix Chair. Now and then people claimed to have spotted phoenixes at auspicious moments, but those sightings were never proven. My phoenix too seemed to have flown.

The wait became long and I wished secretly that she'd never come. The wind howled the lanterns dim and cast us into skidding darkness. Whatever the swift-winged bird in its name, the conveyance I'd sent had to battle the storm with men no more solid now than they ever were against such a battering sky. The astronomers had made a poor choice and Yehenara missed her appointed hour.

She arrived with the day already flush and settled. We prostrated ourselves before the many altars, sought the favour of Buddha, ancestors, all the Manchu spirits, ate son-and-grandson dumplings for numerous future children in the wedding chamber as the crowd outside sang and chanted blessings upon us, drank from the nuptial cup, double happiness characters hung up all around us.

It was my duty to free her from the red shroud that covered her face, approach her, reach out my fingers and raise the obscuring fabric. It was supposed to be a precious moment. Sometimes bride and groom had never laid eyes upon each other before, or had but brief and fuzzy recollections, and this was their moment of discovery, of gazes shy a while, fumbling expressions, a million hopes and questions in a second's look, as newly married husband and wife took in the future.

My fingers stopped short of the shroud, froze, hung limp and stupid in the air. Yehenara sat still and waited. I remembered the girl with a flicker of amusement in her eyes and lips trying to suppress a treacherous smile at the sight of not an emperor, but a bewildered youth with a silly sceptre in his hands. If I were fully an emperor, that girl should have been here hidden beneath the wedding shroud today, and perhaps my fingers would not have hesitated like they did now.

I would have sooner left Yehenara waiting and obscured. Her initial happy glow soon faded after I lifted her shroud but made no further gesture. The wedding chamber was decorated in the festive red proper of such occasions. We sat beside each other on the wedding bed in silence. On the other side of the wall was the place where the Manchu shamans killed sacrificial pigs and boiled meat for offerings.

The quiet crushed us now that the gongs and cymbals were silent and the crowds gone. I stared at the red carpet, better than the "hundred baby" drapery that made curtains around the bed. Even one baby would be luck. There were things they didn't know or didn't want to believe. I didn't want to believe them either and perhaps my fingers would have hesitated before that other girl too, before any girl in this world. Come nightfall, there was only one man in the Forbidden City, the emperor, but I already knew that I was little better than a eunuch.

There were things I couldn't give a wife no matter how many son-and-grandson dumplings I ate and no matter how many hundreds of babies adorned the bed. But oh, how they'd want them from me, Cixi waiting for an heir, Yehenara and those two concubines who came through the back gate earlier that day, each of them hoping desperately to be the bearer of that future heir.

I had the shamans in my head. They were women, danced in a jangle of bells and beat of drums, feathers jiggling, waving their sticks. I saw the knife they wore hanging from their belts. These wild women could turn into birds and fly to the spirit places. And I was the sacrificial pig, these women pressing in to pull out my insides.

During the Ming dynasty, the empresses had lived in this palace. Many buildings in the Forbidden City had changed their purpose since then. We put our shamans here and kept this one red-swathed hall for wedding nights.

Yehenara sat in silence beside me. Her face was long and thin. She stared at a silk painting on the wall, scene of trees, mountains and tumbling water. Horse face, let her gallop off into the picture and fade behind the mountain pass. Could the shamans not call forth the magpie, get another of those magical red berries from heaven and place it in her mouth, like Fekulen on the mountainside? She'd have her heaven-sent child and leave me alone.

We sat a long time like that. Cixi liked to think herself the legendary old man whose hands held the countless threads of fate that bind couples together. She was always making matches for nobles' sons and daughters and even for the palace maids, confident in her ability to place the right people in each other's embrace. Now it was me and Yehenara, her own nephew and niece, whose threads she'd tied together, and she'd surely had a different picture in her head than our two mournful figures sitting stiffly side by side on the wedding bed.

Yehenara finally turned her eyes to me. I saw disappointment there, and hurt. Cixi had organised for us the grandest wedding celebration our dynasty had ever known, grander even than her own son Tongzhi's wedding, but the sumptuous ceremony really was just a hollow facade, like the temporary constructions replacing the burned buildings in the outer court.

Yehenara got all these honours, finery and splendour only to end up sitting rejected throughout this forlorn night. Phoenix, empress, she got mountains of pearls and jewels and fancy robes, the right to wear imperial yellow and enter the Forbidden City through the imperial front gate, so many envied things, but I sensed then that what she wanted most at that moment was a husband.

"Cousin," I grabbed her hands and felt the tears rise. "Cousin, forgive me. I do not mean any offence."

She just stared at me, wordlessly reproachful.

"Know that I respect you," I murmured. "Cousin...Try to understand."

She nodded slightly and looked away. We stayed like that, her hands in mine, sad and silent.

Three days we lived in that red room, came and went for endless banquets and ceremonies, where everyone wanted to see us radiant with newlywed bliss. It all wore me down.

The piles of food, crowds, pretence and Yehenara's constant presence started to choke me. The most lavish wedding any Qing emperor had yet had and it was for me, who couldn't even fulfil its purpose.

Another banquet waited, this time for Duke Guixiang and various other nobles and officials. I said I was sick. The thought of the banquet made me sick anyway, and I felt too tired now to pretend anymore. All the food got divided up and taken on my orders to the nobles and officials. I sent nothing to Duke Guixiang, he'd had enough already.

15

They blamed an irreverent caterpillar. I didn't believe them of course. They had to invent something to explain so fearful an omen. A bolt of lightning struck the Altar of Prayer for Good Harvest at the Temple of Heaven and set it on fire only months after my full assumption of power. The whispers grew loud. The heavens were clearly against this reign, and as if all the endless disasters weren't enough, here was stark proof in the destruction of one of the most sacred sites of all. So they came up with the caterpillar, which had insolently crawled to the top of the temple, and Heaven, incensed by its audacity, sent down lightning in punishment.

The fire in the outer part of the Forbidden City before my wedding had been already bad enough. The omen disconcerted me too. My mind still pictured the small temple on the edge of the village, where the former censor wrote his last protest, put down his brush and drank his poison.

Tongzhi's spirit would never cease its sorrowful wandering. Cixi and the court had only quelled the voices raised against my selection as emperor by promising that my future son would be made Tongzhi's heir, thus putting his spirit to rest, but I had no son. If I achieved nothing else, I at least had to produce an heir, but I could not, no matter how much I wanted to. I feared that the heavens had no need for such an emperor. The mandate was not in my hands.

Very little was in my hands. Again, I mounted the throne in the Hall of Supreme Harmony, again heard the thundering cries of ten thousand years, and I was truly emperor now, no regent, no "rule under instruction", though not much changed in practice.

I held audiences alone now with the court and provincial officials and took care of all the routine business. Memorials sent in by the officials came to me first and only then got sent to Cixi, but I was supposed to agree all appointments and dismissals with her, constantly seek her advice, and let her decide the important matters.

I sensed my hollow part. I had no authority and no one would act on my word alone. They went through the motions with me but looked to Cixi for the real decisions. It was perhaps not her conscious design so much as the fact that almost thirty years of rule lay stacked under her hand, thirty years during which the old men of the court had flattered the one by whose favour they had risen. Her official title became an ever longer string of virtues and the flatterers were unafraid now to compare her even to the sage kings Yao and Shun.

She had a hole in her, a thirsty place that gladly drank attention, compliments and praise. It suited the old men. They had their familiar, well-rehearsed ways of doing things and didn't want to change. They had rusted into place and though I couldn't take them apart like I took apart the clocks, I couldn't find a way of fitting myself into their mechanism either.

I drifted, attended to my official duties and passed the rest of my time studying and reading as I always had. This dull blanket of days made me remember how the eunuchs once wrapped me so tight and hot as to suffocate me and make me faint. Maybe it would have been better if they had. A lacquered coffin was a surer refuge than my books and even my guarded rooms.

Yehenara moved into the quarters just behind my palace, and the two consorts got rooms on either side. Intruders, I ignored them as best I could, tried to shut them out, but I knew they were there, waiting for my call, eager to receive my "dragon seed" and bear the happy harvest that would continue the dynasty.

I wanted them to move to their own palaces, but Cixi thought it best that they stay at my side for now. Only the rituals could drive them away, the fasting days when the rules about not associating with women removed them from my presence. For the sake of being left in peace, I'd have fasted constantly were it permitted.

Cixi knew the records of my night companions were blank. Everything the emperor did was noted in the records – what he ate, what he wore, who he saw, where he went and also who he slept with. The eunuchs kept Cixi informed on that latter point. I gave them nothing to register and caught their sidelong glances as the weeks became months and I left Yehenara and the concubines in lengthening solitude.

"The Empress Dowager, she keeps asking," the eunuch, unhappy record-keeper, came with an awkward look on his face. I could see the appeal in his eyes.

I had no solace for the hapless eunuch, and no solace for Cixi's growing concerns either. She got only my mumbled excuses and stalling words. I pleaded my body unwell or said I was too tired. There was truth in it for my health had never been good. That she even raised these matters and probed the intimate places showed her worry.

Yehenara was a well-mannered girl, just as Cixi had said, pleasant in all the public moments, a calm and gracious smile on her face, but in private she was not so restrained. She would present her morning greetings and I would give a perfunctory nod and wave her away. One morning, she didn't leave, hovered by the doorway. The sun came between the curtains and cast a glow around her.

"You may leave," my voice came out harsh, though I hadn't meant to speak so roughly.

She flinched and hung her head.

"What is it you want then?" I asked, forcing my face mild and tone soft.

"You…You haven't called me even once." She raised her head and fixed me with blameful eyes.

"That's my decision," I said reluctantly.

"But I have my rights, and you have your duties," she murmured.

I felt a twinge of pity for her then, like when I had tried to press what vague comfort I could into her scrawny hands on that cheerless red wedding night.

"Cousin," I sighed, "What will you change with talk like this? This fate isn't of our choosing. I don't blame you and nor should you blame me."

"Don't call me cousin," she blurted out with sudden feeling in her voice and a demanding note I hadn't heard before. "You cannot call me cousin any longer. I was your cousin but now I'm your wife."

I turned away in silence.

"This isn't about fate or blame," she sounded tear-choked behind me. "You have duties. How long are you going to ignore them?"

I looked at her again. She drew herself up and stared at me with a haughty streak in her eyes.

"Remember, I am your empress, your wife, not your cousin," she repeated and hurried away.

A dazzling oblong of sun fell between the curtains where she'd stood. I recalled the dappled wooden lace and the jade sceptre I'd tried to hand to the girl with child's laughter twitching her lips. That girl got nothing. Cixi had Princess Rongshou give the embroidered purses to two plump-cheeked sisters. They became consorts of the fourth rank and were named Jin and Zhen. Yehenara had no cause for envy. She at least received my ceremonial attention, whereas the two consorts may as well not have been there at all.

I tried to steal away from everyone when I could. The pond in the imperial garden was lily-dotted, with flashes of fish between the green. The rosy sky wore the fading trail of another day gone so soon. My rain-leaping pond, I came here seldom now. The garden had grown small and the eyes too many, making it hard to find solitude.

I put the little flute I'd brought with me to my mouth and tried to draw forth the tune in my head. It pleased me to learn these small things in my quiet moments. I loved music and enjoyed playing instruments. Sometimes I tried the flute, like now, sometimes the drums the eunuch musicians played on theatre days. Notes flowed from me smoother than words. I had no polish of craft but I sensed my ear accurate, and my fingers were nimbler and more responsive than my stammering tongue.

Cixi had wept that morning. Her tears had been a flow of anger first, disappointment at a stubborn son, and then she'd turned sad that I shunned her gifts. She wore Yehenara's mournful face in her heart and felt the rejection just as keenly.

"What of little Jin and Zhen then?" she pleaded, seeing me cold to Yehenara's mention. "Why do you ignore them so?"

She had much praise for them, especially for Zhen, the younger of the two sisters. She'd become fond of the girl, seeing in her, it seemed, an echo of herself as a girl just arrived in the palace to take her place among Emperor Xianfeng's consorts.

I had never really thought about what it might have looked like from her point of view back then. I had just the two consorts, but Xianfeng had had quite a few, and so Cixi would have had plenty of competition to catch the emperor's eye and receive his "dragon seed". She hadn't come from a wealthy, noble or well-connected family and had had no particular advantage. She had been just one among many young women and probably acutely aware that it wasn't an uncommon fate for girls to enter the palace but never catch the emperor's eye even once, never get their place in the record books of night time summons, and watch their years fade away, lonely and unnoticed.

Emperor Xianfeng was reputed to have been the "literary" rather than the "martial" type, enjoyed a good poem or painting and loved the theatre. Cixi hadn't just sat idle, praying for the lucky moment, but had spent her days refining her talents so that if the lucky moment ever came, she'd be not just a single brief flower for Xianfeng's delight, but a whole garden of pleasures in which he'd want to roam and linger.

Now, she spied a bit of her youthful self in Zhen. Zhen was younger than Cixi had been when she entered the palace, but she had promise and Cixi decided to cultivate it and brought in tutors to teach her painting and music, the sort of things she'd studied herself while waiting for Xianfeng's call. Her eyes spoke hope that if I'd not take to Yehenara, I'd bestow my affection on the sisters at least, for they were her gifts too.

"Don't hide yourself away in shyness or doubts." Cixi said suddenly, sadness clear in her voice.

Her look strayed around the room. We were as alone as we could be. The maids had retreated from sight and only the girl with the tea was still there, motionless against the wall.

"You know, there are joys in these things if only you would open yourself to them." She let out a soft sigh of memory that ruffled the usual formal surface of our speech.

"These things" – this was as direct a name as she would give to what was actually meant to happen during the night-time summons. We didn't talk about this side of life except in the usual euphemisms. That she laid that language aside now showed her sincerity.

She gave me no more than the briefest flicker of her past. For a moment, I could see in her eyes that she'd not always been a widow. It was just a fleeting glimpse, but her look said then that Emperor Xianfeng was once a flesh and blood man and whatever he had pressed and kissed into her body was still with her all these years later.

She wept then. Xianfeng had poured so much into her that it still brimmed forth in tears whenever his memory seized her. That was no doubt the sort of love the poets and songs spoke of. My tears and feelings were made of many things, but not this aching recollection of another's touch and closeness.

I couldn't play the flute for long. It tired me and my breath was in weak supply. My eyes were wet with the morning recalled,

Cixi's sorrow and reproaches, and with the dusk-painted sky, the remnants of what had been bold with sun not long before. Hovering eunuchs stirred to life around me. I was never the "solitary man", as the long-ago emperors had referred to themselves. In the physical sense, emperors were never alone. Attendants looked to have blank eyes and closed ears, but they only feigned it. I knew they watched me and stole little pieces of me to toss around later on their gossiping tongues.

My eunuchs were silent and stepped in soundless tread as I did. They knew my strict way and stayed mute in my presence. Some power was mine. I could punish the eunuchs myself now and I made use of this right. My eunuchs learned to obey in my presence at least, even if not behind my back.

A slender sound from somewhere close by broke the quiet, a song drifting in the evening air. I didn't recognise the voice, it seemed a child's, and gave the plaintive tune a strangely innocent touch. I looked for the singer. She stood by the incense burner, staring at the bronze dragons, no smoke rising from their mouths. I couldn't see her face, wanted to find out who this unexpected child was. She didn't hear my steps and continued singing to the sunset sky.

"Oh!" She saw me, blushed and hastily tried to kneel.

It was Zhen. I'd seen her before painted thick with makeup, for only widows wore their faces plain, but she turned to me now soft clear skin, a simple dress and few jewels to steal her freshness. She looked much better this way, a truer picture. I smiled at her. She smiled at me too but I didn't linger. I could feel the stealthy gazes of the maids accompanying her and continued onwards.

16

I called Zhen.

I had to try. The eunuchs brought her. She kept her eyes down. Even hidden under her makeup she was still just a child and she waited nervously, knowing what the summons meant. I stood in silence. She bunched herself up in a corner on the bed and looked up at me with mingled apprehension and curiosity.

I really wanted to try, wanted to fulfil my duty and also discover "those things" that Cixi hinted at. But I was hollow.

It all started when the gongs stole my essence away. Everyone had been aglow with the painted faces and noise of the theatre. I sat with smile fixed and thoughts distant, watching the martial figures on the stage. Cixi too had watched the performance with her usual intentness. It wasn't long after she'd agreed to supervise me in government and I was still smarting inside at my defeat.

The martial figures seemed to mock me. They were just eunuchs really, trained as actors, but they looked strong and imposing on the outside at least. No one saw anything martial in me, no sign of resolve and strength, or they'd surely not have begged Cixi not to make me a real emperor, but only the hollow husk of one.

And then they sounded the gong. It gave a deep ring that set my dreams in motion. I liked to wander in the Western Gardens and find my ancestors' presence etched into the characters of poems and woven through the temples and pavilions. I wanted to be like Kangxi, and like Qianlong, a cultured and martial emperor at once, with learning to my name but also battles won.

The gong rang out again. Courage, I realised, came not from a man's stature or warlike costume, but from the feeling deep within. They kept sounding the gong and I grew strong and felt my vigour, a rich hidden source that swelled in me as the sound surged.

But the gongs stole it from me. I was not master of even this most deep and vital part of my own essence. I might feel and desire, but could not control it. Something in me was out of alignment. I consulted the palace doctors repeatedly, but their numerous concoctions brought scant results. Only lost in sleep would that surge sometimes take me, but not of my conscious will.

Zhen knew what she was, a pretty receptacle for my precious substance. She sat meek and patient. Seeing her before me, I realised this bid was foolish. Had I really thought it possible? It was enough to carry my shame within myself, let alone lay it bare before another, and I turned from her and stared at the wall.

"Maybe I could sing to you?" her voice came hesitant behind me after a while.

"Sing if you wish." I didn't look at her.

It was the tune I'd heard in the garden. She faltered at first but her voice soon grew stronger. Muted by distance then, the words came clear now. It was a commonplace theme, woeful tale of a grieving girl torn from her love. I glanced round at her. She looked not at me but at the lantern light. The girl in her song had at least tasted "the joys of these things", while she would never have even their memory to mourn.

"Stop!" My order came abrupt.

"My singing doesn't please you?" she lowered her head once more.

I was silent. My clocks began to chime. I had a lot of them and set them so that all the different chimes ran in harmonious sequence.

"The eunuchs say you know how to fix the clocks," Zhen said timidly when the chiming stopped.

"I do."

"My favourite one stopped working. It had such a pretty chime and I liked to hear it in the night if I woke up. Would you fix it for me?" She gave me a hopeful smile.

"I can try. Have the eunuchs bring it here."

"May I not bring it myself?" she asked. "I'd like to watch you fix it."

I shook my head. "I don't let anyone watch me work."

She pouted a little. "Do the eunuchs watch you?"

"You're not a eunuch."

She forgot her shyness and sat upright, a challenging look in her eyes. "I can make myself a eunuch," she declared.

I just smiled at her words and thought sadly that she'd see more of me as a eunuch than as a concubine for whom I had no need.

The next day, a eunuch came with Zhen's clock.

"Put it down there," I said, gesturing at a spot on the table.

The eunuch set it down gently. I gave his face a brief glance. A delicate young boy with pleasing features. He looked back at me with laughing, mischievous eyes and again, I recalled for a moment the girl I'd been on the verge of making my empress. The boy had spirit. Normally, the eunuchs stood in slightly bowed pose, eyes lowered, in the emperor's presence.

"I haven't seen you before," I remarked. "Are you new here?"

The boy's face broke into a mirthful smile.

"Zhen!" I exclaimed, realising it was she hiding under the little hat and eunuch's robe.

"I said I'd become a eunuch." She gave me a triumphant look.

We both began to laugh.

"So, can I stay?" she asked.

I nodded. She was the only one I ever called. Often though, she came to me not as a girl summoned to the bedchamber, but like that first time, as a eunuch. She became a companion. It was something so new to have this friend beside me, watching me with clear, trusting eyes. There was confidence in her eyes, confidence in me, and she never spoke duty as Yehenara did.

She watched me fix the clocks. Sometimes she sang, and sometimes she just waited in silence while I read, or she would pick up a book and read too. Sometimes she stayed in her eunuch guise, and sometimes I let her dress in my own robes and she would turn all solemn and serious and pretend to be the emperor for a moment.

I came to the garden, looking for quiet again. Pale winter sun slanted through the pine trees and brushed colour on the bronze creature that guarded the gate to the Hall of Imperial Peace.

The garden had a fading look that brought no solace. It wasn't my duties as a husband and hopefully a father that dampened my heart this time, but my fast-waning chance to be a son.

I stared at the sculpted bronze creature, a fierce mythical beast said to have the power to discern the right and wrong in men's hearts. It would be difficult to live if all our secrets and deception were laid out starkly in the light, difficult to be a good and loyal son.

I saw no winter with my eyes closed. I saw instead the spring spread broad and the Western Hills running a jagged line against the sky. I saw my father beside me, finger pointing and face alight as he explained his naval plans. He and Li Hongzhang had come up with the idea of having the navy train on the lake near the Summer Palace. It was supposed to give practical purpose to the money we were spending on all the restoration work there.

The treasury was all but empty. Tutor Weng was head of the Board of Revenue and spent his time turning away supplicants come looking for funds. But there was always money for the Summer Palace, or whatever else might win Cixi's favour.

Unlike the creature gold-dappled in the sun, I couldn't see into hearts and read the truth there. I sensed concealed things and caught the whisper of rumours about embezzlement and waste. I was willing to admit dishonest intent in Li Hongzhang, but, clasped in that springtime memory of my father, I so much wanted to believe his assurances. There was no way for me to see this whole land over which I reigned but through the words of ministers and advisers. It was natural for me to seek my father's voice. I had to believe him true.

He had often seemed like the rest of our clan, living proud and narrow in the warrior past, but as time passed, I heard new words from his lips, words that sometimes echoed my own vision and the different map I wanted to draw. I sought to replace disasters and defeat with modernity and strength and it gladdened me to hear him speak in tune with my desires.

He had been attentive over these months, closer to me in a way. We couldn't see each other as much as we would have liked, but we passed on words through Tutor Weng. Still cautious, my father preferred to stay in the shadows, getting his protégés to speak for him at the morning audiences. I knew now that he was wary lest his honours steal Cixi's special shine or set jealous relatives against him.

He struck me as sad at moments. He'd seen turbulent times in his younger years. When the French and English invaded, he'd followed Emperor Xianfeng to Rehe. He was there when Xianfeng died and Grand Councillor Sushun let his ambitious heart swell. Sushun had been a member of the imperial clan and one of Xianfeng's closest advisers. He had also been among those who'd advised the court to flee Beijing, leaving Prince Gong behind to deal with the foreign invaders.

Lying on his deathbed, Xianfeng had formed a council of regents for his young son, made up of Sushun and his allies. As I'd heard the tale, Sushun started nurturing usurping dreams, even dared to sit on the throne himself when he thought no one was looking, trying it out for size. It had probably been tempting to dream such things when the new sovereign was just a small child and the only obstacle in the way were two young widows with no political experience to speak of, and even more tempting again, no doubt, when Sushun had them all right there in his hands in Rehe.

Cixi and Cian had found themselves effectively prisoners in the sealed-off island that Rehe soon became. Prince Gong was in Beijing, Sushun wouldn't let him come out to Rehe. He and the two dowagers had had to plot in all the best traditions of intrigue, with secret messengers going back and forth between them. My father and mother had aided in that conspiracy.

Finally, the two dowagers and the new little emperor had returned to Beijing, travelling ahead of the funeral cortege bringing Xianfeng's body back to the Forbidden City. Someone then had to ride out to Miyun, a wayside town, where the party accompanying Xianfeng's coffin had halted for the night. This had been my father's task. He galloped through the dark to where Sushun waited, hopefully still unaware of the plot, and arrested him. He was hardly older than me at the time. They were all young then, bold and hopeful.

My father had a curious object at home, a special sort of ancient vessel that tipped and spilled its contents if filled too far. It was a symbolic reminder to be modest, like the humble exhortations he hung on his walls. Only his life had always been too full and had given him so much of what he sought that he had to tread very carefully to keep from overturning.

The light slipped from the bristling bronze creature and left it dull. The spring was gone and the sun was hollow. There would be no miracle this time. The knowledge cut me clean and chill. My father was dying.

Doubts niggled inside me. I never really had been convinced his illness was being treated properly. I'd spoken my fears to Tutor Weng the first time my father fell ill. My words had seemed to trouble him and he gave no reply of any substance. My suspicions troubled me too. Cixi kept sending the palace doctors to his side, but their treatment had no effect. Even those I trusted shied away from the doubts I raised, clearly reluctant to probe the issue or give me any straight answer.

Empress Dowager Lu hovered in the darker reaches of my thoughts. I swallowed my questions, too afraid or unwilling to follow my guesses and see where they might lead me. It was perhaps a blessing not to have that bronze creature's gift of discernment. Life would perhaps look too bleak if I knew too much.

I doubted I could be a father, but I still wanted to be a son. I was emperor, but there was so much I couldn't do. I could smash things, vent frustration on the eunuchs, beat them until their blood dripped forth and they cringed and begged. I could stand as now in the winter light and feel the tightness of tears pushing to the surface.

How much was I really my father's son? For all his elaborate caution over the years, my father had always been ambitious underneath and had even shown a boldness I seemed to lack, if only by joining the plot against Sushun. I could picture Miyun ahead, its houses dim with slumber, the young man galloping forward with his uncertain task, aware that they were all playing for the highest stakes, for life and death. I couldn't help but wonder, if I met my Sushun, if I had to plot, pretend, put my neck on the line and take the risk, would I have the courage?

17

My father's ancient vessel was too full in the end and it overturned. He wasn't blessed with a long life. The winter stole him, just as I feared. No matter the formality of our words and the distance of protocol between us, he was still my father and I felt him snapped from me, as if a piece of my own self had flown towards the hole in the clouds. I cried at this parting. His hand in mine, the last of his warmth still clasped between my fingers, and even that had passed now.

His memory, still fresh, wore the taint of gossip, rumours of embezzlement, money for the navy diverted for the Summer Palace, gifts and handouts to keep everyone happy. The words stung me deep, for I hated these things, but I wanted my father's memory to shine.

The Summer Palace caused me untold conflict inside. I wanted the officials to speak truth in their memorials, but when they grew bold, it was to paint Cixi as a pleasure-seeking woman, indifferent to the country's woes. They didn't see her tears or troubled silence, never glimpsed her doubts and worry. She lived between extremes in their heads, praised or accused.

And I, how was I to know my way through the gossip and the things others hid from my view, sift the truth from the rumours and the facts from the exaggerations? Tutor Weng staked out a dutiful path and prodded me along it. When the tongues grew sharper and accusations piled up, he urged me to take a stand and make things clear, so I issued an edict declaring that the Summer Palace was my own undertaking, a mark of my filial respect, and Cixi had only agreed to it at my insistence. My father had left me a confusing work, but I had to stay loyal to his endeavour. I gave the rebuilt Summer Palace a new name, the Garden for Cultivating Harmony, wrote out the characters and had them inscribed to be set above the gate. My father did not live to see Cixi's laughing eyes as the grand procession bore her from the city, past the fields new with spring and towards the hills now draped in a tumble of temples and roofs bright with the gleam of sun-struck tiles. Nature and craftsmanship merged in fairy-tale creation and Cixi was entranced.

If my father had hoped that his costly work would earn its worth by keeping Cixi busy and distant, he was partly right at least. She came now to the Forbidden City only when the rituals required it. When not at the Summer Palace, she preferred to stay in the Western Gardens. The problem was, though, that my filial obligations meant I had to follow her most of the time.

I would live a brief while at the Forbidden City and then move to the Summer Palace for a few days. And when she lived in the Western Gardens I moved there too. I chose a place called the Ocean Terrace as my residence. It was an island in the southern lake, not a true island, because there was a bridge to the shore, but it had a pleasing tranquillity and had been a favourite place of Qianlong.

It pained me to think of Qianlong. The closest I could come to him was to contemplate the same scenes he'd once admired. He had shone in golden fullness and I was but a sputtering imitation. Even the small things escaped my grasp. I continued my attempts to cut our household budget and force everyone to be honest and frugal, but they always backed me into a corner with claims that the money was for Cixi's expenses, knowing I'd have to approve.

Not even Tutor Weng gave me his full support, despite his Board of Revenue duties and his awareness of how precarious our finances were becoming. I remembered his eyes praise-lit at my classroom words about conserving the empire's wealth for the good of all its people and my condemnation of selfish rulers who spent this wealth on their own enjoyment. I hadn't been just a boy writing essays, I'd been an emperor, conscious that my statements were not idle thoughts but the beacons of my future acts.

In the end, everything was circumscribed and I had no lofty sweep for my noble pledges and no grand scope for my plans. With Li Hongzhang's help, they laid a model railway alongside the lake in the Western Gardens for our amusement, and got us steam launches for pleasure trips at the Summer Palace. Fine playthings of course, but we couldn't build real railways and develop modern shipping, ports and industry.

They were all happy with me as a ruler only if I did nothing of consequence. It wasn't for cruel pleasure that I was harsh at times, especially with the eunuchs, it was my frustration pouring free. I was still that storm water rush at moments, furious inside. How could I shape the country to my vision when not even the Forbidden City obeyed my will?

At least life in the Forbidden City was more relaxed when Cixi and I were apart. Those calmer, freer moments were my father's small legacy too. I was happy to see Yehenara and Jin follow Cixi to the Summer Palace, but Zhen I kept behind whenever I could. Books and eunuchs were my usual companions and Zhen was fresh and different, really more like the friend or younger brother I'd never had a chance to know.

We hadn't a great choice of pastimes in the Forbidden City, but she was uncomplaining, content to watch me read memorials and ask me what they said. The rules forbade palace women from having anything to do with government affairs, but I didn't really know what else to talk about and I shared with Zhen my thoughts and my hopes for the country. She shared these hopes and always nodded so earnestly. It was flattering of course to hear her praise me and to see myself wise and strong in her eyes.

She came to me all secretive one day, wanted to show me something. It was a camera. She'd had the eunuchs smuggle it in from outside.

"I'm learning how to use it," she said brightly. "And I'm teaching my eunuchs too so they can take photos of me."

She planned to dress up and have the eunuchs photograph her in different costumes.

"I could take your photo too," she suggested.

I smiled at the suggestion. I wanted to say yes and join in her enthusiasm, wanted to take that camera and photograph her myself, and everything else around, but my lips stayed silent. I felt sorry for her then. The palace gates never really closed behind her in her heart, and she continued to live as if beyond, a frank impulsive child ignoring the rigid constraints of our life.

The palace rules regulated every corner of our days and our routines. She got her set allowances of everything a consort of her rank was deemed to need. That included money, silks, brocades, food and tea, but not foreign cameras and all the fashionable novelties she sought. The consorts weren't supposed to receive anything at all from outside except for gifts of food from their families on certain special occasions.

Photography fascinated me too, of course. I thought it a marvel, this little box that could freeze a whole slice of life. Outside, it had become quite common and my relatives were all having their photos taken. Here, things were different. The palace was guarded by more than just visible walls and armed men, but Zhen didn't see this.

She found the money from her allowance not enough for all her whims, and she and the eunuchs organised little schemes to make a bit of extra on the side. I was aware of it, but it was a trifle when the whole court was full of corruption. I could give Zhen so little in any case that her small misdemeanours and amusements seemed almost a kind of compensation for this dull and narrow life she'd been forced into. I preferred to leave her free. I had other things on my mind and hadn't the words or inclination to reproach and forbid.

I knew though that nothing we did could stay hidden for long. I warned and reminded her that Cixi took the rules very seriously and not having her or Yehenara around didn't make us suddenly free. There were always the eunuchs to keep watch on us and report to the Summer Palace. My personal eunuchs always included a number Cixi selected especially for that spying purpose. Zhen never really understood how serious I was.

"You're the emperor, you'll look after me," she laughed.

Her words and casual laughter cast shadows in me. Sometimes I preferred solitude then. Her confidence in me gave me both a glow and a sting. I wanted to believe in what her eyes projected, this image of myself so beguiling to my hopes and pride, but I knew deep down that the only thing that could really protect her was to retain Cixi's fondness.

Cixi preferred Zhen to Jin, who hadn't much character compared to her lively younger sister, but both girls still had her favour and she raised their rank. I wasn't so lucky and could sense her growing displeasure with me. Yehenara kept up her sweet demeanour. In public, I played my part too and was respectful and polite towards her. In private we never spoke, at least I didn't speak to her, even if she tried to speak to me.

I wasn't sorry for her anymore, wouldn't take her hand and give her small comfort now. She ran to Cixi instead, let her aunt gather her complaints and tears. I caught the echoes of those sobbing words in Cixi's cooling gaze. My mouth was hasty and rough at times and I chased Yehenara from me when she got too obstinate. Cixi would fix sharp eyes on me then. To insult her niece, the wife she'd chosen for me, was to insult her too.

Even if Yehenara said nothing, the eunuchs kept Cixi informed. It was a sour work that her marital thread had woven, and her sadness was real, but I couldn't conjure up feelings out of nothing, couldn't do more than give her my contrite face and my silence.

18

Evening came. The theatre would play into the night. I'd spent the day looking every bit the emperor, dressed to receive birthday greetings, all the usual auspicious words. Cixi disliked long faces during festive moments. We would soon begin the period of mourning Emperor Xianfeng's death and the joy would flee, but on this day, we had to look happy.

I never learned her generosity of feeling and my laughter was rare on these public occasions, but I was practised in the etiquette smile. On stage, they extolled my virtues. It was the actors' duty to flatter me on this day. Yehenara too was dressed up and smiling. She liked these ritual moments that made her the empress beside me.

The gongs spoke war today, not just theatre imitation, but approaching fire and storms. It was a language I was going to have to learn. Li Hongzhang talked possibilities for peace, but I knew this was a lie. I wasn't just dreaming brave pictures into the gongs' proud sound. I knew in sober reason that Japan had already lit the flames and was now feeding them high.

It all began with a peasant uprising in Korea. The Korean court asked for our help in quelling the unrest and we sent a small force and informed the Japanese of our actions. Now, the Japanese were filling Korea with troops to suppress peasants who'd already laid down their arms and fled. It was just a pretext for war.

The Japanese came and went in the history chronicles mostly as pirates who raided our coasts. That had earned them the name "dwarf bandits". These days, they put on airs and dressed like Europeans. Even their Emperor Meiji wore a European suit and posed for photos. They thought their modern look and vaunted reforms had somehow changed them, but they showed us now that they were still just the same treacherous little bandits underneath.

Li Hongzhang was in charge of our navy, which even the foreigners said was the best in Asia, but all he did was talk mediation. Hopes of peace and foreign help were illusions though. Japan didn't light these war flames out of idle whim, but puffed up in conceit, long picking quarrels with our country. Peace was a tasteless fasting dish. They wanted to feast on war and grow fat in imitation of the Western men whose dress they wore.

Li Hongzhang and others were perhaps willing to let Japan swallow Korea for the sake of peace, but I wasn't. The Japanese would soon want more. Worse still, if we let them take Korea, all the greedy foreign eyes would fix upon us. Russians, English, French, they'd see us weak and would descend on us to scavenge our riches and pick at our flesh.

I ordered Li Hongzhang to prepare for war. He kept on with his Russian hopes. I could guess the price of Russia's friendship. They'd already snatched part of Manchuria. Their own vast empire wasn't enough for them. They wanted our land too. I told Li Hongzhang not to trust the Russians or any foreign power. We would rely on our own strength.

He was at his headquarters in Tianjin. I showered him with orders, but he dithered and stalled, came up with excuses, said the navy was short of funds and ill-equipped. He'd presented such a glowing report only months before, but now he said we were short of everything, arms, ships, provisions for the men. I ordered Tutor Weng and the Board of Revenue to find him the money he needed, but it made him no swifter to carry out my orders. I felt choked by the urgency, trying to use what little time we still had to get our forces prepared, but I depended on Li and he seemed determined to ignore me.

It was easy to forget the Japanese, Li Hongzhang and war at the Summer Palace. The motionless blue sky tempted me to glide like the pleasure boats in the lake's silver tickle and drift away from it all. The Summer Palace was big and gave Cixi all the walks and outings she desired. When the heat grew thick, everyone retreated to the shaded courtyards, where the eunuchs hung up summer reed screens to keep out the beating sun.

Cixi was aware of the storm clouds building up beyond. I could tell from the way she turned silent and withdrawn. She was always like this at difficult moments, would leave us all and go to hide inside herself and ponder. I feared she'd waver and let Li Hongzhang's foreign hopes find shelter in her heart, but she cheered me with her sudden resolve and declared that we had to stand firm.

The Japanese took Seoul and installed a puppet government. The theatre and smiles were over and the days turned bleak enough for our sombre looks not to be out of place as Korea slipped from our hands. Worse news came when the Japanese attacked our supply convoy. We lost more than 1,000 men, their bodies tumbled in the waves, lives stolen before they even had a chance to fight. We'd chartered the ship carrying the troops from the English, and Li Hongzhang's foreign dreams swelled anew as he rushed to assure us that England would simply have to intervene now.

But England stayed quiet. Tutor Weng had said to me on many occasions that we must rely on our own strength. I could see that he was right. I declared war.

My classroom had been my real home as I grew up within these palace walls. Now, I laid my books aside and came to the classroom not for lectures, but to talk war. My robes felt suddenly very heavy, heavier than I'd ever felt them. I didn't like lavish ornament and dressed simply when protocol did not demand otherwise, and yet plain as they were, these robes weighed on my shoulders. I knew them to be stitched of lives and hopes, a blanket of the country's fate I pulled about me.

The classroom hadn't changed, same window, same wall beyond, sun sliding across the room as it always did, same corner of sky now clear, now clouded, but it was hard to know what to do and it made me realise how young I was still.

Tutor Weng was more to me than just a teacher or a court official. He had held me close and dried my tears, woken my mind and shared with me something of the world. I didn't bury myself now in his beard as I had when I was a boy, but I appealed to him morning after morning, seeking his counsel. He became my special adviser on war.

The listless years fell away and my life rang with new and clear purpose. They'd called me stubborn in the past, made it a fault and spoke it with reproach, but here was the chance to make it a quality. Stubbornness got in the way in routine palace life and protocol, in the classroom and in marriage, but war would give it its place and would make it not the sticking point but the rudder holding our course steady.

The memorials I received now were not just ink and paper but came alive before my eyes, true and real, the blood and determination of my people, and I read them with a keenness I'd never known before. They shone with courage and loyalty. Previously nameless, faceless officials, minor men, suddenly became lofty individuals, asking to go off to fight. I was proud that our country had such sons. These were not the abstract "people" of my classroom essays. These were men, Manchus, Chinese, soldiers, scholars, civil officials, from the north and from the south – the differences suddenly unimportant when we all had this one country to fight for.

War was something I'd never sought or desired, and yet the sudden fullness it gave life was more of a tonic than any of the revitalising potions the palace doctors brewed for me. I had little time to sleep or eat, but my health was better now than it had ever been. I didn't wilt and fade, my usual ailments seemed to dissipate in this new urgency, and my mind was sharp and alert.

The night was calm. The eunuchs, in the tales they told, filled the Forbidden City with all kinds of devils and spirits.

They were afraid of the dark. I lay in bed and heard no ghosts or demons but only the sighs of past years that slipped from the shadowy corners. The Opium Wars, the Anglo-French invasion, our lands defiled, our treasures trampled underfoot, this was all in the lessons Tutor Weng had taught me with pain in his eyes.

The sighs I heard now were those of my ancestors. My grandfather, Emperor Daoguang, and his son, Emperor Xianfeng, had both faced loss and defeat. They came to me now in the night, urging me to give them peace and end the humiliation. It was not my one quiet voice alone that promised them their desire, I spoke with the strength of millions and was certain our banners would fly triumphant.

19

We added another character to Cixi's honorific title as a way of marking her approaching sixtieth birthday. This title was growing longer all the time, and each time it grew, so did the quantity of money and gifts that went with each newly added virtue. She was already the benevolent, fortunate, upright and many other qualities. Her latest glowing epithet was conferred with all the proper ceremony and followed as usual by celebrations and theatre.

Autumn turned the gardens gold and scarlet. They were normally festive colours, celebration red, and this bright yellow was the symbolic colour of our dynasty, the colour of my official robes. Our bloodied flags would show these same colours, go underfoot with the mud and damp, like the falling leaves.

Our men fought while we celebrated. The news was grim. Pyongyang fell and most of our naval fleet was damaged or sunk. Cixi too was shocked by our defeats. I hoped her fury lay where mine did, with Li Hongzhang in Tianjin. I sensed her blaming finger pointing that way and was eager to seize my chance.

"You have proposals?" she gave me a querying look.

I nodded. Not just hot-blooded young officials called now for Li's dismissal but even some of the most senior and respected men at court joined the chorus. I should have found it easy to speak my intention, but as always, I froze before Cixi, suddenly uncertain.

I didn't understand Li Hongzhang. My father wrote a poem about the navy once. Cixi had sent him to Tianjin to inspect what Li was doing with the new fleet. I was envious and would have loved to go to Tianjin and inspect the ships myself, but it wasn't allowed. My father got so enthused about the whole experience that it made him lyrical. He saw our German-built warships, went on board, watched the guns fire, observed the ships' manoeuvres and described it all to us on his return. Even the Europeans had lauded our fleet, and they were supposed to be rather expert in such things.

What I couldn't understand was why Li Hongzhang sat miserly on his treasure now, kept his precious ships close, afraid to expose them to battle. It made no sense to spend years and money on a much-vaunted fleet, supposedly our greatest asset, and then not use it when we had a real enemy upon us. I told Li that we had to engage and destroy the Japanese while we could, drive them back before they had a chance to launch a full offensive.

My strategy was in ruins now and I blamed Li for his apathetic efforts and dithering. How could we fight a war if the key commander didn't have his heart in it?

"I want to dismiss Li Hongzhang and strip him of his rank." I tried my best to sound firm before Cixi's probing gaze.

Her eyes lifted to somewhere beyond me and her face took on a thinking look. I sensed it wasn't me she saw now but the man whose fate was in the balance. I knew something of how he'd originally won her trust. Tutor Weng and others had spoken of the Taiping rebellion, a bloody, devastating conflict that had dragged on for years, killed millions and laid half the country to waste.

The Taiping, anti-Manchu rebels from the south, launched their struggle to overthrow our dynasty just as the young Emperor Xianfeng began his reign. They took Nanjing, the former Ming dynasty capital, and promised a "heavenly kingdom", though there was nothing heavenly about its exploitative, brutal ways, or about its leaders, who wallowed in just the kind of luxury and depravity of which they accused us. Then the foreigners invaded and added to the chaos.

Cixi and Prince Gong, the reins of power newly in their hands after they defeated Sushun and his usurping plot, decided to take a gamble on people like Li Hongzhang and the local army he'd put together. They knew, of course, the Manchu fears of putting military power in Chinese hands, but agreed to take the risk. The gamble paid off. That long-sought peace was no doubt worth a lot, and Cixi had defended Li against cries of betrayal and dishonesty over all these years, but now the tide swept in too high.

"To strip him of his rank is punishment enough."

Cixi's look was settled and her gaze was back upon me now, telling me not to be hasty. She'd not hand her favourite to his accusers all in one go, but would give them only a small piece to gnaw on. I knew there was no pressing the case further for now and bowed to her will.

The sighing night grew troubled and sleep refused to steal me away. The spirits of Daoguang and Xianfeng weren't in their tombs. They were sleepless too and joined me here, only it hurt to feel their pleading eyes so close. I got up and read, made the eunuchs jump when I thought of Li and thumped the table.

"Why do you come to me?" I addressed a silent reproach to Xianfeng's troubled presence. "Go to her, the one you chose from among the "fine maidens", the one you loved, the one you raised to empress dowager on your deathbed. Go and beg her from the shadows."

It would be more use than coming to me. The most I could do was watch my plans crumble, watch our forces collapse in battle, and deprive Li of the three-eyed peacock feather and imperial yellow riding jacket that were special marks of imperial favour he'd once received from Cixi's hands.

Xianfeng's spirit didn't heed my advice. He hadn't known what power would accumulate in Cixi's hands. She'd been just a young woman and mother when he died, a favourite consort who'd known how to please and entertain him. She'd had the qualities to endear, a pretty girl who could sing, paint a passable genre scene of bamboo, flowers or fruit, turn out a couplet or poem, and play the discerning companion at the theatre. He hadn't known that Grand Councillor Sushun would soon get his head chopped off at the vegetable market in Beijing, where public executions took place and that his beloved consort would end up deciding the country's, and the dynasty's, destiny. Calls came for Prince Gong's return to the court. The murmurs had been there since the war began but they turned loud now. I'd scarcely seen Prince Gong these last years. He'd become an ill and lonely old man, his wife and his brothers had already departed this life, the gates of the Forbidden City stayed closed to him, and now all these officials clamoured for his return. They believed in him, even the young men who'd hardly known him except through the stories their seniors told.

Cixi rejected the idea at first. The chafing and grievances between the man who many murmured would have made a better emperor than her own late husband, and she, the concubine who'd risen to such elevated status now caused friction, even hostility, but I knew that she too still remembered how she and Prince Gong had harnessed their mettle and ambition in more fruitful works. They'd inherited the broken pieces left by rebellion, war and foreign invasion, but had glued those pieces back together and polished the shine. Her reluctance seemed less about private grudges than about fear that it would be only an illusion for the two of them to relive their illustrious youth now, and that her gleaming memories forged anew would produce nothing more than ashes. Still, there were few options left and she gave in to the appeals and called Prince Gong back.

Prince Gong had been unlucky really. Emperor Daoguang had been a conscientious man, who'd thought long and hard about which of his two most cherished and able sons to make his successor. If the rumours were to be believed, Xianfeng won the day through the cunning of his tutors, who turned his shortcomings into virtues and had him play the model of humaneness beside his brother's boldness and ambition.

The story went that Daoguang had his sons take part in one of the hunting competitions of which my forebears had been so fond. The young Prince Gong produced the most trophies of course, while Xianfeng, his older brother and a less able hunter, made not a single kill. When Daoguang asked him why he'd returned empty-handed, he said, following his tutor's advice, that with spring upon them and nature so filled with new life, he couldn't bring himself to kill.

Humaneness was the higher virtue in the Confucian scale of things and Emperor Daoguang liked his son's answer. The "literary" son became emperor and the "martial" son was made a prince. I needed the martial sort now, and clung to the slim hope that Prince Gong, if he couldn't ever be emperor himself, would at least seize his chance to have the dynasty grateful in his miracle-working hands.

20

My hopes looked increasingly vain. I felt it more acutely than ever during the audience with the foreigners. They came to see the ruler of this vast land, and found a slight, shy boy sitting quietly on the throne. I sensed it in the way they stared. I was uncomfortable with these eyes so frankly upon me. They turned me hesitant.

The envoys' tone was respectful but they hadn't the familiar deference and restraint. My officials, those old men, had little real respect for me, but they had to play their part of obsequious councillor. I made them come to the Forbidden City in the very early hours, night still thick outside, and gave them only stingy light in the audience hall. That way they couldn't see the boredom and impatience on my face.

I was glad that the foreigners stayed at protocol distance below me at least, far enough away to make it hard for them to see my cracks. They'd finally got their way after all these years of wrangling. We invited them to an audience at the Forbidden City itself.

Once, I knew them only through stories and hearsay, as little figures decorating the clocks, the dancing girl in the music box or the porcelain woman I shattered long ago. Their costume preferred the sombre tones, dark like the winter upon us, but their faces were bright and they showed me that their languages too were full of auspicious words.

They brought letters from their sovereigns for Cixi on the glorious occasion of her sixtieth birthday. The words were little different to our own, conveying the same praise of her manifold merits, same wishes for long life and countless other blessings.

It was to deliver these royal sentiments that the foreign envoys were finally permitted to enter our gates.

They'd hoped for the Hall of Heavenly Purity, the palace in the inner court where the main audiences took place, but that was going too far and too fast for our guardians of tradition, who felt we'd already made a huge concession as it was. I received them in the Hall of Flourishing Culture, its position to the side of all the main buildings a symbolic indication of the foreigners' place in our eyes.

It wasn't a particularly grand edifice, not these days, anyway. Our earlier emperors held lectures on the Confucian classics there, hence the culture-vaunting name, but the building was seldom used now. The eunuchs swept it clean and put a throne and a bit of appropriate decoration in there. You could see if you looked hard enough that this was only surface splendour dressing crumbling, flaking walls. We put on all our finery and made ourselves impressive too. Prince Gong and Prince Qing stood solemn at hand and translated the foreign congratulations into Manchu.

In reality, we no longer spoke Manchu in daily conversation. Our Manchu was a formalised administrative language of government, ceremony, documents and records. It wasn't the language we spoke and felt within, Chinese had long since taken over. The sounds pinched deeper at me now though. The Japanese were in Manchuria. The port of Lushun was in danger and so too were the sacred tombs of my ancestors and the cradle of our dynasty.The smooth foreign faces spoke smooth words, as if there were no war and no games going on behind the scenes. Prince Gong and Prince Qing were calm too, wrapped up in their protocol role and seemingly blank and indifferent to the men before us. They put on this diplomatic pretence when really, they were all running round in the shadows, groping at each other's words and hints.

None of us had miracle-working hands, only fumbling fingers and patchy vision in this war-clouded night. The foreigners probably knew all our grasping gestures, all our internal squabbles and divisions.

We covered it all with our protocol masks.

We put ourselves on display here for these foreigners, fresh from the birthday celebrations and feasting days, watching on as our Manchurian homeland fell. Of course, I knew the imperial precedent that made me duty-bound to mark the auspicious date in proper style. When Qianlong's mother turned sixty, he celebrated the occasion with the grandest possible spread of his filial piety and put on even greater shows again for her subsequent jubilees. But this filial piety cost so much money and took up so much time.

They called Qianlong's reign an era of prosperity. Our prosperity today was the thinnest veneer and I could only smile sadly inside at the choice of venue for the audience I gave now, this normally empty, decrepit hall where I played emperor a brief moment for men speaking blessings they knew would never be ours.

The birthday caused Cixi a lot of conflict too. Her fiftieth birthday celebrations had been marred by the war against France and she wanted to make up for it now. Preparations for these sorts of lavish events had to start early. I had issued the edict two years previously. That way, the officials would have time to get their presents ready. She was all joy and anticipation.

But who would speak to her of the empty treasury? Not my father with his palaces, Li Hongzhang with all his gifts and attention, or the grand councillors eager to make her ever more dazzling and grand and gain ever more favours from her hands. Even Prince Gong's once-bold tongue was silent now. Even Tutor Weng with all the virtue he'd taught me and the Board of Revenue knotting him with worry would never let me cut away these endless expenses. I tried repeatedly, but they tied my hands down with filial duty.

Not all of the officials were happy with the plans, especially in the provinces. Some of them sent in memorials asking us to stop the jubilee events. I agreed with their appeals, but the only person with the authority to stop them was Cixi herself, and she would never take that step.

The symbolic dimension ran too deep. If we could shed our lavish leaves so easily, who could guarantee we'd not start pruning the branches too, and even hacking at the trunk? She was the trunk, if only because the officials that mattered and the imperial relatives had all grafted themselves into place and twisted their own tangles around her. The most we could do was shrink the scale a little and dim the lights and colours.

Even dimmed and reduced, the celebrations were still grand enough. Sometimes I thought of my counterpart over in Japan, Emperor Meiji, who was also watching this war unfold, following the armies and battles. I couldn't help wondering how he celebrated his mother's birthday and whether he sat through days of banquets and entertainment while the fighting raged. Did his ministers speak the truth or were they like mine, like Li Hongzhang, only telling me when it was too late that everything was rotten and all the money gone?

I was starting to envy Emperor Meiji. I heard a rumour that he had pledged to eat only the very simplest fare so long as the war continued.

Cixi had more serious matters to deal with. We all knelt before her – I, Yehenara, Zhen and Jin.

"You admit your guilt?" Cixi's tone was icy and her eyes flashed anger.

I caught the fleeting glance Zhen threw my way. How many times I'd called her to my side just to have those trusting eyes on me, just to hear her voice speak confident words and sense her belief in me and support for me. But I couldn't help her now. I burned and raged inside, but my pose remained submissive, humble and contrite.

Zhen mumbled her admission.

She'd gone too far with her little moneymaking schemes with the eunuchs, helping to get a couple of minor posts attributed through bribes. It was a trifle as far as corruption went, compared to the scale of what others were engaged in, but Cixi had got wind of it all and it outraged her.

"And you," she turned to Yehenara, "you disappoint me. So negligent in your duties as empress. How could you just let this all happen? How long has this all been going on?" Cixi's voice and anger rose. "Pursuing frivolous luxuries, meddling in court affairs, and you did not intervene."

Normally, I'd have felt a kind of malicious joy at seeing Yehenara berated this way, but I couldn't at this moment. The Japanese were filling Lushun with death. They killed children who hardly yet knew this world and people already too old to raise a hand in defence. They saw not human beings, but simply flesh to tear into, blood to let free, corpses to scatter through the mud.

I was sure Emperor Meiji did not have to go through the kind of humiliation I was going through now and could devote himself wholeheartedly to fighting this war.

"This 'demon art' of yours, I won't have it here." Cixi directed her ire back to Zhen. "You dishonour our name with these evil pursuits. And dressing as a boy! Going about as a eunuch! Have you no shame at all?"

The "demon art" she referred to was photography. Zhen's camera had been taken from her. We all kept our heads down as the tirade went on and on. Zhen was to be demoted in rank. And flogged. Jin too, for good measure, though Jin had never done anything but sit around and eat and grow fat.

"And you," Cixi finally turned to me. "Do you recognise your guilt?"

I nodded humbly. Oh yes, I was full of it, full of the bitter taste of seeing our people massacred and our armies defeated. What was Zhen but a girl of small cunning who'd secured a handful of petty favours in breach of the rules. It was wrong of course, but there were greater crimes and evils that called for our attention. But then what did I know, I was everything Cixi long ago said I'd become, a muddle-headed emperor, a failure and a disappointing son.

Alone later, I recalled Zhen's eyes, her gaze that had given me hope, kindled ambition in me and fired my sense of purpose. Would those eyes now lose that precious spark?

She had reason to feel I'd abandoned her. Not just she had incurred Cixi's wrath, but so had her cousin, Zhirui. The gossiping tongues ascribed his rise through the official ranks to Zhen's meddling and influence on me, but in reality, I favoured Zhirui because he was young, active and bold.

He came up with a proposal for withdrawing further inland and continuing the war, if the Japanese attacked Beijing, which was looking increasingly possible. I gave that project my approval.

But there was no fighting a war though when most of the court no longer had their heart in it. It all took me back to when I was still a boy and we fought the French over Vietnam. I had felt so torn then, full of resolve inside, but fearing not being in tune with Cixi's views and plans. I was not convinced that Cixi herself was so ready to give in now to the Japanese, but the senior officials, old men, most of them, had little appetite for continuing the fight and were doing their best to incline her towards suing for peace.

The Japanese were sending signals that they were ready to start peace talks and my father's old protégés on the Grand Council painted bleak pictures of the Japanese ravaging our ancestral tombs and breaking through the mountain passes to Beijing if we ignored them and attempted to press on. They knew Cixi's unhappy memories of her flight to Rehe with Xianfeng all those years before, and played now on her fears that life would once again force her to flee the foreign invaders.

These constant stop-start attempts at peace seemed to me a Japanese ruse to stall the fighting a while until the winter cold passed and they could launch a spring offensive. The winter cold was our ally, perhaps a better friend than Li Hongzhang and his like. We were more used to it than the Japanese were. We had this whole great land to withdraw into. Some of Zhirui's ideas were unrealistic no doubt, but at least he tried. The others either urged a shameful peace or, like Tutor Weng, just kept telling me to punish the cowards and order the men to fight harder.

Zhirui was banished to a remote military outpost for his efforts. Ultimately, he was just a minor official, a man I'd only ever seen on a handful of occasions. What difference to me was his fate?

I was good at kneeling and submitting. It had been my constant lesson and was instinctive now. I knew my failings as a son. Unlike Zhen, Cixi would never look at me with confidence in her eyes. I was only an adopted son, only her nephew.

She was the empress dowager and formally above me. I might be the emperor, but if all my forebears had declared that we ruled through filial piety, I could only continue the tradition. It was the great Kangxi who had proclaimed that, but he'd been lucky that the empress dowager in his time had left the running of the empire in his hands, so it was probably easier for him to be appropriately filial.

The war looked ever bleaker, and our family disputes oozed out too now. Everything formed a corrosive mix that stripped restraint from officials' tongues. Some of them were like Zhen, trying to cross the lines we were forced to feel inside even if we couldn't see them. They didn't like what they saw as Cixi's meddling in the country's government. I didn't like it either, but I couldn't afford their audacity from afar. Cixi's eyes read these reports and accusations too, and even if I were to try to hide them, she still had her spies.

Sometimes, for the sake of not spreading war to the domestic front as well, I had no choice but to punish them. If I didn't banish an insolent tongue now and then to Xinjiang's distant reaches, Cixi would wonder if some part of me didn't actually agree with the sentiments expressed. And so I let her punish those who'd trusted me, and others too frank of speech I punished with my own hand. We still had to stand together, still had to fight.

The court pressed hard on me to look for peace. Cixi chose Zhang Yinhuan, our former ambassador in Washington, to go to Japan for peace talks. It was a thankless assignment and Zhang wasn't keen. Even Prince Gong couldn't get him moving and I had to force him on his way.

All the signs suggested the Japanese would attack Li Hongzhang's main naval base at Weihaiwei in a bid to destroy what remained of our navy. We had to hold Weihaiwei because if it fell, the road to Tianjin and Beijing would be open. Knowing the cunning Japanese, they'd try to attack not just from the sea but land their troops and creep up from behind too. I ordered Li to coordinate ships and ground forces so as to protect the approach from the sea and give cover to the surrounding towns as well.

New Year was one of the calendar's biggest holidays, but this time the festive mood fled. The air turned bitter and the snow came thick and wild. They fought at Weihaiwei in this cruel dancing snow. The heavens were not with us and it all slipped from our hands. Li hoarded his precious ships right to the end. I could do no more than threaten them all, strip commanders of their rank and order them to fight to the death. This was the only strategy my advisers could offer. The admiral leading our naval forces killed himself and the ships went down. Weihaiwei fell. The Japanese refused to accept Zhang Yinhuan's credentials as peace negotiator and sent him straight back home. There was only one man they were willing to negotiate with, and that was Li Hongzhang.

21

I had always had more contempt than anything else for the eunuchs, with their slippery, deceitful natures and all that pent-up viciousness they kept inside. In past dynasties, eunuchs often became the real power, pulling puppet emperors' strings.

Not so long before my forebears entered Beijing and established Qing rule in China, a eunuch and a palace milk nurse between them had terrorised the country. The young Ming emperor on the throne at that moment had been practically illiterate and devoted his days to his passion of carpentry. He was a good carpenter, but he was hopeless at fixing the rapidly disintegrating Ming Empire. Officials who opposed this eunuch's power lost their heads or got thrown into prison. My forebears were aware of all that and at first wanted to do away with the eunuchs altogether, but in the end, they kept some on for menial purposes and curtailed their former powers.

The eunuchs needed a strict hand. Give them an inch of leeway and they soon grew lax and impudent. I'd never liked their constant, watchful presence, but these days I found myself even glad of them at moments. I was never without my eunuchs after all. They had to share my grim days and dark places too. I'd sought solitude in the past, but now I couldn't face the shadows alone in the hurting nights.

I lay as Daoguang had lain, and as Xianfeng had lain, eyes wide open and red with defeat, and it was a small solace at times to hear the duty eunuch stir and glimpse his drowsy face demanding nothing more than for the sky to lighten and set him free.

I wished my own sky would lighten and someone would set me free. There was a legend that circulated among the people. They said that Emperor Shunzhi, Kangxi's father, didn't die young, snatched by smallpox, but slipped away to the holy mountains of Wutai and became a monk. This, they said, explained why Kangxi made so many trips out there, because he was going to visit his father, who'd shed his imperial chains and embraced the simple monastic life he really desired.

It was a pleasing story, but it wasn't true. Emperor Shunzhi died in this very palace where I faced the crushing night. I wished I knew how to make the legend real and steal away into the rosy morning as Shunzhi was said to have done. Like Zhen, I could disguise myself, and who would ever know me beyond these palace walls?

One of the expressions for becoming emperor was "ascend to the summit". This summit was the place where the emperor alone could stand. Some things I could only know as emperor. I still carried fading echoes within of that grand feeling from the start of the war, that indescribable sense of oneness with my people and country. There was something unique in that feeling, something surely only the sovereign could experience.

But there was loneliness too at this summit. There were cold-laced heights that others did not wish to ascend. They would have been all too eager to share victory with me and make their part known, but they turned from me now that we faced defeat. No one wanted to put their hand to the knife that was going to have to cut pieces from our land for the enemy to feed on. Afraid this shameful blood might stain them, they left me to wield the knife myself.

The morning lightened eventually but it brought no deliverance. My fantasies of following Zhen's example, dressing up as a eunuch and stealing away in the dawn dissolved in an instant when I looked down on the face summoned for audience that day. It was Li Hongzhang. He came seeking final instructions before setting off to Japan for the peace talks. I'd disgraced him, dismissed him, ordered him never to set foot in Beijing again, and I'd have sent him to the Japanese straight from Tianjin, where he'd been hiding all this time, but Cixi called him back to Beijing.

I assumed she'd done so because she wanted to see him herself, but now she wasn't seeing anyone at all, said she'd caught a cold and was too ill to receive visitors. I glanced at Li's bowed head. We were completely alone. I couldn't help a bitter laugh inside, remembering an official I'd recently banished to Xinjiang for daring to suggest that Cixi meddled too much in government. There was nothing I wanted more right now than for her to get up from her sick bed and meddle, but no, even the supposedly power-hungry empress dowager had abandoned me.

She left me with the quarrelling courtiers arguing around me. Li said the Japanese would demand territory from us. Tutor Weng favoured giving them more money, anything so long as we didn't have to cede land. Prince Qing and my father's old Grand Council proteges said if it came down to it, we'd do better to cede Taiwan but keep hold of our ancestral lands in Manchuria. I kept my words few and vague. We had no money for indemnities, big or small. As for land, I was emperor of it all – how could I divide it into categories of lesser or greater worth? As a Manchu, I could not cede my ancestors' lands, but nor could I bear to lose Taiwan, which those same ancestors of mine had brought into the empire.

Li came to Beijing for the flesh-cutting knife. It had to come from my hands. He said the Japanese wouldn't deal with him unless I granted him clear powers to discuss ceding territory. Powers of that sort required the appropriate status to go with them, so I restored his rank and gave him back his peacock feather and imperial yellow jacket. We had to keep face in the small things, at least before the Japanese. Li would look his imperially appointed part. I knew he was right. We had no choice but to confer the powers he asked for, only for so many years now, every big decision had required Cixi's approval, and this time was surely no exception.

But Cixi was in no way anxious to lend her name to this shameful act. She stayed silent and out of sight. Prince Gong and the others who'd been busy advocating peace talks pinched and squeezed me every way they could to hurry up and give Li the official sanction he needed. I played the obedient son and did what all these courtiers had always taught me to do – solicit Cixi's decision on all -important matters. It was hard to see what was more important than this.

"Do it your way, no need to tell me about it," she tossed caustic words at me when I came to her side with my request for her opinion.

So many frustrated moments when I'd have welcomed those words, but now they sounded mocking. So, was I not to tell her of events and not seek her advice after all these years of being reminded at every turn that it was my duty to beg her wise counsel? Let a day go by and she'd lose her impatience, remember her son and wonder why he'd gone silent and was shutting her out. I tried again, sent Prince Gong this time to get her opinion, but he got no further than Chief Eunuch Li Lianying, who informed him that Cixi was ill and all business was mine to decide.

Now we were alone, Li Hongzhang and I. I recalled my father, the spring-ruffled lake at the Summer Palace and my father's eager talk about the navy, my eyes bright and hopeful as I listened to his words. I recalled him as he lay sick in bed, his trembling hand in mine. His navy had been perhaps more in his fantasies than anything, but he didn't forget it, forcing it from his tongue even as he believed he had thought my gaze upon him for perhaps the last time. Where was it, this navy, the one in the poem he wrote? Where was all the praise from near and far, the stirring newness and metal-glint radiance of our battle might?

Li stood humble here before me. Others he would have bribed, flattered or softened with gifts, but I had no need of these things. I had wanted only a navy that could fight, and this he had been unable to give me. I saw that he was a clever man. I didn't like him, but at the same time, I knew that we had few officials of his calibre, few men as awake to the world as he was, men of practical action and initiative. Though I'd heard Cixi and even my father speak well of him, I didn't trust him. It wasn't the usual Manchu suspicion of Chinese officials, the distrustful eyes that many of my relatives turned on Li and other influential Chinese. I didn't share those prejudices, but I sensed no loyalty in Li, no loyalty to me in any case.

I assumed he no doubt felt as much animosity for me as I did for him. Cixi had raised him through the ranks and his honours had come from her hands. His loyalty was to her and I was just a chance upstart getting in his way. Whatever emotions he had, he kept them hidden. Lying awake in the night, I'd felt suffocated by the thought of what I'd have to say to him now. I had enough trouble putting it in writing in the edict I sent to him the day before. I'd hoped that would be enough. It wasn't.

He repeated what he'd already said about needing an absolutely clear mandate and waited to hear the assent drop from my lips. My mouth turned stiff and reluctant. Li kept his humble pose and the silence grew long. The clocks ticked and I felt as I had when a very small child and they shut me in dark cupboards and left me to cry until all the sound grew mute in me and the clocks grew loud. But this darkness now wasn't a punishment place, it was destiny's heavy hand, and it pressed painful duty on my frail shoulders.

My lips moved. "Yes", I forced the small word. "You have the mandate."

By saying it out loud, I handed him the knife.

He lifted his head an instant. "Then I will leave tomorrow for Tianjin," he said.

He had what he'd come for, my personal authorisation to sit down with the Japanese invaders and discuss which pieces to carve from my country. I stood in my summit's leaden loneliness, abandoned by all but Li Hongzhang. He was now the one man willing to share my shame and lend his name to our disgrace. He would receive the people's curses and I their laments.

The "summit" came from that ancient classic, the Book of Changes. Heaven, Earth and all things in between them were in a constant state of flux. No sooner was the zenith reached than the downward journey began. Every ascent to the greatest heights already carried within it the seeds of later fall to the greatest depths. The old books of songs and chronicles that Confucius gathered together and put into order already spoke of numerous summits and falls, of death and disaster raining from the heavens, kings grown weak and lands famished, sorrow turned deep and realms soon in ruins. The people sighing, no strength left to stand tall and look once more to the azure vault above. Fragments of these laments written down so many centuries before floated in my head now, echoing the tears I'd cry when Li withdrew and I'd be alone in this hall.

I'd read and memorised all these ancient lines under my tutors' guidance. They came back to me not as classroom moments, but in the singsong tone of Cixi's evening voice, silvered and gentle in my distant memory.

"Don't cry my son," she used to say to me, and would sing to me, recite the poems, wipe tears from my cheeks. That voice seemed so faint now, more like the froth of dreams. Cixi herself seemed farther away than the remotest corners to which I banished miscreants and troublemakers. She chose me, wrenched me from the brief flicker that would have been my life, and led me to this lonely golden summit, only to leave me when the light lost its shine.

22

"Li Hongzhang has been shot!"

The news stung me. For a moment, my old resentment fell away. Sunlight angled into the rooms and there was a sense of spring growing firm, all the young leaves and fresh colour speaking life and hope after the chill and bloodied winter.

Only I and Li Hongzhang had been still plunged in that chill and my thoughts had stayed tied to him over these days, following him across the sea to Japan, with him as he met with Prime Minister Ito and the other Japanese negotiators and listened to their absurd, unacceptable demands.

More news soon arrived. Li was in a Japanese hospital and his life was in no danger. A Japanese fanatic had appeared out of nowhere in the street and fired a gun at Li. The heavens must have been protecting him and the bullet only wounded his cheek. That was bad enough for the Japanese, who attached as much importance to ritual decorum as we did. They were all very embarrassed by the attack. Ito, the same one who had been trying so hard to force gluttonous demands down our throats, now came to Li's bedside, all concern, apology and solicitude.

If the fanatic's gunshot had really been able to alter the course of the negotiations in our favour, I'd have been happy to see Li with more than just a bullet-grazed cheek. Ito was soon back to being as tough as ever. He wasn't going to give me the dilemma of choosing between the Manchu lands and Taiwan. Japan demanded both places, and all our money too.

Li and his son in Japan kept up a stream of correspondence with my father's old proteges at court. Again, I sat silent at audience while everyone argued. Li pressed me from over the sea. He needed the words from my mouth once more and said I either had to accept this impossible peace the Japanese were forcing on us, or declare the continuation of an equally impossible war.

I wanted it all to end. Everyone had long since capitulated in their hearts and I knew that they would act behind the scenes, ignore my silence and nudge Li towards signing the peace deal. What I didn't expect was that Cixi would suddenly flare in indignation and speak the resolute words I'd been waiting for all this time. She'd been careful to stay away from the mess at court, playing the ideal empress dowager off in her retirement, following the country's tribulations from afar.

Prince Gong went to see her and returned with her sudden verdict – better to resume the war than to cede territory. This was the Cixi I'd prayed for, the imperial mother who could muster hearts and courage with her authority. The problem was that her brave spirit had come too late. She knew as well as I did that we'd already lost our battles.

Li's telegrams grew urgent, the Japanese were increasingly impatient with our hesitation and were threatening to attack Beijing. Cixi's words were for show, so that she could figure in the records as having urged courage and resistance to the very end. She would be remembered as valiant and I as the emperor who'd led a failed war and given my consent to our humiliation. Over in Japan, Li knew he'd run out of time and couldn't stall Ito any longer. He went ahead and signed.

It lay before me now, the Treaty of Shimonoseki. Japan's Emperor Meiji had already ratified it and they waited for me to do the same. Li Hongzhang lay low in Tianjin and I had the palace walls around me to keep public outrage at bay. The outrage was real. There were protests, and I received piles of pleading, urging words.

Tutor Weng sounded almost like Li now, telling me to hold off putting my seal to the treaty in the hope that the Russians would help us get back our Manchurian lands. Some at court pressured me to hurry up and ratify it, afraid that fighting would resume. As for Cixi, she vanished once more, as was her wont in difficult situations. She caught another cold and couldn't see anyone, again offering no advice but told me to take care of everything myself.

I knew that not all victories came swift and easy. Nurhaci, the founder of our dynasty, fought the Ming, but the Portuguese cannons with which the Ming armed their border forts thwarted his plans. His son continued our forebears' enterprise but did not live to see a Qing ruler sit on the throne in the Forbidden City in Beijing. Not long afterwards, though, the Ming fell and the Qing forces crossed the pass from Manchuria. It had taken three generations.

It took eight long years for Kangxi to crush the anti-Qing rebellion in the south, and even longer to defeat the rebellious Mongol leaders far to the west. The conflicts with the Mongols began under Kangxi, but it was only under Qianlong, more than fifty years later, that the western borders were finally secured. Sometimes, even the ablest commanders and greatest rulers had to wait. Sometimes, patient spirit was a precious treasure.

Acting in this patient spirit, some of our officials said we ought to retreat inland and draw the Japanese into a long war that would eventually exhaust and defeat them. This echoed the earlier suggestions made by Zhen's cousin, Zhirui, the one who Cixi had sent off to a distant garrison as punishment.

In one of those mocking twists of fate, Cixi herself now said much the same thing. She got all fired up with resolve again, still laid up with her cold and unable to receive me of course, but she sent Prince Qing with newly decisive words telling me to renounce the treaty and prepare anew for war if this was what the country desired.

When Prince Qing first came with these words, I stared at his impassive face and felt as though the clouded sky had suddenly broken and sun shafts had pierced us with gladdening light. I saw a chance for the country to gather its dignity once more.

My hopes were only brief. Prince Qing passed on Cixi's fighting words, but he himself continued to oppose the idea of renewing the war. That raised my suspicions. Prince Qing was originally a rather lowly figure from among our relatives, but he was the kind of unquestionably loyal courtier Cixi liked best, and it was she who'd given him the lofty rank he held today. He was a good flatterer, corrupt, but always generous with his gifts, and guaranteed to follow in Cixi's wake.

That he didn't follow Cixi now made me realise once again that her brave words were for the record's sake alone. I had no doubt, of course, that she felt genuine outrage over the treaty the Japanese were foisting on us. But she wouldn't stand behind me if I really did go ahead and resume the war. She'd not abandon Beijing and relive her past. Zhirui was already in distant exile for hinting at the idea the year before, and this was a truer measure of her intentions.

I too was running out of time now. Only a few days remained before the deadline Li and Ito had agreed on in Japan. Prince Gong had been ill at home but even he came now to tell me to sign. Unlike Cixi's colds, Prince Gong's illness was very real. He dragged himself from his sickbed and came to me haggard and worn to tell me that we had no choice and that I had to take the knife in my hands once more and knowingly thrust it into our country's flesh.

I thought of Zhen. To think of her was as much as I could do. I had little chance to see her. She had been staunchly at my side at the start of the war. She believed in me and believed in our ability to win. But these last bitter months had kept her from me.

I was reluctant to let her in anyway, even only as a memory or the object of my roaming thoughts. She was yet another of my defeats. Cixi had confined the two sisters in disgrace, allowing them out by special mercy to take part in important rituals and festivals. That left them in a suspended, shadowy state, still visible when it mattered, hidden from sight the rest of the time.

Zhen had had enough trouble getting used to life behind our walls, and now her life was even more circumscribed, stale and sad. She came to my memory dressed in eunuch's robes. That simple disguise gave her freedom and hid the girl completely. That was partly what annoyed Cixi so much, that Zhen treated her status of imperial consort as just a costume to cast aside at whim. I doubted Cixi had been so frivolous and bold with Xianfeng. Cixi, though, had quickly found a more serious and meaningful role to play by giving birth to Xianfeng's only son. I had an empress I tried to avoid, two disgraced consorts I had scarce chance to see, and still no heir in sight.

The picture of Zhen as a little imitation eunuch came and went in my head. It was that same fleeting fantasy of my sleepless hours. Emperor Shunzhi had outraged his mother, the dowager empress, when he declared his desire to throw aside the emperor's robe to enter a monastery. He even persuaded a monk to shave off his hair in the symbolic ritual of cutting ties with this world.

Even in ordinary families, entering the monastic life was often a great drama for sorrowing parents. It was hard to be a properly Confucian filial son when you abandoned your home and ageing parents to withdraw to a remote mountain somewhere. What then to say of the emperor, who was supposed to be father to the entire country? It created a great drama in the palace of course. Shunzhi left a poem lamenting the fate that made him born into a royal family when he longed for nothing more than a monk's coarse garments and humble begging bowl.

He was about the same age then as I was now. He never became a monk of course. They talked him out of it. That didn't stop me from dreaming my own version of his dreams. Like Zhen could throw off her concubine's finery, I'd fling aside my emperor's role as just a robe to pull from my body, don humble garb, plain and unnoticed, and go small and silent with the dawn. There would be no calls of ten thousand years, no treaty before me, no courtiers trying to turn me cruel and force my hand to hack away our own flesh. Others would gladly take the throne from me. My boastful cousins with their envious eyes, for example, they dreamed of taking my place. Let one of them mount this summit and sit proud atop the ruins.

I'd become a quiet scholar somewhere, happy with my books and simple in desire. But I knew the folly of these thoughts. Emperor Shunzhi never left for the sacred Wutai Mountains. Emperor Tongzhi, my restless cousin, always sneaked back into the Forbidden City after visiting the brothels. They said it was Prince Gong's son who used to lure him out to the entertainment district, where the theatres, teahouses and brothels crowded in the bustling lanes. Alone, he'd maybe not have had the courage to slip away as he did.

The emperor's robes weren't so easily shrugged off. Shunzhi and Tongzhi both wore them until smallpox released them from their imperial obligations. Even that young Ming emperor who was only interested in carpentry couldn't completely shirk his duties. He could leave the country in the hands of illiterate, greedy eunuchs, but he still had to be emperor until illness cut his life short.

I wasn't sure I'd know what to do with myself if I did find a way into the streets beyond and became just another passing figure. I didn't know that life beyond. All I did know was that my war had failed, we had no army to fight with and our navy had sunk. Even my father had deceived me. There was no poem and no promise.

It wasn't I who cut into our flesh. Corruption, deceit, complacency and greed had so long scraped away at it that it simply fell now from our hands. I was tired after these months, scarcely heard the voices around me now. My vision filled with fog. I took the imperial seal and pressed it to the treaty.

There, it was done. No grand councillors, my tears hid them. Only Tutor Weng I saw. He'd hoped so much that I'd be like Kangxi, but I was becoming more like Chongzhen, the last emperor of the Ming, who went to the hill behind the Forbidden City and hung himself on a tree when he saw his dynasty crumble and his courtiers flee. Not even that I could do. I stood numb, unmoving, stared at Tutor Weng and cried.

23

Words flowed sweet and clear from Yehenara's tongue. The table before us was arrayed with auspicious dishes, which I presented, while Yehenara recited the victuals' fortune-filled names. Cixi shed fond smiles and glowing looks. She loved to see us close like this and doing something together as a happy pair. She got to see us act out this pleasing scene twice a month, when we gathered on the set days for the meal at which we served her in another of the many rituals of respect that were part of the rules our ancestors handed down.

My thoughts were far away. These ceremonies were so practised and familiar that I was truly like the fancy palace clocks, able to perform my functions in smooth and absent fashion.

Yehenara made the words a melody and held out a cup, which I filled. The palace cooks came up with all these culinary blessings and names of good augur. We normally ate together only on ritual or festive occasions. Otherwise, we ate alone, served by our own maids and eunuchs. The tables were always laden, but only a portion of all that food was actually worth eating. Part of it was just for show, food that had already gone cold and been sitting round a while, but the rows and rows of dainty plates and bowls looked impressive and made it harder for would-be poisoners. The cooks had a lot of imagination anyway and even just the names of their dishes added peace and blessings to the air.

It wasn't these edible portents that filled me now though. My head hummed with words, very different, English words. I ran through them in silence, fixing them in place in my mind. It was a marvellous pastime to take the world and name it anew. There were benefits to having learned to be a clockwork emperor. It meant I could slide my little personal pursuits into the dull routine. I never spoke much anyway, kept my quiet smile firm on my face, and this was enough.

English was a new treasure I'd found and my secret key to freer moments. English didn't know the Forbidden City, with its rules and rituals. I first started trying to learn the language some years before and had made more or less regular efforts since.

It became more important to me now. I got Prince Gong to find me teachers from the interpreters' school he'd helped set up during Tongzhi's reign. The interpreters' school dated from earlier days and used to train people in the Russian language, as there were regular dealings with the Russians to the north, but Prince Gong had it reorganised to teach other European languages as well. The Europeans who came in Kangxi's or Qianlong's time had learned Chinese and Manchu. It was they who adapted to us back then, but these were different Western men who came to us now, merchants and soldiers rather than scholars and missionaries, and we had to learn to understand their words and ways.

My mouth stayed clumsy and my pronunciation was not good, but the meanings settled inside. I'd always had a good memory and I was disciplined, made time every day for my study. I was impatient now and couldn't wait for the books my teachers had ordered to arrive. I told them to search among the foreigners in the city for books I could start on straight away.

The foreigners had a lot of books, not just in English but also foreign works they'd had translated into Chinese. My eunuchs soon knew where to go. I sent them into the city to gather books from the foreigners' homes. They returned with tales of all they saw in those homes, described to me strange objects, and I sent them off again to get me these things too. No one refused the emperor. The eunuchs brought me back a gramophone and even a bicycle, better than the curiosities they used to bring me from the foreign shop when I was a child.

I wasn't very successful at riding the bicycle, but I read all the books the foreigners could give me. I read their works on history, philosophy, geography, economy, and when those ran out, I read treatises on medicine, science, agriculture, whatever they'd had translated. I even read their Bible. That got their missionary hopes up and they started trying to make Christians out of some of my eunuchs.

"Take it away!"

The eunuch's ringing interruption scattered my English words. His voice broke the silence that had fallen on our meal and made us all look up.

It was my fault, I'd taken too many spoonfuls from the same dish, engrossed in my English contemplation. This was another of the little rules originally designed to thwart would-be assassins. It wasn't so easy to poison the emperor's food if no one ever knew which among the sea of little dishes he preferred to eat. On my own, I didn't care about these things, ate the same few dishes day in day out, and forced the protocol into as unobtrusive a corner as possible.

The eunuchs removed the offending dish and the meal continued. The gates swung shut on me again. There was no point learning English when I was allowed to speak only Manchu before the foreigners, and not even talk with them directly but only through the princes at my side.

I wasn't as serene as I looked. I wasn't really a clockwork construction after all, but a flesh and blood man, and I wanted nothing more at this moment than to grab these uselessly auspicious dishes and hurl them to the floor. That would make them all look up in fright. My eunuchs waiting outside knew I was capable of such wrathful fits. They knew what I was like when Cixi wasn't around to see my smile gone and my calm unhurried manner fall apart. I had learned to suppress and hide the frustration inside, but I had to vent it somewhere.

The foreign books meant much to me. I didn't always understand them, but I valued them regardless, even the simple words in the English primers or the technical works beyond my grasp. They were my journeys and my window. I had no other way of looking beyond my small world.

Li Hongzhang was more fortunate. He was tossing about at sea right now in a French ship bound for Europe, sent to attend the Russian Tsar's coronation. I had never seen the sea and would never see Europe or any foreign land. The books were my ocean-tossed ship. I couldn't follow my eunuchs through the city and enter the foreigners' homes, but I'd have called the foreigners here to my side and poured forth my curiosity, were it permitted.

Once, it was. I lived trussed up in the ancestors' rules, but my ancestors themselves had not always shrunk and constrained their world this way. I envied Kangxi. When the Jesuits came to spread their religion, he didn't expel them as many of his officials desired. He took from them all he found useful, made them work not for their Roman Pope but for our Great Qing, sent them out to map the lands, got them to forge cannons. They taught him music and mathematics and he employed them as astronomers, painters and translators. What he found in them ignorant and foolish he was willing to forgive, and if the gates later closed on them, it was only because they failed to reciprocate this consideration, defied our laws and remained narrow and demanding.

Kangxi warned that these men from the West would make trouble later on. His son, Emperor Yongzheng, could see ahead too. He told the Europeans in Beijing that he knew they hadn't come with ill intentions and only tried so stubbornly to convert our people because their religion taught them that they must, but others would follow, not with promises of salvation, but with guns and ships.

The sad thing was that he was right. Our country was strong back then and the foreigners could not impose their will at whim. We had no such power now. We had turned the ancestors' fields into a barren place we could water only with our tears. We clung to the ceremonial husk of their legacy and let the vital substance rot away. All I could see of the ancestors around me now were these old eunuchs with vigilant eyes counting our spoonfuls. They remembered this rule but forgot countless other words of more important counsel.

I envied Li Hongzhang. He would see the places I read about with his own eyes. I hadn't planned to send him on this voyage. I chose another official to attend the Tsar's coronation, but the Russians didn't want my choice, they wanted their old friend Li.

As emperor, I could do a lot to my subjects. I'd signed orders to have people dismissed, arrested, banished, beheaded, but I couldn't untie myself from this one man. Li hid from me in Tianjin after the treaty with Japan was signed. We had to hand over Taiwan to the Japanese and I made his son go and do it. Li told me his son was too sick to go to Taiwan, but even if that was true, which I doubted, I would have forced him to go. I was determined to make sure they drank this poison with me.

When Li finally came to Beijing, I could hardly bear to look at him. He brought my defeat too close. Taiwan was gone. The first of the indemnity payments to the Japanese was as much as our entire annual revenue. We had to borrow from abroad and that only caused us more problems. The foreigners were eager to lend of course, and fought amongst themselves for the privilege. I didn't want to give the Russians their choice of envoy, but Cixi ordered me to send Li. Life continued, but I was still cold in the shadows. I went guilty and hopeless to Emperor Daoguang in the sleepless nights, my heart stopped up with failed war and plundering foreign hands. I knelt shameful before Emperor Xianfeng, knowing I was not the "glorious succession" my reign title proclaimed, but just the dregs of a once-proud inheritance.

Tutor Weng was one of the few who saw my mood and sensed what sat so heavy on my heart. He was still head of the Board of Revenue, though we didn't really have any these days.

I was grateful to him during those first days after signing the treaty. I had no wish to remain emperor and yet still had to rise every day at dawn, see the grand councillors, hold audiences and read the memorials sent in.

Officials could request sick leave if they fell ill, or retire from service altogether. I had no such privilege. True, history did know of emperors who'd stepped down. Qianlong was the most recent. He'd been on the throne for sixty years by then and stepped down out of filial piety, having vowed not to rule longer than his beloved grandfather, Kangxi, whose reign lasted sixty-one years. But Qianlong was in his eighties and handed power to one of his sons. I wasn't yet even as old as Qianlong was when he became emperor, and I had no son to take over from me.

Tutor Weng tried to shake me from my despair and spark energy and interest in me again. He reminded me how after the foreign invasion that ended in Xianfeng's death, rather than sinking into sorrow and self-pity, the empress dowagers and Prince Gong embarked on a modernising course to reinvigorate the country. I had to do the same.

I knew we had to act. It was no new conclusion in my mind, but I felt it far more urgently now. Time trickled by and my clocks started chiming, jolting me from the blankness into which I'd sunk. I remembered Zhen that first night, when she asked me to fix her clock. She'd worn such an admiring expression as she watched me work the cogs and springs with nimble confidence. She seemed to think my hands would fix anything else as deftly too, not just broken clocks, but the entire country.

I caught myself in a mirror's flash and flicked my gaze away, not wanting to contemplate the figure, too small and frail. I saw this slight boy. Others beyond our walls couldn't see me at all, but their eyes were like Zhen's, trusting, hoping, searching for my capable, fixing hands.

If Cixi, Cian and Prince Gong had done it when the country was in an objectively even worse state, surely we could do it again now, pull ourselves up and make ourselves strong again. I donned my robes of power and sent out an edict declaring that we would strengthen the country by building railways, developing industry, mining, shipping, modernising the army and opening schools.

The country was waiting for this signal. People had been busy sending in reform proposals ever since the war ended. I joined a number of them to the edict and asked the provincial officials to look them over and give me their opinions.

I longed to feel the same swell of unity and purpose that I'd sensed at the start of the war, but it was much easier to rise up against a foreign invader than to fight the enemy within, fight our own ignorance, greed and short-sighted, narrow interests. Even with the best of intentions, it was hard to know how to proceed, especially when even the small things turned murky and got tangled in lies and intrigue.

My secret English learning was a better kind of escape than Tongzhi's visits to the brothels, but it never worked for long. Too many things broke through to return me to our sluggish, stale reality. I had no English words for the conflicts and frustrations in my heart. English was made perhaps for men who came in ships with guns to take others' treasures and land, not for helpless emperors who let their treasures and lands slip from their hands, lived bound up in countless frozen rituals and locked behind moats, walls and constantly patrolling guards.

24

German might have been useful too. I contemplated the ornate clock in my hands. The winter sky was crisp and icy wind bowed the trees. The Forbidden City's walls were perhaps supposed to keep it out, lessen it at least, but it still came bitter down the passageways, got into my joints and my head and turned me numb and aching. The sunlight helped, filtered through the window and spread gentle warmth through me.

It was the quiet time of day. I would have slept a while but my back hurt and my legs ached. The palace doctors were no good. I'd learned a few things in the foreign medical books and suspected that the foreign doctors might be more effective. Here, in private, at least I didn't have to sit upright and official and grow stiff and cold in the draughts.

The clock in my hands had stopped. I'd noticed the motionless hands, at odds with all the others, and reached for it. It was of German make, the clock face set into a ceramic body with delicately painted insets, each one depicting a detailed scene, small ovals of distant Europe, pointed spires of their churches, steep-sloping roofs. My eyes rested on a carriage with horses, and beside it, a gentleman in a tall hat and an odd-shaped woman with a fat billowing skirt and a very pinched waist.

Two Germans. I stared at their smiling painted figures. The foreigners wanted so much from me now for two Germans. Unlike the clock Germans, these two were real people and they were dead. They were Christian missionaries, came to visit a colleague in a small town in Shandong Province. Armed men broke into the room where they slept and killed them. The third missionary managed to get away.

It wasn't very clear who was behind the killing and why, but Shandong was one of those places where all kinds of radical groups, sects and rabble-rousing movements sprouted, and the Christian missionaries had become a lot more active there too over recent years, drawing in converts, adding fuel to an already volatile mix.

I'd always condemned these sorts of attacks and had issued edicts in the past forbidding the persecution of the Christians. It mattered nothing to me that someone was Christian or whatever else. It wasn't important what name a man gave Heaven, for the names were many, and many too the altars and shrines, rituals and prayers. I condemned this murder of course, but the Germans did not care.

We had laws and we were ready to find and punish the killers. The foreign books I'd read spoke of rules and laws that governed relations between civilised nations. Obviously, the Germans did not think us a civilised nation. They might have placed their trust in another country's courts and justice, but from us they wanted Shandong itself. They occupied part of the coast, said they'd build a naval base there, and demanded sole rights to build railways and mines and control the surrounding territory.

The painted clock faces took on a jeering look. Just two Germans. I was sorry for the incident, but what was happening now made a mockery of all the fine words in those foreign books. I'd liked this clock for the gallery of miniature far-off scenes it displayed, but I flung it from me now in a rush of anger. My little eunuch Chun, who entered just then bearing tea, gave a start and nearly dropped the cup. He set the tea down, avoided my eyes and moved towards the cracked clock on the polished floor.

"Leave it!" I ordered.

Little Chun backed away hastily, eyes still averted.

"Recite your words." I softened my tone.

Little Chun kept his face down and knitted his brows in concentration. "I don't remember," he mumbled after a while.

"This here," I pointed at the cup.

"Oh yes," a sudden smile flitted across his lips. "Cup," he said in English. "Tea, book, sky, house…"

"Good." I stopped him and he looked relieved. "Bring me my decoration, the one the Russians gave me."

He soon came with it. A fine little object, I'd seen the foreign ambassadors wear things like this. It had a double-headed eagle with a crown above, a sort of cross with a little man and some foreign letters. The Russians said it was their highest state decoration. They had given it to me the year before, when, using the way they calculated age, I turned twenty-five.

I held it tight and felt it dig into my palm. I pressed it hard against my skin and stared at the marks that remained when I took it away. Tracks across my hand. Little Chun had retreated some distance and tried to look absent. The sunlight grew thin and the warmth faded.

Li Hongzhang brought me gifts when he returned from the Tsar's coronation. I didn't want his gifts. He never listened to me. The Russians had given me this little decoration but they took from me far more. For several years, they'd pressed us to let them build a railway across Manchuria so as to make a shortcut to Vladivostok. I said we would build our own railways. There was no reason for the Russians to do it for us. They wouldn't do it for us but for themselves, like these Germans in Shandong now. I hadn't wanted Li to go to Russia in the first place. When the Japanese asked for him, it ended up costing me Taiwan. The Russians asked for him and I had little hope that he'd return from his journey bearing only an assortment of European curiosities.

Tracks across my hand, biting edge of the Russian decoration. My suspicions were right, of course. Li had long been on good terms with the Russians, and it was no wonder they wanted him to come in person to the coronation. They put a secret treaty together during his visit. Russia promised to help us should the need arise, and in return would station its ships in our southern Manchurian ports and build its Manchurian railway. This was the gift Li brought back for me, and he left me with little choice but to sign it. What else was I supposed to do?

I remembered how Zhen always used to laugh away my urges to be prudent, saying, "But you're the emperor, you'll look after me." And others were little different to Zhen, told me to assert my will, put people in their place, stand up, resist. Like the understandably infuriated governor of Shandong urging us now to fight and not let the Germans walk all over us this way. That was all very well, and I knew he was a valiant and patriotic fellow, but fight with what?

I'd learned my lesson from the war. I wasn't a fool. If Japan could defeat us, what would these Western powers do to our country? We'd only just started taking our first steps in the direction that would hopefully let us do what Japan did, modernise and strengthen ourselves until we could cast off the foreign fetters and stand proud once more. We Manchus had once been unafraid to search wide for what could be useful, weave new strands into our life and thinking. Now we'd become so closed, so frozen in our past. I was trying to change this. I was genuinely curious, tried hard to be open to the foreigners and their ways, eager for their knowledge, but all they did was shame and humiliate me.

It was New Year and I had a new date to write now: twenty-fourth year of the Guangxu reign. It only made me sadder. Twenty-four years seemed a long time, but all I had to show for it was a big list of disasters. The heavens showed their contempt for me as much as the foreigners did. The latest ill omen unnerved the astronomers. They predicted an eclipse on the first day of the New Year, an inauspicious event of the highest degree. Faced with such an ominous sign, I had to play my part as the Son of Heaven and sent out an edict in which I declared myself humble and guilty before this warning portent and promised to make the New Year celebrations modest.

Even in their modest version, the celebrations still tired me. Cixi waited. Cui Yugui, Cixi's second chief eunuch, announced my arrival. Cui was quite different to his colleague, the glib-tongued Li Lianying. He was a big, muscular man and, looking at him, no one would have guessed he'd lost his virility to the knife.

Yehenara was already there, Zhen and Jin beside her. Everyone had to be together at New Year, it was tradition. I knelt in respectful greeting before Cixi, then Yehenara and the concubines knelt before me. Who knelt before who, who sat and who stood – that was all part of the protocol.

Cixi, as the senior among us, could wave the rules aside if she wished, and sometimes she did, dispensed with ceremony and bestowed sudden favours, but not so often that anyone would start to take it for granted. As Prince Gong had learned in the past, she didn't appreciate it when others, even princes, got too familiar.

I knew she'd been worrying about the eclipse, concerned by what this strange message from the skies might mean, but the inauspicious day drew to a close without anything going wrong. She looked relaxed now as we thanked her and took our places. We never said much on these occasions, just exchanged a few banalities before she sent us on our way. I'd never liked all the endless New Year rituals anyway, but I had an added reason to dislike the New Year period since my marriage.

Under the rules, Yehenara had to see out the old year and spend the first nights of the New Year with me. It was her privilege as empress and I never looked forward to the days when she moved into her quarters next to mine and weighed on me with her presence. Cixi, ever hopeful, liked to remind us of our marital duties at this time. She found roundabout ways of getting her hints across, like the year before when she suddenly trotted out the story of the prolific katydids that had given their name to one of the palace gates.

I hoped we'd get no katydids this time, or any other fast-breeding creatures. She had a warm look on her face. I knew how swiftly this look could fade though. She gave me a gentle smile and enquired after my health. She herself was seldom ill. She escaped to the Summer Palace as soon as the weather permitted and spent her time in the gardens, walking the paths and planning excursions to the scenic spots.

It seemed strange to think now that when I was a boy, we hadn't made these constant travels back and forth. It was strange to remember how Cixi had fallen ill and Cian died so suddenly. I could still see myself, little and alone, taking my place in the audience hall and trying to be emperor while Cixi lay sick in bed. I remembered the lamp light flickering on the officials' hat feathers, and I sitting shy on my throne, aware of the emptiness behind me, no curtain concealing my mothers' faces, Cian in her coffin, Cixi hidden in her palace with the doctors at her side.

I'd cried and prayed for her then. She was sick for so long that I saw only her soft moments and forgot how her tongue could sting and her eyes turn me foolish. Even were it possible, I wouldn't know how to speak freely in her presence. We exchanged ritual phrases and I gave her standard answers. And yet the names of mother and son that we used were not bare words but did have flesh and feeling.

There were many things unspoken. I'd often seen her face cloud over with anxiety. I'd seen her tears too. They had mingled with my own when I was little. I'd glimpsed them through my howls in those early days, seen her come to my side looking tired and grey, her eyes all moist. That was the time when the great famines began and starvation drove people into flight.

Our walls kept hunger and refugees out of sight. I had been just a small child and unaware of such things, but Cixi knew what was happening in the empire beyond. Her son had just died. She'd wielded her influence to get me, her sister's son, named the successor, but faced with a sickly, howling child, she perhaps hadn't been as certain and confident as she looked in public.

Her gaze wandered from me to Yehenara, lingered a moment on Zhen standing to one side. I knew her eyes and could see the sadness that welled there. Each year brought its tear-edged anniversaries, remembering husband and child, too soon gone.

The mourning period for Tongzhi had passed not long before. It was Cixi's winter sorrow. She dressed in lesser mourning shades now. The white of fresh loss had given way to the purples and blues of grief grown old, but hearts did not always count years and degrees the same way and she still felt the sadness keenly. Whatever his faults, Tongzhi was her son and he was only nineteen when he died. She seldom shared his memory and I knew little of him beyond the gossip I'd heard and the concubines he'd left behind.

Only girls when the smallpox took him, they joined the collection of widows in the farthest palaces, the small and musty places where we never went. Not able to return to life outside, they stayed hidden behind their walls and grew old, spending their days in needlework and prayers. They lived the Forbidden City's ritual life too and came to present their respects to Cixi on various occasions.

I saw them quite often when I was a boy, especially Lady Yu. She was quite an educated woman and Cixi seemed to rather like her companionship. Lady Yu had been Cixi's favourite even before Tongzhi's wedding day. Cixi had hoped to make her empress, but Tongzhi had ignored her hints and placed the sceptre in the hands of another, Alute, who happened to be Cian's hoped-for choice.

Alute was related to Cian and that probably helped. Her father was a prominent scholar and the only Mongol to have ever come top at the imperial exams. She herself, from what I heard, had been a beautiful, educated and ambitious girl. That had created friction with Cixi, but she'd apparently got on very well with Tongzhi.

I never knew her. She died not long after I entered the Forbidden City. I heard later that she'd killed herself, swallowed gold leaf or starved herself to death, determined to follow her husband into the grave, though the official records said she had just got sick and died. The rumours suggested she'd been a wilful girl, quarrelled with Cixi and shown disrespect. I knew little for certain and never asked about these things. Sometimes it was better to leave the past alone.

It was probably with the memory of Alute in her mind that Cixi had decided to give me Yehenara. Her own niece would not dare insult her the way Alute had. She achieved only a piece of her dream. Yehenara and I were obedient and respectful, but we didn't bring her or each other happiness. The years passed and there was still no heir to the throne.

Cixi asked her questions and I gave my usual protocol answers. There was no need to speak myself, for she was informed anyway. Her spies always took care of that. She knew my dislike for Yehenara and was fully aware of my health problems, but she hoped regardless that fate would take a kinder turn and set things right.

I kept my eyes down. It wasn't just Cixi who watched me. Zhen surreptitiously tried to catch my gaze. Cixi had restored her and Jin to their former rank, but was less keen to let Zhen and I restore our scrap of old complicity, and we didn't see each other often now.

Zhen had lost Cixi's trust and the semblance of forgiveness was just a thin cover for disgrace that lingered, even if no longer so visible. I didn't want to look her way. Corrupt, opportunist officials trussed me up like the eunuchs used to, Germans and Russians grabbed my land, and Yehenara, that thin, stooped little spy, tried to share my nights. Zhen's stealthy glances flashed hopes and memories at me. I had nothing to give her in return. Hopes and memories were all she'd have so long as Cixi remained the power above us all.

25

Prince Heinrich, the German Emperor's younger brother, was coming to Beijing and requested an audience. I straightened up on the throne. The grand councillors looked even older in the dim light. Tired ill men, they had to come before me every morning. I saw them now weighed down with the dawn, court beads hanging heavy round their necks, heads bent with protocol and age.

I looked beyond. The morning grew stronger and cut the eaves free from the last threads of night. The trees gained colour and the walls turned solid. Cixi grew all sorts of flowers in her courtyard. I cared less for such things, but liked to see the trees pressed against the sky and the flocks of crows that would fly suddenly across my little slice of world, on their way to scavenge what they could of the sacrifices and offerings at the temples.

"I will receive this prince in the Hall of Cultivating Blessings," I declared.

It was my old classroom, the place where I'd spent so many years in study, and it seemed to me a good venue. I added too that the prince could enter the Forbidden City in his sedan chair. We'd open the gates to the building for his passage, and we'd put on a banquet in the side hall.

The grand councillors looked alarmed.

"The Hall of Cultivating Blessings is unsuitable," Tutor Weng spoke up. "The east room houses the Empress Xiaojing's ancestral portrait...It wouldn't be proper. And the side hall, it's too small for holding a banquet."

"And that gate...That gate hasn't been opened since the start of Emperor Jiaqing's reign," Grand Councillor Gangyi joined in.

"That's right. It has been closed for more than a hundred years," Tutor Weng continued. "It will have sunk in its fittings and I fear it would be most difficult to open now."

I jumped up in impatience. It was them who'd sunk in their fittings and were difficult to open. I had a hard time fighting back the urge to kick something, throw something and yell at them.

It was such an old debate. They remembered as if yesterday the fusses of more than a hundred years ago when Qianlong was still on the throne and English envoys came hoping to meet him but bristled at the demand that they kneel before him as the etiquette required. They came with gifts and birthday congratulations back then, though they were really hoping for trade concessions. In the end they did kneel, but didn't get what they wanted. The next English delegation was even more recalcitrant. Unfortunately for us, these prickly foreigners weren't long returning with guns and opium instead of gifts for the emperor.

I stared at Tutor Weng and his face turned stubborn. He often had that look these days, zealous defender of all that was proper and fitting. He was still annoyed with me for letting the foreigners ride into the Forbidden City for the New Year audience instead of dismounting and passing the gates on foot, as was the rule.

I granted them this right before they even asked for it, knowing that they expected these things as a matter of course, and didn't realise that to ride into the Forbidden City was a great privilege granted only to a few. Even grand officials had to cross the broad courtyards on foot, with the wind bitter at their tails, sun beating down, rain or snow in their faces, drenched or sweating in their official robes by the time they reached the audience hall. But the foreigners didn't understand these things.

We called them barbarians, and they were in many ways, ignorant of our culture and traditions, conceited and demanding. But they were prickly barbarians, sensitive to the small things and easily slighted, not unlike Cixi with Prince Gong's brusque familiarity really. They were barbarians with armies and might, and it seemed to me we'd get further by using etiquette they recognised than forcing on them protocol they'd never understand anyway.

We still hadn't sorted out the German prince when the Russian ambassador requested an audience. I saw him in the Hall of Flourishing Culture, which looked in better shape now that it got used more often. Tutor Weng stood down below, his face impassive, but I knew he had a sharp eye on me. It was under that same watchful gaze that I'd learned to sit straight and still, keep my aspect solemn and become the silent sovereign, distant on his throne. I had been a little boy in the classroom back then and Tutor Weng had taught me imperial decorum. These days, he no doubt thought me a disappointing pupil, heedlessly casting aside those lessons so diligently learned.

The Russian wanted to deliver a letter from the Tsar. Breaking with the usual protocol, I said I wanted the Russian to mount the dais to where my throne stood, and hand the letter to me personally. Tutor Weng was horrified and said it wasn't proper, as usual.

He'd lauded Kangxi in the past as an example to follow, but what would he have said to Kangxi back when the Jesuits were his everyday companions? Was it proper to sit down with some Italian missionary to play a harpsichord duet, or have French doctors attend him at his bedside? But if there was one thing I'd been learning these last years, it was that there were big gaps between what people taught and the desires they affirmed, and how they applied these things in reality.

We settled on a compromise in the end. The Russian mounted the dais, as I wanted, but laid the letter on the table before my throne rather than placing it directly into my hands. Prince Qing waited for me to make my reply.

I thought of Li Hongzhang and his "gift" – the secret treaty with Russia. I'd always told Li not to trust the Russians.

I stared at the Russian ambassador, solemn and dignified in his uniform, and wanted to ask him why his country had lied to us. Where was the promised help? Russia had looked on idly as the Germans pulled pieces of Shandong from our fingers and anchored their warships at their new base there. Not only did the Russians not deliver their promised aid, they forced us into letting them have the same privileges in southern Manchuria, wanted a naval base of their own on our soil. And then the English, French and Japanese all demanded a bit of our territory too.

I wasn't an emperor, I was just a bankrupt merchant trying to salvage the last of his remaining wares and forced to sell off his goods at the lowest price. But I had to keep on looking dignified and impressive up there on my throne.

The Russian wore a suitably deferential look and waited calmly, knowing I'd not ask awkward questions or speak reproachful words. Frankness and ritual diplomacy did not go together. Prince Qing stood expressionless, ready to translate my protocol Manchu words of no substance.

I smiled to myself, ignored Prince Qing, fixed my eyes on the Russian and spoke Chinese. It took them by surprise. Prince Qing looked flustered for a moment and it made me want to laugh to see him force the composure back on to his face. My smile turned bitter. Was there any point in clinging so hard to our Manchu words and traditions when most of Manchuria was now in Russia's hands? I didn't want to pretend anymore.

My scandalous plans for receiving Prince Heinrich sent the grand councillors rushing to Cixi, the ultimate guardian of all that was right and proper. She soothed their fears by simply decreeing that the audience would take place at the Summer Palace instead. She'd receive the prince first, and then I'd receive him separately. As for the Germans, they were already arguing with Prince Qing and the others from the Foreign Affairs Office about giving the prince a chair to sit on during these brief audiences. Cixi made it clear he'd get no chair from her.

The foreigners were very ignorant at times. Even I could not sit in Cixi's presence unless she granted me the privilege. She hadn't invented that rule, but she wasn't about to change it either for the sake of some German prince.

The Summer Palace wore a welcoming shine. Prince Heinrich was with Cixi, standing. I waited my turn to receive him and went over in my head the words Zhang Yinhuan had prepared for me. Zhang, our former ambassador to the United States, was the one we'd originally tried to send to Japan to negotiate the peace deal, but the Japanese had wanted Li Hongzhang instead. Zhang was an official at the Foreign Affairs Office now, and so was Tutor Weng, which meant they'd both be present when I met with the prince.

Tutor Weng didn't mind managing our empty treasury but he didn't like his foreign affairs post. Confucian ideals as he understood them made it preferable to scrape the financial dregs than to deal with "barbarians". Zhang was just the opposite. He'd lived abroad and was at ease with the foreigners and their ways.

I liked Zhang because I was eager to learn more about the foreigners, and he painted their world for me better than anyone else around. I had endless questions for him and thought up countless reasons to summon him and listen to his stories. We sent him to England the year before for Queen Victoria's jubilee celebration, and the long months of his absence gave me the rare feeling of filling my imagination with someone distant. I hadn't had that feeling since I was a boy and Tutor Weng had returned to his home town, leaving me impatiently awaiting his return. Zhang too I had wanted to hurry back, have him return from England with new tales and impressions to share. I'd never had many chances to just talk with someone about the things that interested me.

I wanted to have a proper conversation with Prince Heinrich, but was conscious of the protocol constraints. Zhang prepared some notes for me. Nothing about the Germans taking over part of Shandong of course. Zhang said conversation had to stick to diplomatic niceties. I'd ask the prince things like how was the German Emperor, and what countries had he visited on his way to China, and I'd say how much I hoped our countries would be friends.

They arrived. I stood up when they came in. Tutor Weng shot me a disapproving look. This Heinrich hadn't come to China for diplomatic chit-chat, but to command the German forces in Shandong. Tutor Weng was a patriotic man, and knowing why the German had come probably added to his quiet outrage as I forgot every lesson he'd taught me, stood up to receive the barbarian prince, shook his hand in the foreigners' manner and bade him sit down beside me. I was good after that, said only the things Zhang had prepared, then Prince Qing and the others took him off for the banquet.

That was my part over. Prince Qing would act as host on my behalf at the banquet. The emperor never sat down to eat with sundry visitors. If I ate with anyone else, it was Cixi. They'd feed the prince and then take him, as Cixi instructed, on a tour of the lake and the sights. But I hadn't finished yet, though the officials didn't know it.

I waited a while, went over to the hall where they were dining, asked the prince if he was happy with everything, and presented him with a Qing state decoration. The foreigners liked these ribbons and medals, covered their chests with them on ceremonial occasions and gave them as gifts to each other. I liked them too.

The prince was pleased and suddenly asked me if I wanted to see his soldiers. That was the best surprise, and all the more so because it wasn't planned at all. Prince Heinrich and I went out into the courtyard together, where the soldiers waited, and he got them to line up and march. I forgot about looking solemn and imperial and smiled happily, nodded my enthusiasm. The men performed a series of precision manoeuvres and I felt as though the clocks had come alive in human form. Prince

Heinrich smiled and even the soldiers sparkled with life under their studied sternness.

Tutor Weng had come out into the courtyard too. His face was smooth, but I knew he was choked with dismay inside. Throughout those long classroom years, he'd awaited my arrival every morning in the side room, there before dawn, sipping tea as the darkness lifted slowly and the eunuchs bore me to my lessons in my yellow-draped sedan chair. We always began with the ritual bows, I took my place first, facing south, as the emperor should, upright and still, and he sat to the side. That was the proper way of things and he'd drilled it all into me, but now I'd jumped up and rushed into the courtyard to watch some foreign soldiers marching, overturning all those years of schooling in a single morning.

26

Summer was on its way, but Cixi had deep autumn in her eyes. She looked down at Prince Gong's weary face. The old quarrels faded and a golden hue lit their expressions. That was nostalgia's glow, I supposed, and all the common memories they had kept hidden were finally allowed to surface. I saw sorrow, worry, even a hint of fond complicity in the way he and Cixi looked at each other now.

He'd been ill for some time. I remembered how he had dragged himself in sickness to the Forbidden City to bring me his sad advice in person and tell me to sign the treaty with Japan. I knew he had been ill at home then and hadn't expected to see him turn up before me. This time, I came to him. We knew the end was close and he'd not get up again.

I left them to their memories and went out into the gardens. They had a lot to remember together. Perhaps they would not take their words too far, but then again, perhaps they would use my discreet withdrawal to speak things they'd maybe not say if I were there. I was eager in any case to wander the gardens a moment. Prince Gong's mansion had perhaps the finest private gardens in all of Beijing. My life consisted of only a limited collection of surroundings, grand though they were, and it made a change to visit Prince Gong's home, though the circumstances reminded me of my father's illness and death.

Rituals took me out of the Forbidden City along the emptied road south in grand procession to the Temple of Heaven, to the other major temples scattered around Beijing's inner districts, or to the special field where I ploughed my spring furrows. Otherwise, only death could break my usual routine.

I got to visit tombs on rare occasions. I'd gone to my father's final resting place a few times. He was surrounded by mountains too, like the emperors. He chose the site himself when he was a young man, didn't shoot an arrow like Shunzhi, but spun a more lyrical thread, devoting a poem to the picturesque spread he thought a fitting place for his long rest. He had chosen a peaceful site, and I liked to imagine that he'd come out from his dark shelter and finally become the quiet poet of his deeper desires, free from the ambitions and fears that had always got in his way before.

The gardens lay perfect before me. The sunlit pond, elegant pavilion and curiously shaped rocks in careful arrangement pleased the eye. The air was warm and silent, tempting me to let my eyes close and drift away in a lazy moment.

I pictured things I'd been talking about with Zhang Yinhuan. I saw an oceangoing ship, distant land on the horizon, newspaper pictures of foreign cities with streetlights and trams, voyages I'd liked to have made, journeys of discovery, not death. Zhang described foreign cities brightly lit. We had electric lights only at the Summer Palace. Zhang said there were trains that carried people around under the ground in London. We had hardly any trains, even above ground.

The ducks on the pond looked so serene, smooth and untroubled as they glided back and forth. These gardens captured a timeless China, distilled it in tranquil refuge from the world. It was the idyll poets described.

My ancestors were entranced when they first went south. Manchuria was a rugged, hardy land of forests, mountains, snowswept plains. South of the Yangtze lay a different world. They had read the Chinese poets and in the lake scenes of Hangzhou and the gardens and canals of Suzhou they saw the poems come to life before their eyes and fill them with richness and colour such as they'd never yet seen. Manchuria was cut from coarser but more virile cloth perhaps, while this Chinese south was delicate silk.

They took it back north with them and wove it into their palaces and gardens. When the heat came to Beijing, they became Manchu again and went north to spend the summer the old way, competing with bow and arrow, showing off their hunting skills and horsemanship. The ancestors had known how to hold on to their essence while at the same time enriching themselves with new things and broadening their world.

Saddened, I watched the ducks. These gardens were all we had left of those days, an imitation Suzhou. We never even went south now to the real Suzhou, let alone venture out to the distant lands Zhang told me about. Peter the Great in Russia, emperor though he was, had donned a commoner's garb and gone abroad in search of new learning, and even Emperor Meiji in Japan had left the centuries of imperial seclusion and travelled around his lands.

I wanted to be like them, but all I got were temples and tombs, and, like now, deathbed visits to relatives. Instead of broadening my horizons, I broke trifling rules and sparked battles amongst the guardians of tradition that surrounded me.

Hidden in the piles of old things from the past, I'd glimpsed portraits of Emperor Yongzheng dressed in funny European clothes and with a wig of curly hair on his head. He'd never gone around dressed up like that of course, but he'd asked the court painters to paint him that way, and he had worn the Europeans' eyeglasses, though it wasn't considered a fitting thing for the emperor to do at that time. He had stacks of eyeglasses made for himself, so as to always have them at hand, no doubt.

My zealous guardians found fault with me simply for turning up to an audience with the French ambassador wearing a French decoration I had been given earlier. I meant nothing by it really, just thought it would please the Frenchman to see me wear his country's decoration.

I tossed a small stone at the pond in a boyish gesture. Ripples spread and the ducks scattered, wary a moment before resuming their smooth sailing. All I did was skim the surface in my attempts to reform. Shaking hands with foreigners and letting them sit in my presence was the most I could achieve, but these were such tiny and laughable victories when set against the whole.

The war with Japan grew distant, months became years, and my orders and decrees seemed to fade in their urgency. The university I was trying to establish existed only on paper. The industrial development I tried to promote was little more than words.

I hadn't seen many foreign newspapers, but the little I had glimpsed put fear in me. In just a few months, I'd been forced to give away territory to five different countries. Where would it stop? Would we become like India, a colony, slaves to a foreign master?

India was an ancient land with a proud heritage. I knew that much. I knew the Buddhist pilgrims once went all the way from China across forbidding mountains and deserts to reach India's cities and seats of learning. Did my officials today even know where India was? Did they see it was a big place swallowed by England, even though England was just a little island and very far away? Not that I had the clearest picture of geography myself. Kangxi had had the Jesuits make maps for him, but me, I didn't even have a proper map of the world.

They'd all grown cautious, even Prince Gong who'd once been sharp-tongued and bold, though he probably knew better than any of them how I felt. He and Cixi would perhaps be recalling the dark days of the Anglo-French invasion. Prince Gong had been ordered to stay in Beijing when the invaders arrived. He saw the skies thick with smoke to the west of the city as the Summer Palace burned. He was forced to put his name to the foreigners' demands, proud emperor's son, had to turn humble and submit.

I felt my tears come. It would be hard for my Sixth Uncle to close his eyes in peace. Nothing had changed since those days. The urgency burned painful inside. The war never faded for me. We still lay prostrate, half-naked in the last frayed threads of our former finery. The foreign powers made a pretence of courting us a little, but they'd soon do away with even ritual politeness and let loose their lustful hands.

I got to my feet and wandered alongside the water. This mansion originally belonged to Grand Councillor Heshen, Qianlong's favourite in his final years. Heshen was a capable young man when he caught Qianlong's attention, and he rose fast through the bureaucratic ranks. They said he came to all but rule the country, almost emperor himself in his wealth and power. He muddied Qianlong's vision with deceit and flattery and painted short-lived splendour to hide a crumbling reality.

When Qianlong died, one of the first things his son, Emperor Jiaqing, did was order Heshen to commit suicide and confiscated all the riches he'd piled up in this mansion. Jiaqing thus managed to replenish the treasury a bit, but he was never able to rebuild the cracked foundations. The age of prosperity was over. A blackened memory of corruption and lies were all that Heshen left. The night came swift on him for all his power and rank. Only this residence remained now in its gentle beauty and sweet shelter from the world.

I did not want to see smoke and ashes as Prince Gong had. Tutor Weng and the others reproached me for not being a filial son and ignoring the ancestors' rules. They had things all wrong. Could a good son watch idly as others plundered and destroyed his ancestors' legacy? Could I be a worthy emperor if I let the dynasty fail and left the country to be raped?

There was no need to fear new things. Shaking hands with a foreigner didn't make me foreign. My fascination with foreign things didn't stop me from drinking in the beauty of Prince Gong's gardens. Studying the world beyond would not make me forget the teachings of Confucius and the wisdom of my ancestors. If they'd made Chinese culture a part of themselves without ceasing to be Manchus, why could we today not cast our vision wider? My ancestors were once so swift on their horses and so deadly with their arrows, but the foreign trains rushed faster than any horse ever could, and the foreign guns were deadlier than any arrow.

The sun descended, sinking light, tinged with approaching end. I did not want to be the sunset emperor, the one to watch the day fade and falter, powerless to stop the night's advance. It was Prince Gong who stared into his sunset now, not me. We were in summer just starting, not autumn with its colours already over. I blinked my eyes hard and pushed the tears away. I would soon mourn my uncle's death, this I knew, but it was not time to mourn my country.

The first character of my reign name was glory, radiance, a word of morning and hope. There had to be a way forward. If we didn't take it, we'd have nothing left to fight for soon. Prince Gong the young man had shown courage and innovation. I only saw the later traces of his younger self. My Sixth Uncle, he'd been one of our dynasty's brighter hopes in these difficult years, but his last words to me after all this time were little different to what the other old men at court said.

Was this his legacy, just more of this caution, this ebbing resolve and sinking sun? I shook my head, sadness and frustration stirred thick together. I refused it. My sun was that of dawn, not dusk. There were voices out there that called with more resonant tones. There were lights that shone stronger.

27

I watched old eunuch Zhang serve the food. He performed his simple motions with loving care, his expression smooth and concentrated all at once. People like him were rare. I could see he took pride in his task and his eyes showed a clear and honest heart. I'd have taken him for myself, but he was Cixi's eunuch.

Cixi always ate slowly, contemplated the dishes, dispensed occasional praise and reflected on the different flavours. Half the time, I wasn't even really sure what I ate. I was the same now as I popped some food in my mouth, got up from the table and wandered about the room.

Things were always more relaxed at the Summer Palace. Protocol shrank and rules grew fewer. That was another reason why no one had ever much liked living in the Forbidden City. I watched old Zhang from the corner of my eye and supposed he was luckier with Cixi. She appreciated his work and it seemed to please him to watch her savouring her meal. All his conscientious efforts would have been wasted on me.

The hours hurried. Time passed quicker than ever when I came and went from the Summer Palace. The journey itself was not long but the organisation was complicated. I had to notify them at least a couple of days in advance of my plans and give them time to close the road and prepare the guards, eunuchs, cooks, palace doctors, administrative staff, all the horses, carts with provisions, medicines and so on, turning a couple of hours' travel into a vast expedition. Cixi's processions were even more grandiose.

Always surrounded by clocks, I was so used to their sounds and little noticed them, but their insistent tick pressed hard on my ears now. They nibbled away at time, and I was still silent, too fat with words to think of food, too aware of the figure at the table, chopsticks in her hand, her slow calm gestures making me grow only tenser.

"I can see that there's something you want to say. Why don't you speak?" Cixi stopped eating and stared at me.

I stood still, eyes on the floor. On the road here, it had seemed easy. It had been stuffy behind the curtains and I peered out, let in some air, saw the hills in the distance and the brighter spots where the light caught cascading rooftops still an indistinct jumble. Cixi's instinct was right. I did have something to say, much more than polite phrases of small substance.

On the road, I had arranged my words in my head, setting them out in neat sequence, but they grew sticky once I arrived. Just like the astronomers checking the skies for auspicious days and hours, I sought the right moment too, but it turned slippery. Cixi spoke of other things and I wasn't sure I could twist her favour my way and hold it firm.

"Emperor, why do you hesitate? Say whatever it is you want to say."

I nodded. Warm and inviting, she pared herself down and turned kind eyes on me, made me feel foolish in my timid fears. I cleared my throat and began, reminding her of two memorials I'd received recently, urging us to go further in the reform effort.

"Oh, that's what it is, is it?" she sharpened her look a little. "What are you thinking?"

"I agree with what those memorials say," I said slowly, eyes down. "I think they're right. We're losing time and the officials drag their feet constantly. I also believe that we need to make clear that reform is our policy, the court's policy, and that it has our support."

Mm," she turned thoughtful. "So, what do you propose exactly?"

"I propose doing as the memorials suggest and issuing an edict declaring our commitment to reform."

She forgot about the food now, laid her chopsticks down and shot me a keen glance.

"Reform…Yes," she nodded slowly, "but what sort of reform?"

"The sort of reform I've been trying to get them to carry out ever since the war," I sighed.

She was silent. I gave her a hopeful look. I needed her support. No one would move without her signal and nothing would change without her approval. Even with her out of sight at the Summer Palace, the officials and governors still sought her out with their procrastinating gaze, reluctant to act on my word alone. If I did issue an edict of the kind the memorials urged, the officials all around the country would know that I had Cixi on my side. They knew I'd never take such a step without her assent. The edict would speak loud, showing them that she shared my view and that I acted with her full endorsement.

"Do you really think it's that easy?" she threw me a questioning look. "Issue an edict and everything will come right?"

"If it were that easy we'd already have accomplished what we're only still just talking about today," I said glumly.

"Yes…" she fell into silence once more.

Old eunuch Zhang took on a wooden pose now and became a background object. Preparing tea and serving food was his sole purpose and occupation, but he gave himself completely to his humble tasks every single time, even after so many years. If only the officials would work like old Zhang did and show the same diligent care.

The eunuchs, when I was a boy, hadn't respected me and the officials now were no better, took constant sick leave, shirked their duties and ignored my orders. It wasn't even reform I needed to impose on them so much as simple discipline. The eunuchs I could have fined or flogged, but I had to find some other way to shake the officials from their torpor.

"We have to make them understand that there's no other way." I tried to nudge her into a response. "Otherwise… otherwise…there won't be anything left to reform…"

"Yes, I realise that," Cixi cut me off. "Maybe it's worth trying. I'm just afraid…"

She broke off and gave me a long hard stare that made me shrink. I dared not ask what it was she feared.

"If only he hadn't left us." She looked away and sighed. "We need someone like that now, someone with experience… balance…"

She meant Prince Gong. I was still dressed in mourning for him. We took part in the funeral rites and gave him the fullest honours. The court bestowed on him the posthumous name of "Loyal". He had been loyal to the dynasty and loyal to Cixi too, in the end. The old conflicts lost their sharpness and it was his docile final years that she fingered now in lingering regret.

She blinked and I caught the shine of tears in her eyes. This was one of the moments when the layers fell from her, leaving her ageing and vulnerable. She made me freeze up even more inside when she was like this, made me feel guilty and inadequate. She was supposed to abandon herself to the carefree years of an honoured old age and pursue her little pleasures in the fairy kingdom my father had built for her, confident that the burden of governing had passed into the hands of a wise and strong emperor. But it had never happened.

This was Prince Gong's legacy too. He couldn't be emperor himself, but he came close by ruling jointly from behind the scenes with Cixi and Cian while Tongzhi was a child. Tongzhi's very reign title said it all – "joint rule'", it proclaimed. Prince Gong probably never imagined then that his action would whittle away the whole notion of what it meant to be emperor. He no doubt saw just a six-year-old boy too young to rule and two young women who knew nothing of government. He saw his own chance for influence and took it.

It had worked well for a while, until Tongzhi grew up and started ruling in his own right. And that was where my memories began, hiding in the bamboo and seeing Sixth Uncle and my father tense and angered. Now all of them were dead except for Cixi, and her eyes turned moist with sudden nostalgia.

The country needed more than our sighs and tears. We hadn't come so far since those days in Rehe after Xianfeng's death. We were still crushed by the foreigners' demands, still hostage, not to Sushun the would-be usurper, but to the perhaps more dangerous foes that were our own ignorance, prejudice and short-sighted vision. I knew Cixi's idea of experience and balance. Her officials surrounded me. They'd had their merits once perhaps, but they were old men now. They lived on the past, still victors inside, outwitted Sushun and his gang, ended the bitter years of war and rebellion, and brought if not prosperity then at least stability.

Now they clung to this stability turned stagnant. There was no cunning Sushun eyeing the throne now, but the urgency was no less great. Someone still had to ride out into the night and arrest the foe, like the way my father had ridden out to Miyun, where Sushun guarded Xianfeng's coffin and waited for dawn to come.

The old men wouldn't do it. They hadn't the resolve for such things any longer. My father had done it back then. It was the one act of courage in his life maybe, but more than I could claim. I would prove myself his son in this deed at least. I knew the moment had come and I didn't need astronomers to tell me. My own Miyun awaited and it was time for me to set out into the darkness. But the order I would carry had to come from Cixi's hands.

"Whose voice will you listen to?" Cixi dabbed at her eyes and spoke softly. "Whose advice will you follow? These reformers, they have good intentions perhaps, but they have no experience, you know."

I nodded. She was old too and forgot now that she'd once had no experience either.

"I will listen to everyone." I assured her.

"Will you?" she gave me a quizzical look. "It seems to be mostly Zhang Yinhuan who has your ear these days. The rumours about him lately are very unsettling. You know what I'm talking about," she continued.

I lowered my eyes, silent. There were allegations floating about that Zhang had taken a bribe from the Russians. The gossip implicated Tutor Weng too, though I didn't believe it. Tutor Weng wasn't the bribe-taking sort, and if he ever did take a bribe, it certainly wouldn't be from foreigners.

"These are serious matters, you know," Cixi prodded me again.

I nodded. Quiet fell, only the clocks still loud and distinct in my ears.

"This edict on reform," she pulled me from the ticking, her voice decisive now, "yes, I suppose we should try. Go ahead with your plans."

The road back to the Forbidden City was different. It was always a relief when the gates closed behind me and the tension melted. I always breathed more freely in Cixi's absence. I sat in the same yellow-curtained stuffiness and grew stiff as we hurried along, but my mind and body tingled, alert, elated even. I didn't open the curtains this time to glimpse the villages and fields or the city walls drawing closer. The air felt fresh and new. It was inside me, a sudden flood of hopes.

Prince Heinrich had got his soldiers to march around for my inspection. I wouldn't need to watch a visiting German's soldiers now but would have my own, whole armies of them, modern, well-armed soldiers. I'd have my university, my mines and railways, banks and factories, and schools teaching not just the world of Confucius' time but the world of today. I'd been trying for so long now to assemble the pieces. The mechanism was there, and all we had to do was set it chiming.

Tradition demanded that they close the road when I passed. All the crowds vanished inside and the windows were shut. People were chased out of the way to stop them from watching my procession.

I had never been comfortable in others' idle gaze. It wasn't the people's stares I sought but their ideas. Now, I would open the road of speech wide. The Grand Council and the small group of officials with the power to submit memorials was too tiny a stream. I wanted a great river of opinion and I'd be the fisherman plucking talent from its waters. I breathed freer than ever. I had Cixi's blessing. My urgent night seemed not so dark after all and the dawn lit my way forward with summer promise.

I got Tutor Weng to draft the edict and the result pleased me. It called on the entire nation, from highest nobles to humblest commoners, to lay aside their resistance and work together for reform.

Lamps turned the night soft. These rooms where I'd grown up had so often swelled with sighs and shadows. It was maybe just my imagination, but they always seemed to me my ancestors turned restless with hopes or reproach. The shadows were gentle tonight. I ran my eyes over the familiar surroundings, the bed that stayed empty, Yehenara's place. It never served its purpose and she spent her days at the Summer Palace, an arrangement that suited me just fine.

"Forge ahead daily." I glanced at the board above the bed, inscribed with the three large characters I hardly noticed usually. Cixi had written those characters. I smiled to myself. It was a fine sentiment, but she had never really let me forge ahead, afraid I'd leave her behind somewhere on the way.

I'd show her that there was nothing to fear. She could let me go and I'd not abandon her. We could forge ahead together if we swallowed our hesitation and harnessed ourselves in harmony.

The ancestors didn't come tonight from their hiding places to reproach and torment me. I heard only the eunuchs and the clocks. I wasn't the small boy afraid of darkness, loud sounds and thunder now. I was the emperor and I had work to do. Sleep came swift and peaceful.

28

Rain cast a drab shroud and my misted thoughts ran together. I had a heavy head and dull ache inside, and I wanted to sleep. Tutor Weng's words ran together too. Awareness broke apart for a moment, but I forced my eyes open and sat up straighter. This lethargic, head-drooping feeling reminded me of my first years back in the classroom. I was always tired then, words fraying around me as dreams stole my attention.

I glanced at Tutor Weng. I hadn't forgotten his hand on my hot little forehead all those years ago, and his voice turned kind in my ear. They would have been bleak days without the warmth and encouragement he had given me then.

The other grand councillors stood impassive now as he spoke about rules. He said they were going to draw up a new code of protocol for my meetings with foreigners. I knew, of course, what had sparked this new proposal. Tutor Weng resented the way I threw aside convention and followed my impulse. Rituals had always been important. A country that let its rituals fall apart would soon fall apart itself.

This I knew from the classroom years, of course. Confucius and his followers all said it. But they didn't say that we had to let rituals strangle us like vines could strangle trees, choking the lifeblood from them until only the husk remained. It seemed to me that the scholars and officials too often turned Confucius himself into a hollow shell, not to mention the rituals and rules. Tutor Weng had been different. He'd meant so much to me not just for the simple human things, but because as a teacher he had tried hard to keep the lifeblood flowing in the classic texts and had fed me not tasteless pages but real flesh and colour.

This old man talking rules before me now suddenly seemed a stranger, and his words were dull. He still had that business with Prince Heinrich fresh in his mind. The prince had asked to see me again before he left Beijing. He had a telegram from the German Emperor for me. He refused to come out to the Summer Palace where I was staying, so I came to him instead, travelled into the city and back all in one day just for his sake, shook his hand and let him sit in my presence once more.

The German Emperor bestowed on me a decoration and informed me through Prince Heinrich that our navy could also use the bit of land the Germans had grabbed in Shandong for their naval base. It was very kind of the Germans to give us access to our own territory. Only a symbolic gesture really, because we hadn't much of a navy now anyway, but in our current situation, even symbolic gestures were better than nothing.

That was the whole point behind my willingness to shake foreigners' hands, let them sit on chairs and in the halls they wanted, and leave them to bow as they wished. I was anxious to avoid disputes with the foreign powers, afraid it might disrupt my reform plans. It was humiliating of course, but it was better to play meek and friendly for now and concentrate on the tasks at home.

"Have the Foreign Affairs Office draft the new code then," I cut short Tutor Weng's explanations and nodded my assent.

Tutor Weng took his place again and silence fell. I thought I could hear the rain's sad voice but that was just my imagination. I liked the rain when it swallowed my world's usual outlines and clothed everything in delicate mist that let my fancy grow. I liked to see its silver drops cling in small pearls to leaves and windows, and I liked the sky-catching puddles it scattered. I couldn't see it now, just sensed its dreary curtain. The air was warm, damp and unpleasant.

The Summer Palace was big and open, unlike the Forbidden City, and it was often tempting to wander the lakeside and watch the temple pagodas disappear as the rain shrunk the hills. Mornings were for duty, though.

Back in the Ming dynasty, there were emperors who simply refused to work, hid in the palace depths and turned away officials who came bothering them. The emperors of our dynasty were hardworking and always up at dawn, even at the Summer Palace. Kangxi's successor, Emperor Yongzheng had made sure of that. Like Cixi, he hadn't liked living in the Forbidden City, and after the mourning for Kangxi was over, he moved back out to the lakeside where he'd lived as a prince. Some of the officials feared this would lead to an idle, self-indulgent life, but Yongzheng showed them otherwise. He had an audience hall built and called it the Hall of Diligent Government, and he meant it too. The officials had to get up in the middle of the night to make it out there from the city on time for the dawn audiences, so Yongzheng decided it would be simpler to have them all live nearby.

Yongzheng's old parks and palaces got destroyed when the French and English invaded, but our rebuilt Summer Palace had its Hall of Diligent Government too, and our dawn audiences continued.

I wasn't feeling very diligent today. Tutor Weng had a lot of words this morning. He waffled now about having newly appointed senior officials send letters of thanks to Cixi. I didn't listen to his words but watched his pointy beard waggling away. It wasn't done to grow a beard until you reached forty, and I was a long way off that age. I'd always known Tutor Weng with this pointy beard. I liked its prickly feel when I was a boy and remembered pressing my cheek to it, hiding myself in Tutor Weng's arms.

"Have an edict drafted to that effect," I nodded at them. There was nothing to debate when it came to things like thanking Cixi. We were all filial sons and had to show our gratitude. What did it matter to them that keeping her as the sole star in the sky made it hard for me to find my place? The emperor was supposed to be the North Star, but if the sun never set, the North Star never got a chance to shine, and these grand councillors were all determined to make sure that Cixi's sun never set.

The beard was still, and Tutor Weng silent once more. I remembered now that today was his birthday. I had thought him rather an old man when I first saw him all those years ago. He hadn't been old then, it was just the grave demeanour that did it, but he was old now. For more than twenty years I'd seen him almost every day. I knew he had a life beyond the Forbidden City of course. He had family in his home district in the south and had always gone now and then to see them and be the filial son at his parents' graves. That was all abstract to me though. My vision was simple and reduced people to their official functions. I was the emperor and saw people only in relation to myself and my plans, only so far as they furthered or frustrated my desires.

I had never really thought about what Tutor Weng may have carried in his heart and it only now dawned on me that he was jealous of Zhang Yinhuan. I'd never had much reason to consider my officials' emotional tangles.

It was a chance thing that alerted me to Tutor Weng's inner conflicts. There was this fellow called Kang Youwei, a scholar from Guangdong in the south. He came knocking on Tutor Weng's door when he first came to Beijing, looking for a way to move up and make a name for himself. It was the normal thing to do, look for a scholar-official with standing at the court and colleagues' respect, and try to insinuate yourself into his circle, make an impression, pull the right strings. Tutor Weng, with his decades as imperial tutor and all his government posts, attracted bright talents looking to be put to use. It flattered him no doubt and he did speak with me about some of the scholars who came his way, including this Kang Youwei.

Though a Confucian scholar schooled in the usual traditions, Kang was interested in foreign countries and their experience, so I put him to work writing accounts of reform in places like Russia and Japan. Tutor Weng knew about that project of course, and I told him casually one day to ask Kang to send some more copies of these accounts. It was just a little message to pass on, but Tutor Weng was oddly stubborn and when I pressed him, said he'd broken off contact with Kang and didn't think he could be trusted. He'd read Kang's latest work on Confucius and realised that here was a slippery fellow he'd rather avoid.

I wasn't interested in their academic debates about the veracity of this or that portion of the Confucian texts. Tutor Weng was stubborn the next day too when I repeated my request.

"Oh well, if you don't want to see him yourself, pass it on to Zhang Yinhuan," I said, conciliatory. "Tell him to go see Kang."

"But Zhang sees you every day. Why don't you tell him to go and see Kang yourself?" he said, his tone suddenly rather peeved and surly.

That was what opened my eyes, this tiny incident and peeved remark that slipped from his mouth. There I was, imagining Tutor Weng and Kang had fallen out over texts from 2,000 ago, but it was much simpler and stupider, really.

Kang and Zhang Yinhuan were on good terms. They came from the same part of Guangdong. Zhang didn't really see me every day, as Tutor Weng suggested, but his visits were already too frequent for Tutor Weng's liking. Looking into Tutor Weng's eyes that day, I realised he was jealous of Zhang. He saw me as his and feared that I'd slip free of his grasp and Zhang would lead me beyond his easy reach.

Tutor Weng's beard shed its memory fondness and returned to being just the usual attribute of a man past forty, respectfully still and waiting now, its owner's head inclined in ritually submissive pose. Only ritually submissive. His eyes were lowered, but not in genuine deference. This I was starting to understand now, along with the fact that his words were not always as sincere as he'd have me believe.

Kang's unorthodox views weren't the issue. He'd called Kang a bright fellow with a wild streak in his thinking, but he'd said it with indulgence, not reproach, and now he suddenly claimed this was a man who couldn't be trusted. He wouldn't be happy knowing that I'd summoned this same untrustworthy Kang for a personal audience next day.

The heat rose. The stuffiness was in me rather than the room. Tutor Weng's proposal to have officials thank Cixi for their appointments looked like just a minor point of etiquette, but its real purpose was to remind me of my place. The officials had to thank her because it was she who ultimately decided, and I wasn't to forget that, wasn't to imagine that just because she'd given her blessing to my reform plans I could finally shrug off my subordinate role. That was what Tutor Weng was trying to tell me.

Sometimes, when the frustration got too much, I exploded at the grand councillors and flung abuse at them. Today the rain wrapped me in its soft dull blanket and turned me slow and lethargic. It felt a little strange to know Tutor Weng envious at the thought that I sometimes summoned Zhang Yinhuan and was smiling attention before his stories. It was stifling enough already being Cixi's adopted son. I didn't want anyone else trying to turn me into their personal possession, not even the teacher I'd trusted and valued all these years.

But I had more interesting matters to attend to now. We had started modernising part of our army at least, and these newly trained troops were going to hold exercises in Tianjin in the autumn. I'd envied my father when he went off to Tianjin to inspect Li Hongzhang's navy. They thought I was still only a boy then and wouldn't let me go.

Things were different now and I planned not just a journey but a whole symbolic statement. Cixi and I would travel together to Tianjin for the occasion, and we'd do it by train.

Our officials went back and forth now this way. To have Cixi and I make this train journey together would be an excellent way of showing our commitment to progress and modernity, plus, I simply longed to travel in a real train.

Tutor Weng's face grew long as I announced my plans. He didn't approve of me and Cixi travelling by train. It wasn't proper. Now I really felt like when I was a small boy, once more seated before my teacher with his books and learned look and the great clock on the wall ticking the morning away. I used to go and stand in my stubborn corner back then and I could do the same now, play deaf and motionless. I didn't feel like arguing with him and so I ended the audience altogether and left the Tianjin issue undecided.

The rain still fell. Once it had tumbled joyous from the sky, and I hadn't forgotten that either, hadn't forgotten how I'd prayed for its cool streams, leapt in the wet morning and made Tutor Weng's eyes shine when he heard. I was such an earnest boy, always chasing that elusive virtue of the sagely kings he and Prince Gong had spoken of at my very first lesson. I'd trembled at the hugeness of my task, cried lots of lonely tears, but I had never run away. I'd believed my teacher, sincere and diligent, tried as hard as I could, fought my fears and weakness and let him lead me forward.

A strange bitter wave rushed fierce through me now. He was the one who'd taken me, a silent stubborn child, and kindled the spark of hope and purpose inside me. I'd have had no heart at all and no joy to taste without the learning, books and ideas he'd shared with me. He'd wanted me to be like Kangxi. Kangxi was only fourteen when he cut himself free and began to rule. I was twice that age and still bound tight, the filial son forever seeking instruction from my august mother, the endless pupil under my tutor's watchful eyes, not allowed to seek out those, like Zhang Yinhuan and Kang Youwei, who could help me broaden my horizons, not even allowed to make one small journey on the railways I sought so hard to develop.

My chest felt constricted and I breathed in deep. Experience and balance were the qualities Cixi lauded. Tutor Weng had those things, always trod a careful path, frank at moments, flattering at others, an instinct he'd developed over his long years at court. But he stumbled now. The path came to an end and he didn't see it. Praising Cixi wouldn't help him. He'd forgotten who I was, not his pupil but his sovereign. I would remind him now.

The eunuchs prepared the paper and ink. With them came a distant memory of winter light and my old eunuch Fan with his soft, slightly fretful voice, asking me what I wanted the ink and paper for. I'd seen Cixi write auspicious characters in her best calligraphy as gifts for nobles and officials. I'd taken the brush and stood as I'd seen her, intent. Two characters I wrote then in my childish hand, "good fortune" and "long life". The New Year was coming and these were going to be my presents for Tutor Weng.

The ink was ready. The emperor's special vermilion ink. I'd learned to use it under Tutor Weng's guidance, commenting memorials and writing edicts, preparing for my future rule. He gave me Kangxi as a model but had me beg Cixi to continue her regency. He taught me values only to then stop me from applying them. He encouraged me into war but wavered when I most needed someone to stand firm. He got enthused over progress and development as laid out in books but shied from the reality.

The ideal Confucian ruler did not jump up from the throne to shake some foreign prince's hand and run off to watch his soldiers. Nor did he board a train amidst smoke and noise, with no grand procession and no symbolic yellow sand spread along the imperial way. But I wasn't an ideal ruler. The heavens had warned me every year of my reign, no matter how earnestly I'd tried. I was a chance ruler, and only half a ruler at that, obeyed on the small things, ignored on anything that mattered. Surely Tutor Weng must have realised he was sowing future conflict inside me, feeding me impossible hopes and ideals and giving me examples I could never emulate.

And yet he'd meant something to me. The rain fell mournful. The vermilion ink seemed to be my own blood and substance and all the memories of that long-ago boy of the tired classroom mornings. I forced my hand to write. I was a frustrated son, still submissive as taught, still chasing kingly virtue, still dreaming of Kangxi. Only if I really were Kangxi, I'd have wrested myself much sooner from Tutor Weng's grasp. In my last act as his pupil, I wrote an edict as he'd taught me in the ink that was my privilege, all my anger and sorrow mingling in the bright colour before me.

I wrote his dismissal, gave standard pretexts of the kind the emperors always used when they just wanted to get rid of someone but lacked valid grounds for doing so or didn't want to state their real reasons. I said he was insolent before me, arrogant in manner, mismanaged state affairs, and there was no reason why I, the emperor, should tolerate these things anymore.

Everyone would know this was just a cover for whatever real conflicts would become the subject of their gossip and guesses, but they'd swallow it quietly on the outside at least. As for Tutor Weng himself, he would no longer come with the dawn to kneel before me every morning. Old and tired man, he'd laboured long and I sent him back now to his hometown in the south. It was my vermilion mercy, light punishment for what on paper were serious faults.

I sent the eunuch to call the grand councillors back, all except for Tutor Weng. I sensed them surprised by my edict but they tried to keep it from showing. The trip to Tianjin would go ahead. I issued instructions for the arrangements, including the train journey. There were no objections this time, they stayed silent and acknowledged my orders.

The sky was grim, but that was inside me. Tutor Weng was beyond my sight. He'd not celebrate his birthday today. "Good fortune" and "long life", it was a different ink I'd used then, a grateful boy with pure intent, creating a small gift I'd put my crumb of heart into.

Tutor Weng would kneel when the eunuch came to read out to him my edict announcing his dismissal. He'd bow his head to the ground and thank the emperor for his kindness, following the rituals till the last, and then he'd leave the long years behind and vanish in the rain.

29

Zhen and I sat together at the Summer Palace, the evening heat clinging to us still, and she cursed the stupid repetitious life we lived. Cixi was giving her something of a second chance these days. I didn't see a lot of her even so, too busy with my reform efforts, but moments like this one now were still precious.

I read memorials and only half-listened to her words. She hadn't given up her "demon art". She was still full of her fascination with photography. It was the speed she liked. Cixi had had drawing tutors teach her to paint but she hadn't the patience to tug scenes slowly from the inks and brushes, wanted something more immediate and complete.

"My eunuchs say that outside, they're talking a lot about Kang Youwei." she tried to nudge my attention her way.

Kang Youwei was the controversial Cantonese scholar and ardent reform supporter who Tutor Weng had called a wily, untrustworthy sort.

"Oh? What are your eunuchs doing running around outside?" I gave her a stern look. "You know that's against the rules."

She half-pouted, half-smiled, took a little cake from the plate on the table and examined it a moment. "Everything's against the rules," she sighed, putting the cake back down untouched.

I nodded. I knew she was back to her old ways, sending her eunuchs out on whatever little errands. It was all to do with this photography passion of hers, some kind of commerce they had going. I didn't know much about it and didn't ask. I hadn't time for worrying or warning now. A private moment together like this was rare enough. She kept her bright eyes on me, didn't want me to go back to the memorial I was reading.

"So, what are they saying about Kang outside?" I asked a little reluctantly, not sure I wanted to hear her answer.

"Well, they say he comes to the palace at night for secret meetings with you."

"Really?" I smiled slightly. "And what else do they say?"

"Just that he has your nightly ear, spends hours at your side, feeding you subversive ideas," Zhen said with a look that suggested she wished it was she in Kang's place.

I laughed, dismissively. They were just foolish rumours. I'd given Kang Youwei one single audience, at the Summer Palace, after I dismissed Tutor Weng. I could still picture him, frank, sincere, full of urging words. He was just a minor official, already forty, and had passed the imperial examinations in the twenty-first year of my reign, in the midst of our defeat in the war.

Hopeful candidates had come from all around the country to take the exams in Beijing back then, and they had been among the most vociferous protestors against the peace deal, adding their patriotic appeals to the already-burning air. Kang would have been among them, clamouring away too.

It wasn't unusual to be getting on for forty and still doing the exam rounds. Some people spent their entire lives at it and looked more like venerable old scholars than students by the time they finally earned their degrees, if they ever earned them. Others just gave up along the way.

"Kang doesn't really come to see you secretly in the night, does he?" Zhen wore a mischievous smile on her face that suggested she was rather taken by the idea.

"You know he doesn't. How could he?"

Ronglu, an old favourite of Cixi's, now governor of Zhili, the province surrounding Beijing, had called Kang arrogant. Ronglu was a Manchu and a military man and his judgement didn't surprise me. At the audience, Kang had spoken in a respectful but forthright manner, and if that was arrogance, I preferred it to the endless euphemisms and empty talk that I normally heard.

"Do you wish he could come to your side like the rumours say?" Zhen asked.

I gave a slight nod. "I wish not just Kang were free to come to my side at will," I said, smiling at her.

It was one of the scholars at the Hanlin Academy who'd recommended Kang to me. The scholar was lavish in his praise and urged me to take Kang on at court as a reform adviser, suggesting that everything would be easy with a talent like Kang assisting me.

Everyone was always dreaming of the past. This scholar drifted in visions from 800 years earlier, when young Emperor Shenzong of the Song dynasty gave his backing to an ambitious reform programme led by the scholar-official Wang Anshi. Wang Anshi rose high, all the way to chancellor, the highest an official could go in those days. Kang and the scholar who'd recommended him would know that story through and through, of course, and I imagined they would love to repeat it now, but I didn't want to.

I had good reason for that. Emperor Shenzong didn't live very long and spent his time battling the empress dowager's opposition. After he died, the empress dowager promptly got rid of both Wang Anshi and his reforms. It was one of those stories with an inspiring start but a daunting end and I had no desire to see my efforts go the same way.

In any case, just as I couldn't simply dismiss all the old officials overnight, I also couldn't simply throw the palace gates wide open to Kang and keep him at my side. Unlike the empress dowager of Shenzong's time, mine was still on my side, still supporting my plans, but maybe that was precisely because I didn't have a Wang Anshi to flame tongues and passions high.

"Does she know about the rumours?" Zhen asked, referring to Cixi, of course.

"If your eunuchs are spreading this gossip, I expect hers are even better informed," I replied, feeling my lips twist in a momentary grimace.

Zhen too had sudden shadow in her expression.

"Do you think Kang could end up like my cousin?" she asked softly.

I looked away. She hadn't forgotten how her cousin Zhirui was exiled during the war against Japan.

I shook my head. "Things are different now." I tried to reassure her, and myself at the same time. "Reform is the official policy now. Everyone knows that. There'll always be rumours, always someone to stir trouble somewhere, and I know some people don't like Kang, but he hasn't done anything wrong."

"What did my cousin ever do wrong?" Zhen murmured.

I saw her out of the corner of my eye, trying to get me to look up and meet her searching gaze. I kept my head down. I hadn't been able to protect Zhirui. I hadn't been able to protect Zhen either.

"I think things really are changing now." I put optimism in my tone. "Look at all that fuss about Zhang Yinhuan. She didn't win this time. I didn't let her have him."

"She has a long memory." Zhen smiled a little. "She doesn't like losing."

Cixi, the unnamed "she", hovered behind our gazes and thoughts constantly. Zhen hadn't changed her mildly scheming ways, even after being flogged and demoted, but the grand councillors were even worse, still up to the same old tricks. They had accused Zhang of taking bribes from the Russians in a bid to get Cixi to dismiss him, but I had managed to reverse that decision. It was a tiny victory, but it boosted my confidence even so.

I took Zhen's plumpish hand and gave it a squeeze.

"Who's winning and who's losing?" I said, more to myself than to her. "That's the whole thing, if we're in competition, we all lose. But I think she's starting to understand that now."

Zhen didn't answer, just looked at me with eyes that wanted to believe but didn't appear very convinced.

The sun turned fierce next day and scorched the hills brown and bare. The heat was still oppressive. It cloaked the Forbidden City in a suffocating blanket, though I'd have stayed there in that furnace if it weren't for my duties towards Cixi.

She was in a good mood and wore a laughing face as she pointed at the eunuchs running around, waving their arms and shouting to each other on the shore. One of the boats had run aground and the eunuchs were scurrying about trying to get it free.

"Huh, they've done it again!" Cixi flashed me a smile. "It doesn't matter how many times we sail this way, they always run aground. I'm sure they do it on purpose, you know."

I nodded. Of course they did it on purpose. They knew how much it amused her to watch their frantic performance. Chief Eunuch Li Lianying had them all trained, he was clever that way, noticing and remembering all the small things that gave Cixi pleasure.

The water shimmered, too bright in the sun. It hurt my eyes and made my head ache. I started feeling dizzy.

"Emperor, you've gone pale. Are you ill?" Cixi noticed and peered at me in concern.

I shook my head, "It's just the heat."

"Hmm," she stared at me a moment. "I fear you're pushing yourself too hard. Perhaps you should slow down a little?"

I couldn't help a grimace. We'd waited too long to be able to slow down now, left ourselves no choice but to hurry. What Cixi was trying to say made sense of course, from the point of view of personal health, but the moment I slowed down, everyone else would slow down too and nothing would ever get done.

I stared at the boats, whole flotilla around us on the lake. There was Yehenara ahead, Jin and Zhen with her.

"Emperor, you need to think about your health. You look tired, you should rest more." Cixi drew me back to the sparkling water and heat-swelled sky.

She spoke with a caring note. I nodded and promised I would follow her advice. Those were lying words to soothe her. I wouldn't rest now that the momentum had gathered. Only small weeks had passed since I'd issued the edict on reform, but I had accomplished more in this brief time than in the whole twenty-four years since they made me emperor.

I reformed the centuries-old imperial exam system. It was all very well and good to write rigid classical essays and demonstrate one's ability as a poet and calligrapher, but these were not suitable selection criteria for today's needs. Our people would learn for the modern world, our children would study at the new schools I ordered opened in the provinces, and those of talent would enter the new university in Beijing or be sent abroad to study.

I wanted practical learning, ordered the provinces to establish study programmes in agriculture and industry and turn little-used temples and shrines into schools. I established a board to develop mining and railways, and approved a translation bureau to translate foreign works into Chinese. I lowered taxes, decreed cuts to the bloated military and provincial administration, and placed orders for new warships and arms for our country's defence.

Sowing the seeds, as I was doing with my edicts, was only the start. My ploughing yet to come would not be the ceremonial furrow of easy toil, but a difficult haul through stony ground. Even so, I much preferred this exhaustion born of labour to the frustrated weariness of empty days, and when I pictured the harvest ahead, it was with real exhilaration. We only had to hope the weather held good. Rumours like the ones Zhen shared with me were smudges in the sky, but hopefully would not become storm clouds or the dark stains of locusts on the way to devour our crops before they'd had a chance to bear fruit.

Eunuchs clustered on the shore and chair bearers waited to carry us up the steep slope. I disliked these outings with all their crowds and ceremony that swallowed the hours, all to light incense in some temple, sit a time with the view spread wide, and eat our meal in a different setting. I did not always accompany Cixi on her walks and little boat trips, but now and then I was expected to add my presence to her procession.

The big yellow umbrellas did little to keep the beating sun away. The chair bearers climbed the hill with step so smooth I could close my eyes and feel no more than a level motion as they bore me onwards. They sweated in the heat, silent and concentrated. They'd practised this seemingly simple task to perfection, and it was the same with everything within our walls, polished skill, strict and unswerving procedure, minute and precise organisation that seldom failed. If only it were so easy to achieve that same coordination and precision beyond the palace gates too.

The view today was not so grand, dissolved in the heat haze, the colours dried and faded by the sun. A sprinkle of temples, pagodas, pavilions scattered across the hills caught the eye here and there and the lake glittered below, green where the lotuses overran its calm surface. It was slightly cooler on the hill and the faintest hint of breeze stirred the air.

Cixi and I were quiet at our meal, separate, dissolved in the haze too, each in our own thoughts. We'd already spoken about the substance earlier when I came to present my respects and we discussed the latest appointments and decisions.

"Ah, so you're sending that Kang Youwei to Shanghai?" she raised her eyebrows at me then.

Of course she knew the rumours too, and I knew she was wary of Kang. He had a strange knack of making people either love him or hate him. Personally, I rather liked him and thought we needed people like him. He didn't sneak into the Forbidden

City for secret meetings under cover of darkness, but I kept the door open from a distance at least and made sure his memorials got to my hands.

When I was a boy, trying to puzzle my way through the rivalries and intrigues I glimpsed, Cixi had talked of compromise and balance, said I'd need to learn those lessons, and said they weren't always easy.

She was right. Kang's detractors did their best to tarnish his name, and his supporters continued urging me to make him my modern-day Wang Anshi. Weighing them in the balance, Cixi and Kang, I needed Cixi more, of course, if we were to get the reforms off paper and into practice. That much I had learned, no matter what my instinctive liking for Kang and his ideas.

We had a project to start a new government newspaper based in Shanghai, and when some of the more cautious reformers recommended that Kang would be a good person to head it, I decided to take their advice. He and his controversial reputation were becoming something of a liability in Beijing. I didn't want a Wang Anshi who would goad Cixi into doing like Emperor Shenzong's mother and battling the reformers and stopping their reforms.

Cixi nodded slowly that morning when I told her that yes, Kang would go to Shanghai to head the newspaper project.

"Hmm, I'd say it's for the best to get him out of Beijing. He's a troublemaker, that one".

I made no reply. Her words confirmed that my fears had been right and it probably was for the best that Kang kept a low profile for now.

The palace chair bearers learned their skill by carrying a cup of water, placing it on the chair and practising going up and down until they could bear their load without spilling a single drop of liquid. My reforms were like that cup. I felt more than ever how hard it was to keep the cup level and the load moving forward.

The shimmering haze beyond was too bright for my gaze to linger long, my head still ached and I felt weak in the blazing day. I had no secret key that would let Kang come stealthily in the night with subversive ideas and I didn't know where these rumours came from. I was no collector of rumours anyway. I saw Kang only in the neat rows of characters written by his hand, and what he wrote was a language I sought, straight-cut proposals of sense and value, comparisons and examples that helped me make my choices. His ideas chimed with my own notions of what direction we should take and gave them form and fabric that I could turn into edicts.

As always, Cixi was slower and more absorbed with the food than I was. My eyes kept straying back to the lake. Zhen had said the evening before that she wished we could take a little boat and wrap ourselves quiet in the evening's lingering light, row with the young moon upon us, simple and alone. She spoke my old fantasies, said she wished we could leave the walls for a time and go disguised through the city, or head for the mountains, not to the tombs but to places untouched and alive.

There was a lot we couldn't do. I would have rather liked to have Kang and his friends come at the quiet hours, slip through the gates to my waiting welcome. I had ordered a map of the world from Shanghai, a proper one that I could have mounted on the wall and see every country spread before my eyes. I would have liked to add new companions to my palace shadows, men who'd help to bring the world in close and discuss it with me, plotting out the future. But no matter what the rumours, or what our dreams, it wouldn't be so, and couldn't be.

Something clouded inside me, a troubled feeling through the seeming calm. Cixi finished her meal and was ready to move on. We walked a while, Cixi in the lead, always brisk in her stride, made us all hurry.

The people had a saying that the heavens were high and the emperor far away. Here, it was the world that was far away, only we were here in this summer indolence, strolling the shaded paths in proper file, watching Cixi stop to inspect flowers here and there. Her face was serene and her eyes mild, they held no more than the flowers and this swathe of nature enriched by a clever hand.

Perhaps I still had something of my old thunderstorm fears still sticking to my guts, memory of the sky in sudden grim flood and the swollen summer turned angry. I looked up through the lace of trees at the blue above, bright pieces set amongst the leaves. Cixi hurried onwards and I followed.

30

It was the time to mourn Emperor Xianfeng and Cixi returned to the Western Gardens. She recalled her grief every year as the summer began to fade and the days turned kind and golden a while before the cold crept in. I accompanied her sorrow and I too thought of Xianfeng. He seemed sadder to me now, perhaps because I was twenty-eight now, creeping slowly closer to his thirty-one, and it was such a small amount, a brief life, reaching the summit only to come tumbling down so fast again and die broken and uncertain as the summer waned.

I lit incense and did my ritual rounds. Cixi was quiet, subdued in her past pulled close again. The shadows were thin and indistinct in my Ocean Terrace pavilion on the little island where I always lived when Cixi stayed in the Western Gardens. They never came as solid and insistent here as they did in the Forbidden City. Even there, they had been distant lately. I sensed the ancestors at peace. The shadows had no cause to gather and reproach me. Some of the living accused me of overturning the ancestors' rules and abandoning their road, but I felt my forebears' silent blessing upon my actions.

The darkness thickened and my lights still burned. Tiredness reddened my eyes and my back and shoulders ached from sitting bent over documents.

"I heard it said that Emperor Yongzheng worked like this, late into the night." my chief eunuch Zhao let the comment slip as he handed me the memorial I'd asked for.

"You heard right." I unfolded the memorial. "You'd better all keep his example in mind."

Zhao let out a faint sigh. He knew the night would be long again.

"I've heard it said too that it was his hard work that brought him to an early death," he blurted out suddenly, then looked afraid at having said such an inauspicious thing, the sort of words forbidden within our walls.

I glanced up at his worried face. "That's called selfless dedication," I said. "Isn't that a virtue to wish for?"

Zhao's look suggested that sleep would be preferable, but he said nothing and nodded humbly.

The characters blurred before me. I lifted my eyes to the windows and blinked hard. Exactly what caused Emperor Yongzheng's sudden death, I wasn't sure. Popular gossip said that a young woman trained in martial arts had infiltrated the palace as a maid and chopped his head off as revenge for her family's sufferings at his hands. That was nonsense, of course. He had perhaps got too carried away with Daoist remedies, or maybe it was like Zhao said and he just overworked himself. That he worked very hard was true, and he had had the habit of staying up late into the night, sitting like me now, bent over documents, dotting them with lengthy, cramped comments in the special vermilion ink.

My eyes roamed a moment and fell on a snuff bottle set among other objects in a wooden display case nearby. It was a fine little thing with a pair of rabbits painted in delicate strokes and black edging that set them off well. I smiled to myself. That snuff bottle was made for Emperor Yongzheng. He'd had a thing about snuff. I was partial to it too, it helped to keep the mind alert.

I thought about Yongzheng a lot these days. He'd been an emperor plagued by gossip, and not just about whether or not he died with his head still on his shoulders. The rumours said that he had poisoned his father, Kangxi, with a bowl of soup, altered his will and usurped the throne. I didn't believe those legends. I thought about him so often now because he'd been a reformer. He'd probably not have used the same words I did, nearly 200 years later, but reading records from his times, I found much that was familiar to me. He'd sought honest and efficient administration, and if he'd worked so hard it was mostly because the only way he could find to achieve it was to bring it all before his own eyes and take it all into his own hands.

I was starting to understand now why he had to do so much himself and push everyone so hard. My reforms were still just so many decrees, and the officials openly ignored me. I had to keep my eye on every order, every case, repeat myself over and over, urge them on, write my anger and disappointment. The provincial governors did nothing and the officials in Beijing were no better. Some imagined me truly the Son of Heaven, dictating my will to scores of obedient subjects, when in reality I could not force them to take even the smallest steps.

I turned my gaze back to the memorial. I knew its content and had already made my response. Emperor Yongzheng was said to have been a rather harsh ruler, harsh from the scholar-officials' point of view at least, because he got fed up with their infighting and obstructive ways, and the fact that someone might be a brilliant poet or very learned in the classics was no protection from dismissal or demotion during his reign.

I was starting to wonder if I shouldn't follow his example and take a harsher approach. I'd tried so far to stick to my promise and listen to everyone, tread a delicate line, but maybe they'd all become so used to thinking me a weak young boy that I'd never get them moving if I didn't give them a proper shakeup.

Weariness fell heavy on me. The clocks were cruel and the days swift. The Grand Council kept falling behind in its work. The number of memorials rose steeply now that all could send me their words. I read very fast and slept less and less, carving out time from the night, but it was more than any one man could swallow. Emperor Yongzheng kept up thirteen years of this intensity. Not even three months had passed since my reforms began, and I was already worn out in the constant struggle with these foot-dragging officials.

I leant back and stretched my neck gone stiff, caught a hopeful flicker in Zhao's eyes. He tried to hide it, looking quickly to the floor. No luck, I hadn't lost my stubbornness either, called for tea and resumed my work.

The mourning rites ended, Cixi returned to the Summer Palace, and I had only two days to myself at the Forbidden City before having to go back out to see her. She wasn't happy with me this time when I arrived. I'd gone for Yongzheng's tactic and fired the top officials at the Board of Ceremony for their obstructionist ways. One of the dismissed officials was a well-connected Manchu and must have already come running to Cixi to complain. I knew him, and I knew too that he was a thoroughly corrupt man and no loss to us.

Cixi fretted away about how I mustn't go against my own people, mustn't lose the Manchus' support. I did my best to reassure her. I wasn't just throwing everyone into the street. It was a matter of shifting people to where they could be more effective. She wasn't entirely convinced but didn't press the matter and withdrew into a brooding silence that I knew was never a good sign.

Zhen was at the Summer Palace too and seized her evening chance. I gave her only the thinnest sliver of my company, the sight of my drooping eyelids and nodding head. I dozed off beside her and dissolved into dreams. My dreams were usually full of the same walls and palaces as my waking life, but this time I saw narrow streets, women in kimonos and men in European dress. I knew instinctively it was Tokyo. The sea was somewhere nearby, and mountains too, turning the city even more narrow and bustling. Sky made thin lines between the eaves, rosy with dawn, and from one of the windows came a song, a quiet voice that lifted and fell, elusive.

Jerked into awareness again, I saw that it was Zhen singing to herself, eyes on the gathering night. She didn't notice that I'd woken, seemed far away in her own thoughts. It was an old memory she sang, maybe not conscious of it, just humming a tune in the quiet evening, but I still remembered the contemplative child who once stood before the big incense burner in the Imperial Garden, peering into the dragons' cold and empty mouths. She sang then of stolen love but she'd been just a young girl looking for the smoke and fragrance that would bring the dragons to life and kindle flames in her heart.

I took her hand and stopped her song. She turned silent and pensive.

"Who is he, this Wang Zhao?" she pressed my hand tight between hers and caught me with a curious gaze.

Wang Zhao was a minor official at the Board of Ceremony who'd been the cause of all the latest fuss. He'd tried to send a list of proposals to me, but his now dismissed superiors had stopped him.

"Why do you ask about him?" I pushed a more serious look on to my face.

She lowered her eyes, hesitant. She knew she was supposed to be of quiet virtue and pretty things, and not wrap inquisitive ears around government affairs.

"What did he suggest that caused such a tumult?" she asked.

"Ah, just imagine, he suggested that I go to Japan and take Cixi with me," I smiled.

"Really?" her face came alive. "Will you go to Japan?"

"Of course not," I laughed. "It's an impossible idea."

"He said impossible things but you promoted him and dismissed all those officials?" she gave me a dubious look.

"Yes, because he wasn't afraid to say it, and because what's impossible now isn't necessarily always going to be impossible."

Zhen nodded eagerly at those words. "I'd rather go to Europe though," she mused, "France maybe, or England..."

I leaned back on the cushions and closed my eyes again. The map they were making me in Shanghai was the closest I'd get to those distant lands. It was enough for me to know I'd take the train to Tianjin. The date had been fixed now for that trip. From there, the ships sailed to Japan, and were I not the emperor I really would have liked to sail with them.

Of all the foreign reform histories that I had Kang write for me, his work on Japan interested me the most. It maybe wasn't by chance that I dreamt myself in Tokyo just before. Japan wasn't an abstract distant land. The things Kang wrote about were tangible, close in time and place. Emperor Meiji was my contemporary, Ito and the other reform architects weren't in the history books but in my here and now. The humiliation of our defeat in the war smarted in me still, but we'd get nowhere by simply turning our backs in wounded vengeful feeling. It made more sense to learn from those who'd inflicted this defeat, swallow our pride and do with Japan as it had done with the Western powers, learn what was needed to become a strong and modern nation.

I wanted to send our bright young people to Japan to study, and the Japanese were willing to take them. It didn't ultimately matter if knowledge came from friend or foe, it was important only to gain it and use it well. I couldn't do as that little official Wang Zhao suggested and go to Japan myself. His heads at the Board of Ceremony, when they finally did send me his memorial, added a note of their own warning me about the treacherous Japanese assassins lying in wait to kill Cixi and I should we be so heedless as to follow Wang's rash advice. I was obviously just a silly boy with no sense of judgement in their eyes and their mock concern for my safety didn't fool me.

Assassins did exist, of course. A very real would-be assassin had tried to put a bullet into Li Hongzhang, after all, and there were enough anti-Manchu types roaming around abroad, plotting their coups and revolutions. It wasn't fear of assassins that could stop me from really going to Japan. Tradition simply weighed too heavy for now. No emperor of China had ever travelled to a foreign land. It was a tempting idea for the future, but in the meantime, I wanted to at least give others the opportunity.

Zhen's hand was warm. She gave her fantasies voice. She'd dressed herself in foreign clothes for her photos and she cloaked herself now in dreams of where we'd go someday across the oceans.

"I've heard that foreign kings and emperors travel abroad," she said.

"Yes, many of them do." I nodded.

"What about their empresses?" she asked.

I smiled. I didn't know if foreign empresses ventured abroad, but Zhang Yinhuan and Li Hongzhang both said, after they came back from England, that no one closed the roads when Queen Victoria travelled her lands, and the people could watch her pass as they pleased.

Zhen tossed her hopes high, soaring festival kites. She pictured the walls gone and all the people come to watch her pass. The looks she threw me as she spoke her dreams were louder than her actual words. I knew those looks well. We didn't say their meanings out loud, just shared their implications in silence. The spark in her eyes spoke of youth and tomorrow.

We knew the day would come when Cixi would join Emperor Xianfeng once more. The funeral rites would begin. All we'd done for Cian when I was a boy, we'd repeat for her. The Forbidden City would fill with wailing and we'd all cry, Zhen too, and I, bowed before the lacquered coffin. Yehenara would cry bitterest of all, knowing that, freed from Cixi's restraining hand, I'd remove her as empress and put Zhen in her place. That sort of thing was common enough in history too.

Zhen's eyes were just the flimsiest cover for all these thoughts now. Her face shone with the knowledge that age and time were on our side. Her lips stayed mute but her gaze went racing off ahead.

31

My hand felt too weak to write. I hadn't the chair bearers' skill, lost the balance and overturned my precious cup. Its sustaining liquid ran away and left me empty and blank. I was alone with my eunuchs, told little Chun to bring me the foreign cigarettes. In privacy I smoked them sometimes.

Emperor Yongzheng had been content with snuff and had tried to ban tobacco, but he'd maybe had his Daoist pills to help him through those long nights. I had my occasional cigarette. Little Chun did my bidding. He opened the small foreign box and his face wore ill-concealed questions.

I knew he could see my pallor and the tremble that seized me. I waved him away. There was something calming in the cigarette. Thin wisp of smoke curled upwards, I followed it, lost myself in its twists and turns, broke apart with it.

The paper lay unrolled before me, empty and waiting, but it was hard to know how to begin. I got up and wandered the room a moment, tried to shake the stupor from me and clear my head. Anger and sadness clenched too tightly together for me to smooth them over so easily. I lit another cigarette and its tiny tip of fire held my gaze.

There had been no such burning point in Cixi's look when I came to her upon my latest arrival from the Forbidden City. She was quiet and a bit absent, drifted somewhere in her own thoughts, bade me sit with her, gently inviting. She had apples piled in a bowl nearby, round and polished. They were a comforting symbol of peace and calm. I stared at the apples and let her draw me out with small questions. Flower fragrance floated in the air. She looked tired and I caught a faint melancholy in her expression. She'd been that way these last weeks but kept her feelings silent.

Her storms were different to my mother's long-ago thunder bursts. They were worse, in a way. It was enough for her to turn on me that cold belittling stare to make me a frightened boy again. That same look crept across her features when I came to her this time.

The apples and flower fragrance couldn't hide my stains and cover the suspicious whiff she caught about me now. It leaked from the memorials I passed on for her perusal, foreign notions of constitution, parliament and other seditious talk. Personally, I saw it no crime to speak these thoughts. Emperor Meiji in Japan had a constitution and a parliament and neither he nor Japan seemed to have suffered. On the contrary, they were doing very well.

I didn't ask for so much. Even Kang thought it too soon for a parliament, but we did want to establish a new council of policy advisers for a broader debate on all these sorts of ideas. I was trying to pursue the balance that Cixi had taught me, wanted to fill my new council with reformers and make it a counterweight to the old men on the Grand Council who weren't very keen on even discussing reform, let alone implementing it.

"Foolishness!" she interrupted my attempts to reassure her, the hard edge abrupt in her voice. "You stupid boy, you're letting them lead you into this nonsense, that Kang Youwei and his friends. You'll lose the people's trust. Who are you giving your ear to? You'll lose the people and you won't even be able to hold on to your own throne. Is that what you want? You want to lose everything?"

Her words rang in my memory now. I felt my face twist bitter, sat down before the blank paper once more. She thought me just as stupid as those narrow-minded fools I'd fired at the Board of Ceremony. Yes, we now had people suggesting I visit Japan, or move the capital, or convene a parliament, but no, I wasn't about to follow their advice, though, objectively, none of those ideas in themselves were so outrageous. Numerous dynasties had moved their capitals, including our own. I had no such plans, but it wasn't as outlandish as Cixi painted it, and nor were parliaments and foreign travel, even for sovereigns. I wasn't stupid though, knew there were limits to how far I could go.

Cixi thought I'd already gone too far.

"You did not see fit to consult with me," she said, the ice in her eyes contrasting with the weary disappointment in her tone.

It was that disappointed tone that lingered with me now as I stared at the empty paper spread before me. I'd made a few new appointments and i hurt her that I had dared to act on my own judgement. Oh, gone were those days during the war, when she caught such frequent colds and told to me to decide everything myself. Give up Taiwan and agree to humiliating peace terms, that I could do on my own, but dismiss a handful of recalcitrant officials and make a few new administrative appointments, for that, I still had to come running to her first, every time, every single time. Like my foreign cigarette, my anger too smouldered and fell away. Sadness clasped me. My apples were the small sour ones of days not warm and ripe yet. Only conflict I gathered, whole armfuls of misunderstanding. I could see Cixi's trust waning and feared the result. It had never been my plan to cast her aside or shut her out. It wasn't my desire to lie to her or hide things from her gaze, and I did so only when forced to.

She left me no choice. I wanted us to be like the apples in her bowl, everything peaceful and calm. I wanted her to trust and support me but she turned hard and deaf. She heard not me but those of shriller tongue, who came with rumours and poison, petty grievances and selfish laments. How could I consult with her when she gave my arguments dark, deceitful shades before I'd even had a chance to state them? How could we discuss when she thought me a foolish boy running too fast and going too far? And not because the country told her so, but because toadies and flatterers anxious not to lose their own little privileges sowed these seeds of doubt and fear in her heart.

I'd tried to share as much with her as I could, though I did have to deceive her to some extent about Kang. He hadn't departed for Shanghai as ordered. I knew he was still in Beijing. But how could I speak of Kang to Cixi? She saw him in the blackest colours, and I couldn't scrub him a cleaner shade with my halting words when others had swift tongues so well sharpened and so much more adept at grabbing her ears.

It was all not enough. If I really were a palace chair bearer, I'd have stumbled on the stairs and sent Cixi tumbling to the ground. I couldn't let this happen. I had to keep her with me. She said I would lose my throne, but if I didn't continue the reforms, I would lose my country too. It had never been properly mine anyway, this throne, and it meant less to me than these lands and peoples who'd been entrusted to my hands.I was like a sneaky boy at the meeting with the Grand Council next morning. I'd appointed four young secretaries to help deal with the enormous volume of memorials now coming in – a decision that had sent Cixi into a fit. I summoned one of these young men now and slipped my piece of paper into his hand. It summed up my thoughts of the night grown hazy with the cigarettes from the little foreign box. It was a call for help, really. I was sending a secret plea to the reformers to think up some way of keeping Cixi's trust, keeping her with us.

It was said that medicine had to be bitter to be effective, but for Cixi we needed to sweeten the taste and come up with ways to continue the reforms and replace the old officials that would be gentler on her, more palatable. If they failed, then only conflict remained, and this was a war I feared.I woke from disjointed scraps of sleep. The Forbidden City's narrow closeness pressed in harder after the Summer Palace, but I didn't suffer from its oppressive weight as Cixi did. My tight cramped places were inside me, not in these old walls and time-dimmed passages. I breathed freer within these solemn confines since

Cixi abandoned them for my father's costly endeavour. For all my thrifty instincts, I had to be grateful that he'd catered to her whims so readily in some far-sighted intent that left me moments sweetened by her absence.

It was no doubt this absence that gave the morning its happier tint and made me hopeful. I relaxed a little and felt the tension subside. Even the grand councillors weren't so irritating, though that was perhaps because Zhang Yinhuan joined them this morning. What interested me was not Zhang himself, but the business he came with, our arrangements for my audience with former Japanese Prime Minister Ito Hirobumi next day.

This Ito was a name on everyone's lips. He was notorious as the man who'd sat opposite Li Hongzhang at the peace negotiations, wrenched Taiwan from our hands and burdened us with crippling indemnities. But it was also he who'd given his country a constitution and was the architect behind the reforms that had made it possible for Japan to defeat us in the first place.

I had been informed of his plan to make a private visit to China. He'd arrived in Tianjin and was met by Ronglu, who'd arranged a suitable welcome. Ito didn't ask me for an audience. The decision to meet with him was my own. He wasn't a prince like that German Heinrich, or even an ambassador, but I saw in him my most significant visitor yet, for all his formal lack of status. I'd heard and read so much about him and now that he was in Beijing, I wanted simply to see him for myself and hear his thoughts on reform.

I dismissed the grand councillors for the day and was about to end the morning's business when the eunuch messenger came in and announced Prince Qing's arrival. This was odd, since I hadn't summoned Prince Qing. He was with the Foreign Affairs Office too, but I'd just taken care of the arrangements for Ito with Zhang and there was no other foreign affairs business so urgent as to bring Prince Qing to the Forbidden City in such haste.

"The Empress Dowager wishes to inform you that she will return to the Western Gardens on this day at the ninth hour," Prince Qing announced.

I stared at his narrow, bearded face. He had Cixi's confidence and surely knew the reason for her abrupt decision, but he kept his eyes blank and lowered, letting me glimpse nothing of her intent.

We had to start moving then from the Forbidden City to the Western Gardens. It was all close by, nothing difficult to arrange, but unplanned like this, it was strange. I caught an anxious flicker on my chief eunuch Zhao's face. The unsettled mood thickened. I sipped tea and tried to collect my thoughts. In all these years, I had never known Cixi to return out of the blue like this. There was just one time I could recall when she'd come at short notice, and that was when Prince Gong was dying, but even then she'd given a day's warning.

Protocol left no room for spontaneity. Cixi usually gave longer notice than me as to her movements, because with her there was always more to move. More than six hundred people, more than five hundred horses, that was her usual procession, and all the actors and musicians followed her too from place to place. You couldn't just gather all that up and leave on a whim.

Only the day before, I'd been with her at the Summer Palace, had held audiences and settled business, and had spent a while watching the theatre with her. I'd left her to continue her entertainment and returned to the Forbidden City. Her eyes had been clear of unexpected plans. I felt certain this hurried return hadn't been in her mind at that moment and I couldn't see what might have changed in a single night for her to break habit and convention this way.

The hours trickled away and I had to get ready to go out to kneel at the gate in welcome as custom required. I sensed Zhao trying to keep his expression empty, though his tenseness was visible.

"Did you hear anything yesterday? Do you have any idea what's going on?" I asked him.

It was Cixi who'd chosen him for me, and she too who'd recently raised him in rank. She liked to keep her eyes and ears among my eunuchs. I wondered if Zhao might not have caught some snatch of rumour or hint of trouble floating in all the gossip the eunuchs gathered.

"Nothing, nothing at all." he shook his head earnestly. "I don't know anything about it."

"Why the worry on your face then?"

He stood silent, awkward, feigned not to hear my question.

"Well?"

"Master of Ten Thousand Years…It is just so very sudden…I fear it does not bode well." His words came out a mumble and he hung his head.

There was nothing for it but to go and take our places. We arrayed ourselves in colour and ceremony, the musicians with their instruments. My whole suite and I got into position and they all watched me, ready to kneel at my signal.

We knelt for her every departure and again for her every return, performing the whole ritual in smooth routine, not really conscious or present because we'd done it so many times. But we'd never done it like now, never with such ill-suppressed nervousness and eyes filled with guesses and doubts. The early autumn sky slid gentle towards evening, but it felt more like the grim chill of winter upon us. She didn't see it though. We gave her the usual calm and respectful faces and she bade us rise in her usual voice.

She kept that ritual dress of a serene look pulled about her as we proceeded in her wake and let it slip only later when I came before her in her palace.

"Tell me, why exactly do you wish to see Ito?" she gave me a searching stare.

Ito? I felt the stare in my eyes too. She'd come rushing back because of Ito? But she already knew I planned to see him. I was at the Summer Palace when I made that decision. And she hadn't made any mention of Ito the day before either.

"Well, he is a man who did much to reform and strengthen his country," I said calmly, as if not noticing the ice in her gaze. "He can share his experience and I would like to hear it."

"He already shared it with the Foreign Affairs Office. Is that not enough?"

"I would like to hear it myself."

She looked unconvinced at my response, sat silent a good while, her eyes picking their way over the surrounding objects, darting an occasional glance at me.

"There is talk going round that you want to engage Ito in some kind of official capacity and give him powers of decision." She spoke again, eyes still now.

"If there is such talk, it is just ill-founded rumour. I have no such plans," I said, forcing my voice to stay firm.

"But this is not what I have heard." Her tone had a worried edge.

She tried to pierce me with her gaze, searching me for certainty, for something she could trust. It was true that some of the reformers suggested I planned to offer Ito some high position or take him on as an adviser. They may as well have proposed I give Ito not just Taiwan but the whole of China. What official post could I possibly give someone like Ito, the former prime minister of a country that had defeated us in war?

But past wounds aside, I did want to see him, and I did seek closer ties with Japan. I was far from the only one. Plenty of our officials shared this desire. I wanted to do my bit too. Foreign affairs had changed. The tangle of protocol and tradition that kept us at a lofty distance put us at a disadvantage now, trapping us between our ignorance of others and their misconceptions and prejudices towards us. I thought my touch of personal goodwill might benefit us more than the isolation we'd pursued in the past.

"Some memorials have called on you to hire Ito." Cixi cut into my silence.

"Yes, but that does not mean I intend to do so,"j I objected.

"Who knows what you intend to do?" she sighed. "How can I guess your intentions when I hear out of the blue that you've fired everyone at the Board of Ceremony? How can I know your plans when you suddenly appoint new officials with who knows what kind of powers, and without consulting anyone? How can I be sure who you'd contemplate hiring when you take on people like Kang Youwei?"

I said nothing, not knowing what words would be of any use, looked down and sensed I had the same reluctant, awkward manner as my eunuch Zhao had had before me earlier.

"Emperor, this is the man who dictated our humiliation!" She raised her tone, exasperated by my silence. "Think of Taiwan, think of Lushun, think of all we suffered and all we lost!"

"I think of it constantly." I raised my head, quiet and serious.

"Do you?" she looked doubtful. "Do you know what you're doing? For goodness sake, are your eyes open? There are British warships just off Tianjin! Haven't you seen Ronglu's telegrams? These meddling foreigners are all over the place now. They say they're just missionaries, but in reality, they're busy stirring up revolution, like that criminal Sun Yatsen, all in the same gang. Don't you see it? And now Ito turns up and you rush to offer him an audience, and before we know it, we'll all be in the hands of Ito and the English!"

I just stared at her, taken aback by this sudden, confused torrent. Somewhere in that tossed and murky rush, I seized the jostling current of her thought. She saw plots and conspiracies of which my audience with Ito was a part, and she had come back to prevent it, or at least try to get a clearer idea of whether or not her fears were founded.

I could see that, angry as she was, a part of her still hoped I might convince and reassure her. I felt it in the almost pleading stare that belied the hard lines her face had taken. She wanted me to set the lights ablaze with steady shine, but I held only my flickering candle with its hesitant glow.

It was like my eunuch, Zhao, had said, it was all so very sudden. I was sure this plot she tried to lay before me now hadn't reached her ears yet when I left her the previous day. She loved the theatre and she too could act, but not to that extent. She wasn't happy with me, of course, for stepping on too many self-important and loudly complaining toes, but that had been the usual fare of these last weeks. She certainly hadn't suspected I was about to put Ito in charge of the country.

Something had happened then after I left her watching the theatre performance. Something or someone had got her alarmed in just that single evening. But I didn't know what and she was silent, named no names, gave no details, and that made it even harder for me to dispel the rumours. I did my best to stay calm and assured, show her I had nothing to hide and nothing to fear. Doubt still clung to her corners, but her expression softened a little, sank with the day, its jagged surface wore down into weary sadness.

Ocean Terrace, my little island, waited for me in the tree-rustling twilight. I'd always liked its gentle solitude. The last colours played on the water as I crossed the bridge. Shadows swelled between the buildings, just night stretching down its first fingers, but there was something alive and unpleasant in it. I tried to read but concentration fled. I sent for the foreign cigarettes again, but the smoke had too thick and acrid a taste now and made me feel ill.

Finally, I set a music box melody flowing, sat with the trifling object before me and made it play its tinkling tune over and over. I still liked these little things. Its foreign lullaby caressed my rumpled senses, soft in sleep-inviting touch. The eunuchs were very quiet and went about their tasks in silent careful movement. The song was something that distant mothers sang to lull their babies into dreams. I saw only the eunuchs' faces growing sleepy around me.

32

The sky grew light and forms turned solid in the dimness. I had preferred them as wavering outlines. Dawn made them just the grand councillors again gathered before me in the Hall of Diligent Government. My eyes roamed, settling on old Gangyi. I wondered what sort of doubts and suspicions this old fellow had been feeding Cixi. Gangyi matched the hall's lofty name, a diligent man who prized order, discipline and tradition.

The business was routine, military matters and preparations for the rites I was due to perform. The abstinence period had begun and the small abstinence tablet I wore in ritual reminder was fitting dress. There was no substance to flavour the morning. I gave them no new laws, proposals or reforms today, just plodded through the morning's work item by item. Gangyi would like it this way, nothing to stir his fears, conservative old Manchu. He thought me young and foolish but knew I'd behave now with Cixi's gaze close by. He'd think it a great kindness that she'd finally reached out a restraining hand.

Yuan Shikai came for instructions before heading back to Tianjin. He'd also been at the Summer Palace the day before, come to present his thanks for the promotion I'd just given him. He worked under Ronglu's command. Ronglu was a good commander and not a stupid man, but I knew that, ultimately, he'd always be loyal to Cixi rather than to me. I wanted someone of my own in the military, someone who'd owe their career to me and whose loyalty I could count on.

Nearly everyone spoke Yuan's praises, including Kang and his reformer friends. Everyone was saying good things about his work with the modernised army in Tianjin, and I'd soon see the results for myself at the upcoming military exercises. I knew

Yuan had started out as one of Li Hongzhang's little protégés and that made me a bit wary of him. Tutor Weng too had said at one point that he didn't think Yuan could be trusted, but Tutor Weng had said the same thing of Kang also, only he'd trusted Kang at first and then changed his mind, while he'd started off with doubts about Yuan but later spoke his praises.

We were all still in the dark about what was actually going on at Tianjin. Ronglu reported sighting English warships in the waters nearby, but no one knew what they were doing there and there was nothing I could say to Yuan except to return to his troops, continue his good work and prepare for the exercises later in the month.

The sky was open and clear now, but I was dampened inside as I thought of the short distance to Cixi's palace. She waited there for me to come present my respects for the day. Suddenly, even the dull routine had gladder taste. I gave my instructions for the next day's schedule, which included one happier item – Cixi's departure back to the Summer Palace. I would be more than glad to kneel this time to see her off.

I was rejoicing too soon. She met me with the same preoccupied look she'd had the evening before and said she'd decided to stay on in the Western Gardens until the day I was due to leave myself for the Summer Palace.

"We'll go back together," she said lightly, but her eyes were solemn.

I had to pretend at least a crumb of welcome, expected to be always pleased to have my imperial mother's presence at my side.

"Can you tell me why Kang Youwei is still in Beijing?"

She put the question abruptly and took me by surprise.

"He isn't in Beijing," I gave a hasty reply.

I did not know that for certain. He would certainly know of the official order I'd issued, instructing him to leave immediately for his new duties in Shanghai. At the dawn audience the previous day, I had also summoned Lin Xu, one of the four young men I'd recently appointed to work as special secretaries at the Grand Council, helping to deal with all of the reform proposals and memorials that were flooding in since I'd opened the right to petition the emperor to all.

I knew that Lin Xu and Kang were on good terms and had him come to the audience the day before with the sole purpose of slipping him a secret message to take to Kang, telling him to hurry on his way for Shanghai and giving him hope that a day would soon come when I'd be able to offer him more.

I assumed that Kang had seen my message and had departed the city. If there were rumours that Kang came and went at will from the Forbidden City, it wasn't surprising there should be rumours too that he was still in Beijing. I had no way of finding out. The four new secretaries would probably have surer information, but they worked shifts at the Grand Council offices with the other clerks and I never saw them aside from two occasions when I'd used them to pass on my messages.

"He is a dangerous man," Cixi declared. She made it firm and fixed.

I was silent and she watched me with something undecided in her expression. I waited for her to continue but she just sighed and looked down at her clasped hands.

"You have this audience with Ito now?" she glanced at me again.

I nodded.

More silence, her thoughts were thick around her but she gave me no more than a hint of what they contained.

"You had better leave then and get ready." She waved me away.

The eunuchs helped me into my ceremonial clothes, draped me gold-and-dragon-embroidered before I set off for the Hall of Diligent Government once more. It all felt like a bit of a farce now and I hadn't any of the anticipation I'd felt the previous morning, discussing the arrangements with Zhang Yinhuan.

Japan was the land of dawn, of the rising sun, and I knew that they looked on us now as a sunset land with its vitality gone. I used to fear being the sunset emperor, but over these last months of reform, it came to me that perhaps our sunset had already passed and I was in fact leading us through the fog-tinged darkness of the waning night, and if I held the course, we too would see our dawn soon break.

Our sun, when it rose, would be even stronger, even brighter. My splendid gold and dragon robes would have been fitting adornment for this vision. I had hoped to see Ito as emperor of a country that was proud, but not so proud as not to learn what others could teach. Now I came with a sense of having turned into the little clock man again, like when I was younger, a small mechanical contraption they could wind up and send in to whir away a moment in inconsequential chit-chat. These shining, impressive robes only made me feel hollow.

Ito had no golden shine. He dressed in sober costume like the Western men, turned calm and clever eyes on me, and I felt his gaze sharp through its discreetness.

"I've long since heard much about you," I said in welcoming tone. "It gives me great pleasure to have this chance to see you today."

Cixi's raised voice the evening before came back to me, Taiwan, the war, our defeat. Ito, how I'd hated that name. My hurting nights in the blameful shadows had been his doing. Greedy, deceitful, Japanese dwarf bandit. We'd had not just a sea between us but the vast gulf of war, blood and shame. He was my enemy, a devil and torment in my heart. But here I was, welcoming this man with his neat little beard and modest but dignified manner, looking at him with hope, not hatred.

We had the usual polite exchange. I was pleased to hear he'd had a safe journey and Emperor Meiji was in good health. No one could quarrel with those words, and they had not a whiff of conspiracy about them. In any case, I had Prince Qing here beside me and knew full well that he'd report my every word to Cixi once the audience was over.

I really did not feel hatred now. The memory still burned, but there was no sense in hatred. In his own land Ito was a victor and a patriot, and it was not the man who'd forced humiliation on my country I was glad to see, but the reformer whose achievements shone broad.

"It was under the guidance of your hand that your country undertook the reforms that led it to prosperity, made such a deep impression, and earned such admiration all around the world," I spoke resolutely now. "My heart too is filled with admiration."

Prince Qing shot me a sharp glance. This wasn't the way an emperor talked. Visitors were supposed to express their admiration of me, not the other way round.

"Our countries belong to the same part of the world and we are not so far apart," I went on. "We too are now undertaking reform. You have practical experience of what works best and what pitfalls to avoid. I would like to hear your thoughts on this subject, and I hope that in your meetings with my princes and ministers you will share your views and give them your advice."

Ito was a lot older than me, nearly as old as Cixi. He'd spent long years in politics, travelled to different countries, fought many battles. He was no doubt skilled at reading the small hints and signals, took them in with his perceptive eye now too and seemed to know that my invitation for meaningful conversation came with no valid stamps and seals and was better left untouched. He kept his words to himself, reminding me humbly that he'd already met with my ministers a few days before and shared his thoughts with them.

"It is my hope that from this day our countries will build an ever-closer friendship," I said not looking at Prince Qing.

Wishes of friendship and peace were always safe topics. I didn't need to look at Prince Qing to know he preferred this bland stuff and was glad I'd dropped the praise and reform talk.

Ito nodded politely at my words and agreed that we should surely develop stronger ties. I knew there was no point now trying to nudge him into real discussion, and so I just asked him about his travel plans and wished him a safe journey onward. It was all over very quickly and they led him off to the banquet prepared in his honour.

I stared about me, empty and sad. Ito's sharp gaze lingered and I regretted this meeting now. It was just more humiliation. He had defeated us in war from out of sight across the sea. Now he came to us in person, curious to see our reform efforts, but his clever eyes would notice only our division and weakness.

The rumourmongers painted his name threatening enough to get Cixi rushing back in panic from the Summer Palace, but I did not see in him my foe. The only real enemy I saw was our own blindness and resistance. My biggest foes were not this clever, cunning Japanese man in his European clothes, nor the British warships that were rattling Ronglu in Tianjin with their mysterious presence. My foes were right here in Beijing, but just who they were, and when and if they planned to strike again, I didn't know.

33

Little Chun watched me write. I didn't chase him away. I traced English words in a careful hand, copying the loops and curls of the letters as I saw them in the book before me. I was strict with my eunuchs but indulged their inquisitiveness if it might further their education. The Ming dynasty's founding emperor put a ban on giving eunuchs learning for fear they would meddle in government affairs, but that soon changed and they opened a school in the Forbidden City to teach the eunuchs to read and write. The eunuchs did meddle in government and became the Ming dynasty's curse, though I didn't think that could be blamed simply on the fact they'd got a little education.

I didn't like ignorance around me, coarseness of mind and manner, and so I educated my eunuchs myself, those among them who seemed worth the trouble, anyway. Little Chun was intrigued, a puzzled expression gathering in his eyes as he followed my hand's movement.

"Why do you write the characters across the page and not down it?" he asked finally.

"They're not characters," I said. "They are letters of an alphabet. You put them together to make words."

"But why across the page?"

"I don't know," I admitted with a slight smile, "the books don't say."

There were better things I could do with this idle hour, but my thoughts were skittish and my body restless. Cixi was probably taking her afternoon rest, it was the usual time for it, but I felt no tug of sleep. Meaning fled me when I tried to read. There was too much clutter in my mind, and so I copied the

English words instead. They absorbed me enough to shroud the troubling day a little and steady my nervous insides.

"Master of Ten Thousand Years," Chief Eunuch Zhao entered with an announcement face.

"What is it?"

"A eunuch has come with a message from the Old Buddha."

"Show him in."

I waved little Chun away and felt an anxious twitch. So Cixi was not sleeping either. "Old Buddha" – emperors getting on in years had often got called that in the past, and Cixi, after she reached her venerable sixty years, took a liking to it too, perhaps flattering herself that she was something like the name implied, sitting serenely above worldly cares and quarrels. Somewhere over these last days, her stocks of infinite serenity and compassion had run low though. Her eunuch informed me of her summons. I was to go immediately to her palace.

It was only a short distance but I tried to draw it out and cast my eyes wide across the landscape, suddenly hungry for the sparkle play on the lake's surface, the wind ripple of autumn-mottled leaves, layers and shades of sky, eaves and gates and even the guards' stony faces. Sticky details to hold me a moment longer on my way and fill the space between me and whatever Cixi had in wait.

I assumed she wanted to have another go at me about Ito. One of Kang's friends among the censors just that morning sent yet another memorial urging me to offer Ito an official post and make good use of him. Prince Qing would have related all the details of my audience with Ito too by now and Cixi would know I'd strayed beyond the usual polite talk.

I knelt and she bade me rise, though I'd have sooner stayed face down to the floor rather than look into her eyes gone cold and closed.

"These are perilous times for our country, don't you agree?"

I wasn't sure where she was heading, but I didn't like it. Her words weren't stained with storms and emotion now, as when she first came back, but seemed to be the product of quiet reflection.

"Yes, these are difficult times," I nodded my agreement.

"To plot harm at such a time, gang up with others in secret and treacherous intent, spread false and dangerous words, would these not be serious crimes?" she continued.

"Such acts would be serious crimes," I said, still trying to guess what she was getting at.

"What would you do with the perpetrators of such crimes?" she narrowed her eyes.

"I would have them punished in accordance with the law."

"Good." She held her hands tightly together on her lap and pressed her lips thin. "Then you will give the order for Kang Youwei's arrest".

I stared at her, surprised. "But he has committed no crime," I objected quietly.

"Has he not colluded with the censors, submitting memorials under their names?"

"That hardly constitutes a plot or..."

"Well? Is this not the case?" she cut me off, blunt and already decided.

I nodded.

"But you persist in defending him?"

Again, I nodded. Her eyes locked on to mine and I saw a flicker of hesitation there. She hadn't expected me to defy her. It was only a moment that she wavered, and then her storms returned and broke in a great jumble of accusations she tipped before me. None of what she said made sense. If all she said was true, Kang was a truly devilish monster, whose tentacles reached from officials banished years ago to the anti-Manchu revolutionary, Sun Yatsen, who'd long since fled abroad, Ito, and the British. They all colluded now to bring down our dynasty and had me snared in their treacherous hands.

"So, will you issue the order?" she ended her torrent and put the question once more.

Slowly, I shook my head. "There is no reason for it," I murmured.

"You refuse?" her voice rose again.

"I have no reason to give this order," I repeated softly.

It wasn't for Kang that I refused. I had already compromised over him, never gave him the lofty posts his friends thought should be his, sent him to Shanghai to get him out of the way, sacrificed him, proving that I had heeded the lessons Cixi taught me.

I'd learned that I could not get too attached to men, knew I had to weigh them on the scales of circumstance and expediency, as she'd weighed Prince Gong and my father. But things had gone too far now. What Cixi demanded was not an order to arrest a single individual, but to stop my entire reform effort. She thought it was I who'd got entangled in some menacing plot, but it was she who was caught in the choking vines of rumour run wild and gossip turned to poison.

I had always given in before, but I would not this time. These reforms were my one desire and achievement. If I could not make a single move, utter a single meaningful word, take a single measure of any real effect, and have any say about the people I appointed and their fate, what reform could we speak of? What possibility of action did we have if anyone who acted risked falling victim to plotters and rumourmongers?

Cixi looked away, studying the bracelets round her wrist. The clocks turned loud and made our silence all the heavier.

"Who would have thought it would come to this?" she sighed. "I gave you my trust and my support, and look what you've done with it, put it in the hands of those who would bring us down".

"No," I shook my head. "Let me explain…"

"I've heard enough." She cut me off again. "I'm tired now."

She motioned with her jewelled, sharp-tipped fingers and maids appeared from the shadows. She wanted tea and her water pipe. The maids vanished again. They seemed hardly more than shadows themselves.

"Tomorrow morning you will go to the Hall of Central Harmony as planned." She addressed me again in a dry and weary tone. "After that, you will come here to me."

I nodded. I had my order. It sounded more like a sentence, as if she'd decided that, failing to get Kang's head, she'd have mine instead.

"Now go!" She flung me a last look and I saw it bleak with disappointment.

Dawn was only just breaking when I left in lamp-lit procession for the Hall of Central Harmony in the Forbidden City. I sensed that something strange was going on, for the guards were not at their usual posts. The Hall of Central Harmony was calm though. It was here that the emperor rested between ceremonies and prepared for various rituals. I was here now to review the prayers for the rites next morning at the Altar of Land and Grain.

I'd come countless times like this in the early hours and felt the night's lingering cool pinch my cheeks. I lingered too with the darkness now, watched it break slowly apart and saw the walls and roofs grow clear in the dawn. The Hall of Central Harmony was part of the outer court. We were higher here than elsewhere in the Forbidden City, had views and majesty before us. It was all so familiar to me of course, but now, I seemed to see it all anew. The outer court was a place where the emperor projected himself in every step and stone, every colour and column, every symbol carved into the surroundings. There were no sudden whims or flights of fancy here. It was deliberate grandeur, a statement of power in physical form.

I looked out across it all. It existed for me and I was its centre. That was a strange thought when I sensed myself such a chance and inconsequential element, and yet it was so, for I was the emperor, the symbolic North Star, the Son of Heaven, the core around which all this power, majesty and ritual turned.

Cixi couldn't undo that, could only regret the choice she'd made on that winter night so long ago after Tongzhi's untimely death. The thought of Cixi drew my gaze to the brightening lines of the white stupa perched on the little hill in the North Lake. That was over in the Western Gardens, where Cixi waited.

She looked bright and fresh with morning, but that was just a surface impression. She always took great care over her appearance. Underneath, I could see that she'd spent a sleepless night and had the same weariness in her eyes as the previous day. She made the same request as the day before too, only this time, as well as arresting Kang, I was to arrest his younger brother too.

"Will you give the order?" she asked again.

I looked down at the floor. In wanting to arrest Kang she followed some clouded logic at least, some plot pulled from dank and vicious places beyond my sight, but what Kang's younger brother had to do with it all I couldn't imagine. I had never met him, knew nothing about him, and had no idea what wrong he was supposed to have done.

"You still refuse?"

"Who is saying all these things? What proof do we have of their crimes?" I ventured.

"Ah, you stupid boy, have you been deaf and blind these last months?" she snapped, eyes flashing impatience.

"If I have, then I beg you, tell me of these crimes, give me their proof, name the accusers." I made my voice and expression as humble as possible.

"Have I not been warning you, counselling you?" she asked. "You chose to listen to Kang instead of listening to me. You have let yourself be misled over these last months."

"You have gone too fast and too far," she continued, giving me no time to speak. "You have set too many people against you and your actions have created too much instability and discontent."

I swallowed hard to keep a bitter laugh from my throat. Yes, I'd been terribly misled. I'd let myself be misled into thinking I could be true to the teaching and expectations of my years of preparation, become the virtuous ruler they'd hoped for and work for the good of my country. I was foolish to have tried to fight petty greed, corruption and ignorance, and get rid of parasites and privileges we could not afford. I was wrong to have thought first of the millions and paid small heed to the hissing tongues of the fortunate few grown fat with rank and complacency. I'd gone too fast, yes, because they had left it so long that there'd been no choice but to raise the knife swift and cut away the rot before it spread further. And yet for all my alleged foolish haste there was still no real result. The reforms were still just a pile of paper, a stack of edicts not yet gone into effect.

"Do you acknowledge your mistakes?" she asked.

"I have made mistakes, but not those you speak of," I said, my voice, never strong, hardly more than a whisper now.

Her fresh morning mask cracked into anger and surprise. "You mean to say that you would continue this way?"

"We have no choice," I said, speaking firmer this time.

"Others think differently," she said grimly. "Read this!" She took a document from the table beside her and held it out.

It was a memorial from Censor Yang Chongyi. I knew this name. He had caused me trouble in the months after the war with Japan, making accusations against reformers and calling on me to close down the "study societies" they set up. The first time he came with his charges, I actually believed them and did as he asked. None of the officials, not even Tutor Weng tried to stop me, though they all knew full well that Yang was levelling spurious accusations.

I paid him no attention after that. If a bunch of scholars could save the country with study societies, so much the better. He did though succeed in worming himself into Cixi's favour, and it was to her he'd gone to now. He must have found a way of bypassing me and getting his memorial directly into Cixi's hands.

It lay clear before me now, this tangle of plots and blame Cixi had been speaking over the last couple of days, all tied together by Yang into a strange, illogical knot. His accusations were ridiculous, but the implications were grave. Under the influence of Kang and his seditious gang, I planned to hand the government over to Ito, and in order to stave off this betrayal of the ancestors' legacy, Yang and others entreated Cixi to intervene and place my rule under her instruction once more.

Her mind was made up. I could see that. I knew too that it would be in vain to argue and explain, show her the flaws and falsehoods in Yang's charges. Like she said the day before, she'd already heard enough. My voice didn't count and my arguments had no weight. I could not speak with her but only from below her, only as the obedient son ever respectful of her wise opinion. I knew what it meant and my hand shook. The memorial slipped from my fingers.

"So, will you give the order for Kang's arrest?" Cixi spoke softly.

"No." I pushed the sound from my trembling lips.

My fate was sealed anyway. There were greater dangers, enemies of more imminent threat than whatever they imagined Kang could bring upon us. I had spent these years signing treaties I did not wish to sign, punishing those I did not wish to punish, approving waste and extravagance I had no heart for, promoting men in whom I saw scant merit and curbing the tongues of those who spoke bitter but sincere truth. I did not wish to add to it now and only further blacken my integrity.

"You realise what this means?" Cixi raised her eyebrows a little.

I nodded.

"I am not doing this of glad heart, you know," she sighed. "They give me no choice. You too have left me no choice. We must go on now, show that everything is under control and business continues as usual. We have to work together." She gestured at the table. "The ink is ready. Write the edict."

I stared blankly before me and didn't know what to write. Tutor Weng's lessons had not prepared me for this. The vermilion ink was supposed to be the mark of power, not the instrument with which I wrote my own disgrace.

"Here is a draft to help you along. Copy it out, improve it if you will." Cixi handed me a piece of paper. "Only do it quickly. There is all the day's business to attend to yet."

I did as instructed. "The nation's affairs are in a perilous state," the draft began. "There is everything to put in order. I toil day and night with my utmost effort but have the constant fear of being overwhelmed in the flood of work."

I stared at the words from my hand. These statements were not untrue, for it was a difficult time and a vast labour that awaited, though I was not afraid of hard work.

"Since the start of the Tongzhi reign…" my hand went faster as I wrote out the sixteen characters of Cixi's official title, all her marvellous qualities, and described with what great skill and benefit for the nation she'd handled the affairs of government during her two periods of regency.

"Moved by my deepest regard for the nation's welfare, I have beseeched her repeatedly to have the gracious kindness of instructing me in government, and I have received her assent. This is the guarantee of prosperity for our entire nation and people."

I gave her the finished text. She read it through and nodded slowly.

"That will do," she sighed. "Come now, the grand councillors will be waiting. We will see them together and you will announce the edict."

I followed her. The old men would be happy to have me silenced. I took my place beside her in the audience hall and declared myself unfit to rule. That, after all, was what the edict meant. It was all so simple and undramatic. I became the emperor in name only, and my reforms would surely follow me into disgrace.

Cixi sat beside me with a solemn face and sombre gaze. She wasn't lying when she said she had no gladness in her heart. I knew her well enough to sense her conflict, sadness and frustration. The old men of court, my ignorant and envious relatives, the whole privileged caste with their personal interests to defend, they all crowded behind her, pushed her on, played on her worries and stoked her fears. If anyone had all banded together in a plot, it was them.

She said they gave her no choice, but it was a choice whom to support, whom to trust and believe, and it was them she chose. She gave her initial blessing to reform but kept silent when the laments and accusations began. She played distant from it all, retired in her summer gardens, sighed to me over the officials come running to her with their complaints when it was no longer her affair, a convenient hypocrisy when every one of us knew how the system worked. It was no secret that it was she the central pillar in this precious balance she'd tried to teach me, she the ultimate authority whose word would tilt it one way or the other.

She could have chosen me. She could have spoken her support not just in the gentle touch of summer but also when the winds turned chill. Would they have dared rise against her, the same princes and ministers who'd spent all these years praising her name? Would they have turned on me if they saw her resolute beside me? It was her choice to raise me to the summit, and her choice to let me fall.

34

The tarnished sky turned the lake cold. I sat in the thinning light and watched the shadows grow, felt a shiver run through me. Chief Eunuch Zhao noticed and threw a glance at the sinking sun.

"Master of Ten Thousand Years, the wind is not good and the chill is coming," he observed.

I made no response. The bit of strength I still had trickled off between the stones and joined the lapping ripples. I was nothing but my two eyes turned large and fixed on the waning day. Fading light softened the lines of the pavilion on the opposite shore. Pink-tinged sky cast its last fragments upon the water and let its colour grow old. Something snapped behind me, the crackle of fallen leaves underfoot, I broke my stare and turned abruptly but there was no one there. I shivered again.

"Better to return lest you fall ill." Zhao advised solicitously.

I smiled faintly at his remark. My smile was a brief ripple on the surface, quick and gone. Sadness squeezed my throat in suffocating choke. I remembered when I smashed the clock face all those years ago and turned my hand bright with blood. I saw the glistening shards of glass and Tutor Weng's eyes alarmed. It stayed buried in me somewhere, this shattering urge and wish to let the blood flow free. I was my mother's son and there were storms in me, but I sat still and numb.

The pavilion across the water slowly lost its details. Qianlong had had it built for admiring the moon. Now was the time of year for that. It lit the night with such a round and glowing pearl, and I'd gone to that moon-watching pavilion too in the past, not to compose poems as Qianlong had, but to let my dreams and thoughts race me away towards that tempting orb.

No moon had risen yet. The only person who ever made it there was Chang E in the legend, after she drank the elixir of immortality her husband had hidden. Her curious sip brought her no happiness and life on the moon was lonely and sad, but year after year, she lit its pale glow in the hope that its shine would bring her a glimpse of her beloved left behind in the world below.

I didn't need to go to the moon. I had solitude and sadness enough where I was. Four days had passed now since I entered my disgrace. After placing my rule back under her instruction, Cixi gave the order for Kang's arrest herself later that same day. They searched Beijing for him but he'd managed to flee the city in time and they only got his brother. Cixi figured Kang probably hadn't got far yet. He'd no doubt try to escape by sea, and that meant leaving through Tianjin. She sent an order to Ronglu telling him to be on the lookout for Kang and arrest him if he came that way.

A brittle calmness settled after that. I played the clockwork emperor again, sat docile beside her at audiences, used my vermilion ink to write words of no consequence on matters of no substance, and led everyone in performing the prostrations before her at the ceremony marking the formal start of what was effectively her third regency. As a small reward, she even tried to comfort me, saying she wasn't changing direction so much as simply reining in my excesses.

I had to go to her as always to present my daily respects. That was clockwork too and I wondered, on one of those occasions, why the usual command to rise didn't come and she left me kneeling. Was there any need to keep me in that pose now that the edict kept me permanently on my knees before her? I stole a glance at her face, the same face that had tried to speak scraps of comfort such a short time before. Now it was livid.

"You said you had no reason to arrest Kang," she said in a slow, quiet voice after finally letting me rise.

I nodded. Her restrained tone didn't match the emotion whirling in her eyes.

"You're trying to say you did not know what he was plotting?" her voice sharpened.

"You mean getting me to put Ito in charge?" I sighed, wondering if her bringing up Kang again meant they'd finally caught him.

"That too," she said drily, "but I'm referring to his plans to seize power by force, using the military."

"That's absurd," I murmured, staring at her.

"Yuan Shikai does not strike me as a man given to speaking the absurd," she said. "Oh, I know that he has links to those reformers of yours, but he is not a fool. You say these allegations are absurd, yet this is what he told Ronglu upon his return to Tianjin. Ronglu is busy investigating the affair right this moment."

Yuan Shikai, the name came like a blow. I recalled his cautious eyes on me in the audience hall when he came to thank me for his promotion. The man around whom I'd hoped to build my own support base in the military now tried to add to my defeat? Was this how he'd interpreted my hints? I had dangled before him the future day when he'd no longer be Ronglu's subordinate, and he had twisted my hopeful words into a foul conspiracy?

"And you," Cixi hurried onwards, "What have you got to say about it all? Are you still going to maintain Kang's innocence after this?"

I didn't know what I could say. According to the edict I'd written at her command, I had been toiling day and night with my utmost effort. Where was I supposed to have found the time for plots and conspiracies? None of it made sense. Was it not enough already that Kang was bringing down the dynasty with Ito? Did they have to sour the bitter brew yet further with these strange new accusations?

The plot, as Cixi told it, was vague and muddled, but the consequences came swift and sharp. They started arresting the reformers. Three of the new secretaries I'd assigned to the Grand Council got arrested that same day. The fourth, Lin Xu, the one who'd taken my message to Kang, was taken away when he arrived unsuspecting for his shift at the Forbidden City the following morning. Kang's friends among the censors got taken in too, and so did Zhang Yinhuan. Cixi cancelled the plans to leave for the Summer Palace and postponed our departure a few more days. There was too much urgent business to take care of for now.

"Master of Ten Thousand Years, the light is leaving fast," Zhao gave me a pleading look.

I nodded slightly. The coloured streaks dissolved and thickened into approaching night. I recalled Zhang Yinhuan when he returned from Queen Victoria's jubilee in England barely a year before. I made him describe everything then, the people, the places, their customs and thoughts. He told me about his years living in America too.

Zhao was right, the light fled fast. Our darkness had none of the electric glow that made yellow streams through foreign cities. Ours was black and ignorant. Ours were the jail cells that closed now around Zhang and the others. Zhen's melancholy song came floating into my mind, the one she sang to the smokeless bronze dragons when I first saw her and marvelled that such an innocent, carefree child had strayed into our world.

She'd suggested Kang might meet the same fate as her cousin Zhirui and find himself banished. Her guess was too mild. She too had shared my dreams and now had to pay for it by sharing my disgrace. She'd never completely cleansed herself of her previous stains anyway in Cixi's eyes.

I wasn't allowed to see her. They kept her shut away in her rooms and wouldn't let her out even for the ceremonies. The only glimpses I had of her were in the words little Chun brought back to me from his stealthy meetings with her eunuchs, but these were tiny crumbs that contained nothing but fear, anger and sorrow.

My feet and hands were chilled. I felt the cold easily and it crept deeper inside me as the darkness grew. I almost wanted to fall ill as Zhao warned. My body would cover my pounding thoughts with ache and fever. I almost wanted too, to be shut away like Zhen. It would be better than rising with the dawn as always to attend to the routine and listen to the reports from the Board of Punishments on how the arrests of all my "plotters" were going. It would spare me too the torment of having to come each morning before Cixi.

She'd had more questions for me that morning. I could see immediately that she was in a particularly foul mood. Not everything was going as smoothly as she hoped. The foreign ambassadors were making a big fuss over Zhang's arrest, and memorials were coming in from the provinces in my defence.

She launched into the same old round of plots and crimes, Kang, Ito, Zhang, English missionary friends of the reformers, prodded and picked at me in what had become a tedious, endless circle of interrogation. I knew she wouldn't listen to me anyway and so I didn't even bother trying to offer some response now. My silence was abrasive to her and she lost her calm.

"This can't all just come from nowhere," she flung at me, pleading and furious all at once. "You know as well as I do that there's no smoke without fire. Now speak the truth to me."

"I already have," I sighed. "I feel unwell. I need to go and rest a little."

My head ached. Tiredness throbbed in my forehead and her questions pressed too hard.

"Unwell?" she stared at me, her expression thoughtful all of a sudden. "Yes, I've noticed this. You have been unwell. You were always calling the doctors these last weeks. Their treatment doesn't seem to have had much effect."

I nodded. "They've never been any good. Their remedies don't work."

"Hmm," she kept her stare on me. "Yes, you're right, you know. Your health needs attention. Actually, I had wanted to suggest that you put out a call to the provinces to recommend their best doctors and send them to Beijing, like I did that time I was sick, you recall? How about we do that?"

"Yes..." I gave her an uncertain glance. I had no faith in the palace doctors and welcomed the thought of finally getting more competent help, but there was something disconcerting in her abrupt change of tone.

"Shall we do it then?" she asked.

I nodded hesitantly, uneasy. I could see from her eyes that she had her mind set on it anyway.

I really did feel ill when I saw the order written in my name and realised the purpose of her suggestion. "Since the fourth month, I have been repeatedly unwell, and though the days pass, the treatment I have received has had no effect," it began.

The fourth month was the month I issued my edict to the nation on reform and started cutting away the rot.

I raised my head from the paper before me and stared at her in dismay. She was trying to get me to state loud and clear that my whole reform effort had been nothing but the product of an unwell mind.

"But I cannot accept..." I began, before my voice started to stammer and I was left with my mouth open and stunned.

"I'm afraid you've given yourself no choice," she spoke sadly. "What else can we do now? This is what your foolishness has brought us to. Look at what's going on out there. Everything is in such a febrile state, all these wild rumours flying around, all this raucous outcry, and now the foreigners are sticking their meddling fingers into it all. It's only making the whole situation more unstable. We can't let gossip rule the streets. We have to give an explanation to calm the mood."

The lakeside night swallowed Zhao too. I was alone. Only within our walls all seemed so calm. Outside was as Cixi said, febrile and awash with rumour. Cixi tried to sweeten the taste of what she was asking me to do. My relatives were all against me, pressuring her to simply force me off the throne altogether, and then there was the growing unrest, the need to silence the doubts. She spoke words of higher purpose, presenting it all as some kind of noble sacrifice on my part, destroying myself but saving the dynasty from potential turmoil.

I had known illness all my life and it had been of small concern to anyone but myself. Only now did it become the perfect pretext. They made all my work of the past summer just a symptom of my sickness, decisions made in judgement impaired by whatever ailments afflicted me. Such an emperor could not be left to rule unaided.

Zhao hadn't vanished, just kept silent. He knew my stubbornness and stood beside me in gentle resignation. If I did not send him away he had no choice but to stay and see the night swallow everything in its sameness.

The moon rose, full and pure as always at this time. The mid-autumn festival was due in a few days and Cixi planned for our return to the Summer Palace by then. This was the time when Chang E lit her sorrow and looked down on her memories. The elixir of immortal life took her to the moon but gave her no way back. Down below, we would light lanterns to send her a little cheer and make her feel less lonely.

The footsteps behind me were real this time. Glowing circles bobbed their way through the dark. It was my eunuchs, afraid we'd be lost in the night.

35

If I closed my eyes the right way, I might erase everything between the moment when I rose at dawn and now, when darkness fell once more outside my windows. There was surely some way of shaking the mind free of all that pressed and hurt it. When I was a boy, the eunuchs would shake me to clear my stomach of the food I stole and stuffed into myself in hasty fits of greed. I'd have been happy to have them take me now and shake the day from my head.

Drowsiness tugged me downwards and I did see eunuchs, not come to shake me, but to push my face into the steaming yellow bowls and make me feast on all that fresh warm flesh inside. And when I shrank from it, they laughed at the little glutton turned so fussy now, and they held me still and forced it down my throat, chunks of freshly slaughtered meat, like the boiled pigs the shamans pulled from the ritual pots.

I threw my eyes open again. My stomach hurt. The pain went across my back and down into my legs. It was uncomfortable lying down and I pulled myself more upright and hoped my eyes would not fall shut again in that unhappy way.

I reached for the foreign magazine on the small table. It was American, one of the things left from earlier months. Maybe Zhang Yinhuan had given it to me or maybe my eunuchs had got hold of it somewhere in the city. I couldn't remember now how it turned up. I didn't understand much of it, just looked at the pictures and figured out fragments of meaning here and there. I flicked through it, looking for distraction. A plump-faced man stared at me from a photo. The caption said he was a senator. I wasn't entirely sure what a senator was, but the man had something smug and slippery in his well-fed face that reminded me of Yuan Shikai.

I ripped out the page with the slippery senator and tore it down the middle, right down the smug face, and threw the pieces on the floor. I didn't need this foreign magazine now, so ripped all the pages free and let them fall around me. I sat surrounded by the scraps of paper and stared at the black beyond.

Apart from the search for Kang, the arrests only began in earnest after Yuan Shikai began speaking conspiracy to Ronglu. Were it not for Yuan, it surely would have been enough for them to have me disgraced, and Kang at least in exile, if not in jail. It sickened me now to think of my hopes and plans for Yuan, that deceitful lying dog.

Ronglu arrived from Tianjin the previous day and went to see Cixi to report on the details of Yuan's allegations. Cixi summoned me after Ronglu left her. I couldn't help a movement of surprise when I saw her. She seemed to have shrunk suddenly, grown old and small in just the space of hours. She said nothing for a long time, just fixed me with a betrayed gaze.

"I still remember it so well," she sighed and finally spoke, wistful and grieving. "You were afraid of everything. How you feared the thunder, I can still hear your cries now. I brought you to my own room and calmed your tears in the night, sang you to sleep, nursed your sickness, tried my hardest for you."

"Your son has not forgotten…"

"You dare call yourself my son!" she cut me off in a sharp jolt of emotion. "What son behaves as you have? What son would think to harm his own mother?"

I gave her a bewildered look, not knowing what she was talking about.

"Kneel!" she ordered.

I knelt, stared at the floor, heard her sniff and snatched as much of a glance at her as I could. Her eyes were moist and she dabbed a handkerchief to her cheeks.

"Is it true?" her voice was hardly more than a whisper. "You and that miserable Kang, you planned to imprison me?"

"Never…I never had such a thought," I felt my lips tremble.

"That is not what Yuan Shikai says."

"I…I do not know what Yuan Shikai says," my words came out in a whisper too.

She told me in a voice choked with tears and anger. According to the plot we'd conceived, Yuan was to kill Ronglu upon his return to Tianjin, send his troops to Beijing, surround the Summer Palace and imprison Cixi. Yuan said he got these instructions in the middle of the night from Tan Sitong, one of my newly appointed secretaries. Tan had been dispatched to him by Kang, who was acting on my orders.

It was too far-fetched to be believable. Ronglu evidently didn't really believe it, or he'd have acted more swiftly and with more decisive hand. I wasn't certain that Cixi completely believed it either, but even the possibility stung her deeply.

"I wonder what means more to you, the ways of our ancestors or the ways of Kang Youwei? Is it so easy to forget those who raised you and follow that vile little man?" Her tone was harsh but her eyes showed pain.

I stared at the floor and we were silent a good while.

"Go!" She waved me away. "It hurts too much to see you."

She had to see me again the next morning. Under her instruction, yes, but I was still the emperor, expected to attend audiences, read memorials and put my name to decisions taken.

Cixi stayed locked in her silent agitation. The English and the Japanese pressed hard for Zhang Yinhuan's release. Our own conservatives called for Zhang and the others to be dealt with as swiftly as possible, on the pretext that the meddling foreigners might compromise the course of justice. Cixi feared confrontation with the foreigners, but she feared too the potential unrest if she didn't show a strong hand.

In the end, they thought it better that we compromise the course of justice ourselves. Who needed an investigation and all the usual time-consuming procedures? They decreed the immediate execution of six of the prisoners, my four young secretaries, one of the censors and Kang's younger brother. Grand Councillor Gangyi was sent to oversee the act.

While they prepared the executions, we watched theatre. Cixi saw no chance now of returning to the Summer Palace for the mid-autumn festival, so she had all the actors come to the Western Gardens instead and rescheduled the performances.

The gongs and cymbals sounded and the actors whirled. Cixi had her favourite little nuts and fruits in bowls, nibbled away, dissolved her worries in the entertainment. She perhaps managed to dissolve me away too, though I was at her side, accompanying her like a proper son. My gaze followed the movements on the stage, but my thoughts were deep in the city at the vegetable market, where they chopped off heads. It was there, years before, that Sushun's head fell from his shoulders.

I had never actually seen an execution, though it was I, as emperor, who sealed each sentence and stood between the condemned and heaven. Autumn was not only the time for admiring the moon; it was also the time for cutting off heads. The way our world fitted together, autumn was the season that belonged with the west, sundown, the white glint of metal, gathering the harvest and reaping the crop of condemned heads too. It was every autumn that I reviewed sentences passed and gave my assent to the executioner's sword.

The condemned had always been just names on paper in the past. I didn't want to see them take solid shape in my thoughts, but I suddenly saw Lin Xu. Mere days had passed since that morning at the Summer Palace when I told him to urge Kang on his way to Shanghai. It was his youthful confidence I saw, those bright eyes with their mirthful spark that shone through the humble demeanour he had to wear in the emperor's presence. He was still so young. I had taken him from Ronglu in Tianjin. I should have left him with Ronglu. Ronglu would have been better protection.

I didn't want to see them arrive at the vegetable market, rumbling through the streets in their wheeled cages, dressed in convicts' clothes and put on show. I didn't want to know the look in their eyes, see the vulgar crowd with blood in their gazes, the sky still pure above the tawdry setting, the light that would sparkle a second on the executioner's blade. I watched theatre with Cixi as they knelt in position, necks bared and ready. Old Gangyi saw them die. The families would collect the bloodied bodies from the ground and try to sew the severed heads back on before burial, for completeness in the next world.

Alone now, Cixi and the theatre behind me, nausea rose in thick pressing rush. I couldn't hold it back and vomit spattered across the torn pages of the foreign magazine lying on the floor. Little Chun came running. The eunuchs cleared the mess. Little Chun brought the spittoon and warm water to rinse my mouth out. I saw his eyes, bright like Lin Xu's, youthful. He was just a boy. Amongst the eunuchs, I tried to choose the ones with modest quiet manner and honest look, and he had these things, it seemed.

I felt exhaustion wash over me and lay down again. There would be more theatre next day and I'd have to attend. Cixi found it painful to look at me, but she didn't trust me enough now to leave me too long out of her sight.

Zhang Yinhuan and the old Hanlin Academy scholar who'd been too ardent in recommending Kang were still in jail, still alive for now at least, their fate undecided. Kang himself got away. After missing him at Tianjin, they lay in wait for him in Shanghai, searched all vessels arriving from the north, but he was already gone. Judging from the first rumours coming through, it seemed the English had smuggled him out.

New shadows roamed in the night beyond, the darkness restless and foreboding, tapping at the windows with grasping fingers. Little Chun made to leave, knowing my preference for distance from them all.

"Stay," I murmured.

He nodded, posted his silent presence close by. I was afraid to be alone. His touch of life, colour in his skin, and the faint rustle of his clothes when he moved gave faint comfort to the night.

36

I was as if back in the classroom, only this time my assignment was set not by Tutor Weng, but by Cixi, who'd ordered me to write an edict explaining the previous day's beheadings.

Autumn sun gilded the roof tiles. Beyond the window, branches slowly shed their leaves and an arrow of birds shot by, made a dark streak, close in formation, perfect in their sudden upward turn. I'd watch the birds as a boy and Tutor Weng would snatch me back to his side. He'd had a smile for me then, knowing a child's dream to follow the birds skyward, but said that if I wished to fly, the only wings I could wear were those he offered, those made of books and learning. Only learning lifted us free and let us soar and glide with broad view and swift movement, and, persuaded, I'd put my wandering eyes back in his hands.It had been hard at moments when I was a boy to pull strands of thought from the sticky mass of unwell feeling inside me and weave them into something coherent.

I felt the same now, dull, tired, couldn't sharpen my mind into anything that would make sense. We couldn't just execute six men without offering a valid reason. We had laws.

"Kang Youwei is the leader of the subversion and now he is on the run," I wrote. I didn't know what to write next. There was Kang's younger brother. He was dead now, but I had no idea what crime he'd committed other than being Kang's brother.

So far, they'd all been charged only with ganging up together to plot subversion. Formally speaking, Kang had broken the rules with the censors, writing memorials for them, using their names, and that perhaps constituted ganging up. I decided to stick it in for lack of anything better, added the guilty censors' names and said they "did indeed gang up and plot subversion".

I was no doubt subversive too, after all, I'd been fully aware of this "ganging up" between Kang and the censors, only the conservatives couldn't just throw me in jail and behead me. The most they could do was disgrace me and repeal my subversive reforms.

That had already begun. There was no need now to hear the people's voice, and the right to petition the throne was taken from them. As for political reform, I'd been cautious enough there, but now there'd be not even a hint of discussion on the subject. Some of my education reforms were allowed to continue, but the old examination system was restored, and my plans to convert little-used temples into schools were abandoned, as was the government newspaper project.

Cixi reinstated the people whose toes I'd trodden on. Even that corrupt fellow I'd fired from the Board of Ceremony got a decent new job. He'd used all his connections and his standing as a Manchu with access to Cixi's ear to get his revenge on me. It turned out it was he who'd taken Censor Yang's poisonous accusations to Cixi at the Summer Palace, setting all these events in motion.

I stared at my two measly sentences and felt my head so heavy my vision seemed to blur. Cixi used to follow my studies very closely, asked to see practically everything I wrote, read every essay and poem I composed. The subversion had already been there. She should have glimpsed its nascent kernel in my words, but instead she praised my virtuous thinking, my concern for the people's welfare and desire for upright and just government.

She said I'd abandoned the ways of the ancestors. What would she have said to Emperor Yongzheng, who reformed pretty much the entire system of government in a bid to make it more honest and efficient? That the Grand Council even existed was only because he decided to establish it. I'd only tried to make us true to the ancestors' legacy. But this was all subversion now.

I supposed I had to say something about the four hapless secretaries, whose heads had fallen the day before. I wasn't sure how they were all supposed to have ganged up with Kang. Two of them had been recommended to me by the governor of Hunan Province and had nothing to do with Kang. Their only fault was to have been chosen to help me in my work.

"They were deceitful and arrogant at audiences, eager to promote criminals of their own kind, all of them villainous in the utmost," I wrote after a while.

I shook my head at my composition. Arrogant behaviour was the same empty charge I'd used to justify Tutor Weng's dismissal too. In the case of the secretaries, it was hard to imagine when they might have been arrogant at audiences. Two of them I met only the one time when I got them to be my messengers, and the other two never saw me at all. But they were all dead now and I had to write something.

I recalled Cixi's agitation over the memorials warning of potential unrest and the threat of foreign meddling if the investigation were left to run its course. Hastily I wrote a few lines about the urgent situation that allowed for no delays. To make sure these criminals didn't escape the net of justice, we had to execute them immediately.

I looked over what I'd written. The crimes still didn't look very convincing. I couldn't think of anything further. Like when I was a boy with my essays, Cixi took my finished work and read it through, only this time she had no approval on her face.

"What am I supposed to do with this?" she held it out before her in disbelief. "You call this an edict? It makes no sense."

I nodded in humble agreement. Of course it made no sense. Nothing made sense these days.

"Do it again," she ordered, "and do it properly this time."

"I can't," I mumbled. "My thoughts won't come."

She stared at me a moment, exasperation in her eyes. "Oh, all right then," she sighed. "Leave it. We don't have time to wait for your thoughts to come."

They turned it into a much lengthier document in the end, scattering my handful of words among the accusations they spun. They found better crimes than me too. Most damning of all, of course, was the charge that Kang and his gang plotted to surround the Summer Palace and imprison Cixi. A crime like that left no doubt as to the need to behead these villains as swiftly as possible.

It became another vermilion edict from my hand, issued to the nation to calm the mood and explain the wisdom of our actions. To appease the foreigners, they cleared Zhang Yinhuan of the charges against him and released him from jail the same day, though in reality he got banished to distant Xinjiang, well out of the foreigners' reach.

We continued the same routine as the day before, took care of business and then went to watch the theatre. It was hard to say who was living the greater pretence, we, or the actors on the stage. Maybe it was the most fitting way to pass the time after all, a lot of movement and noise with the ending already written.

They called me the Son of Heaven and so maybe it was natural I should watch the sky so intently. I hadn't much else to do anyway. Sometimes tears came in silent trickle down my cheeks. It surprised me I still had some when I felt so shrivelled up inside. I was as if a porcelain figure with painted eyes fixed wide and lips serene in small smile of duty. They bore me to my morning obligations and returned me to the Ocean Terrace when my presence was no longer required. And then I sat and stared at the sky.

Confucius said the ancients preferred to keep silent for fear of shaming themselves lest they fail to keep up with their own words. Few had need for his wisdom now in these days of chatter and gossip. I had never learned in any case to speak with ease or swell my voice loud. I was silent even when my heart burst with protest. No one would have heard me anyway.

Cixi gathered the rumours that trailed in Kang's wake as he slipped through Shanghai and sailed for Hong Kong, where the English would protect him. The arrests and dismissals continued. Some of the reformers fled or went into hiding. It didn't matter if they'd been connected to Kang or not. The governor of Hunan was dismissed. I'd read with my own eyes his memorials against Kang. But he was the only one of the provincial governors who actually tried to implement my reforms, and that was sufficient crime in itself.

Had things continued as I planned, Cixi and I would have been in the midst of a very different kind of noise right now, boarding the train for our journey to Tianjin. I'd looked forward to that trip, filled with the anticipation of a hopeful surprise in store. I'd already imagined the clatter and steam, seen myself not an emperor but a railway passenger, curious face at the window, eager to glimpse the land roll by outside.

Cixi cancelled the Tianjin trip the day I wrote my muddled attempt at an edict explaining the beheadings. I wouldn't get to travel by train.

I'd thought that was maybe the end of it all and they'd leave me alone now. But Confucius was right, words ran swift and their speakers seldom kept pace. The rumours said now that I'd given Kang secret orders to flee abroad and secure foreign help to save me. Kang, they said, claimed that everything really had been as the rumours had it all summer. He had indeed been sneaking to my presence at night, constantly at my side.

The foreigners only lent more credence to these rumours, smuggling reformers out of the country and beefing up their troops, supposedly to guard their embassies. The foreign ambassadors spoke their discontent. It wasn't hard to make a grand plot of it all.

Cixi slackened off with her interrogations. She hadn't always the strength now to steel her tone and ice her eyes cold.

Sometimes she just cried. She was too torn up inside by the thought that she'd made me her son only to reap my deceit and treachery.

Her heart wasn't as stony as her eyes could be. Tongzhi had been too much her own flesh, a strong-willed boy, gave her quarrels and battles. I was the quiet one, even my name was a name of quiet. She'd approved it for me. It was the family rule for princes' sons to receive their name from the palace, and my father too had gone to the Forbidden City to seek for me a name of good omen.

She wanted quiet submission, but she wanted love too. They all praised her and cloaked her in their assurances of devoted feeling, and she wanted it real, hoped its glow had warmth inside, and sought sincere intent in the flattering words. It cut her deep to think the gentle-seeming boy could have conspired against her and hidden a lying heart behind his tranquil smile. I saw it in her tiredness and tears, and even in her anger that spilled forth. My heart wasn't cold, but it was numb.

I sensed footsteps approach and stop at a respectful distance. It was Zhao.

"Master of Ten Thousand Years…You have eaten nothing today…"

I ignored him. His duty was silence. He was to speak only if I addressed him.

"Let me at least bring you tea," he pleaded.

I nodded. My mouth felt dry. Zhao said no more. I took the cup he placed on the small table and he retreated. I lifted the lid, felt a wisp of steam brush my cheek as I bent forward and peered down at the pale colour.

"Tea"…the English word popped into my awareness in sudden random recollection. I'd not studied any English for a while. There'd been no time during the summer. Now I had time but my will was gone. I did nothing, just stared at the sky and feared the sleepless night.

The words were still there in a disjointed list that ran through my head. I recalled little Chun and his face screwed up with concentration as I tested his memory, saw how his eyes lit up as he found the words and flung them gladly from his tongue.

I doubted he had much life in him now, not after 200 strokes of the rod. Even if he recovered, nothing would light his eyes again. He would be a prisoner, sentenced to wear the heavy cangue around his neck until the day he died. Those were Cixi's orders.

She had three of my eunuchs and one of Zhen's beaten to death. They were charged with meddling in government affairs. Little Chun, three other eunuchs of mine and one of Zhen's were charged with ganging up together. Zhen's eunuchs had always been courting trouble over the photography business of course. Mine, I couldn't have even said what they all got up to. I had more than ninety of them.

Those with whom I had the most direct contact, like little Chun, I tried to improve in what small ways I could. Those caught breaking my rules were always punished. But I could not know everything, and nor did I seek to. I'd never seen the eunuchs as more than a necessary evil and generally assumed they were probably up to no good. For all my severity with them over the years, I'd never punished them this harshly.

What made things worse was that two of my eunuchs panicked and fled from the palace after hearing that their fellows had been beaten to death. One of them managed to sneak back in with a knife later, planning who knew what kind of revenge, but he got caught before he could do anything. Zhao, and my other chief eunuch, Hao, weren't spared punishment either. They were fined a year's wages. Cixi had chosen them both to oversee my eunuchs, and they'd failed to live up to her expectations.

I cradled the warm cup in my hands, sipped the hot liquid and turned back to the sky. Noise from the workmen rose in the air. They were blocking up the side entrances to my building. Cixi didn't trust what I might get up to in the night. Rumours abounded that subversives from Kang's gang would sneak their way in and try to rescue me. My runaway eunuch had stolen back through the walls with a knife, after all. Cixi felt it safer to brick me in and make it easier to keep watch on me.

I forgot about the tea. It turned cold and I sat with my hand around the cup, motionless. Darkness came. The birds had gone and the sky hid. There was an emperor of the Song dynasty, Huizong. History judged him a bad emperor but a good artist. He'd had a particular eye for the birds and had painted them often. Once he painted a dream he had, auspicious cranes over the palace roofs. His cranes were nothing like the bronze ones that decorated our audience halls. His were free and joyous, a circling crowd in the dawn sky, wheeling over roofs rising from gold-edged morning mists.

Huizong's real life didn't turn out as auspicious and gold-edged as his dreams. His capital fell to the Jin soldiers come down from the north, my own distant ancestors from Manchuria. They took him and most of his family prisoner and led them off into Manchuria's cold reaches. He spent eight years in the bleak wastes of what his life had become before death released him.

I wondered if he saw them sometimes in that exile, his auspicious cranes in the happy light, all unfettered motion. I wasn't sure I'd have the strength to last so long in such sadness, left with just the tattered shreds of dreams.

37

I came out into the cold, solemn-faced Chief Eunuch Hao just behind me. I stopped abruptly and gave him a questioning glance. A rhythmic pounding sound rang crisp in the winter air, rose from down by the shore.

"They're breaking up the ice again," Hao said.

I nodded. The ice created new opportunities for furtive plotting. My Ocean Terrace was already on an island, joined by a single bridge to the surrounding land, and that was easy enough to guard, but winter froze the lake and gave me a potential new escape route. Cixi was careful not to leave me any chance of slipping away with Kang's emissaries and sent the workmen out to hack up all the ice around my shores and free the cold dark water from beneath. I stood where I was, still in the frosted morning, felt the chill make my skin tingle. The foreign women were coming but I had no wish to be put on show for their curious eyes.

Hao's look said we had to leave. Soon I sat at Cixi's side. She was in the centre, of course, a table with fruit and flowers before her. The foreign women were just a small group, ambassadors' wives. Our officials and princesses stood to the sides and watched.

The foreign women had their own way of making curtseys, like their men had their own kind of bowing. I'd only seen painted or sculpted ones before, the ones from clocks, snuff bottles, vases, boxes or photos. There was also the bare-legged woman who'd twirled in my long-ago music box. These women all kept their legs covered. They were pinched at the waist, and feathered, looking like richly plumed birds.

Zhen would have loved to see them in their foreign fashions. Those things interested her. She'd have been eager to pinch and plume herself like they did, her love of costume and ornament dressing the dullness a little. That had always been her small attempt to disguise the days and make holes in the walls so that chinks of novelty would shine her way.

Yehenara and Jin were with the princesses off to the side, but the foreign women wouldn't know who they were. They probably didn't know of Zhen's existence and certainly wouldn't know that she was now shut away in one of the tiny northeast halls at the very back of the Forbidden City. Those small quarters were places of disgrace, mean and forgotten. She was locked in, her eunuchs dismissed, a couple of maids left to serve her.

This was the first time the foreign women had ever had an imperial audience. They could thank Kang for the unprecedented privilege. Safe now with the English in Hong Kong, he turned a caustic tongue against Cixi. They fought a war amongst themselves and did it in my name. It was my name on the edicts that had left Kang's brother and friends dead in the vegetable market, and my name too on the banner Kang flew as he fired his venom-tipped words Cixi's way. Their combat was so much more personal now, so much more bitter, but I hadn't the strength or desire for it. I had sought unity not war.

Cixi didn't want to be hated. Of course, Kang would not love her for having his brother executed, ending his hopes and sending him into flight, but that he could deliberately blacken her before the world struck her into shock and fury. It made her loathe him even more, and revile too those who'd brought him to my notice.

She remembered Tutor Weng then, who was no doubt passing quiet days with his family in the south. I'd already punished him but she made me write another edict of blame.

They had to rewrite that one too and make Kang figure big on the list of offences.

Now, she wanted to wipe clean the stains of these past months, wash away the sludge of rumours and show if not the foreign ambassadors then at least their wives that all was tranquil within our walls and the gossip was just a pile of vicious lies.

She smiled away as she listened to Prince Qing make the presentations. The foreign women stared about them much more openly than I'd ever seen their men do. One woman studied the carpet on the floor with an odd expression on her face. Another stared at the princesses in their Manchu robes and headdresses, and a third had her eyes to the ceiling. Only the Japanese ambassador's wife was more discreet. She wasn't a rich-plumed bird, she wore the dress of her own country.

Most of all they stared at Cixi and me. I felt their eyes narrow in on me and kept my gaze down, throwing only fleeting glances their way. At first, they'd all thought I was dead. That news came from Shanghai when the hunt for Kang was on. Some official down there said that Kang had poisoned me, thinking that might make the foreigners more cooperative.

Kang and his allies added rumours of their own. If I wasn't dead, I was tortured and imprisoned, and if I was still alive, I wouldn't be emperor for long. They'd force me to abdicate. No wonder the women stared at me now. The whole purpose of having them come, apart from endearing Cixi to them, was so that they would see me alive and well and still on the throne.

There wasn't much to keep me on that precious throne. I wasn't publicly a criminal, just ill since I'd got the idea of reform into my head, unable now to govern on my own.

The provincial governors did answer the call for assistance that Cixi wrote in my name, and sent their best doctors to Beijing. They came one morning with the palace doctors to examine me. I was very candid with them and gave them thorough descriptions of my symptoms. My body's failings had always caused me much anxiety. The recent events had sapped my spirits and eroded my strength further of course, but if I could finally get some competent medical help, that would be one small blessing at least.

I never guessed at that moment that Cixi would order the doctors' report sent out to the government officials as proof of my incapacitated state and unfitness for my duties. It was unheard of. The emperor's health was supposed to be secret, but my officials now had every intimate detail of my complaints before them.

The foreigners answered the call for doctors too. Cixi didn't want to take up the offer, but the foreigners kept up the pressure and she finally decided to play cautious again and let them have their wish. They chose a French doctor. He arrived the morning after Cixi divulged my medical report. Cixi and I sat in silence, waiting for Prince Qing to escort him in. We were all silent for a time after the Frenchmen made their bows. The doctor didn't know Chinese and had with him an interpreter.

I stared at the doctor. He stood looking back at me. He had rather a lot of hair, neat beard framing his face, moustache, thick brows over serious eyes. I had prepared for this visit, had written out a history of my illnesses and description of my symptoms, and I had it with me now, tucked down my boot, but they seemed to expect me to speak with them.

"Have him examine my pulse," I murmured in Prince Qing's ear. That was what our doctors always did to diagnose a patient's condition.

The Frenchman did as I requested. He wanted to do more than take my pulse. He had a curious instrument that he wanted to use to examine my chest, but for it to work I first had to remove my clothes. I looked across at Cixi. Our doctors never did more than examine the colour of the face, tongue, eyes, take the pulse and ask some questions. It was unthinkable for the emperor to expose any more of his body than that.

I was prepared to do whatever the doctor asked if it could help him treat me more effectively. Cixi had a calm expression.

The light shone on the silky blue of her gown and gave it a rich sky-filled look. She nodded her consent.

I wasn't dressed in all those fancy dragon robes today. I never wore those robes unless I had to. I usually dressed in simple robes of plain dark shades, only the button on my hat distinguishing my status, but I doubted the Frenchmen knew the meanings of our different hat buttons. I couldn't remove all my clothes before them, kept one layer on. The doctor bent close over me. He looked odd with two ends of the instrument in his ears, while the other end he placed on my chest and moved it about, an intent look on his face.

Prince Qing had an intent look on his face too. Cixi made no effort to disguise her curiosity, following the proceedings with great interest and questioned the doctor about what he was doing and why. I gave the French interpreter the account I'd written of my illness. All the battles and rumours had brought me this one rare chance to see a foreign doctor, and I hoped it might bring me some crumb of good.

The doctor concluded I had a kidney complaint and recommended that I drink nothing but milk. It was lucky for him that I was a Manchu, for we did drink milk and always had it supplied to the palace, not that I actually ended up drinking it, as the Frenchman's advice was swiftly forgotten.

The doctors from the provinces examined me every day for a while at Cixi's orders. This sudden medical attention was not to treat my illnesses but to prepare the way for my removal. I was in poor health and couldn't produce an heir. Everyone knew it now. The foreigners opposed my abdication, and that was the only reason they sent their Frenchman. He concluded that I was ill perhaps, but not in any mortal danger. That wasn't what my cousins with their covetous eyes wanted to hear.

Too sick to assume my responsibilities as emperor, and yet I performed my many duties unfailingly, day after day, even now when I had nothing but despair inside. Too ill to be left to govern, and yet I had known sickness from before I even entered these walls, and it had long been clear too that I would not produce an heir.

My cousins would have tossed me aside in an instant, but Cixi was more cautious. She feared the foreign protests. Any rumour of abdication and the foreigners stirred into action and found some pretext for needing to see me. After the French doctor, the Japanese suddenly said they wanted to present me with a decoration from Emperor Meiji. That too was to check that I really was still alive and still emperor.

Cixi took the initiative this time though, inviting the foreign women to come and meet her and throwing me in as an added surprise, the hope being that they'd return now to their husbands and paint glowing pictures of all they'd seen. They saw only pleasant things. Cixi gave them warm and friendly smiles, presented each of them with a ring, which she herself placed on their fingers. I shook hands with them, nothing much at all in my expression, and I was glad when Prince Qing led them away for their banquet with the princesses.

After that, the days went back to their routine, no more foreigners to see. I watched the hours pass, sat at the window and stared at the afternoon. A tree branch was hung with drops of silver melting in the winter sun. It was just water and the sun had no warmth, but it gladdened the eye even so. The eunuchs were at work again on the ice. I could hear the muffled pounding. The day's chilled brightness lifted me a little. I spotted a pigeon in the sky and watched it spiral into a strange string of acrobatics it performed for no apparent reason or audience. It was all alone in the blue with its fancy dives.

I felt a stirring inside. I was still young. There'd been times when I'd grown so tight with duty and restraint, so sick of sitting still and so filled up with words and thoughts that I could no longer concentrate. Sometimes, I had the eunuch musicians get out their gongs and drums and perform, and I would join them too at moments, beat the time, lose myself in the rhythm and feel my body relax.

Watching the pigeon's senseless spirals, I had the urge to do something too and the musicians came to mind. I'd have them come with their instruments and I'd join them in their tunes. I called Chief Eunuch Hao and sent him off with my order. He came back looking even more downcast than usual.

"It will be possible only with the Old Buddha's permission," he sighed.

I sighed too and hurled a teacup at the wall. It would have been a greater mercy if the foreigners kept their tongues quiet and forgot about me. It was surely a sweeter fate to be cast aside than to live as I did now. But no, the Guangxu reign continued, I was still emperor, though truly now no more than the little man in the ingenious clock, writing characters down the scroll on command every hour, endlessly obedient and unchanging.

Sometimes, turning over all the events of these past weeks in my head, I couldn't help but wonder what things would be like if everything Cixi said was true and Kang and I had plotted Cixi's arrest. Had Cixi, Prince Gong and my father not done the same with Sushun, plotted his capture and removal? Sushun and his allies had seen a country in a weakened, dangerous state and would have thought themselves far better equipped to address the challenges than a small boy and two young women with no knowledge of politics.

But Cixi and Prince Gong had been bolder. My imagination, when I thought of my father's ride to Miyun to arrest Sushun, had always pictured a black night and lurking foe, but really, Cixi, Cian and the boy emperor were already safely back in the Forbidden City by that moment, half of Sushun's allies had already been arrested, and my father rode out to complete the task knowing that power had already slipped from Sushun's hands. It was only Sushun himself, keeping his vigil by the late emperor's coffin, who didn't yet know how drastically his fortunes were about to change.

Kang and I hadn't plotted Cixi's imprisonment. I had been shocked when she'd first spoken of it. Now though, I couldn't help thinking that the Summer Palace wasn't the worst possible prison. We'd have surely left her the actors and musicians, her walks and boat excursions on the lake. We'd not have bricked her in. As it was, it was I who was the prisoner now.

I was only twenty-eight. I was young, and if the French doctor was to be believed, not in any mortal danger. I got up from my place and stared about me as if to see what else I could smash.

"Master of Ten Thousand Years..." Hao began, his eyes on the cup's shattered fragments.

"Ten thousand years?" I cut him short. A strange laughter burst from me. "Whatever will I do with ten thousand years?"

Hao looked uncomfortable and didn't answer.

I laughed. Then I cried. Then the sky lost its bright look and I stared at nothing, just sat still and grew stiff with time.

38

The hot still air broke apart in sudden shouts that jerked me from my book. I knew all the guards and eunuchs' calls. These voices were different and didn't belong to the palace.

"Go and see what's going on out there," I sent my eunuchs out to take a look.

The summer shone blue beyond and here all was shaded calm around, but my heart was tight. The storm had already started its grim march. It surely would not be long now. These frenzied shouts alarmed me.

A few days had passed since we declared war. The foreign armies had already entered Tianjin. They would no doubt take the city and then march on Beijing. We faced not just Japan this time, but eight countries all at once, the world's great powers. My country was slipping into madness.

"There's a crowd at the gate," the eunuchs hurried back in. "It's Prince Duan and Duke Lan, and they've got the Boxers with them."

"What do they want here?" I asked.

The eunuchs glanced at each other. "Uh...They're looking for secondary hairy ones," one of them said finally.

I shook my head slowly and laid aside my book. "Hairy ones" was an old name for Europeans, because to our eyes, they were very hairy, especially with that penchant for long beards they'd had in the old days. "Secondary hairy ones", by derivation, was the name the mostly poor, uneducated and rabidly anti-foreign Boxers, so called because of their mystical martial arts practices, gave Chinese who'd become Christians or who sympathised with the foreigners and knew their ways.

Prince Duan had already brought the Boxers to the Summer Palace to search for Christians among the eunuchs. The Boxer leader he brought with him on that occasion said he could see a cross on the forehead of Christians. He spotted one on a couple of the eunuchs and they were taken away and killed.

"You're crazy," I murmured.

It was Prince Duan I spoke to from my shelter grown thin. He was my cousin, one of Fifth Uncle Prince Dun's sons. Prince Dun died not so long before my father, but his sons were very much alive. Duke Lan was another of them, and just as bad.

That family all bore grudges and wanted to turn their fortunes around. Prince Dun never had his father, Emperor Daoguang's, favour. His mother had somehow disgraced herself in Emperor Daoguang's eyes and it had stained her son too. Emperor Daoguang had him adopted out to continue the male line and title of a childless relative. That was a common practice in our clan and emperors had frequently shuffled imperial sons, nephews and so on among the clan's different branches, so that everyone would have an heir after their death at least, to console their departed spirits.

Prince Duan met the same fate as his father and was adopted out too, this time on Emperor Xianfeng's order. It put them outside the immediate imperial family, so Prince Duan was never considered as a successor to the throne when Tongzhi died. I was chosen instead.

Now, Prince Duan was just a step away from achieving his life's desire. He couldn't be emperor, but his son would. The only thing in the way was me. I couldn't produce an heir, so Prince Duan graciously offered the dynasty his son, Pujun. He'd have pushed me aside and had his son proclaimed emperor immediately, but the final decision wasn't his, and Cixi, true to her nature, took a cautious approach. Ronglu, her trusted favourite, opposed the idea. He was back in Beijing now and had become a grand councillor.

The succession debate went on for months. They finally made it official at the New Year. I had to issue an edict for the occasion, in which I once more declared my sickness, proclaimed my endless gratitude to Cixi for instructing me in government, reminding everyone that I hadn't been in the proper line of succession anyway, and designated Pujun heir-apparent and successor to Tongzhi.

Pujun did much better than his father or grandfather had in terms of being adopted out, he got Cixi's own son as his new ancestor. I wouldn't have an heir. They'd leave my spirit to roam disconsolate.

The edict set off fresh rumours that I was about to die, and I had to show myself before the foreign ambassadors, not very healthy-looking but still alive. Prince Duan would have liked me to be as ill as the gossip suggested and searched my pale thin appearance for signs of imminent death.

Pujun too wanted to hasten me on my way. Cixi had him come to live at the palace so that he could receive the appropriate training for his future role under her watchful eye. That wasn't an easy task. He was an ill-mannered boy of fifteen and didn't look like promising material. He was somewhat afraid of Cixi at least, but had only contempt for me and liked to remind me that he would take my place soon.

The shouts outside grew louder and my eunuchs looked frightened. Prince Duan and Duke Lan did as they pleased now, ignoring even Cixi. They swelled insolent with war, bragging and conceit, the Boxers an unsuspecting tool in their hands.

The Boxer trouble started in Shandong. Shandong was that sort of place, poor and restless, frequently hit by floods or drought, and half-colonised by the Germans these days. Our dynasty had always had to keep a vigilant eye, stamping out anti-Manchu sentiment wherever it stirred, suppressing secret societies and crushing rebellions. It was no different with the Boxers at first too. Cixi feared they were getting out of hand

and sent Yuan Shikai to restore order, making him governor of Shandong.

In the mouths of movements like theirs, calls to rid China of all foreigners usually meant throwing us out too, and they had called for this at first, but if the Manchus were excluded the idea gained sudden appeal. Prince Duan and others at court saw their opportunity and soon the Boxers had a new slogan: "Defend the Qing, destroy the foreign."

I knew my cousins. They burned with desire to cast out the decades of humiliation we'd suffered. They saw in the Boxers what their name proclaimed -- a righteous fist to strike those who'd thought to ruin and enslave us. The Boxers had magic, the protection of heaven, fire a bullet at them and they'd not fall. Prince Duan tried to spin Cixi giddy with his boasts. He brought some Boxers to the palace and organised a demonstration for us to prove his claims. It was all just clever tricks, but Prince Duan believed it fervently.

Cixi had little love for the foreigners, especially with Kang and his exiled friends still slandering her from abroad. She wavered. Prince Duan wooed her with his visions of a loyal patriotic force, and she was tempted, but she never liked to commit herself to matters of unclear consequence. She sent two of the grand councillors to investigate the Boxers. One of them was that old conservative Gangyi who, unsurprisingly, shared Prince Duan's vision and presented a favourable report. His colleague went along with him.

Things moved fast once they had the court's support. Boxers came streaming into Beijing, Prince Duan and Duke Lan in charge. Soon, the city was on fire, the Catholic cathedral aflame, and the Boxers ran wild, searched out "secondary hairy ones" and left them dead and scattered through the streets.

Cixi took fright then. Flames and chaos just beyond her walls weren't to her taste at all. She had troops sent to end the rioting and told Ronglu to organise protection for the foreign embassies. We were back in Beijing by then, returned from the

Summer Palace just before the rioting began. Cixi gathered us all for consultations. I'd seldom seen true and vigorous debate among these officials, but faced with the prospect of war, they spoke their hearts now. They were split in their views and Cixi hovered between them, looking one way and the other, trying to decide.

Prince Duan hadn't a scholar's nimble and reflective mind. He had only his glaring eyes and dreams of seeing his son on the throne. He needed war. It would create brief chaos, and when the dust settled, I'd be gone and the foreign devils vanquished. His arguments were blunt and simple, and he spoke them with menace in his tone. We had to keep the Boxers with us. In our hands they would fight our war, but if we lost their hearts, they would turn against us.

"More riots and disorder, this is the popular support you would have us rely on?"

Everyone looked my way in surprise, and I was as surprised as they were. I was just a mute fixture usually, but my words blurted out before I had time to think.

"You speak of war so lightly today." I figured I may as well continue, now that I'd started. "Remember the suffering we went through after going to war over Korea. All these countries now, their strength would be ten times greater than Japan alone. If they all unite against us, what chance would we stand of defending ourselves?"

Prince Duan gave me a hostile glance. Cixi too had her eyes on me, curious it seemed to see what else I might blurt out in my sudden burst of life.

"There's absolutely no way in the world we can start a conflict with all of these countries at once," I said, pleading, and fell silent again.

Cixi was quiet, retreating inside herself and sat with a thinking look. The consultations ended with nothing decided.

She called us together again the next day. This time her face was grim and her lips tight and thin. The foreigners had sent a list of conditions we were to agree to if we wanted to avoid war. Essentially, they were asking us to put the running of tax and military affairs in their hands. Cixi read out the document and stared hard at us all. Anger and sadness ran together in her voice. Now war was on her tongue, too. She sighed, said there was no way out. Fight and we faced grave danger, not fight and we'd certainly perish.

Prince Duan had no such doubts and rushed to reassure her. He really thought the Boxers with their magic incantations and talismans would throw the foreign hordes into the sea. He'd wrapped himself up in these foolish superstitions and was willing to gamble our country's fate for the sake of putting his son on the throne.

"How can we talk of war with our country as weak as it is and no army to rely on?" I spoke out again. I had but the name of emperor, but I could not undo myself. So long as I wore the title, I had to put my heart into it, had to try. Tutor Weng was doubly disgraced now, first by me, then by Cixi in her fury over Kang, but his lessons echoed in me even so.

"Is that what you think of your people, is that all you think they're worth?" his words came back to me. It seemed only yesterday, his disappointed gaze on me, trying to prod me out of my torpor and make me take genuine interest in preparing for the ploughing ceremony. It was for all those people after all that I was emperor, not for Cixi, Prince Duan or anyone else in this room.

"You want to use a rioting mob to win a war?" I continued. "What luck can you possibly hope for? What have this rabble to offer but their own flesh and blood? You speak empty talk of keeping the people's hearts with us, but you want to make the people's lives a plaything in your hands?"

They stared as the previous day, surprised I still had so many words in me.

"It's an illusion to think that loyal and righteous spirit alone can fight a war," I hurried onwards. "These people have no training. When the day of battle comes, how long do you think they'll last amidst a rain of bullets and forest of guns with nothing but their bare fists before the enemy?"

Cixi shot me a look that suggested I'd said enough and could close my mouth now. I ignored her, stared down at my cousins, appealing to whatever crumb of reason they still possessed.

"Alone, no one can take on a whole horde of enemies. If we couldn't defeat one country, how do you imagine we will fight eight of them?"

I stopped. Cixi was still grim, but she was silent now. Again, the discussion ended with no decision taken.

The debates continued the following day. The foreigners were readying for war no matter what we did. Prince Duan wanted to attack the foreign embassies. That idea sent the officials from the Foreign Affairs Office into a flurry of protest. Cixi looked from one group to the other.

Ronglu wanted to speak. I felt my gaze intent on his face. I knew just how much Cixi trusted Ronglu and knew that whatever he said would carry weight, maybe even decide her. He spoke good sense: no declaring war, no attacking the embassies. Aware of the volatile situation in Beijing now, he proposed getting all the foreigners out of the embassy district altogether and sending them under the court's protection to Tianjin.

"Emperor, what do you think?" Cixi glanced at me.

She always asked me what I thought for the sake of appearances, and I always gave the same answer, said I agreed with her opinion. Now I threw my clockwork face away and showed her my earnest eyes.

"I think Ronglu is right," I said, hoping my small voice might add another drop in favour of peace.

Seeing Ronglu speaking frankly against war, others finally started joining in with their support for his view. I felt a sudden hope, but it was brief. I knew Cixi's face too well and the look she wore said she'd already decided. Refusal choked me. She was ill-informed, led along by my cousins gone mad, but she wasn't stupid and there had to be some way of making her stop this senseless rush into destruction.

My eye fell on a huddle of the foreign affairs specialists standing among the officials. One of them had been our ambassador in Europe and had already spoken out against war at these discussions. Seized by a sudden panic, I left my place and went down to him.

"You know the foreigners," I grabbed hold of the former ambassador's arm, "is there really any way we can fight them?"

He and his neighbours shook their heads gravely and lapsed into sighs.

"But there must be a way we can still save the situation," I pleaded, tearful now.

The officials too had faces heavy with emotion. I was vaguely aware of Prince Duan pointing at me and saying something to Cixi.

"Let go of him," Cixi caught me with her sharp tone.

I did as ordered and returned to my place.

Prince Duan won the day in the end. The unfortunate former ambassador whose sleeve I'd grabbed and his colleagues were arrested and we all prepared for war. Prince Duan and Gangyi gave whatever orders they pleased now. They didn't need Cixi's edicts anymore. These days they simply wrote their own.

Now, I sat with my frightened eunuchs, the crowd still yelling outside the gate. Their calls grew louder. They wanted me to come out. I'd heard the rumours about the little chant they'd dreamt up, "kill a dragon..." The dragon was a euphemism for the emperor. It was me the dragon they hoped to kill.

"Come out, friend of the foreign devils," the words filtered in across the yard.

The eunuchs glanced at each other with worried eyes. They'd be qualified as secondary hairy ones too, no doubt, with a master like me.

"Devil's apprentice, come on out!"

I grimaced. That was what Pujun the future emperor liked to call me. He was probably out there with his father, happy to throw his books aside and run with the warlike mob. Cixi had appointed two imperial tutors to teach him to become emperor, both of them staunch supporters of Prince Duan and the Boxers. Pujun had no love of study anyway.

The shouts clanged in my ears. I sat still, jaw clenched, nervous thump in my heart. I didn't know how to fight. I felt hot and afraid, and almost wanted to put my hands to my ears and make the madness go away. The noise finally subsided. The voices lost their vigour and grew ragged, slowly moved on. This time, they'd only wanted to give me a fright.

39

I lit incense, performing rites in memory of Emperor Xianfeng. The fragrance and my words of prayer muffled the strange wails that cut through the first glimmers of dawn. My thoughts crumbled into small things. Eunuch Liu would come soon to shave me. It was his day to come. I hated being shaved.

The strange wails continued, seemed to come from all directions. I thought it perhaps the cats that roamed around the Forbidden City at night, but these howls came from somewhere beyond and had a different note I'd never heard before.

The wails had been going for a while now, starting in the sleeping darkness, a troubling call that woke the eunuchs and sent them staring into the yard. I was already awake, pulled back the curtain and asked what was going on, but the eunuchs saw nothing more than the murky night sky.

They huddled in whispers, fell into a hasty hush and broke apart when they saw me. Normally the eunuchs' gossip didn't interest me and stayed a vague murmur beyond my hearing. They'd been muttering away amongst themselves since the previous evening and fear hung thick about them now as the sky kept wailing. One of them bent before me, arranging the offerings on the altar. He seemed nervous too and threw apprehensive looks towards the breaking night.

"What's got you all so afraid?" I asked him when the rites were completed.

He darted a glance at the ceiling full of dark shadow. "It's that sound…" he murmured reluctantly.

"What about it?"

"It's… It's…" he put his eyes to the floor and shuffled awkwardly from one foot to another.

"It's what?"

"It's an unhappy spirit," he said finally.

The Forbidden City teemed with devils and spirits in the eunuchs' minds. Most of what I knew about such matters I had learned from them. Each hall, each palace had its own collection of ghosts and demons that seeped from their hiding places and ran free when darkness fell.

"What unhappy spirit?" I pressed the eunuch, sensed he was hiding something from me. "There are unhappy spirits here every night. Why is this one wailing now?"

"It's lamenting its unjust end," the eunuch sighed.

"Who is? What unjust end?" I gave him an odd look.

The eunuch shook his head and backed away a little. He was half-swallowed in the shadows, lit in fragments by the candles and lanterns. His face tensed up in fear and the wails from outside only added to his anxiety.

"Speak!" I ordered.

"It's…I don't know anything, I only heard from the others…"

"Speak whatever it is you heard."

He took a deep breath. "It's…It's Mistress Zhen…"

"What about her?" I stared at him.

I hadn't seen Zhen since the reforms were defeated and I was forced to give all power back to Cixi. They kept her shut away in her little prison behind the Imperial Pharmacy and no one ever mentioned her name. I wasn't much better than a prisoner myself, better kept than Zhen, of course, but closely watched the whole time. It was the most I could do to see her in a dream or memory, amongst all the other things I'd lost.

"Go on, tell me," I pressed the shrinking eunuch.

The eunuch gulped more air. "They threw her down the well," he murmured.

"Who threw her down the well? What well?"

"I don't know anything," he whispered. "It's just a rumour. They say Cui Yugui threw her down the well by the Gate of Chaste Obedience yesterday."

The eunuch was pale. His voice trembled. The sky kept howling.

"Go," I said softly.

I stayed alone with the candle flicker and incense-perfumed air. Cui Yugui was Cixi's second chief eunuch. He wasn't a demon, and he couldn't take an emperor's consort, even a disgraced one, and throw her down a well at a whim. Such a thing, if it was true, had to come from Cixi's hand.

I raised my face and listened. The wails in the sky were closer now. They were not the wild creatures or unhappy spirits the eunuchs feared. They were the sounds of war.

The frightened eunuch rushed back in. "A eunuch has come from the Hall of Happy Longevity," he announced.

A eunuch come from Cixi. I went out to see what he wanted.

"The foreigners are here, they've broken into the city, the Old Buddha sends for you to come immediately to the Hall of Happy Longevity," the eunuch spoke in a breathless rush.

The dawn was just a thinning dimness giving way to morning low and sad, sky squatting grey on the roofs. I felt grey and damp too. Nothing stirred in me and, listening to the distant guns, I wondered vaguely how much longer I would see these walls, or anything at all.

We knew the foreign troops would arrive sooner or later. Our guns had been firing at the foreign embassies for some weeks now, firing above them rather, because Ronglu was in command of our troops and appeased Prince Duan by making a show of attack while at the same time getting his men to fire at pretty much anything but the embassies themselves.

The embassy district was just beyond the palace walls and we'd had the noise follow us through the days. Prince Duan and Duke Lan tried to persuade us to stay at the Summer Palace, but Cixi wanted to be in the Forbidden City. She had her memories. She'd already fled from the Summer Palace once, and when she came back only ruins remained.

Cixi had her maids and eunuchs around her. Many of the eunuchs had fled over these last days. They retreated to the sides on my arrival.

"Duke Lan reports that the foreigners have broken through the city gates," Cixi said hurriedly. "He says we're going to have to flee."

I stared at the floor. What was there to flee for? My gaze strayed across the precious objects, little boxes, vases, bowls, clocks, curious stones, snuff bottles, jewellery. The foreigners wouldn't know the stories of these things, wouldn't know the meanings of the small statues in their shrines, the fine calligraphy, the objects of good omen, wouldn't know the fineness of jade, coral or pearls, perhaps at most would see silver and gold with their ransacking eyes. They'd smash and pillage, trample heedless through it all.

But did Cixi herself know the value of things? Or was she like me as a little boy with the ancestors' clocks, when I grabbed the delicate porcelain woman and smashed her to pieces on the hard stone floor? Was it so easy to take the laughing face and sparkling eyes of a girl she herself had chosen for me once and have her thrown down a well? Were we so different to the barbarians about to descend upon us? Were we not all now sick with the same pitiless hearts and brutal madness?

I wondered if it was true that they'd killed Zhen. The eunuchs' gossip often got things wrong. I couldn't see Cui Yugui anywhere. Only Chief Eunuch Li Lianying was there, looking exhausted.

"But how can we flee if the foreigners are so close?" I asked quietly. "They will capture us. If we have no way out, we should surely just stay here, where we belong. It would be better than letting the foreign soldiers capture us on the road."

"They won't capture us," Cixi spoke through gritted teeth, her face locked tight in new resolve.

She looked me up and down. I had already prepared myself for the day's affairs and wore my imperial robes. Court beads hung around my neck.

"You can't go like that, everyone will see immediately who you are." She had an urgent look in her eyes, and called Li Lianying over. "Go and see if the guards don't have something fitting for the emperor to change into," she ordered.

I soon looked different. No one would know I was the emperor. The clothes were too big for me, plain old blue robe with no belt, trousers hanging loose, little round hat with no mark of distinction.

Cixi was still in the midst of transformation. Li Lianying did her hair in the style of the Chinese women and she had her maids cut off her long nails. Yehenara and Jin arrived, got their share of commoners' clothes from Li Lianying and went to change. They too got rid of their Manchu hairstyles and distinguishing look. Tongzhi's widowed concubines turned up, but stayed dressed as they were. They were to remain in the Forbidden City.

The walls seemed so narrow and close as we filed towards the gate. Like the eunuchs said, all the demons and spirits breathed the walls alive and made them curve in on us and reach out dawn-dampened fingers to stop our escape. The fateful well was there, just to the side. I kept my eyes fixed ahead. We had to pass it. A cold circle of stone wrapped tight the inky blackness below. Was it here this last line of sky Zhen saw, these last few steps, this gate up ahead?

The Gate of Chaste Obedience was the consorts' gate. They came through it on their wedding day and were forbidden from ever stepping back out to the other side. Cixi went through. Tongzhi's widowed consorts stood with tears running down their cheeks. They could go no further.

Cixi gathered us in a huddle around her and ordered us to keep our mouths shut and speak not a word on the road. She particularly speared Pujun with her gaze, well aware of our future emperor's foolish head. Then she assigned us our places on the carts and took Pujun herself so as to keep an eye on him. I found myself sitting with Pulun, another of my relatives. Yehenara and Jin had to crowd into the one remaining cart with the maids.

The foreigners hadn't yet broken through from all sides. A thick crowd besieged the city gate, everyone trying to escape in a chaos of carts, animals and people pressed together in haste and panic. The morning was leaden with windless heat and the sky was black-edged and ominous. Cui Yugui appeared now, dressed as a cart driver. He came and went, scouting out the road ahead.

I sat with Pulun, silent as ordered. If I closed my eyes, it all grabbed me even stronger, the steaming heat, the noise, the stink of the animals. Mud and dung lay thick underfoot and we were stuck in the middle of it. No one would close the roads for us and clear the mess and the populace from our sight. No one knew who we were. Our clothes, our carts and our sorry appearance weren't much different to this throng of people around us all trying to get through the gate and flee to safety.

Cui got us through. He suddenly caught sight of Grand Councillor Qiao, not in disguise as we were but in his official robes, and got him to use his authority to clear a passage for our little group. More fleeing people streamed out of the city on the other side, soldiers roamed about, and Boxers, wrapped in their distinctive red strips of cloth. Hunger, defeat and fear stamped some faces and others wore marauding looks. There was no stately imperial procession this time, only this escort of war and suffering, and the city as we'd never seen it before.

Even in flight we took the only road we knew. The Summer Palace opened its gates and we entered our familiar world. Protocol was forgotten as maids, eunuchs, all of us together on the carts, entered by the same gate. The quiet hurt. It made my ears ring and I couldn't shake my head clear. I saw grim things when I closed my eyes.

Soon all went silent with brief sleep. Cixi was taking a nap. The sullen day cast shadows. Perhaps because it was the young autumn time when we remembered Xianfeng's death, it was he who came to me today from the dim reaches, a little mocking it seemed that I should have sought so earnestly to change our fate and yet was now repeating his journey. Had I thought to do better than him, I who had never truly ruled at all, except perhaps for those brief summer months two years before, and that too ended when the autumn arrived.

They all came seeking shelter behind our walls now, all my martial clan so eager for war just weeks ago. Cixi called an audience. Prince Qing was there, ready to take flight. He'd wavered this way and that at the Foreign Affairs Office, and now there were no foreign affairs for him to take care of, only war. Prince Su turned up. He lived next to the embassies and the foreigners had taken over his residence and filled it with Chinese Christians. Prince Duan too arrived, his brave talk silenced now.

Cixi wanted us to get moving again before the foreigners worked out that we'd fled. She was afraid they'd guess our route and come looking for us. Prince Duan was especially eager to hurry out the gate as quickly as he could. He probably knew that if the foreigners did catch us, he'd be one of the first to pay with his life.

Cixi organised our departure and it was all very orderly. We travelled in small separate groups so as not to draw attention to ourselves. My group was the same as in the morning, only we'd requisitioned some carts from the princes and weren't so crowded together now.

I still had Pulun with me. We were as silent as before, swayed and rattled through the muddy dreary land, pressed down by the grim furnace above. We had no provisions. I felt the thirst and sweat, my throat parched and my clothes grown damp and sticky.

Cixi had brought along some money but there was nothing to buy. All the shops were shut and most had been looted. There were no laws anymore. We saw men who smashed and stole, uncaring, and we just stared and continued on our way.

We came to a village and stopped for the night. It was a Muslim village and we found shelter in an old mosque that was going to ruin. The eunuchs went out to look for food. We got a little porridge made of some kind of bean. It was better than the old millet canes the maids had tried to boil into a mush earlier in the day. The eunuchs brought in some water to drink, but I couldn't force it down. It was cold and discoloured.

Cixi sat silent on the brick bed. There was nothing in the room except for some broken old junk. Insects were everywhere, they bit us and flew into our faces, crawled over our clothes. The princes arrived and gathered outside to present their respects. Cixi told them to leave.

The maids came to help Cixi get ready for sleep. They filled the room with smoke to drive out the mosquitoes and turned everything dim and fuzzy. I had a cushion from one of the carts, sat in a corner and leant against the wall. That was my bed.

The darkness settled. Cixi lay wrapped up by the maids and I sat in my corner. We were alone now and we said nothing to each other. It had been a long time since we had slept in the same room, not since I was a sickly four-year-old boy afraid of the thunder.

There were no clocks here and the silence was troubling. My skin itched and hurt where it was chafed by the coarse unfamiliar clothing and bitten by insects. I closed my eyes and I was swaying on the cart, rolling through the mud and ruin.

Prince Duan was somewhere in the dark outside with his son, my hopeful successor. I was too parched inside for tears. Pujun would have nothing to inherit. Not even Xianfeng came from the shadows now. Not even he had sunk this low. It was a grand procession that took them to Rehe when the Anglo-French armies arrived, imperial pomp and splendour spread forth as if the emperor were not fleeing at all but simply going north for the hunt, like in the old days. That was Sushun's ruse to keep the populace calm.

The night was empty. I would die but this shame would forever carry my name and become part of the twenty-sixth year of Guangxu, written in the annals, stored in the archives. This war, this disaster and this shameful flight would lie upon my shoulders. They would not see that I had tried, only that I'd failed. My dreams were discarded and only my defeats would remain. All our prejudice, petty ambition and rivalry, I wore its sweat-stained coarseness, ate its pitiful substance, rested now in its dismal embrace.

Prince Duan wanted to make Pujun the Son of Heaven, but heaven had turned its back on us. We'd lost heaven's mandate. We did not even dare show our identity now, lowered our heads and joined the scavenging refugees. I, Emperor of the Great Qing, sat dirty and hungry in a corner of a ruined mosque and stared at the smoke-thickened blackness.

40

The sky swallowed the world in anger. We were caught in the mountain roads and came to a standstill as sudden rain came down. The narrow paths and steep slopes squeezed us in and trapped us as the thunder rumbled through. I never lost my fear. Pulun couldn't see it. I sat glazed and blank.

First the rain drenched us and then the heat steamed us. The clouds hung fat and black and tried to squash us between the peaks. We stopped at a post station and they found us a little soup to eat. No one had anything much to give us. The soldiers and Boxers had already taken everything, horses, food, ransacked the houses and shops. We still saw them roaming about, looters and scavengers.

We came to the pass. The Great Wall climbed high through the steepness to where the sky sat heavy. The solid squat gate rose up before us and our carts filed through the brief dimness into the silver-grey circle of unknown world beyond. My ancestors had once travelled the other way, crossing the passes into China. We unworthy descendants now straggled miserably back into the wild places.

Gunfire bounced across the stones and brought us to an abrupt halt. Someone was shooting at us. Cui Yugui and Li Lianying rushed to surround Cixi and Pulun jumped out to protect me. We all retreated to the pass and waited a time until everything seemed quiet ahead.

The walls of a town came into sight, it was a bigger place than the day before, but the Boxers, themselves fleeing the foreign attack, had taken over, smashing and setting fire to things, the streets were all a mess and the people hid away.

We found an empty house in which to spend the night. There was nothing much there, but it was a little better than the old mosque. The princes, grand councillors and various other officials had made their way out of Beijing much as we had, following in our lead. They arrived in a trickle and gathered in the muddy yard. Cixi and I stood on the porch while they prostrated themselves in the mud and wished us many auspicious years. There was nothing to say and Cixi dismissed them all.

It would have been better perhaps if one of those bullets on the mountain road had caught me while I was numbed and frozen and snatched me from this farce. It was all too sad and stupid. Our grand officials and nobles knelt on the sodden ground while beyond, the Boxers and soldiers roamed about destroying and pillaging, and back in Beijing, the foreigners were no doubt doing the same.

I stood before them, wet and dishevelled. They used the grand-sounding royal euphemisms, calling our pitiful flight a "tour of inspection" and our humble stopping place a "wayside palace", just like Kangxi or Qianlong when they'd set forth in splendour to travel their lands. The pretence sickened me, pathetic shreds of power and protocol we clutched about us to the last.

When I was a boy, I had dreamed of those "tours of inspection". We had seldom travelled even to the tombs. But I had no dreams now. The sky stayed low and we continued through the mountains. Roaming soldiers mingled with our procession and there was no way to make them leave. I was covered in grime, the long braid of hair down my back was all in disorder and coming undone, and the hair grew thick on the part of my scalp that ordinarily should have been shaved.

I had no change of clothes. None of our swelling crowd of court dignitaries thought to offer me anything to wear. They were always cautious about seeming too well-disposed towards me lest Cixi and her supporters interpreted it as a desire to help get power back into my hands. Not even the eunuchs really bothered about me. Only Li Lianying made some effort. He was careful that way, knew I was young and that Cixi wouldn't live forever, and so he tried to ensure my favour too.

The rain returned in fierce torrent, sky split and shook, we stopped again and it all streamed down on us and sent the soldiers scrambling under the carts. We wanted to draw water from a well at the roadside but the eunuchs found corpses and severed heads there, so we hurried onwards.

Cixi never complained. Bloated flies flew around us, we sat in a sweltering room at another looted post station, excrement stink wafted from the street, we were unwashed and thirsty, we had no food. Cixi said nothing. She'd said hardly anything ever since we left the Forbidden City.

The district magistrate from the next town arrived. He came in court dress and even knelt at the roadside in welcome, followed every rule of etiquette. It made a strange contrast with the chaos all around. He said he'd ordered the post station to prepare food but the soldiers stole it before we arrived. We ate the little bit of porridge they'd managed to save. The magistrate, whose name was Wu Yong, was still quite a young man and seemed a conscientious official doing his best to keep order. He was the first local official we'd met anyway. The others all hid or fled.

He'd done his best to prepare for us, dressed his little town in fragments of festive look, put red paper with auspicious verses up on some of the gates, but it made me sad in the middle of this desolation. I got a proper room with a real bed to sleep on and Wu Yong brought me some of his clothes to wear. We finally ate a decent meal that evening.

Cixi took Wu Yong with us. She took his cook too. Our number swelled as more and more officials and soldiers arrived. Our soldiers looted just as much as the ones we'd seen on the road earlier. Some were executed as punishment, but there were too many of them and no one could control them all.

We travelled in more comfort now. They finally found someone to shave me in one town we came to. We stayed there a while. Cixi took a liking to Wu Yong and questioned him at length about various affairs. He had the naive honesty and frankness of someone who didn't yet know the ways of the court and seemed to think everyone was as honest and sincere as he was.

I sensed his puzzled glance on me at moments. Whenever we stopped, we called the grand councillors for audiences and kept up a semblance of government. Cixi always asked me to put my questions first and I said the same thing every time, asked if the lands were at peace and the crops were good. It was all that ultimately mattered, like in the ancient days of Yao and Shun, peaceful fertile land and the people well-fed and content.

I looked stupid. I never spoke other than to ask my two questions and present my respects to Cixi, so Wu Yong never had the chance to work out if I really was as stupid as I appeared.

The time passed slowly and idly. I had no books to distract me and sat motionless and empty. No one paid me much attention and I ignored them too, sat on the floor and drew random scrawls on sheets of paper. Perhaps because there was so much empty time for thoughts now, the things I normally suppressed swirled thicker in my head. Defeat, betrayal, humiliation and loss, they came out in the demons and spirits I scribbled on the paper, bringing to life all the things I'd learned from the eunuchs with their tales of the teeming multitude that kept them frightened at night.

Some of the insect bites and sores from the damp, chafing clothes turned pus-filled and foul, as if the festering stench of these days was eating right through me. When I closed my eyes, I could still feel the rocking motion of the carts on the narrow mountain trails and hear the tinkle of the little copper bells around the mules' necks. A quiet elegy for our sinking country tinkled in my ear as the scenes rolled by again and again in my memory. What Grand Council business was there to discuss when the towns were burnt and plundered and severed heads lay in the mud around a roadside well?

We were past those horrors now. The skies cleared and the mornings were edged with autumn crispness. The mountains rose stark against the blue, and were I still a boy with dreams I'd have felt my heart seized by the majesty of it all. Pujun enjoyed it, anyway, sang his happy thoughts in a clear, strong young voice. All his playthings and amusements had joined him now and were piled into more carts behind.

I wasn't a carefree boy like Pujun though, and it didn't matter how grand the view, I saw my own memories spin before me in endless bleak circle. These princes and officials around me were fragments of my shame and hate. They disgusted me. They resumed so easily the motions of court life and government business from one little town to the next and seemed to have already wiped from their minds that not long before we had been hungry, dirty and sleeping in whatever corner we could find.

Cixi's spirits picked up too. We reached another pass in the Great Wall and the mood took her for a little sightseeing. We all had to go along for the excursion, came through the pass to the wind-scoured landscape beyond, desolate place with barren mountains rearing up around. The sky was deep and pure. The wind whipped us, flung sand in our faces and chased us back to where we came from.

My eyes seized its bold spread even if my heart stayed damp. Walls and rules had kept me in narrow places all my life, but I had travelled far on the roads and rivers that wound their way out of books, poetry and music, all the tales, words and tunes that could wrap vastness in small form and bring it to my sheltered places. I had dreamed of seeing not just my country but the whole world, sailing the ocean to distant lands as Li Hongzhang and Zhang Yinhuan had done.

Li Hongzhang was back in his old role of negotiator again. He'd been down in the south, demonstrating his political astuteness by staying out of the Boxer mess, ignoring orders from Beijing to send troops and refusing to join the war effort. It was tempting to think that had he been more active, he might have been able to influence Cixi for the better, but if Ronglu hadn't been able to, Li probably wouldn't have succeeded either.

Maybe he'd sensed that and had preferred to keep as far away from the Boxer madness as he could. He'd kept out of the way too when my reforms were stopped and I was disgraced. All he got for it was the downward spiral of self-delusion we'd entered ever since then, and now the court came to confront him with the shattered pieces and get him to negotiate a peace agreement with the foreign powers.

As for Zhang Yinhuan, he was dead. They killed him in his place of exile in Xinjiang. It looked like just another murder amidst the general chaos, but the orders came from Beijing. Maybe it was Prince Duan, maybe Gangyi, perhaps even Cixi herself. I didn't want to know who sealed his fate. It was all pus within me, and I was sick of them all. I had no hopes and dreams. If I had to choose, I would have preferred the eunuchs with their stunted, vicious little hearts and I sat with them on the floor and played stupid, no longer caring what anyone thought.

The future looked to me as desolate as the rocky, sand-scrubbed lands beyond the pass. Drought and famine had struck my country in the very first year of my reign when I was still just a tiny boy screaming my fear of the thunder. War, hunger and disaster were my constant. I used to write in my essays and poems for Tutor Weng of my love and concern for the people. But only now did I really see this people for the first time in my life. Peace and good crops, if we could give them this alone it would be a miracle. Ensuring peace and good crops were the emperor's paramount duties. I'd been a studious boy and I remembered my lessons, even if everyone around me had forgotten.

41

Eunuch Liu was losing at chess again. "Master of Ten Thousand Years, you are too clever for me," he sighed, nodding his head slowly.

I gave him a vague smile. "You're not trying hard enough, that's all."

"Oh, I always try as hard as I can," he laughed. "But all my skill is in my hands, not my head."

Liu was the one who used to come to shave me. He caught up with us on the road and Cixi assigned him to attend on me. He brought news from Beijing. The foreigners and Chinese Christians had burned down Prince Duan's residence, together with everyone in it, all his servants anyway, because Prince Duan himself had fled right at the start.

Some of those who'd supported the Boxers committed suicide. Pujun's imperial tutors both killed themselves. One of them, the father of Tongzhi's empress, Alute, who was said to have killed herself after Tongzhi's death, had his entire household take their lives along with him. Liu said the Forbidden City was more or less calm and Tongzhi's consorts were looking after everything as ordered.

My eyes wandered. Normally I was concentrated when I played chess, got absorbed in it and forgot everything for a while. Now I felt tired and distracted. I hated this place. It wasn't so bad when we first arrived in Xian, but then we moved to new quarters and Cixi put me and Yehenara in the same rooms. Only a screen partitioning the middle room kept us separate.

I tried to avoid Yehenara but she always found me. She thought she could wear me down with her stubbornness.

Sometimes I had to throw things at her to make her leave. She seemed to hope that Cixi would yet find some way of forcing me to play my part, turn me docile and make me submit with her as with everything else. Not even Cixi had that power. If I hadn't submitted yet, I never would.

I was careful with Yehenara around, knowing that she reported on my mood and behaviour to Cixi. I did nothing, said nothing, stared out the window for hours and sometimes played chess with the eunuchs. The months passed this way. I knew the eunuchs' whispers behind my back. They thought I was sick in the head, turned into a log, not even really alive anymore.

Maybe I was sick in the head, too disillusioned now to be anything but a log. It was safer to be a log, mute and stupid. Liu saw his luck changing on the chessboard and gave a happy chuckle. I didn't really see the pieces.

Pujun would find himself knocked off the board soon, sacrificed to practical concerns. The warmongers were all falling now, cut away as the foreigners pressed their demands, and Pujun, as one of the main warmonger's sons, would have to go too. Prince Duan would never fulfil his imperial dream.

The days ran together in my head. It seemed sometimes that we'd barely arrived in Xian, and other times it seemed that our journey was already so distant. Naïve Wu Yong was sent off to the south to do some tax collecting while we were still on the road, in Taiyuan. The grand councillors arranged that, plotting to get him out of the way. They had no need for an honest voice, especially not one with Cixi's listening ear.

We reached Taiyuan in the mid-autumn days when the great round moon silvered the night. We too were silvered and splendid by then, our procession rich and grand. We were greeted with feasts and pomp, a fat spread of kindness and flattery that Governor Yuxian threw upon us.

The foreigners sent their list of heads to Taiyuan. Yuxian was on it too. He'd incited the Boxers right from the start, and when he saw their star burning bright in Beijing, he'd rounded up the foreigners in Taiyuan and had them killed. Cixi savoured his banquets and thoughtful gestures and showed him with good favour, but there was no lingering with those condemned. Yuxian made an awkward host before the foreign eyes watching from Beijing.

Cixi wanted to be as far away from the foreigners as possible, fearing they might want her head too. She decided to press onwards, further into the interior. The winter was approaching and we left for Xian.

Unlike Taiyuan, Xian was not just some provincial centre, but had been the illustrious capital of many former dynasties. I hadn't my books to fill the hours, but I saw their pages turn real, catching the echo of the great roll of events of which we were just the latest fragment. We were small in this city, an insignificant stroke in the long chronicle that still seeped across this mountain-ringed plain.

Nearby had been the capital of Qin Shi Huang, the first emperor of China. Here the Tang dynasty had built their great city of Chang An, to which men had come from all the strange and distant countries with tribute, travelling the Silk Road with exotic goods and crossing the seas from Japan in search of learning.

I sat with my dull frozen look and saw only the screen separating me from Yehenara, or the hated faces at the audiences. But history was closer and vaster here, and I could sense the dynasties risen and fallen, all the dawns and twilights. The broad blue skies wore a laughing look at moments, the heavens telling us they'd already seen our sorry performance. They'd seen everything here, every tyranny and treachery, every foolishness and vanity. And who were we? Those emperors of old would have called us a barbarian people, a wild tribe from the outer lands.

The Ming emperors too had thought us a barbarian people to be kept safely on the other side of the Wall. My ancestors crushed that disdain and made our name proud, but it crumbled now like so much else had crumbled before it. Prince Duan, my cousin, was born in the wrong time. Eunuch Liu said all his skill was in his barber's hands, and Prince Duan was the same. He rode his horse swift and shot his arrows with skill. He was a man of movement and vigour but not of thought. He should have lived at the beginnings of our dynasty, when he could have become a bold Manchu warrior and seen his name renowned and praised.

The foreigners wanted him dead but Cixi issued an edict exiling him to Manchuria. The foreigners wanted Gangyi too, but Gangyi died his own death, fell ill while we were still on the road and did not make it to our stopping place. Duke Lan was banished, and some of the others were granted the privilege of committing suicide rather than being executed.

"I've won," Liu gave me a half-smiling half-uncertain look, not sure whether it was proper to beat the emperor at chess.

I looked down at the board. "You have, yes," I nodded.

"Perhaps it is you who was not trying this time," Liu said.

"Perhaps that is so", I agreed.

Wu Yong came back from the south and found his absence hadn't cost him any of Cixi's favour, but he still had much to learn if he wished to keep it. He thought one day to speak in defence of the officials who Prince Duan and Gangyi had thrown in prison for opposing the war during the consultations back in Beijing. They were executed not long afterwards. Cixi turned grim with her stormy look. She gave Wu Yong her version of events.

"Ask the Emperor, he was there too," she said.

Wu Yong did not ask me and I stayed silent. Cixi hated people reminding her of past mistakes and didn't like to take responsibility for wrong decisions. It was easier to cling to a distorted version of events and put the blame on others, and I would not cause trouble for myself by questioning her words.

She liked Wu Yong and soon turned soft again, but I was still nervous inside, feeling my stomach clench tight. I'd never lose it, every time the same. She paralysed me, squeezed me tight with anxiety.

"Shall we have another game?" Liu suggested.

I shook my head, "No, it's enough now."

Liu put the chess set away and I went back to staring into nothingness. I hated my weakness and fear. It all made me bitter. After so many years of trying to be what Cixi wanted, so many years of giving her unfailing respect and submission, she'd believed Yuan Shikai and imagined I'd have the audacity to imprison her. How little faith she'd ever had in me, what little trust she'd accorded my words, and how willing she'd been to believe the lies of others and turn deaf to the heart of the one she'd made her son.

She was kinder now though. The failed war and our sorry flight relieved me a little of my guilt in her eyes. She heaped anger and blame instead on Prince Duan, Gangyi and the others who'd encouraged the Boxers. They weren't there to hear it now.

Sometimes, I still wanted to cry but nothing came. There were no tears in a log. When we were in Taiyuan we had fine quarters in the governor's offices. They'd been built as lodgings for Emperor Jiaqing, who was to pass through the town on his way to the holy Wutai Mountains. Emperor Jiaqing never used them in the end. He died before he could set out on that pilgrimage. Everything they'd prepared back then got sealed away, and when we came, Governor Yuxian had it all brought out, furnishings, ornaments, all dusted off and finally used for the first time.

The Wutai Mountains were not far from Taiyuan. I lay in bed there amidst the finery that Emperor Jiaqing never saw and remembered the legends about Emperor Shunzhi slipping away to become a monk. It was a tempting image in the night to go silent from them all and seek simple shelter in the holy place, run from the futility of what my life had become. I was not so guarded here, not bricked in, and watched closely. There was nothing to go on for, nothing to go back to. I was only thirty and it was sad to live a life so frozen and defeated.

I lay there in Taiyuan and saw myself like Shunzhi in the legends. I'd had that thought before, only the road had been longer. I cried then, small silent tears, because I knew I'd never do it, just as Shunzhi remained emperor until the day he died, forcing his mind to stay conscious through the last of his illness while he arranged his succession. Even as the last crumbling page in our dynasty's chronicles, even as the sunset emperor, I had to bear my fate, stay to the end and watch the night come in. It was Heaven's will.

My dreams were of this broken stuff and my life this fraying fabric, yet there was no casting it aside and going free into some brighter morning. I would always see Tutor Weng and Prince Gong giving me my first lesson in being a virtuous emperor. I would always carry Cixi's voice inside me no matter how far I ran. It was the way of Heaven and I could not go against it. It was as Confucius said: he who wronged Heaven would have no one left to pray to.

42

I sat quietly through the months in Xian, asked about peace and the crops, wished Cixi everlasting happiness and played my part in docile silence. My ears stayed sharp though, and I followed the negotiations and events as best I could, while keeping the thoughts from my face and judgement from my lips. On the surface, I seemed to have been cleared of disgrace and lifted back up into a freer, kinder life, but I knew it was better to play safe and keep my head down.

That list of conditions the foreigners had sent to Cixi back during those days of impending war, and which had so infuriated her, contained one more condition that she did not read out at the audience then – my full return to power.

I only found out about that later. It had always angered Cixi that the foreigners seemed to prefer me to her. The foreigners had smuggled out Kang and some of his friends, got in Cixi's way, stopped the court from tossing me aside completely, and then had the gall to demand that I be put in charge again.

We later discovered that that list of conditions was a fraud. It hadn't come from the foreigners, but most likely from Prince Duan and his allies, hoping to goad Cixi into losing patience and declaring war. The document might have been a forgery, but it lingered nonetheless in everyone's minds, seemingly believable. Even just the hypothetical thought of such demands made the conservatives ill at ease. They didn't want to see power in my hands. They feared I'd be vengeful after all they'd done to me.

They had little cause for fear. I had no more desire to be a hollow plaything in the hands of the foreigners than I had to be an empty figure decorating my own clan's imperial stage. It was one thing to be the devil's apprentice with a chance of stealing the devil's knowledge, but to be the devil's puppet was not a privilege I sought.

I'd read all the historical chronicles of course and knew the countless stories Xian and its surrounding hills could tell. No matter what the crimes and mud Kang and his sharp-tongued friends flung Cixi's way from abroad, it paled beside the truly ruthless women who'd ruled in fact, if not in name, from Xian in their day.

Cixi was a shaky, timid flame compared to their cruel glare. But behind her temperamental eyes were others who could forge and flatter, prod and provoke, and knew that, empty clockwork thing though I looked, something still stirred inside me, and my eye still saw them, still remembered. It was prudent for me to remain humble and harmless. It was the best way to survive.

Sometimes, it seemed as though we would never leave Xian. There was even talk of forgetting Beijing and making Xian the capital once more, as it was so deep inland and hard for the foreigners to reach. I could only smile sadly to myself at the irony. Cixi had reproached me bitterly for allowing others to share with me proposals of this sort. Back then, such words were crazy and seditious. Now, people could speak them as if a normal thing.

Xian became our capital in all but name in any case. The officials trickled in over the months, bringing with them the archives and records, and the court took on a flowing routine that carried away memory's irritating grit in its soothing currents.

Finally, Cixi proclaimed our return to Beijing. Even the foreigners had started urging the court to come back, but Cixi waited until it was certain that she wouldn't appear on any list of heads and no one would force power from her hands.

It was autumn again when we finally set forth on the journey home. We did not flee this ancient capital as we had Beijing. Borne aloft in our sedan chairs of imperial yellow and dressed in all the splendour of our rank, we came in stately file through the gates. No mud, dung and panicked sweat of crowds and mules this time, the streets were lantern-lined and fragrant with flowers. The city walls rose up ahead, the gates wide and clear for our passage. There was no crush of refugees now. The officials knelt as we passed and there was nothing to hinder our way.

We headed for Kaifeng, another former capital of a vanished dynasty, the Northern Song, swept aside by my own people's distant ancestors, who in turn then saw their glory crumble under the Mongol horsemen's hooves.

Some officials on the way gave us a modest reception and diverted funds allocated for our welcome to their own pockets instead. Others squeezed their people for money and greeted us with lavish excess. We'd fled as commoners piled into carts, a few silver coins our only provisions. Now they tried to restore our dignity and erase that unhappy image. The riches flowed as if we'd already forgotten the huge indemnity we'd have to pay the foreign powers.

It wasn't the palaces and feasts that impressed me, but nature's broad sweep. I wished only that this chance had come to me at a brighter and more hopeful age. I'd have been stretched tight with joy to see the mountains unfurl, the rivers tumbling or drifting wide and slow, the sudden cliffs and caves and the smears of autumn colour. I'd have thrown my arms wide to embrace it, cast my eyes as arrows to the horizon in every direction, with the world grown vast below and not a wall in sight. It was a journey to have made in happy boyish spirit with lively snatching gaze.

But inside, I was the sky already clouded and the winter growing close. We climbed summits and saw views turn grand, but when filtered through my saddened heart, they were filled with twilight before the sun had even set. I glimpsed the shadows of all the past travellers on these roads, the poets, soldiers, scholars, officials, emperors, exiles, all the spirals of favour and disgrace. The chrysanthemums bloomed and the autumn perfumes floated. I smelt the earth, its damp and deathlike odour, and saw the flowers already faded and gone.

We came down from the heights where the lands had been rumpled ridges running distant, wound our way towards the Yellow River. Beijing was far from our sight but a telegraph drew it close. Li Hongzhang was dead. He'd telegraphed earlier to say he was ill. Others informed us now of his passing. Cixi cried at the news and my heart too was subdued.

Li inspired in me many contradictory feelings and I had often had harsh thoughts for him. In private revenge for his personal loss of face at my hands, he'd joined those who brought me down when I tried to take my country forward. There had probably been missed chances, opportunities lost and buried in personal rancour, but it was all too late now for anything but regret.

Cixi had often defended him and intervened to keep his punishments more symbolic than anything, but he hadn't escaped so lightly over these years. It was a thankless fate he'd shouldered to have always negotiated our defeat. It was courage in a way to wear the spitting looks and take the shameful place before enemy and invader. Although, the way I saw it, he'd played his part too in bringing these humiliations our way, and I felt it fair that he had to share our disgrace and drink our poison to the end, fair that we kept the bitter cup pressed to his lips. At least he never flinched or turned away. Many others would have let it fall.

The court expressed deep sorrow and gave his memory full respect and honours. The sorrow was very real in Cixi's case. Her tears were sincere, and she reminded me of how she'd been when Prince Gong died, her age and sudden weakness showing, her lost and exposed sensation perhaps even stronger now, for there were fewer and fewer of her valued and trusted people left.

Li received tears and posthumous honours. Others received honours they could enjoy here and now, including Yuan Shikai. Everyone knew how much I hated Yuan Shikai. It was always my seal on the edicts proclaiming promotions and rewards, of course, but the generous hand was Cixi's, not mine.

What she gave, she could also take away. Kaifeng was where Pujun left us, stripped of his heir-apparent title. He cried many tears that day. I wasn't sorry to see him go. They could say he was only a foolish boy, not yet polished by the years, but he had a bullying heart and no respect, threatened me, even shoved me, laughed to see me helpless. His hadn't the kind of nature one could polish into something of more noble aspect. He hid no pure jade inside, only layers of spoilt life and arrogant gaze on the world.

One face shone youthful amongst all the officials thronging to Kaifeng to make reports, receive honours and present their respects. My eyes turned keen as I saw his figure enter the audience hall and take his kneeling pose.

My younger brother Zaifeng had returned from a journey far longer than any I'd ever undertake. He'd crossed the oceans and came now to meet us in Kaifeng. One of our Manchu soldiers had shot dead a German baron during the Boxer troubles in Beijing and the Germans demanded that an imperial prince go and apologise in person to the German emperor. They wanted Zaifeng. He was only eighteen, but he was my brother and that had weight in the Germans' eyes.

We were not brothers by the same mother and I had never had much chance to really know him. He inherited my father's title, a boy still when my father died, and had become the second Prince Chun. I had only a faint notion of what world he kept inside him, but even through the audience formality I sensed a widening in his eyes and new sparks of knowledge that had not been there before. He seemed to have grown older and become more serious.

I wished I could have taken him aside in private and let him tell me all about his travels. He had seen the German Emperor in Berlin, and he'd played the foreigners' game of protocol pride too, refusing to kneel in the way they desired. He had visited

France and England and seemed to have made a generally good impression on the foreigners.

I couldn't help the murmur of envy that fate had made me emperor and not the one to sail the seas and travel to foreign lands. Cixi was pleased with Zaifeng and gave him a kind welcome. She too was curious to hear his account of the voyage. I listened with interest, but thought it too sad a thing that we and the foreigners knew each other only in this way: they came conquering, and we went with apologies forced from our lips.

Winter approached, snowflakes spotted the ground and whirled in the wind. Cixi's birthday had passed and we were preparing to depart for the final journey back to Beijing. The officials cast anxious looks at the snow-streaked scene out the windows and shuddered with the naked bending trees, but their faces relaxed when the morning came shining and blue. The sun turned bright and the wind was kind, a gentle breeze to ruffle the banners unfurled in long silken stream.

The sky stretched clear above as we sacrificed to the river gods before boarding the boat to cross the Yellow River. It sparkled gaily in the sun that day and the oarsmen sent its waters into bursts of little jewel drops flying through the air.

We travelled north now and reached Zhili Province. Yuan Shikai came to meet us. I tried to make my eyes blind to his presence. He was big in Cixi's favour right now because he had opposed the Boxers and taken modernising steps in his province, opened schools. Cixi was so impressed that she issued an edict commanding all the provinces to follow his example and open schools.

Had I not tried to do the same three years before? Had I not shown Yuan favour too, only to earn his treachery? We needed the schools and I was glad of Cixi's resolute mood, but she could have been this resolute in my summer of reform, before war, ruin and foreign demands came to force her down this road.

My practised smile was slipping and my sadness melted through. They repaired part of the railway line and we were to make the last stretch of the journey by train. One summer morning three years earlier, Cixi listened to me tell her about Yuan Shikai and his army reforms, and we planned our visit to Tianjin to watch the military exercises. We were going to take the train and be modern. But then the chill autumn arrived and Cixi sent the workmen to brick up my already shrunken and guarded world.

The astronomers set the auspicious hour for our return. Cixi feared we might miss it and she was awake and ready with night still thick outside, anxious to get moving. We were already on the station platform when the dawn came.

They'd prepared the train in suitable fashion for imperial conveyance. Cixi, Yehenara and I travelled in separate carriages decorated in keeping with our lofty status. Cixi was eager and inquisitive, welcoming this sudden novelty. I felt only a stinging regret deep inside, couldn't forget that I had already hoped to offer her this same novelty and thrill with the trip to Tianjin that never happened.

I felt something in spite of myself, of course, tasting the gathering speed as we pulled out of the station and slowly picked up pace. The chugging sound and rocking motion washed over me. I pictured the train as a gleaming, steam-plumed arrow cutting a hurried path across the countryside. Laying railway lines was no easy task. Many officials opposed them and local people feared they would damage burial grounds and disturb the spirits. But sooner or later the lines would come, no matter the opposition. This was why I had wanted Cixi and I to travel to Tianjin by train back then, so that people would see there was nothing to fear and would understand that just as they'd once cut canals in long ribbons across the miles, they would now lay tracks for these steam-trailing arrows to fly swift through the fields.

We did not miss the auspicious hour. Throngs of officials greeted our arrival. It was all so splendid, as if we were coming home in triumph rather than returning defeated from inglorious flight. I hurried from the show, knowing I'd not succeed in fitting with the joyful decoration, fleeing straight to the waiting sedan chair and hiding myself behind its curtains.

Much had changed. The people clambered on to the rooftops to watch us pass. The foreigners too came out to view our procession. We never used to have all these eyes on us. Peering through my curtain, I saw all the curious faces straining to glimpse my brief presence. They became a passing blur. I was fixed and still and it was they who flowed by, onlookers, soldiers, even foreign ladies clustered by the city wall. They lost their shape and distinctness. The colours merged into a grey formless mass that rolled on in some direction of its own, away from the road I travelled. My bearers took me with solemn step back into the past.

43

I left all the clock pieces strewn about and went into the yard. There was something I hadn't got quite right yet, and the music refused to come. The dust in the air had gone now and the wind had fallen to a mild breeze that jiggled the pine needles. I wandered a few steps this way and that and undid the stiffness I'd gathered sitting bent over the clock parts.

The day caressed me with its glad cleanness, the sun gentle on my face, and I felt the urge for something wider. Here at the Summer Palace, they'd bricked up parts of my yard too, though those bricked-up places served little purpose now, only reminding me of my past guilt. Eunuch Sun hovered nearby, discreetly watchful. I'd come to a standstill in the middle of the yard and stared at where the tower rose on the hill, shining brightly in the afternoon light.

I stood a long time, hands hanging at my sides, picking out the details, contrasts, all the tiny strokes that fitted together to make the scene. Buds on the trees, small petals of pinkish hue, leaves that rippled gold and green in quick-flitting succession, made me think of the fish in the lake when they flashed and turned for a second near the surface.

Perhaps it was because I'd been staring at the clock parts for so long that the picture seized me in its sudden richness. My eyes had grown sore with the closeness of my work, and now the memory of the broader view flooded back in.

Sun looked almost startled when I finally moved, walked over to the gate and looked toward the lake. I had sat so obstinate with the clock, putting it together and taking it apart, determined to get it right. I had a lot of perseverance and didn't really need to eat or even sleep.

I didn't sleep well at night anyway. Sleep came during the audiences and I didn't fight it, drifting in and out of dreams while Cixi discussed things with the officials. I just had to wake up every so often to say I agreed with her. The officials fell apart into curious fragments and dissolved into my dreams, and it was better that way. I didn't want to see them solid and clear. It was easier to have my senses dulled and go through the motions of my duties with dimmed awareness.

The Hall of Jade Billows was the name given to my quarters at the Summer Palace. It was right close to the water's edge and also very close to Yehenara. I was still watched. Cixi made sure to know always where I was, what I was doing, what I said, how I behaved. It could have looked like simple concern. I was supposed to be sick after all.

Whatever real sickness I had got scant attention. Cixi was well versed in herbal remedies and had the maids and eunuchs pluck certain grasses and leaves that were made into medicines for her use. She would now and then send pills or potions in kind gesture to favoured officials she'd heard were ailing.

I could call the palace doctors to my side but I didn't trust them and I knew that Cixi meddled with their prescriptions. I had little confidence in their abilities anyway. That French doctor had struck me as competent, but he had only come once, and only then because circumstance had forced it on us.

I saw from others' eyes that they perceived in me a sickness of the spirit rather than the body. Time went by and so many now knew only the nervous, mute figure, the little imbecile.

The new foreign ambassadors came to present their credentials shortly after we returned to Beijing. Protocol had all changed now. I sat above the foreigners and officials, Cixi above me. They addressed their words to me as the reigning emperor, but it was to her they spoke. She had never previously been present at such ceremonies. Prince Qing had a smooth look, happy now to know that the days when I'd spring surprises on him were over. I'd never dare be so bold with Cixi watching.

I sat quietly and caught faint flashes of pity in the foreigners' glances when they looked my way.

The old protocol tussles were over. They could dictate their demands now and got all they wanted. They rode right up to the gates of the inner court and came before us in the Palace of Heavenly Purity. This had been the private quarters of Ming emperors and of our ancestors Shunzhi and Kangxi too. It was here that the emperor lay in state for a time when he died. We'd restricted the foreigners to places of less symbolic importance before, while they had always wanted the equal treatment that they never gave us in return.

It didn't really matter now that everything had been violated. The foreigners had desecrated the Temple of Heaven, stolen objects from our halls and rooms and pillaged our shrines. They didn't spare the Western Gardens and the Summer Palace. We found buildings damaged by fire, parks and gardens ruined, precious things lost. It all greeted us forlorn and stripped of home, battered, emptied and cold.

The foreigners thought themselves more civilised than us, but they too failed to live up to the broad words and bright light of their books. Not knowing or understanding our beliefs and culture, they gave them no value, stole them as trophies or curiosities at most, or let them smash and burn. Fire consumed the Hanlin Academy and made ashes of our written treasures. They came to fight people they thought savages, but they were just as narrow and brutal in the end.

As for the Boxers, they were cut down, brave only with the foolhardy courage of ignorance and their misplaced patriotic ardour. Their amulets were no protection, of course, and the red cloth strips they wore mingled with flowing blood. The foreigners killed them, peasants from flood-ravaged or drought-stricken places, hungry men of angry heart led on by vain, ambitious fools. Prince Duan made of them a ragged horde, red-wrapped in fervour, called them an army and sent them to fight, but he did not stay to see them die.

The scars were less visible now, the damage repaired or hidden at least, and the Summer Palace shone. Birds broke the quiet and sun warmed the wood and stone, turning it pleasant to lean on. The shadows would lengthen soon and the light would grow sad.

I returned to the clock pieces strewn on the floor. Eunuch Sun brought me tea but I forgot it and it turned cold. I could get the clock to tell the time once more, but not to play music. The melody was wrapped into a small spiked cylinder that was supposed to start its motion at a precise moment, pressing the little hammers that sounded the notes. It intrigued me how time lay hidden in the notches and springs and the clever way they fitted together.

It didn't work and I pulled it apart again, frustrated, sat staring at nothing, the pieces once more scattered about me. I could only make the time pass but could not set its tune. I felt a wry smile on my lips. They would report to Cixi that this was how I spent my time, sitting on the floor, dismantling and reassembling clocks, obstinate and silent.

Knowing her superstitious heart, she'd read inauspicious meaning into my choice of pastime. Clocks were a symbol of death in our vocabulary. A close coincidence of sound made them a delicate word one took care with lest they strike not just another hour but the end. Only whose end? This was what Cixi would be wondering. Whose final days did I see creeping closer?

It was my own end I feared. My heart trembled in the night and my youth protested when morning came with new fullness. I sensed the slender threads pulling tighter. Spring had come, but they all wanted me to stay in the autumn and the sunset.

I could call doctors to my side, but they'd not give me any real treatment, and I could live seemingly free, so long as I spoke only with whom Cixi wished me to, and only words she wished to hear. Memories were always short. Those new foreign ambassadors saw that perhaps Cixi and the conservatives were right and I was feeble, a colourless creature compared to this vigorous old woman who seemed to have a firmer, clearer grip on events.

She was a reformer now herself anyway. She revived my ideas, orders and edicts, the same ones that she'd earlier repealed and dismissed. They could reform without me, take what they'd thrown aside as my folly and violation of the ancestors' laws, my plans drawn up with the help of criminals, and make it their own. It had taken so much death, suffering and ruin to get them to this point. Even I had begun far too late and had let war and humiliation ride over us before I'd been able to make my attempt.

I didn't spoil her polished new image with unhappy echoes. This belated effort to reform was better than nothing at all, and so I agreed with her proposals and never recalled the past. The reforms would be hers, unstained by the blood of men whose heads had fallen from the executioner's blade, or by exiles whose barbs continued to prick her hatred.

Only I wasn't sure there was much hope left. That ominous clock in pieces on the floor, I'd had it telling time right, but couldn't get the melody to work in harmony. I wasn't sure that Cixi now had either mechanism in her hand, just the surface gleam still shining in what light was left to us. Her informants, Yehenara and the eunuchs, wouldn't see so deeply, wouldn't think that the end I sensed ahead was not just my own but that of our dynasty and our country as we knew it.

In the meantime, Cixi took pains to wash away the foreigners' doubts. Before the ambassadors she was regal and solemn, but the foreign ladies she charmed with a kind and simple manner and they were won over, came full of smiles and sweet talk. Cixi spoke sorrow and regret, made the Boxers and the war a sad mistake that distant Prince Duan and the others who were dead could bear upon their absent shoulders.

The foreign ladies were reassured by what they saw. Not that they would ever see much, only the performance we put on for them. We chose a fitting decor and showed them but a carefully arranged fragment of our lives. Cixi was not in the habit of throwing her world open to others. Even when I had been just a trusting child beside her, she had always kept her thoughts tightly shut away. This was her nature. Others' hearts had to be bright-lit before her, but of herself she gave only the moments of her choosing.

The foreign ladies saw only what she wanted them to see. They saw Yehenara full of grace and simplicity, a smiling young empress and charming hostess at ease with the foreign ways. Jin straggled along behind with the other court ladies, and the foreign women wouldn't have even known who she was. She was an object to be kept safely in the background.

Zhen was more awkward. She was dead but the rumours had flown far. Cixi knew the ladies would not love her if they thought she'd had my cherished consort thrown down a well, so she gave Zhen a noble fate and issued an edict when we returned to Beijing, saying that Zhen sacrificed her own life to protect her virtue.

Many girls, fearing they'd be raped and dishonoured, threw themselves down the city's wells during those chaotic weeks, and the story was that Zhen did too, left behind as the rest of us fled, escaped her locked and barred little hall behind the Imperial Pharmacy and flung herself to her death.

I never did learn for certain what happened that day before we fled the Forbidden City. I knew only the rumours, and I knew too that Cixi had dismissed her eunuch, Cui Yugui, and sent him away from the palace. He was the one supposed to have pitched Zhen into the small, dark circle. He'd obviously become too uncomfortable a presence to have around.

When spring arrived, Cixi granted a special favour to Zhen's family and let them enter the Forbidden City to retrieve the corpse. Concubines' families were never allowed in ordinarily. The only time a consort could hope for a visit from relatives was if she bore a child, and mine had no such chance.

The spring wind was gritty with dust, still cold with ice-touch. I didn't go to see them at work by the well. They burned incense and prayed first to calm the spirits and keep the demons away. The well was narrow and it took them a long time to get Zhen out. They had to break part of it away to get at the body. Jin was there. She'd been jealous of her sister, the only recipient of my favour, when she was alive, but now that Zhen was dead the memory hung sad and she set up a simple shrine by the well, free of any words that might raise questions.

I had grown so numb and indifferent on that long road west. Death had come to Zhen swiftly and I'd barely had the time to realise it before I was on that cart with Pulun and rattling off towards an uncertain horizon. I'd felt dead too, only mine was a slow process, something flaking and crumbling, a tree gone hollow inside, the branches curled and withered.

Now summer reached out its melting caress and let the memories loose. Sky streaked with evening shade and I heard echoes, remembered once more Zhen's plaintive song drifting in the Imperial Garden. Many small recollections, a face alive, a hand still warm, eyes that looked at me with trust, laughter sprinkled through the moments.

I had laughed with her too. I hadn't always been a wooden effigy, and I hadn't been stiff and serious every minute of my life. Sometimes we'd been young and filled with sudden mirth. Sometimes we forgot the rules or for a moment didn't care. Sometimes Cixi had been at the Summer Palace and we'd filled the gloomy narrow places of the Forbidden City with our own small light.

Her family took the body away for burial. Cixi's edict declared her chaste and obedient, praised her virtue and gave honour to her name. No one wanted to live now in the Palace of Great Benevolence. That was where Zhen had lived before disgrace shut her away. Everyone feared her spirit would linger on there, and so the building stayed empty.

By tradition, aggrieved spirits stayed close to the makers of their misery, seeking their revenge, but I knew Zhen better. She'd not linger within our walls, not even to torment us.

44

Sunlight hit the brass of all the foreign instruments and made them seem a dazzling yellow river. There were too many people crowded around, all the princes and officials, the princesses in their streams of silks and jewels, all these swivelling heads and sneaking glances. I hid behind a pair of opera glasses, but they were only small protection.

Everyone had come to see the circus perform, and I was curious too, only I didn't like being on display like this. They all seemed unrestrained, as if the foreign entertainment released them from the usual strictness. It was a novelty, and everyone was lively and impatient for the show. None of us had seen a circus. We hadn't much idea what one even was. This one was Russian. Cixi had heard rumours of their act, grew intrigued and invited them to the Summer Palace to perform for us.

They set everything up in a field, imperial colours, symbols and all, and we took the boats across the lake and came in sumptuous procession to the venue. I was glad of it really, even if shy in the crowd. The Russians were a change. We'd had various theatre troupes come to the Summer Palace, but never a circus.

I stole glances at the faces around me. The American woman artist was there, her expression keen and happy. She'd been with us a while now, painting Cixi's portrait. It was to be sent to some exhibition in America, but was taking a very long time to finish.

The artist spent her days at the palace and her nights at my father's residence nearby. My father never got to live there long. Cixi granted him the residence after he first fell seriously ill. He had to move out of the old residence in Beijing because I had been born there and the place where an emperor was born took on special significance and could no longer be used as an ordinary house.

The artist spent a lot of time among us, but I never spoke with her. She didn't know Chinese. I knew some English, but I wasn't supposed to speak to foreign visitors at all except to deliver the formal minimum required at official occasions.

Cixi gave instructions to make sure no one had any unsupervised contact with me. She told everyone I had a strange shy disposition and might unwittingly offend people. The foreigners probably believed her. They seldom attempted to talk to me, anyway. They never saw me alone and if any of them did think to suddenly ask me something, Cixi would answer for me.

I didn't try to break the rules. The eunuchs, maids and court ladies all had to report to her on everything everyone said and did. I was mostly under her eye in any case. She fretted if I was too long out of her sight and would send the eunuchs to find me and see what I was up to.

For Cixi, having the portrait done was also a big novelty. The American ambassador's wife suggested it as a way of giving people abroad a chance to see just who she was, this empress dowager of China. Cixi was very sensitive about how others perceived her. She hated the thought that people abroad might believe the things Kang Youwei and his friends said, or associate her name with the killing and chaos of the Boxer troubles.

Having portraits painted was nothing so strange of course, but we didn't sit and pose for them. Perhaps it was because our painting style and what our brush tried to seize were different. Even when the Jesuits had painted our earlier emperors, they probably just did so from memory. But this American woman said that Cixi herself would have to sit and pose. Cixi agreed. She had a curious streak that battled with her conservative instincts.

I was impatient for the artist to finish her portrait and leave. Cixi had long since grown sick of it and didn't want to pose.

She was kind and affable with the artist, gave her favours and smiles, but she too wanted her gone. She was always worried the artist might glimpse things better kept hidden, and see what lay beneath the palace life's courteous and pleasant facade.

I wanted the artist to leave so that Yu Geng's daughters wouldn't have to spend all their time keeping watch on her. They were there now in the sunny afternoon, faces eager as the Russians began their show. Yu Geng was one of our Manchu officials. I knew him from when he was our ambassador to Japan. He later went to France, but that was after my reforms were stopped.

His daughters had grown up abroad and they knew foreign languages. Cixi took them and their mother to live at the palace, got them to be her interpreters at audiences with the foreign ladies. It was a strange thing to see them, Manchu girls, arrive in their French dresses. I thought them pretty in their foreign costume. Their dresses had shapely lines that brought out their youth and grace.

They wore their foreign clothes for quite some time. It added different tones to our everyday picture and I always looked out for them, liked to catch sight of them and see what new look they'd put on. After they'd displayed their French wardrobe enough, Cixi made them Manchus again and they now dressed the same as the other court ladies.

The Russians brought out trained animals. They were very obedient and performed fancy tricks, but their eyes were sad. They did the same thing every day under their masters' gaze until it was a perfected routine. It was just forced repetition.

We had no circus masters here, but our eunuchs did similar things. They trained birds to fly not into the skies in search of freedom when released from their cages, but to return to the one who set them free. That was one of Chief Eunuch Li Lianying's tricks to make Cixi happy. She let the birds go free every year on her birthday, and every year some of them would circle briefly in the sky and return to her side.

The artist seemed quite absorbed in the circus but it was hard to tell from her expression what she really thought of it. We had no experience of these foreign things and so no gauge of quality, and I was curious to know her impression. There were so many people around and everyone had their eyes on the performance, but I did not dare approach the artist myself. I told Sun, my eunuch, to ask her in English what she thought.

I'd started teaching my eunuchs English again. I spent most of the time at the Summer Palace in my Hall of Jade Billows and that name described my feeling well, a rippling sea inside me that lifted me and let me fall in incessant motion. It was hard after my defeat to muster the will and energy to discipline myself and not let the hours pass unused. Everything hung heavy with futility and I had no heart even for the books I loved.

That was why I was so glad of Yu Geng's daughters. They stirred something in me and were a little bit of dawn amidst the shadows. They knew English and I began to catch them with my questions, asking them how to say this and that.

They knew music too and played the piano. We had some pianos at the Summer Palace and I asked them to teach me. I had learned to play Chinese instruments on my own, but I wanted to try foreign instruments too. The girls taught me some waltzes and I carried the lightly turning melodies in my head and let them sound inside me when my heart grew sombre. They had a soothing feeling. I liked the touch of my fingers on the keys, the sense of merging with the instrument and the music. Only there was often too little time and I had to learn in brief snatches.

I liked to ask the girls about the customs and life of Europe. They were our own people and so I was allowed to talk to them, but at the same time they were like foreigners and had much of interest to tell. I spoke with them about the different countries and ways of doing things, and listening to them, I felt regret sigh in me that I had this searching nature but was so confined.

I wanted really to know jade billows, travel tossing ocean roads and see distant Europe grow solid on the horizon.

Cixi had revived one of my old plans and was sending young Manchus abroad to study. Kang Youwei had proposed it just after the war against the Japanese. I remembered it among the reform ideas I'd sent out to the provincial governors. It had been one of my cherished hopes. I'd wanted not just our Manchus, but as many young people of talent as possible to study abroad. That had seemed to me a surer way towards strengthening our future, not chipping away at our riches but adding to our wealth, like these daughters of Yu Geng. I saw they were educated girls, and even Cixi was making use of their foreign learning and saw its benefits.

Were I still just the prince's son I'd been born, I would have been eager to be among those young Manchus chosen to leave for foreign lands. I was a student by temperament and would have been delighted to pursue learning among the foreigners. Were it not for strange twists of fate, I'd never have been emperor, and I maybe should not have been. I did not have the right qualities. But then again, had I not become emperor I was not sure I would have lived to even think these things.

I saw much less of Yu Geng's daughters since the artist had arrived. They came and went with her every day, lived at my father's residence with her, there to help her, translate for her and keep her under watch. Cixi hoped the artist would not sense she was under constant surveillance, and it seemed she didn't from what we could tell. Yehenara spent a lot of time with her. The foreigners all liked Yehenara. She was sweet in manner, took the trouble to learn their etiquette, sat down at table with them and played the charming hostess.

I missed not having the chance to talk a little with Yu Geng's daughters and I especially regretted the lack of occasions to practise English and music. But it was Cixi's order that they stay with the artist. She trusted them and grew quickly fond of them.

The older of the two in particular won Cixi's favour and seemed to think she could use it to encourage reform. In small things like having the portrait done, it was possible. I would have liked her to succeed in something bigger, but such dreams were an illusion.

She thought it enough to sow yearning for change in Cixi's heart, but it was not as simple as that. Even were it her burning desire, Cixi alone hadn't the power to truly reform our country. The officials stalled and played on her cautious instincts. They all fed off each other's wariness of change, locked in a trap of inertia. Many of the officials opposed reform, while Cixi realised now it was inevitable but hovered around the edges, convinced that she'd yet find a way to balance the new demands with the ancestors' legacy as she understood it.

There was a pause in the circus and the bands began to play. They were Chinese, the men in rows puffing away on the foreign horns and trumpets. One of the bands was trained by the Englishman who'd long since been running our maritime customs office, and the other was Yuan Shikai's military band. Yuan had used Germans to train his soldiers and he'd probably got them to teach his musicians too. They played foreign martial tunes.

Yuan really did supplant Ronglu in Tianjin, but Ronglu moved up to head the Grand Council. He was dead now. Illness took him in another blow that threw Cixi into a silent grieving mood for a time. All her old favourites were gone. Corrupt old Prince Qing headed the Grand Council now, and Yuan was busy with his flattery, hoping to step into the place that Li Hongzhang and Ronglu had left vacant.

Yuan was an unwelcome thought. His smug round countenance took me back to those autumn days of betrayal and despair. They called him modern-thinking and reform-minded, and Cixi too praised him on occasion, but I knew that whatever he did, his only commitment was to himself. If what was good for Yuan happened to be good for the country, he'd support it, but if the country's welfare and his own interests diverged, he'd go with himself first.

Cixi looked around. She seemed in buoyant spirits and appeared to be enjoying the circus. She enjoyed most new things at first and then the novelty faded, and she'd start picking fault in what she'd found so intriguing just a short time before. She had a measure of curiosity but it was not big enough to hold a shifting, swelling world. She'd graft little fragments here and there on to our swaying construction as it suited her, but to reinforce the whole by adding some pillars of foreign inspiration was beyond her will or ability.

It was the small fruits she culled, and most of the time she found their taste not nearly as sweet as what our own gardens gave. Yu Geng's daughters could paint some new streaks in her world, but they couldn't build her anew. It was too late for that. She was almost seventy and had lived most of her life bound up by rigid laws, locked in frozen ritual and tradition. It was not going to melt away so easily now.

The artist was polite of course. She told my eunuch that the circus was good and sent a smiling look my way. I put the glasses back to my face. The artist's eyes seemed to reach deep. Maybe it was her profession that made it so. She seemed to study us all. I wasn't sure I would have liked her to paint my portrait. It was never proposed anyway. And maybe she wouldn't even be interested. I was not a fascinating figure like Cixi.

45

I was alone as I could be, only the eunuchs trailing me. At the Summer Palace, I at least had a little more freedom of movement these days. Cixi's spies surrounded me anyway, reporting on my every mood and move.

I came round a building, into a courtyard I thought empty at first, until I caught sight of a slight girlish figure leaping about in a corner, quite oblivious to her surroundings. It was Yu Geng's younger daughter. She'd taken her shoes off and was dancing barefoot, jumping and twirling like the European woman in my music box long ago.

"Ah, the little mischievous one," I said with a smile, approaching her stealthily.

She whirled around in fright and was about to drop to her knees in the ritual greeting.

"No need." I gestured for her to stay as she was. "So, this is your dancing?"

She blushed. She'd been copying the kind of dance steps she'd seen in Europe – what they called ballet.

"Do they do it barefoot?" I asked, glancing at the shoes on the ground nearby.

She blushed even harder. "They have special shoes," she said. "But in these shoes" – she gestured at the dainty shoes affixed to a wooden platform that the court ladies wore – "it's not possible to dance. It's easier barefoot."

"I'm sure it is," I nodded in understanding. "But people here don't dance. They don't take their shoes off and leap about barefoot. You little mischievous one, I know you'd rather be free to whirl about, but you're in the palace. It's best to be careful."

She nodded, gathered up her shoes and put them on again.

I hated being the warning voice and dampening presence. I only did it because I didn't want the girls to suffer. Cixi liked them and showed them much favour, but I couldn't forget how fond she had been of Zhen too at first, finding her a lively, talented, clever young girl.

Cixi wouldn't have welcomed the barefoot ballet in the courtyard though. It was her time of sombre colours and sorrowing season. She repeated the rituals in memory of Emperor Xianfeng, a young emperor now more than forty years dead. She remembered him alive, of course, as vividly as ever, and her old grief would still surface at these moments.

This time, her tears and prayers were not for her long widowhood alone, but also for the latest war. Once again, our country was a battleground, though we were not even combatants on this occasion, merely bystanders watching as Russia and Japan went to war in Manchuria and did their killing on our soil.

We were powerless. Manchuria was ours in name only. The Russians had sent a lot of troops there during the Boxer troubles and never withdrew them after peace was signed. Japan looked on, unhappy. Both countries had their greedy eyes on the region. All we could do was declare neutrality in the conflict and try to guess who might win.

A sense of panic set in as the war flared and spread. Eunuchs started fleeing again, like they had during the Boxer troubles. Telegrams arrived with news of the battles. Cixi, as always at such times, spent long hours shut away, worried and distant. Wordless, she received my kneeling greetings in the mornings, and I'd soon retreat and leave her to pick through her thoughts and cares.

She called frequent audiences to question the officials and military commanders on developments, glancing at me too now and then to see if I'd offer some opinion or advice. Her eyes wanted it at moments, seemed even to plead with me all of a sudden to share the burden with her, but I didn't stray beyond my usual words of agreement with her decisions. I stood at her side each morning and read the memorials and telegrams, adding my insubstantial remarks where required, and continued the routine we had worn smooth over these last years.

I only looked indifferent to it all. In reality, I followed every step of the war as closely as I could. That pleading look in her eyes was an illusion. We were all trapped in one way or another. I had been willing to carry the burden, but she hadn't trusted me to do so. She'd trusted those who called for her to take it on her own shoulders. There wasn't any going back, only biding time, and I left her, old and weary, to carry this weight that no one wished her to share with me anyway.

I did care deeply about what was happening, but I had learned my part and I knew no other would be accorded so long as Cixi remained alive. In any case, there seemed very little we could do. Our dynasty was failing and the cracks were growing.

About the only good thing was that the artist had left and Cixi's portrait went off to America. Yu Geng's daughters had time again and my English made new progress. The older girl gave me lessons, read me dictation and tried to teach me correct pronunciation. Cixi got her to translate foreign newspaper articles into Chinese, mostly about the war, but sometimes other news came up.

She came to me one day with one of the newspapers she'd been translating for Cixi. I followed her guiding finger down a column of small black print until my gaze seized the familiar name – Kang Youwei. He was in Singapore. We hadn't known for certain where he'd got to after fleeing abroad. There'd been rumours of all these assassination plots and uprisings he was supposedly organising, and our officials had made attempts to track him down and seize him abroad or lure him back to China. I knew very little for sure about all these affairs. I tried to find out more, but I had so few means of getting information and had to be extremely cautious about anything to do with Kang.

"She's seen this?" I asked, referring to Cixi.

De Ling – that was the older girl's name – nodded. "She had me translate this for her this morning."

She looked at me as though imagining that now I'd open up and talk with her about Kang, those three brief months of my reforms, and about my own thoughts about all that had happened since.

But I didn't. I trusted her, but I didn't trust the many spies around. I didn't really believe all the stories about Kang and his plots. It seemed that everyone was organising assassination attempts these days and there were always rumours of revolutionaries wanting to kill us. Cixi fumed about foreign governments sheltering criminals, but to no effect. The court set a bounty on their heads, but the criminals kept themselves safely out of sight.

With or without wars and plotters, the autumn always brought its first damp hot days draped in old mourning forXianfeng, and then the moon grew round and perfect and I performed more rites and the lanterns filled the evenings with light. The leaves decorated our strolls around the park with their brief burst of colour. The gold soon dimmed and autumn's crimson cloak faded. The only colour that stayed after that was the festive red of paper decoration for Cixi's birthday.

I was still the filial son and gave the order for lavish celebrations as the cold crept in. Seventy years was a meaningful mountain of time, what they called "the rare age", for so many lives never made it that far. She was unlucky yet again. Her jubilee dates always seemed to coincide with war. The French had spoiled her fiftieth birthday, the war against Japan had ruined her sixtieth, and now here was this conflict in Manchuria to cast a pall over her seventieth. She said we should be quiet and modest at this time of hardship for our people, and I had to make a due show of insisting that we follow tradition and give her a proper display of our respect with all the extravagance that entailed.

The days had turned to snow by then. We stayed on at the Summer Palace a little longer. The rooms had grown cold and the gardens bare, but Cixi lingered, not yet wanting to embrace the winter or the Forbidden City's dark confines. Here we had light at least. The buildings and grounds were lit now by electric light, while at the Forbidden City we still used candles.

Cixi liked the snow. I had too once and remembered trying to hide in its falling flakes as a boy and sink into its unswept softness. I'd tried to make the eunuchs leave it where it fell, stopping them from clearing it away, wanting to do as Kangxi had advised and wear each season as it came and not shelter in false comfort that would only make me weak. But I'd had purpose then and more will to forge myself stronger.

Cixi had her own plans for this white-brushed world. She wanted to capture it in the camera she'd grown to love.

That too was the doing of Yu Geng's daughters. They roused her curiosity when she saw their photographs, and they got their brother to bring in his camera and take pictures. It appealed to Cixi in that it was so much faster and more flexible than a portrait. She would hurry now through duller duties, eager to run to this new amusement. She posed on her own, with the court ladies and even with the eunuchs, dressed herself up as Guanyin, the Buddhist embodiment of mercy and compassion, and thought up backdrops and settings, just as she did for the theatre.

She never suggested I too pose with them. In truth, I would rather have learned to use the camera myself than to pose for it. Its appearance in the Summer Palace's life sent sad echoes through my heart. Little Zhen was still just an impulsive girl when she fell in love with that alluring box that turned the world upside down, reversed all its shades and put it back together in such perfect likeness. She was always recreating herself in various guises, and she too had got the eunuchs to join in, roamed the Western Gardens looking for scenic spots to offset her laughing face.

She had been too soon with her passion. It was indecent, a "devil's art" when she'd sought to learn its secrets. Now, it was innocent and fun, one of Cixi's favourite pastimes. But Cixi did not like to look back into the past. We didn't speak of Zhen. Cixi flavoured the past with whatever made it easier to digest. There was a set version of events, and we kept to it or stayed silent.

De Ling came to me with her English books, but I could see she was distracted.

"It's my father," she said, when I asked. "His health isn't improving. He wants to go to Shanghai and get treatment there."

I knew that Yu Geng had been unwell lately and that Cixi had been sending the palace doctors and all kinds of potions to his bedside.

"And you'll go to Shanghai with him?"

She nodded. "That's what he wants. I'd worry about him if I didn't go."

I knew what it felt like, this separation. I still remembered my own father dying in spite of all Cixi's attention, and I remembered my crushed heart in the dawn, listening at audience to the updates on his worsening health and wanting to be just a son and not a sovereign far away at the moment of need.

"The thing is," De Ling added after a moment's thought, "I do think I can be useful here. The Empress Dowager is well-disposed towards me, and I feel that I should make use of that and do my bit to help the reform effort along."

I looked around. The duty eunuchs this evening didn't include any who I knew to be obvious spies.

"It's an illusion," I said quietly. "You'd do better to go to Shanghai. Take your talents somewhere where you can put them to better use. Here, you'll never do more than provide a moment's novelty."

She stared at me a while and let out a sigh.

"Are you sure?"

"Yes, I'm sure."

I knew Cixi. Just as she rearranged all the decoration whenever foreigners came to visit, she'd liven our backdrop with a dab of foreign notions here and there. It wasn't worth the sacrifice of happy youthful years. Our life was novel to the girls at first but it would soon become dull and they'd lose her hopeful glow.

They did not belong in our world. Even dressed in Manchu clothes, they stayed that little bit foreign at heart. I loved in them that note of otherness that chimed amidst our routine gestures.

"If you stay," I added, "she'll arrange a marriage for you."

De Ling nodded slowly, her look turning serious.

Cixi would surely find some Manchu noble for her. She was of marrying age and Cixi never tired of tying people together with her marriage thread even if it chafed and hurt them. She married off the nobles, the palace maids and sometimes even the eunuchs. She wed a cousin of mine to Yehenara's younger sister in a marriage that ended in disgrace. She was quick, too, to tie down my brother Zaifeng after he came back from Europe, married him to Ronglu's daughter, and Zaifeng dutifully pretended happiness that was not really there at all.

As for De Ling's younger sister, my "little mischievous one", she brought such smiles to my face with her spontaneous ways. She had a bittersweet echo of Zhen about her, Zhen as I'd first known her, singing alone in the garden or becoming my friend by donning a eunuch's garb.I wanted her to keep dancing. I didn't want her to become like the birds the eunuchs trained to soar glad into the sky, circle a moment and return to the waiting cage. She wasn't like Zhen, hadn't entered through the Gate of Chaste Obedience, bound by our laws never to return to the other side. She could leave and I would not keep my fingers closed around her. She was not the music box girl to twirl for my delight every time I opened the lid.

In the end, Cixi's pills, potions and palace physicians were all powerless to hold Yu Geng and his family in Beijing. She realised she couldn't delay them any longer. She let Yu Geng go and his family followed. They departed on the day and hour Cixi chose as auspicious. She looked sad to see them leave.

"Good luck," was all I said by way of parting words. I said it in English and watched them a moment, hoping they would manage to keep their world broad and free. They would have oceans and music and foreign sights. I had the fasting time ahead, and sacrifices to prepare for.

46

Darkness cloaked the Temple of Heaven. The night shook in the wind, torch flames trembled, trees stood black and thinned by winter. Our line of dark figures moved in slow procession. It was time for the grand rituals.

Nothing spoke now of those days during the Boxer troubles when the foreign soldiers filled these grounds and buildings with their soldiers and made off with the things they found there. The healing years had passed and everything was as before, ready for the prayers and sacrifices that linked us to the wider universe beyond, and also to emperors and kings all the way back into the depths of time.

My tread was slow and stiff. Emperor Qianlong reached the age of seventy before he finally found the way too long and had a shortcut made, the entrance to which was closed now. No emperor since had ever gone through that gate because Qianlong forbade it to anyone still short of the requisite age. I was far from seventy but my body protested and my legs were swollen with pain. I made an effort though to slice away these distracting things, to push my body's ills from me and leave the heart untainted. I entered the Palace of Abstinence to prepare in the silence.

Mine was a nature made for abstinence. The ritual calendar was full of these fasts and I had never found them hard to bear. It did not grieve me to renounce the delights of flesh or table. Heaven had made me only half a man, and the pleasures of banquets were lost on my indifference. I had so little to renounce anyway. If anything, I gained something during these ritual moments, tasted a sense of shelter and purpose I little knew elsewhere.

No one but my eunuchs could follow me through these doors. It was the same at the Forbidden City, and I often felt my spirits lift when I entered the Palace of Abstinence there and knew myself shielded from even a glimpse of Yehenara's spying eyes and tattling tongue. I was shut away from Cixi too and could savour the moment, unfold in timid blossom and open up the tendrils of hopes and feelings spared by the chill.

Cixi shared my road as far as she could take it. We lived at the Summer Palace most of the time, but the altars and temples were all in the Forbidden City or beyond in the quarters of Beijing. She did not want to let me go anywhere alone and so we all moved back and forth as the ritual calendar demanded. It was simpler in winter when we lived in the Western Gardens and there was not so far to move.

But her road had its limits. The Temple of Heaven was mine alone. Cixi couldn't follow me out and take the road south, not that it really made much difference, for she always had her loyal eyes and ears around me anyway, even now, there among the eunuchs, officials and imperial relatives.

My whole life had been abstinence these last years, an endless chain of fasting days. As I feared, Yu Geng's daughters had been my last bright leaves and scented petals before drab winter set in. Their departure seemed just a short time before in my memory, but the months had already become years and I'd had little happiness since then.

The wind howled outside, blind and cold as it threw itself against the walls. I was on my knees to beg the ancestors' blessings, but my heart was unsteady, rocked by all the recollections the wind seemed to hurl through the cracks. Cixi was with me in spirit, even if not physically present. I saw not the tablets with my ancestors' names, not the offerings, incense and candle glow, but Cixi's dark eyes and that way they had of veering between mother's tears and punishing lash. What could I implore of my departed forebears? Her voice was louder, her light shone stronger, and I had scarcely even known how to stand beside her, only how to kneel in greeting, guilt or disgrace.

We did need the blessings of Heaven and ancestors. We were weak and our road was unsure. Were Cixi a man and were she emperor, she'd have had the right to use Qianlong's shortcut gate here at the Temple of Heaven, for she had passed her seventy years. She'd have been the first since Qianlong to do so. None of the emperors after him had lived so long.

He had perhaps lived too long, long enough to grow complacent and sink into the soothing image his favourites spun for him. Perhaps this was not so much Qianlong's fault, but simply that old age naturally preferred the picture of a past unsullied and a successful work complete. Even Kangxi had grown weary over sixty-one years on the throne and had closed his eyes to troubles, sighing that to deal with them all would only create even more problems.

Cixi thought highly of her abilities as a ruler, but splendour so often proved a short-lived thing, and I doubted she could succeed in the task she'd taken on. Just as the prayers never had effect unless they came from a sincere heart, so reform had to come from a hand that genuinely wished it, not just out of urgency and as a last resort, but out of firm conviction that this was ultimately the safer, surer road.

This wasn't the case with Cixi. She thought it would be like the electric lighting at the Summer Palace, adding new shine to familiar surroundings and pouring greater light on a life otherwise unchanged.

Life was changing on the surface to be sure, and much faster and more dramatically than anything I'd been able to do with my small scraps of power and Cixi's restraining hand constantly on my shoulder. But that was because the rivers were about to flood and the officials were all hastily trying to build dykes to hold the waters back.

Looking through the chronicles, so much in our history had been about waterworks, dams, dykes and flood prevention.

Ability to manage the rivers and their temperamental flows played a huge part in determining who had been a good emperor and who a selfish, spendthrift fool.

I wasn't a good emperor. I'd done not even a fraction of what was needed, aware of the resistance I'd meet. Perhaps I really should have been the plotter they imagined, with soldiers at my beck and call and enough courage to seize the night and put Cixi into the gilded confinement into which I'd found myself locked instead. But I hadn't had that kind of courage or desire, and we would have had to fight not a single swift battle but many.

The court had felled heads, filled prison cells and sent people into flight after my reforms were defeated, but that was only a small trickle of blood compared to the swollen stream I'd have had to set flowing if I had done what they accused me of planning. How many reformers had there been, after all, and how many more people ready to struggle to the bitter end for their crumbs of privilege and certainty?

Kangxi had been decisive when young, audacious even, and Yongzheng fought painful battles for the changes he sought, but I was not them. I was Zaitian, the tranquil flow and gentle current, the timid boy afraid of thunder and loud noises. I was the emperor's little cousin who, had it not been for Cixi's destiny-changing hand, would have faded quietly away, my mother never understanding why her love and fear mingled in such a sorrowful result.

My mother left me something of herself that night they came to take me from my sleep. She gave me her sudden oscillations, her frozen silent aspect that broke abruptly and violently, like that pond in the Imperial Garden where the rainwater burst in fat flood after the storms.

I had little to be proud of, no more than helpless futile gestures that had brought me nothing but humiliation and defeat. There was nowhere else to pour out my anger. Before Cixi I stayed quiet and meek, true to the name she'd approved for me before she ever knew I'd become her son. I still woke the eunuchs at night, cursing at the words I read in my sleepless hours, memorials thick with stupidity and deceit, made them jump in fright when I'd slam the table or smash what came to hand, but that anger was those same streaming waters from the pipe's mouth, leaping into the pond and going no further.

I failed to pray with clear and concentrated heart. My thoughts scattered and my body was unworthy, not solid enough to hold my will together. It was time to wash and put on the ritual robes. The sky was still dark as we began our procession again in a solemn stream, ponderous music ahead, nervous flames and strange-lit faces around me.

I mounted the Altar of Heaven, took my place in the centre. Unlike the other ritual places, here there was no roof, just the dawn-edged sky above. This altar modelled those of all the past dynasties in their past capitals and mirrored in its stone circles the universe around us. This small central ring was the symbolic summit of our world. Above me was Heaven, and I took my place now on behalf of all that lay below, all the lands and peoples who looked to me to pray for their welfare.

I'd had no power for a long time now, and I never really did. But here, I was still the emperor, still the Son of Heaven, and I could only hope that Heaven might look more kindly on this son than did my imperial mother. I knelt as ordered and bowed my head to the stone. Three times I put my forehead to the ground, rose, knelt again, repeated the prostrations, just as my subjects did when they came before me.

I'd performed this rite many times now, but I tried to make it precious and new each time, not let it become worn and lose its meaning. If I was still Cixi's obedient son, I was still Tutor Weng's diligent pupil, too.

I heard that he had passed away. I did not see our later conflicts now but recalled his earlier words. He never achieved his hopes with me, and I never achieved the dreams his training had led me to imagine should be mine. I failed his expectations, and he left me disappointed and frustrated. And yet there were truths that never faded and lessons that stuck fast. I might have been even more despondent, grown indifferent and not even tried at all had he not pushed me. He'd been right to always nudge me from my sorrows and remind me of the people.

I'd had hardly any notion then of who they really were, this people, knew nothing of their lives. It was only later that events threw me into their midst for a brief chaotic moment, as we fled from our mistakes. My reign had brought them little good and I had failed them in my attempt to strengthen their foundations and brighten their future. It was all I could do now to pray for them in earnest and beg Heaven's protection.

The sky was starting to change as dawn firmed. I felt weak in the blustery remains of this night. The wind rose and fell and bit my fingers as I raised the ritual jade in offering. Even with all Tutor Weng's lessons, it was hard at times to keep myself from slipping completely into apathy. I had to force myself to do this more and more these last years.

There was nothing to wake for. I continued my study on my own after Yu Geng's daughters left, read my English books, sometimes put my fingers to the piano keys and tried to recall the graceful waltzes they'd taught me. I read all I could on many subjects, attempted to follow the world and keep my mind nourished. But sometimes I despaired, and then I'd sit and stare blankly, a wooden thing again, motionless for hours.

My days flowed through the clockwork routine and from one rite to the next, and it was hard to keep them real and give them purpose. But I would pray for my people as best I could. Heaven had thought to entrust them to my hands and make my quiet voice speak on their behalf. It was a strange fate that never should have been mine, and I had not the stature to bear this load. But I would not deny them my sincerity at least, would not leave the ritual hollow.

I was alone at the centre of the altar, but conscious of all the faces unseen and names unknown whose hopes I carried. I was not the "brilliant succession" my dynasty had sought. I was the fading light, and I had to muster my strength now to send my small flame skyward. I lifted my eyes in silent appeal to the blackness above.

47

Beijing filled with fires. The spring usually brought wind and dust. Now it brought choking heat and smoke that made it hard to breathe. Some said it was Heaven's displeasure, the fire god come down to wreak havoc for a time, and others said it was the revolutionaries up to no good.

The clogged and stuffy air pressed my eyes closed and I saw the eunuchs, the ones I'd had during Cixi's long illness when I was a boy. Laughing, they wrapped me in layer after layer and I sobbed helpless in their hands, dizzy with heat. They hadn't undone me yet. I was still trussed up tight and waited for them to come and release me from this foolish torment.

A soft voice sounded beside me and I thought it my long-ago eunuch Fan, with his eyes sleepless and red from my crying and his sighs that I was too small and fragile a child for him to attend to. It was a eunuch, but just little Li bringing me tea, and I was far from those small boy days. I pushed myself upright and took a peek outside. The hazy sky still let down enough sun to beat into the courtyard. The heat lingered on even after darkness fell, made the night a furnace and kept me from sleep.

"Master of Ten Thousand Years, you still have your medicine to take," little Li reminded me shyly.

I shook my head. "Why take it? It does no good."

The eunuch looked worried. "Maybe, but the Old Buddha always asks. She likes to hear that you are taking your medicines properly."

"Let her ask," I sighed. "You know, I suspect that too much medicine may be even worse than too little."

"Is such a thing possible?" little Li gave me a doubtful look.

"Oh yes," I nodded. "Doctors and potions can help, but they can also harm. By not taking their medicine, you at least maintain the mean. The body might not improve, but nor will it worsen."

Little Li lowered his eyes and said nothing. I could see that my theory didn't convince him. I turned my gaze back to the yard. I felt like I'd swallowed the day's sultry weight and there were hot stones inside me. My back ached and no position was comfortable for long. I wanted to walk and unstiffen myself but even this simple act was hard now, for my legs had swollen in the heat and pained me.

"The doctors of renown from the provinces are on their way," little Li offered, seeing my dejected look. "They will surely bring medicine of greater effect."

"I hope so," I sighed again. "It has been so long now."

Nothing stirred in the heat beyond. The sky had smoky haze but no promise of rain. It had been almost ten years since the doctors from the provinces first came at the end of my brief summer of reforms. They hadn't been brought in to cure me then, only to prove that I was sick and unfit to be emperor. The French doctor had said I wasn't seriously ill and would improve if proper treatment were followed, but it never was. The palace doctors came regularly to take my pulse, each then writing his prescription, and Cixi oversaw it all, chose from among the remedies proposed, and made alterations or additions of her own as she saw fit.

I could do nothing but watch my slow decline, knowing that they were all waiting for me to wilt and fade away. It made it harder to keep any sense of purpose alive. I struggled with the despair that ebbed and flowed inside me and fought my failing health, but it was wearing me down, leaving me glazed and dull.

But it was too soon to surrender. Between the fading chill and the fires that flared, the spring whispered encouragement, and I summoned the resolve to ask Cixi to let me see other doctors. She hadn't been in such good health herself these last months and had lost some of her former vigour. She often looked weary now, her emotions close to the surface and eyes quick to moisten with tears. Perhaps that made her more willing to finally agree and put out a call to the provinces to send their best doctors, as they'd done ten years earlier.

My eunuch was right. The doctors from the provinces did soon arrive and some of them made a good impression. I particularly liked the look of one doctor from Zhejiang who had common sense in his head. I complained that I'd been feeling quite unwell for the last couple of years, but none of the treatment I received ever had any effect.

"That's because you can't just take any old medicine any old how," he said. "It's not the quantity that counts, but choosing exactly the right treatment for the right effect. Taking even a couple of hundred doses of this or that potion won't help, especially not when we're dealing with problems that have built up over time and not just appeared overnight."

He'd already taken my pulse and told me what I could guess for myself, that my general condition was weakened and my kidneys were in a poor state. Cixi was with me, as she always was when the doctors saw me. The doctor from Zhejiang darted glances at her and looked a little nervous, but she sat attentive and still, and let him speak.

"What you say is very reasonable," I smiled at the doctor. "Have you the right treatment with the right effect for me then?"

The doctor proposed some tablets and I gave my strict order to have the prescription drawn up accordingly and not changed in any way. I didn't want anyone meddling with it as they usually did. The Zhejiang doctor pleased me and I felt my hope rise a little at the thought that he would stay now in Beijing and come to treat me.

I forgot though that my wishes mattered nothing and little around me was ever sincere. Cixi wasn't interested in effective treatment – for her own ailments perhaps, but not for me. They came up with an absurd system, organised the doctors into three teams of two doctors each, with each team supposed to treat me for two months. The Zhejiang doctor and another doctor of promising reputation formed the last team, so it would be another four months before they came to treat me.

I had only just started taking the Zhejiang doctor's new medicine and now it was back to the old flood of useless potions and getting told to drink wine by one and chicken broth by another, with no one seeming to have any real idea of what they were doing. They inundated me with their prescriptions in just more of the same senseless routine I'd been trapped in all these last years. I didn't take the medicines they gave me. I already knew it was pointless and I told them so, but no one paid any attention. I despaired of getting through the four months before I'd finally see the doctors I wanted.

It was a wonder I'd still had enough foolish hope to imagine in the first place that Cixi would genuinely try to help me. There was no reason for anyone to make an effort for me. They'd hesitated at first to push me aside altogether because the foreigners had made clear their preference to keep me on the throne, but Cixi was a reformer now and the foreigners had forgotten me over these ten silent years. They thought me just a timid, empty-headed boy. I was observant even if I seemed mute and dull, and I saw how they perceived me.

They could perform the rites without me. When I was a boy, my uncles and cousins performed them in my stead until I was old enough to do it myself. Cixi had already chosen the next emperor. When she married my brother Zaifeng to Ronglu's daughter, she was already thinking that if they had a son, he would be next on the throne.

They did have a son, Puyi. He was not officially proclaimed heir-apparent, as Pujun had been, and for now, he was just my nephew and lived in his father's residence amidst nannies and servants, a tiny boy with no idea of the future already set aside for him.

Cixi sometimes spoke to me in a tender tone, but it was the tone of memory, not of the present. She recalled the boy with timid eyes raised hopeful, eager to earn her praise and put a smile on her lips, the gentle son of quiet manners and earnest heart. She'd felt something for that boy, as much as it was possible amidst the formal restraint of our everyday lives. Her tender tone was the sigh of nostalgia and the lamenting note of regret for a son she'd lost ten years before.

And I, the one at her side these last ten years, the one who came every day to present his respects, walked beside her as they bore her to the audience hall each morning at dawn, shared meals and endless theatre, and played his part in the many rituals, I had been dead to her all this time, only a shadow and echo of her recollections. She'd cried her grief-hot tears for a loyal and devoted son in that autumn a decade ago, when everyone spoke of treachery and lies. Her mourning was old now. I lingered on but had no place or meaning.

I had no family of close bond and a wife I tried my best to ignore. Zhen they had tried to keep from me, and then parted us altogether. I had no children, and the small boy who waited his turn for the throne would be successor to Tongzhi, not me. There was no one to make an effort for my sake and no circumstance that made it necessary.

The heat faded and autumn unfolded its colours. Cixi was no doubt glad to have the provinces' best doctors at her call too, along with their palace colleagues. She had fallen ill with dysentery that summer but was looking better now. I couldn't say as much. I still had the first team of doctors attending me and saw no improvement.

It was the dawn hour when we held audiences. I hated this time more than ever since Cixi had brought devious Yuan Shikai on to the Grand Council the year before. He still carried his whiff of slippery intent and flattery with him. He'd spent the last ten years buying Cixi's growing favour with costly gifts. She'd always fallen for flattery in her need to be loved.

He even sent her a motor car, and a marvellous machine it was too, only there was no way for her to use it because the driver would have to sit beside her and the ancestors' rules did not permit such disrespect, though I figured the ancestors, unlike Cixi, would have simply adapted the rules to the changing circumstances.

The autumn season, the knowledge of ten wasted years passed, and seeing Yuan's smug face brought Kang Youwei drifting into my thoughts. I'd heard nothing about him for some time now. It was near impossible for me to get information anyway. Occasional wisps of rumour drifted in, but he'd become the lesser threat now, and the anti-revolutionary efforts these days were directed against Sun Yatsen, who people claimed was the one behind all the fires that spring.

It was here in this hall that I'd given Kang his single audience. I glanced at the bronze cranes and could still recall his words, his eyes full of haste to seize their chance, his hurrying southern-accented voice. He'd compared our country to a crumbling house back then, said if all we did was patch it up here and there, the rain would sweep in and the ruin would continue. We had to mend the foundation, build it anew.

Cixi and the officials accused me of having been too impatient. I saw my own body crumbling because no one had let me mend it in time and the rot had gone too deep. And I saw my country the same way.

We had perhaps still had a chance ten years before. I'd seen the enthusiasm my reform effort kindled, not among the old guard with their privileges to protect, of course, but among many others. But we'd lost that chance. The revolutionaries were stronger in number and more active than ever now, and they were not ignorant Shandong peasants whose discontent we could take hold of and manipulate in our favour, as we'd tried with the Boxers. They were the very people I'd hoped would form my new foundation – students gone abroad to learn, overseas Chinese with money and skills to invest, young people impatient for change and opportunity.

The court had no need for me now, and these people had no need for our dynasty. We'd failed them. The old slogans returned: Overthrow the Manchu! There was no twisting it round now. They called not just for our removal, but for our murder. There had been sympathy for me as a reformer ten years before, a willingness to support me, even though I was a Manchu, but that was then. Now they wanted to kill me. Time faded the memories and they vilified me too. I was the Manchu oppressor and a hated symbol, my short months of reform too brief a flame to have left any lasting mark.

Cixi forgot now how she had rebuked and scorned me for wanting to discuss things such as parliaments and constitutions. I had left them as just the vaguest future possibilities then, knowing that no one would let me go so far so fast, in any case. Cixi talked of these things herself now, not in hints and whispers as I had, but proclaimed them to the country and sent a commission off to Europe to study the options.

She met resistance too, of course, the officials stalled and obstructed just as they had during my reforms, only unlike me, she could dismiss them without anyone coming along to reverse her decisions. Whether her talk would become reality though was another matter. There were reasons, after all, why ambitious men and women had fought for a place at the summit throughout history, and once there were seldom willing to climb down again and join the masses below.

I could have done it, perhaps. I never had enough power to get such a taste for it, and only wanted to use what I had in the best way I could. Like with Cixi's motorcar, where using it would require the driver to sit as an equal beside his passenger, if ensuring our country's strength and future meant sharing my summit with the people, I was willing to do that.

Cixi's offer to share came too late. The people didn't want it now. They wanted to toss us aside and occupy the summit themselves. The revolutionaries hadn't undermined us, we had done it ourselves, became our own enemy, and instead of rebuilding our foundations, we'd spent years laying the road to our downfall.

It was the thirty-fourth year of the Guangxu reign. In our dynasty only Kangxi and Qianlong had reigned longer. Thirty-four years of lost opportunities. I raised my eyes a little and saw Yuan Shikai. He had all the honours we Manchus could give a Chinese, like Li Hongzhang before him. Would the time come when he too would negotiate our defeat?

It hurt to think about. This was all the thirty-four years of my reign had come to. The foundation was more rotten than ever, with power in the hands of Yuan Shikai and the likes of corrupt old Prince Qing and his son.

Pain grabbed me tightly. I'd been feeling worse these last days, but it came sudden now, gripped me sharp inside. I felt myself go pale, tried to suppress it and stay still and calm on my seat. It was too strong and I felt myself starting to sag. All eyes swung my way. The pain enveloped me and I didn't care how they stared now.

Cixi looked a bit perturbed to see me doubled up and gasping.

"The Emperor has been unwell for so long now", she said to the grand councillors. "Can none of you recommend a good doctor to treat him?"

I clenched my teeth at her words. Just more words for the record, more pretence so that they'd all see her attentive and caring to the end. Good doctors had already come, but she didn't let them treat me.

I heard old Prince Qing speak. "I had a serious bout of illness when I was sixty-nine," he said. "A doctor recommended by Yuan Shikai cured me, a man trained in Western medicine."

Yuan joined in with eager confirmation. I bit my lip in pain. It didn't matter now, and I had no choice anyway.

The doctor came one morning soon after. Yuan Shikai knew a lot of people and they weren't necessarily all traitors and liars like he was. The doctor seemed just that, a medical man, professional and calm. Cixi was at my side as always, watching closely. Her face had its closed-off thinking look. I didn't want to know what was going through her head.

48

The autumn grew cold and we returned to the Western Gardens. I was back on my guarded island, sat watching the evening quiet. All was dusty disorder in the room around me. The eunuchs made no effort now, didn't even pretend. They were out of sight, gossiping in their corners no doubt. It only took a few days for discipline to fall apart.

They sensed their master slipping away and shrugged off their dutiful mask, turned lazy and insolent. It was just like back when I was a boy, Cian in her coffin, and Cixi sick in bed. She'd taken to her bed again now. She had tired herself out with theatre and ate too much fruit and rich food at her birthday celebration, which brought on a relapse of the dysentery she'd had in the summer.

From what I could gather from the scraps of rumour that came my way, it sounded serious. She'd always prided herself on her vigour but that was crumbling fast. She was old and had been carrying the burden of government a long time now.

The sky was aflame. One of my clocks began to chime, striking the hour before its time. My senses sharpened and I heard them all ticking away, all my many clocks that had measured out the long days and years of my humiliation. I sighed. They were all getting out of time and some of them had stopped altogether. I'd been too unwell to get up and set them right, and the eunuchs were no help.

But I smiled a little at the clock's tinkling chime. I was feeling better now. This was no thanks to the first team of doctors, who were as useless as ever. But Yuan Shikai's doctor came every day and I took his medicine, despite my initial misgivings. In the state I was in it was worth the risk. Fortunately, the medicine was working, the pain retreated and I sensed that I was finally starting to improve.

The sky glowed rosy. The setting sun threw a flaming carpet across it a moment and then snatched it away. The change was abrupt, the burning clouds so fast extinguished and the light so swiftly dimmed. It had often seemed that Cixi would last forever, like the immortals of legend from her fairy theatre world, or the saintly incarnation of mercy flowing from age to age. She'd float forever in the lotus lake, dressed up like in the photographs she'd had done of herself at the Summer Palace.

But no, no matter how many thousands of years they wished her, no matter that she was Old Buddha and a string of virtues, and the long-suffering mother of us all, that birthday fruit had got the better of her. I knew my senses waited for more than just the ill-adjusted chimes and ticking of my clocks now. One of these days, the wail would go up, taken from palace to palace until it reached even my little island. All the maids, eunuchs and ladies of the court would howl in grief and the officials in their robes and beads would dissolve in laments.

I would cry too and come weak from my bed, pale after sickness, white in my mourning clothes, and would prostrate myself before her cold remains. Always the good son, I'd keep vigil beside her coffin. They'd lacquer her up inside with pearls and precious things. She'd become the phoenix flown away to the western paradise of Buddhist promise, and leave behind empty rooms where I'd no longer go to kneel in filial duty, and an empty throne in the audience hall, still echoing her presence of nearly fifty years.

The monks would pray and chant. She'd lie shrouded in auspicious symbols as the mourning days passed. We'd fill the sky with flames lit by our own hands, scatter paper wealth to follow her on her journey west, burn paper effigies of boats and carriages, maids and eunuchs and all the valuable and pretty things she'd want in the next world. We'd send her to her tomb on the day the astronomers thought of best augur, bury her with all her favourite objects and disperse the rest as mementoes among relatives and officials worthy of the honour.

Her tomb was ready and waiting. She'd been building it all these years, as lavish a palace for her night as had been the palaces of her sumptuous days. She'd be next to Emperor Xianfeng, their long separation would end and her tears would dry.

The sky lost the last traces of its glow and the night took form. A tune floated through my head, one of the waltzes I'd learned with Yu Geng's daughters. I'd forgotten how to play it on the piano but it came drifting back into me now, clear and distinct. When I sent Kang Youwei on his road to Shanghai ten years before, I tried to give him hope by speaking of a future time when talents could be put to use and something real accomplished. I spoke the same words to Yu Geng's daughters too, before they took that same road south.

I'd tried over these dreary years to keep myself prepared for that future time. Now it was upon us. The clocks rang again, right with the hour this time, only they were few to sound, for many had stopped.

I closed my eyes and remembered Zhen come to my side dressed as a eunuch, her eyes curious and attentive as she watched me bent over the mechanical things inside the clock she'd brought me to fix. I knew how much she'd longed for the moment when Cixi would depart, not just to the Summer Palace for a few days, leaving her spies behind to watch us, but for good. Instead, she'd had the long months shut away in the Forbidden City's forgotten corners, and then the brief plunge through narrow, stone-ringed darkness into the chill well water below.

She'd not share this patiently-awaited future with me now. No one would. Too many people did not want my return. It had been their unspoken fear all this time, Cixi's years and my youth, the gnawing knowledge that sooner or later there'd be no empress dowager above me and I'd take my revenge for the treachery and suffering they'd forced down my throat.

As for Cixi herself, she'd tried her best to keep me in her sight all these years, and she'd not want to let me go now. It wasn't out of fear that I'd resume my reforms of course, for she'd belatedly set them in all in motion anyway. It was fear that I'd not be as filial after her death as I had been in life, that my heart let loose and tongue unfettered might undo the work she'd made of herself over these years, crack the image and stain her legacy's lustre. She, Yuan Shikai and the old guard officials, the eunuchs, they all knew me well and their memories were good. They knew I only seemed the quiet one. They knew I also had a furious torrent inside.

They had all let me slowly decay, hoping that I'd turn the logic of time, spare them their fears and be the first to go. They would be kinder to me dead. But I had such a stubborn nature.

Unlike Cixi, I did not have a tomb prepared. It was the custom for the emperor to prepare his tomb during his lifetime, and Cixi had approached me on the subject over the years, but I always refused to discuss it and had done absolutely nothing about it. I wanted to build for our people, for those who were alive, and not for my useless corpse. Perhaps there was not much hope of building now, not with our foundations as cracked as they were. But if there was anything to salvage, any road to try, I had to do it, so long as heaven still gave me the chance and I still wore this emperor's title.

I called for tea but it was a long time before anyone answered. The eunuchs were all with Cixi. I was mostly alone now, and those eunuchs who did turn up were perfunctory and indifferent. They'd learned over the last ten years that I had no standing and they needn't show me much respect. Only Yehenara was diligent in coming to my side, following Cixi's orders to keep watch on me. The solitude weighed heavy and I felt daunted and vulnerable in this cold autumn, but I had no desire to see Yehenara. I chased her from me as in the past.

I shivered. The thin branches of trees merged with the darkness. I'd spent so many hours looking out from these rooms and knew all the moods and changes of expression in the scenes beyond. I'd chosen this place when I was a boy still, liked it for its quiet seclusion and gentle perspective of water, sky and the other shore. The entrances had not been not bricked up back then and the ice was left to form thick in winter. Sometimes we'd sped on sleds across it, wrapped in furs and laughing. Zhen had always enjoyed that, her cheeks reddened with the frosty chill and her eyes full of fun and swiftness.

I had seen her and so many other faces gone and voices silenced, but I wasn't ready to join them yet. The night had come but dawn would follow and in spite of everything I still wanted to wake with it. I saw the wind dance and the birds glide. I saw the sun paint golden streaks and the rain come trailing silver sadness. There'd often been little else, just this scrap of world beyond and the endless books I read. But I didn't want to let go and I'd refused to even consider a site for my tomb.

The shadows thickened. In these now abandoned halls they seemed more solid and had hands that grabbed and grasped. I shook my head at them. Let them go to Cixi first. She was the one grown old, not I. The stopped clocks with their hands still, stuck in their different hours, seemed suddenly to wear mocking grins on their dusty faces. The shadows pressed closer and reached cold into my heart.

I shook my head again. It was too soon. The rains would sweep in and nothing was ready yet. The winds would turn fierce and our shelter was too flimsy. The whole edifice would collapse around our people, and who would think of them in the storm? Yuan Shikai, Yehenara and that tiny boy who was next in line for the throne? The revolutionaries?

Not that I was any strong pillar of course. My lungs were not good, and I often felt my breath choked up. I'd always been a weak and faltering emperor, never found the virtue of kings, only its vague outline, only cried helpless tears for my land and its suffering. But then again, I'd never had power either, never had the chance to act beyond the most constrained limits, never had much substance to my emperor's title. All I'd had was a sincere heart, and I still had that now, even if little else. It wasn't much to go on with, but it was a start.

The shadows rustled with all the furtive fearful things the past could pull out from within these palace walls. The gossip had painted Yongzheng still a prince creeping quietly to his dying father's side with a bowl of ginseng soup laced with death. It hadn't been so in reality, but such things had happened so many times in history and this was what the shadows whispered now.

They'd not let me rule again. I'd be no more emperor with Cixi dead than I was with her alive. I wasn't even sure they'd let me see that moment. They'd let me die slowly these ten years and they'd be anxious now to hurry me on my way. All I could do was wait, cold, ill, alone, afraid. There was no one to call but the indifferent eunuchs. They came with medicine and food. In my weakened state, if I didn't take it, I'd worsen for sure, but if I did take it, I couldn't guarantee I'd see this dawn I desired.

I sat amidst the dusty clutter, stared into the night and tried to keep the shadows away. I wanted to live. I'd show them yet my stubbornness. I'd held on this long, weak as I was. The clocks had always been my friends and I had learned from my boyhood punishment days to lie still in the dark places and listen, listen for the sound of time, tears, my own quiet flow of breath, and the glimmer of that faintest hope beyond.

EPILOGUE

A few days later, Emperor Guangxu's condition took a sudden turn for the worse. Doctor Qu, the doctor recommended by Prince Qing and Yuan Shikai, was called to the palace and noted the abrupt change in the emperor's condition. What struck the doctor most of all was that the emperor complained of serious stomach pains that seemed completely unrelated to his previous troubles.

Doctor Qu found the emperor's residence lonelier than ever. Only a couple of eunuchs were still about, and everything was in neglect. No one bothered anymore.

The next day passed in silence. The doctors were not sent for. Only in the night were they finally called back to the palace. They entered at dawn when the gates opened and later that day were taken across the bridge to Ocean Terrace, where Guangxu now lay unconscious. They were not there to treat him though, only to record that he was beyond help.

He died the following day, November 14, 1908, as evening faded into night. He was thirty-seven. From that moment, rumours went out that he had been poisoned. Forensic tests conducted in China 100 years later confirmed that this was the case. Arsenic was the murder weapon, but identifying the murderer with certainty is a harder task.

Upon hearing that Guangxu was dead, Cixi immediately issued an edict naming three-year-old Puyi emperor and his father, Zaifeng, regent. Already exhausted by illness, she spent the night with the grand councillors, taking care of the arrangements for the succession and the mourning period. She died the next afternoon.

One of the first things Zaifeng, Guangxu's younger half-brother, did as regent was dismiss Yuan Shikai from all his posts. He attempted to continue the reforms that had begun, but it was too late to stop the storm from sweeping in and bringing down the crumbling edifice.

The dynasty held on for another three years until an uprising set revolution spreading across the country. The court, needing Yuan's military influence to attempt to suppress the uprising, called him back to Beijing. After much deliberate stalling, he finally came, replacing old Prince Qing, who'd become the first prime minister in a reorganised Qing government. He promptly pressured Zaifeng into stepping aside as regent and then, with Prince Qing's help, persuaded Yehenara, now the Empress Dowager Longyu, into signing the act of Puyi's abdication, thus ending the Qing dynasty, which had ruled China since 1644.

Prince Qing became very wealthy and went off to enjoy his riches. Yuan Shikai put his power and armies to use and became president of the new Republic of China. Being president wasn't enough. He proclaimed himself emperor, declared the founding of a new dynasty and even performed the rites at the Temple of Heaven. His "dynasty" lasted three months. Society was not ready for another emperor so soon and resistance was too strong. Another three months later Yuan died of illness.

Kang Youwei remained loyal to Guangxu and ultimately, loyal to the Qing. He took part in a failed attempt to restore the abdicated Puyi to the throne in 1917 and remained an advocate of constitutional monarchy for China until his death in 1927.

Guangxu never prepared a tomb, but Yuan Shikai ensured he got one. The work was still unfinished when the dynasty fell, and Yuan's government provided the funds for its completion.

ALSO BY IJEN KIM

THE SNUFF BOTTLE BOY

"A rich, artistic novel, Kim's debut reads as much like poetry as it does prose... the ebbing naiveté recalls the novels of Kerouac—though with far less whimsy and far greater consequence."
— Kirkus Reviews

One does not think of North Korea as having a 'foreign community, but it does, and this is a story from within that world. North Korea is much in the news, but only as an almost too absurd to be real 'other'. This novel gives that 'other flesh, colour and life. Anyone curious to get beneath the regimented surface of Pyongyang and its people would find here a different vision, a hidden world lurking behind the seemingly identical facades lining the monumental socialist streets. This is North Korea with a lyrical, human touch, warm, sad and funny all at once.

Fate and family tradition demand that Mickey becomes an artist and trains under the eye of Mr Jin. Mickey comes from North Korea's Chinese community, the only long-term and fully established foreign community in that country. He grows up not just with art, but with the stories of his erstwhile aristocrat great-grandmother, and dreams of his mysterious grandmother, Lily, who left for Moscow as a young woman, taking with her one of the family's two precious snuff bottle heirlooms.

Navigating an often treacherous world, Mickey finds himself caught up in journeys and events far beyond what he'd thought possible. Lies, deceit and hidden dangers abound, but so do friendship, generosity and love. Through it all runs the sustaining power of imagination and an ability to see light and promise in even the darkest corners.

Printed in Great Britain
by Amazon

52468971R00200